Prai

# OWL DANCE

"A rip-snorting, Wild West steampunk extravaganza with a touch of Arabian Nights that comes alive with authentic insight into the magic, peoples, and landscapes of the Southwest. Satisfies as both science fiction, and a western that is fantastic, and comes alive with realism. The kind of book that makes me proud to live in Aztlán." Ernest Hogan, author of *Cortez on Jupiter* and *High Aztech*

"*Owl Dance* is a great western-style steampunk science fiction tale. Summers knows science, and it shows in really fun ways in this one, keeping this wondrous. If you like steampunk or westerns or just a having a really great time, give *Owl Dance* a read. I think you'll really enjoy it." Trent Zelazny, author of *To Sleep Gently* and *Destination Unknown*

## Other Books by David Lee Summers

*The Solar Sea*
*The Astronomer's Crypt*

### The Space Pirates' Legacy Series
*Firebrandt's Legacy*
*The Pirates of Sufiro*
*Children of the Old Stars*
*Heirs of the New Earth*

### The Clockwork Legion Series
*Owl Dance*
*Lightning Wolves*
*The Brazen Shark*
*Owl Riders*

### The Scarlet Order Vampires Series
*Dragon's Fall: Rise of the Scarlet Order*
*Vampires of the Scarlet Order*

# OWL DANCE

A Novel of the Clockwork Legion

## DAVID LEE SUMMERS

Hadrosaur Productions, Mesilla Park, NM

Owl Dance
Hadrosaur Productions
Third Edition: October 2021
First date of publication: September 2011

ISBN-10: 1-885093-97-7
ISBN-13: 978-1-885093-97-4

To
Rebecca Petithory-Hayes
and
Gary Hayes
Whether traveling back in time to the Wild West
or forward in time to an optimistic future,
you are great companions to have on the journey.

# ACKNOWLEDGEMENTS

First and foremost, I would like to thank David B. Riley. In a very real way, there would be no Owl Dance without him. I created the characters of Ramon Morales and Fatemeh Karimi for a story called "The Persian Witch" that first appeared in his anthology Trails: Intriguing Stories of the Wild West. One of my goals in that story was to create characters I could go to again and again as I needed them. Over the last few years, David purchased several of Ramon and Fatemeh's adventures for his magazine Science Fiction Trails. Because of David, I created these characters and I kept going with them until I had enough material to create a book. For that I'm very grateful.

In that same vein, thanks to David Rozansky, for asking to see an outline for a steampunk novel. That helped me figure out just what Ramon, Fatemeh and the alien Legion were up to. Because of that, my loose collection of stories developed an arc and a path to a story that could be completed.

M.H. Bonham is another editor who made an important contribution to this book with her comments about the "The Clockwork Lobo" which subsequently appeared in her anthology WolfSongs2.

Many thanks to Ernest Hogan, Anna Paradox, and Laura Givens who read early drafts of this novel and made comments that were taken to heart in the editing. Each brought valuable insight that made this novel much better than it was before.

Thanks to Maya Bohnhoff for a valuable, in-depth discussion of the Bahá'í Faith.

I'm very grateful for the work of editors Matthew Delman and Carol Hightshoe. They poured over the novel very carefully and helped strengthen the writing, plot and characters all the way through.

Last but not least, thanks to Kumie Wise and Myranda Summers who acted as proofreaders as every chapter came out of the computer. Moreover, Myranda was the one who suggested that Ramon and Fatemeh meet a clockwork lobo and she created the character of Larissa Crimson.

# OWL DANCE

# CHAPTER ONE
## THE PERSIAN WITCH

"Sheriff, I hate to spread rumors..."

Ramon Morales tipped his hat back on his head. The blurred form of a small, hunched-over woman silhouetted by the light of the setting sun was in the door of his office. "Rumors? What...?"

The woman inclined her head and planted her hands on her hips. "I'm talking about the curandera who rode into town last month in her fancy wagon." She looked from one side to the other, then stepped close to the desk. Mrs. Chavez's face became clear then. "I think she may be practicing black magic," she said in hushed tones. "She might be a bruja."

The sheriff sat upright and put on a pair of wire-frame, round-lensed spectacles. "What makes you think that?"

"That wagon of hers is full of strange potions and powders." Mrs. Chavez's breath smelled of garlic and onions. Ramon scooted back, putting a few inches between himself and the irate woman. "She gave Mr. Garcia a potion that cured his liver and he took up drinking again. She told Mrs. Johnson there wasn't anything she could do about her straying husband."

Ramon shrugged. "Alfredo Garcia's a drunk. Of course he started drinking again when he felt better." The sheriff inclined his head, confused about the second point. "I'd think you'd be happy she couldn't help Mr. and Mrs. Johnson. You're a curandera, too. That's more business for you."

Mrs. Chavez heaved an exasperated sigh. "That's not the point. They went to *her* first, even though she's not a local. She doesn't even go to Mass." She straightened and pointed a long, gnarled finger at the sheriff. "But that's not the worst of it. You should see the owls. They're her familiars."

1

Ramon stood. This nonsense had gone on for long enough. "She lives out by Old Man Seaton's farm." He firmly took hold of Mrs. Chavez's elbow. She tensed and her eyes narrowed, but she did nothing else to resist as he escorted her toward the door. "There are always owls out there. They aren't a bad omen. They just hunt the mice in the field."

"You *would* sympathize with those creatures—with a name like Búho Morales." She clucked her tongue. Ramon rolled his eyes at the use of his nickname. "Mark my words, Sheriff. She's trouble."

Ramon didn't like the sound of that. He'd heard rumors of witch hunts in other parts of New Mexico Territory. Some had turned very ugly. Still, he wanted Mrs. Chavez out of there so he could focus on more immediate concerns. "I'll go talk to her soon," he said.

She pursed her lips and seemed to consider that. Finally, her shoulders relaxed. "Thank you, Sheriff."

Ramon sighed and gently closed the door behind the old woman. Socorro, New Mexico had been part of the United States for less than twenty years. In that time, it had swollen from a population of about 400 to nearly 4000. Many of the settlers came to work the silver and lead mines in the surrounding mountains. Others were ranchers who had moved in from Texas after the Civil War, looking for new land to feed their cattle. Meanwhile, farmers did their best to hold onto prize soil near the valuable waters of the Rio Grande. It was a rough and tumble town that failed to attract many educated folks like doctors. Ramon was pleased at the prospect of a new healer in the town, but frustrated others would not welcome her.

Ramon shook his head and tried to put thoughts of Mrs. Chavez behind him. It was Friday night of a warm spring day. That meant there would be bigger trouble than squabbling curanderas. The miners would be coming in from the hills and the cowboys would be coming in from the ranches. They would collide in the saloons that night. The sheriff turned around and resumed his place at the desk. Just as he removed his glasses and tipped his hat over his eyes to get a little more rest, the door burst open.

"Sheriff!" Deputy Ray Hillerman was breathing hard. "We

already got our first fight down at the Cap!"

Ramon returned his glasses to his nose and pulled the pocket watch from his vest. "It's not even 6 o'clock," he grumbled. "It's going to be a long night." He closed the watch's lid, placed it back in his vest pocket, then strapped his six-gun around his waist. He followed Ray out the door. It was a short, brisk walk around the corner to the Capitol Saloon. Socorro might have been the second largest town in New Mexico Territory after Santa Fe, but it was hardly a huge city like San Francisco. Ramon and Ray met one of the other deputies, Juan Gomez, at the door. Just as they stepped inside, a gun went off and the big mirror behind the bar shattered.

Ramon gritted his teeth. He would much rather go home for a quiet dinner than break up a bar fight between the miners and ranchers who had taken over his town. He drew his gun and fired a couple of shots at the ceiling. "All right, everyone!" he shouted. "Drop your weapons real peaceable-like." A couple of guns clattered to the ground and a cowboy flew in the sheriff's direction. He stepped aside and the cowboy continued on out the door. The heart of the fight was still going on in the back corner. A cowboy cracked a miner over the head with a pool cue. Ramon sighed and holstered his gun. The sheriff and his deputies waded into the fray. Juan hurled three of the cowboys toward the bar. The sheriff pulled one guy off another while Ray pushed a miner into the wall.

A miner had a cowboy pinned to the top of a pool table, beating him senseless. Ramon motioned to Juan who grabbed the miner's arms and pinned them behind his back. The sheriff drew his pistol again and looked around. "Now boys, this is not the way to start the weekend."

One of the miners with grungy clothes and dirt-encrusted eyebrows stepped forward. "One o' them thar cowboys said we's nothing but a bunch o' earthworms."

"I don't care who started it." Ramon was startled to realize that he really *didn't* care. The only person in the room who actually grew up in Socorro with him was Juan. "Everyone who has a weapon, drop it now. We'll take 'em over to my office and you can pick 'em up tomorrow when you've sobered up enough." Several pistols clattered to the floor. As one of them hit the ground, it discharged and the bullet caught Ramon in the shoulder. He spun around and fell back onto the pool table, landing on top of the cowboy the miner had been beating. Juan and Ray ran to the sheriff's side. "I'm all right," grunted Ramon. "It's just a graze."

"You better go see the doc," said Ray. "Get that cleaned up, anyway."

The sheriff struggled to climb off the pool table, then looked at the fellow lying there. "I think Doc Corbin's going to be busy with this guy. Ray, you better get him over there while Juan rounds up the guns."

"But what about you?" asked Juan.

The sheriff looked around at the miners and cowboys. They seemed to have calmed down somewhat. Some were packing up to head off to other saloons while a few were going to the bar. One cowboy even bought a miner a drink. The sheriff thought that was a good sign. He looked down at his shoulder, and gritted his teeth. The wound needed treatment, but he wasn't in the mood to see either Doc Corbin or the curandera, Mrs. Chavez, just at the moment. "I think I can tend to this myself."

"I hear that new curandera is pretty good," said Juan. "I bet she could fix you up right quick."

One look out the window told Ramon it was early yet. The sun was still shining. There was a barstool in Socorro for every man, woman and child living in town. That meant there could be plenty more fights to break up before the night ended. The sheriff realized if he tried to treat himself, he could be out of action for a while. Looking at Juan, he nodded. "Maybe you're right. I'll go see what she can do for me."

Sucking in his breath, Ramon followed Ray out the door. Meanwhile, Juan began collecting the pistols and the barkeep swept up glass from the floor. Ramon frowned as he walked back toward the office. Every Friday night he seemed to understand a little more why his mother and cousins had left Socorro.

Back at the sheriff's office, Ramon collected his horse and rode down toward the Rio Grande, past Old Man Seaton's farm and up a slight rise to where the new curandera had moved into an old adobe. Next to the house was the fancy wagon Mrs.

Chavez had mentioned. It was painted and built all of wood, not covered with a canvas tarp like so many others. It reminded the sheriff more of a chuck wagon or a gypsy wagon from Europe than a Conestoga.

As Ramon climbed off his horse, he heard odd little whistling sounds. When the whistling stopped, he heard the chirping of a burrowing owl. Stepping around the wagon, the sheriff saw a woman dressed in black, sitting on an old crate near a fencepost. Atop the fencepost was a small owl. The woman whistled and then paused. The owl would move from one foot to the other—almost like it was dancing—then it would chirp. Enchanted, Ramon watched this for a few minutes, but the orange glow of the setting sun reminded him time was short. He had probably not seen the last fight of the evening. The sheriff cleared his throat. Startled, the woman looked up and the owl flew away.

Ramon was struck by the woman's bright green eyes and lovely, smooth features, which quickly shifted from astonishment to impatience and finally to concern as her eyes settled on the wound. Noticing the direction of her gaze, Ramon realized he should say something. "Pardon me, ma'am, but I heard that you're a curandera."

Without a word, she stood and stepped close. Carefully, she extracted the fabric of Ramon's shirt from the wound so she could see better. At last, she nodded without taking her eyes off the injury. "Come this way," she said. She led Ramon toward the house and paused to light a lantern that hung outside the door before taking it down and going inside. She reappeared a few minutes later with a black bag, like a doctor's.

She opened a door on the back of her wagon and instructed Ramon to sit down. He could smell assorted herbs from within and wondered what all she had in there. Opening the bag, she retrieved a bottle and some cotton. Far more gently than Doc Corbin would have done, she cleaned and dressed the sheriff's wound. "You're new in town, aren't you?" Ramon asked as she worked. "What's your name?"

"Fatemeh Karimi," she said. "I'm from Persia."

"Pleased to make your acquaintance." He watched her climb into the wagon. She might not be a local, but somehow her gentleness and concern for a stranger reminded him of many good people from his youth, who had since moved on. She searched through a few drawers and finally climbed down next to the sheriff. She handed him a small bottle.

"Drink this, it will help ease the pain but it won't cloud your mind."

Ramon sniffed at the contents of the bottle and made a face, but he did as she instructed. "That was quite some trick you were doing—whistling at that ol' hooty owl," he croaked, trying to hide the tears that came unbidden to his eyes from the potent flavor of the herbs. "It was almost like you were talking to it."

She smiled. Ramon wasn't sure whether she was amused by his reaction to the herbs or by the question. "That was no trick." She stepped over to the well and retrieved a ladle full of water. "I am Bahá'í. We believe all humanity is one family and that family should live in harmony with the world. The owls are my neighbors. As you'd say, I'm doing my best to be neighborly."

Ramon took the ladle and drank the water. He was grateful it cleared the taste from his mouth. "Why did you come to America?" He handed the ladle back to Fatemeh.

"In Persia, women must wear veils in public. A friend of mine resisted." She looked down to the ground and moved a few pebbles with her boot. "She was arrested, and strangled with a silk scarf. When she was dead, they hurled her down a well and piled rocks on top of her." She looked up and a tear ran down her cheek. She reached up and wiped it angrily away.

"It would be a shame to cover such a lovely face."

She laughed bitterly. "I didn't come to America to escape the veil. I came to America to escape what the veil represents— that women should remain hidden and unheard."

The sheriff sighed, thinking about Mrs. Chavez and some of the others he knew around Socorro County, like Bishop Ramirez. Then, he looked into Fatemeh's eyes and smiled. "I've never liked it when one person says they're better than another. I suppose that's why I stayed in Socorro when so many in my family left. It's why I became a sheriff." He looked down at the badge pinned to his vest. "Still, it pays to be a little prudent," he cautioned. "You may have freedom of speech here, but that doesn't keep some people from spreading rumors... like Mrs. Chavez."

"Why should I be afraid of her?" She folded her arms across her stomach and snorted. "She only pretends to be a healer while she charges people huge fees to read cards and make phony love potions."

"I'm afraid she does have some powerful friends." The sheriff suddenly realized his shoulder was no longer in pain. He touched the bandage, but pulled his finger away when it still stung. He snorted thinking Fatemeh had done a better job than Old Doc Corbin and certainly a lot better than Mrs. Chavez could have done. "I'm impressed," he said, tipping his hat. "How much do I owe you?"

"Nothing today. In your line of work, I suspect you'll be back. You'll also meet others needing a healer."

"Fair enough." Ramon started toward his horse. "You let me know if Mrs. Chavez or any of her friends come around here and bother you."

She inclined her head and narrowed her eyes. "Why would they do that?"

"This is a good country with good laws, ma'am, but sometimes people forget those laws." He pulled himself into the saddle. "It's my job to refresh their memories."

She smiled slightly at that and looked the sheriff up and down. Although Ramon was flattered by her attention, a shiver traveled down his spine at the intensity of her gaze. "I think I'm going to like it here, Sheriff..."

"Sheriff Ramon Morales, ma'am. My friends call me Búho." He gathered the reins and spurred his horse down the trail before it got too dark to see. As he rode, he reflected on his nickname which meant "owl," and like the owl on the fencepost, he supposed he was falling under Fatemeh's spell.

Ramon found the rest of Friday night surprisingly quiet. He suspected the cowboys and the miners got all the fighting out of their systems early. He slept in late on Saturday. Mrs. Gilson, who owned the rooming house where he stayed, helped him change his bandages the next day. The wound still stung, but it could have been a lot worse. Things remained calm on Saturday night and Ramon decided to go to Mass at San Miguel. He hoped Father Esteban would be saying Mass, but was surprised to find Bishop Ramirez behind the pulpit. When he looked around at the pews, he noticed the bishop's brother-in-law, Mr. Dalton, who owned one of the biggest mines in the area, sat two rows ahead of him. The sheriff slipped out early and made his way behind the church to the little parsonage. He knocked and Father Esteban appeared at the door with a warm smile.

"I was just about to open a bottle of wine. Would you care to join me?" he said, ushering the sheriff inside.

"I didn't know priests drank."

"Not often and not to excess," said the priest, "if we're behaving ourselves." He winked

Ramon dropped into a wooden chair in the main room of the parsonage while Father Esteban poured two glasses of wine. He placed one in front of the sheriff. "What brings you here tonight?"

"I was wondering if you knew what a buh-High is?" Ramon did his best to pronounce the word Fatemeh had used. Even though Father Esteban was Bishop Ramirez's junior, he somehow struck Ramon as the one who spent more time with books.

The Father took a sip of his wine. "I take it you've met our new curandera."

The sheriff nodded. "She said she's from Persia. I was wondering if she was saying she was some particular type of Persian, like an Apache is a particular type of Indian."

Father Esteban chuckled, then took off his spectacles and placed them carefully in his pocket. "No, it's more like how you might say you're a Catholic or how your Deputy, Ray, would say he's a Baptist. Bahá'í is a religion from Persia."

Ramon set the glass of wine on the little table and thought about the priest's description. "Are you saying she's a kind of Mohammedan?"

The priest shook his head. "Not really. As I understand it,

the Bahá'ís believe all religions are a little bit right. They believe Christ, Mohammed, Buddha—all the great teachers—hold some of the truth and they were all teaching us to worship the same God."

The sheriff took a hefty drink of his wine as he evaluated the priest's words. "I'm guessing Bishop Ramirez wouldn't hold to those teachings."

The young priest's smile seemed a bit sad. "No, I suspect the bishop would consider her belief heresy. It might not take much to convince him Fatemeh is the witch Mrs. Chavez says she is."

"You don't think she's a witch…"

Father Esteban took another sip of his wine. "Don't tell the bishop, but I wonder if the Bahá'ís are on to something."

"What would the bishop do if he thought someone was a heretic?"

Father Esteban took a deep breath and let it out slowly. "He's pretty old-fashioned. I wouldn't put it past him to burn a heretic or a witch at the stake…or worse."

Ramon shuddered. He remembered the witch trials he'd heard about in other parts of New Mexico and decided he didn't need to know any more.

The wine was starting to go to his head. He put the glass down and thanked Father Esteban, then walked back to Mrs. Gilson's rooming house with his hands in his pockets. Stopping before he stepped onto the porch, the sheriff looked up at the stars in the sky and wondered who understood God better— Fatemeh or Bishop Ramirez.

The timbers of the rooming house rattled, startling Ramon awake. He rubbed the sleep from his eyes while trying to figure out what had shaken the room. The smell of Mrs. Gilson's coffee convinced the sheriff to dress, and then trudge down the hall to the kitchen. He poured himself a cup of coffee and sat down at the table. Soon after, Mrs. Gilson appeared with some flapjacks. "Did you feel that tremor this morning?" she asked.

"Shook me awake." Ramon reached for some of the preserves. "Suppose it was an earthquake?"

She shrugged and returned to the kitchen. A few minutes later, Juan Gomez stepped through the front door of the rooming house and pulled up a chair. "A rider came into town. He said a dynamite shack exploded up at the Dalton mine. There's a lot of miners hurt. I sent Ray to fetch Doc Corbin."

Ramon nodded as he shoveled flapjacks into his mouth. "Was there a cave-in?" he asked around a mouthful of food.

"Nothing like that, but there's a lot of debris scattered around from the explosion. They can use all the hands they can get to clean it up and help with the wounded."

The sheriff pushed the empty plate away. "You get going. I'll be right behind." He ran back to his room and grabbed his gun and his hat. As he hurried out of the house, he remembered to thank Mrs. Gilson for the tasty breakfast.

The sheriff climbed on his horse and started to ride toward the mine. He could see a plume of smoke and dust rising from the area. As he considered the wounded, he realized Doc Corbin could use all the help he could get, and Fatemeh had proven herself to be a good healer. Ramon turned his horse and rode out to her place.

Aromatic smoke wafted from the chimney. It seemed she was getting ready to cook her own breakfast. He climbed off the horse, then stepped over to the door and knocked.

"Just a minute," came Fatemeh's voice from inside.

Ramon checked his pocket watch, then stepped around the corner of the house, looking in the direction of the mine. The angry dust and smoke plume from the explosion was dissipating. He couldn't afford to waste much time.

"Ouch!" cried Fatemeh.

Ramon whirled around and saw Fatemeh clutching her ankle and examining her foot. Apparently, she had opened the door and stepped on the threshold with her bare foot. Several needles had been driven into the threshold in the form of a cross. Ramon closed his eyes and swore under his breath. "Damn it, Mrs. Chavez. I don't need this right now."

Looking down, Fatemeh saw the needle cross. "What in the world...?"

Ramon sighed. "It's a way to tell if the person inside the house is a witch. A witch can't pass a cross of silver needles."

"It sure kept me from stepping outside."

Ramon looked back toward the mountains. "We have a bigger problem than this. There's been an explosion at one of the mines."

Fatemeh looked up from her foot. "There has? Can I help?"

"I was hoping you would." Ramon grimaced, thinking the words came out sounding sappy, even if they were true.

Not seeming to notice his tone, Fatemeh nodded. "I'll get my things...and some shoes." A few minutes later, she reappeared at the doorway with her black bag. Careful to step over the needles this time, she climbed into her wagon and loaded some bottles into the bag. She reappeared, then darted around the back of her house. She rode out on a sleek Arabian stallion a few minutes later. Together, she and Ramon rode to the mine.

As they approached the mine, the smell of smoke, gunpowder, and dust hung heavy in the air, burning Ramon's lungs. They heard wails of agony. Riding closer, they saw the remains of the dynamite shack. A severed arm and leg lay nearby. Ramon's horse reared. Patting the animal's flank to calm it down, he looked around and saw the reason for its agitation. A severed head lay in the horse's path, its eyes staring up and mouth open in surprise.

Worried about Fatemeh's reaction, Ramon looked around. Her expression was neither shocked nor scared. Instead, her eyes were locked on the mine entrance, her brow furrowed in anger. "This is a cursed place."

They rode forward, past a man with a wooden plank embedded in his chest, lying in a pool of blood. Finally, they came to a place where Doc Corbin knelt beside a man who kicked and thrashed. The man's arm was only attached to the shoulder by some tendons and muscle. "Quick! Give me a hand. I need to get this arm amputated and the wound cauterized."

Fatemeh ground her teeth, then climbed off the horse. "They've desecrated the earth. No wonder it struck back." She stepped over to the wounded man and opened her bag. "Sit him up," she commanded as she produced a vial of greenish liquid.

The doctor did as he was told. The man screamed and Fatemeh poured the liquid down his throat. He began thrashing even more. "Help us hold him," called Doc Corbin.

Ramon clambered off his horse and grasped the man's legs while Fatemeh and Corbin held his upper body. A few minutes later, he relaxed and began breathing gently.

"You can tend to him now," said Fatemeh. She looked up and rushed to a man trying to staunch the flow of blood from another man's leg.

Ramon quickly turned around to avoid watching Doc Corbin saw off the wounded miner's arm. He found himself face to face with Randolph Dalton. The mine owner's velvet coat and silk vest were pristine. "Why did you bring her?" asked Dalton. "Talk of cursed places striking back will spook the men."

Ramon looked around at the men lying on the ground, bleeding and broken, many scarred with powder burns. Some wailed in agony. Others were only strong enough to whimper. "All due respect," said the sheriff, "I think these men have just learned the fear of God."

Dalton ground his teeth. "That may be true, but the minute they start thinking the shack exploded because of a curse…" He threw his hat to the ground. "Mark my words, if my men start to pack up and leave, there'll be Hell to pay." He stormed away.

"I think Hell has already had a say," muttered the sheriff under his breath. Despite that, Ramon could understand why Dalton was upset. The explosion cost him a lot and men who were upset and distraught reacted in all sorts of ways. Anger was certainly possible. The sheriff looked around and found a mine supervisor. The man put him to work clearing debris.

By the time it passed noon, the sheriff and his deputies were covered in sweat-streaked dust and soot. They had done about all they could usefully do. Ramon saw Doc Corbin packing up. Fatemeh, whose black dress was matted and stiff with blood, patted the hand of one of the miners and spoke quietly to him. She stood up and moved to another. As the sheriff climbed onto his horse, he couldn't help but notice Mr. Dalton watching Fatemeh like a hawk.

On Wednesday after the mine accident, Ramon waited at the sheriff's office for the mail to come. He sorted through the letters and opened a packet containing a fresh set of wanted posters. Rifling through them, he was at once relieved and disheartened to see no one he recognized. "Even the outlaws are all strangers," he muttered.

Standing, he stretched, then put on his hat and stepped out into the sunshine and decided to take a walk. As he stepped into the street, a young boy named Elfego Baca ran headlong into him. Behind him, his friend Juan Fernandez skidded to a halt, kicking up a cloud of dust.

Ramon put his hands on his hips and glared down at the boys. "Shouldn't you two be in school?"

Elfego and Juan stared up at the sheriff with wide, rounded eyes, then looked at each other. Finally, Elfego sputtered out an explanation. "Mrs. Chavez...she offered to pay Juan twenty-five cents if he would draw a circle around the new curandera."

"A circle?" Ramon's brow furrowed. "What for?"

Elfego straightened up proudly. "They say, if a boy named Juan draws a circle around a witch, she won't see him and she'll be trapped."

Juan smacked Elfego's arm. "You talk too much. Mrs. Chavez said we weren't supposed to tell anyone what we're doing."

Ramon removed his glasses and rubbed the bridge of his nose. These were small and annoying things, but he didn't like the sound of it. "Boys, you get back to school now." He pointed his finger right at Elfego's nose. "I don't want to hear anything about the two of you harassing Miss Karimi." He pointed his finger at Juan. "Understand?"

Both boys swallowed and nodded rapidly. "Yes, sir," they said in unison.

Ramon watched the boys run back in the direction of the schoolhouse. Instead of going for his walk, he decided to unhitch his horse and ride out to Fatemeh's house. He knocked on the door, but she didn't answer.

He tried the latch and the door opened. Light streamed in from a window and landed on a table. On it was a scrap of paper. Scrawled on it was a note in Spanish. It was difficult to read because of the poor handwriting and some water drops— perhaps tears—that had fallen on it after it was written, but Ramon finally figured it out. "I lost my husband because of the curse you placed on the Dalton Mine, Bruja."

Ramon sighed and put the letter in the pocket of his shirt. As he stepped out into the sunlight, he saw Fatemeh approaching, carrying a set of traps. "Can I help you, Mr. Morales?"

"I just came by to see how you were doing?"

Fatemeh snorted. "Fine, except for some annoyances. Someone decided to set these traps over by the owl burrows." She tossed the traps in a heap by the wheel of her wagon. "And I found a strange note tacked to my door this morning."

Ramon lifted the note out of his pocket.

"That's the one," said Fatemeh. "Unfortunately, I don't read Spanish. I wasn't sure what it said."

"It's someone blaming you for what happened to the mine," explained the sheriff.

"That's ridiculous!" Fatemeh shook her head. "Why would they think that?"

"People get crazy ideas when they're scared."

"Like trapping owls?" Fatemeh looked down at the traps. "You'd think farmers would want the owls to eat rodents!"

Ramon dug in the dirt with his toe. "Some people think owls are the servants of witches." He took a step closer and looked at the traps, then back up into Fatemeh's eyes. "Someone is trying reduce your 'power'."

"I am most certainly not a witch." Fatemeh folded her arms.

"The thought never crossed my mind—but it has crossed some others." Ramon shook his head. "Hopefully they'll get over it, but if you have any more problems, come to me."

"Thank you, Sheriff. It's good to know I have a friend around here." She smiled and Ramon felt his cheeks grow warm. Despite being embarrassed by her scrutiny, he found he liked her smile and was glad she thought of him as a friend.

He tipped his hat and cleared his throat. "Well, I best be

getting back to town, ma'am. But let me know if you need anything at all."

"I will, Mr. Morales."

On Friday night, Ramon strolled through a surprisingly quiet and peaceable town. He saw lots of cowboys and hardly any miners. Finally, he ambled into the Capitol Saloon and noticed the barkeep already had a new mirror installed. He ordered a beer. "Quiet night tonight. Where are all the miners?"

"Most of 'em are gone," said the bartender. "I hear Mr. Dalton's blaming it on that Persian witch. He says she placed some kind of curse on the mine."

Ramon took off his hat and tossed it onto the bar. "Not that again. How could she have anything at all to do with a dynamite shack explosion?"

The bartender shrugged. "I have no idea, but Mr. Dalton and the bishop aren't too happy at all. You know the bishop owns several shares in the mine, don't you?"

Ramon nodded. He knew that fact all too well. "She didn't place a curse on the mine. She didn't like it much, and may have said that too loudly, but it wasn't a curse." Ramon looked at the bottle of beer and sighed.

The bartender pulled a rag from his apron and began wiping down the too-empty bar. "Well, you tell that to two powerful men who see themselves losing money for every hour the mine is under-manned. Men have been packing up and moving elsewhere. If the owners can find a way to convince folks they've made the mine safe, they will."

Ramon frowned and nodded, not surprised to hear men were moving on. The mines up north in Madrid and Raton were said to be a lot safer than the mines around Socorro. After an accident like the dynamite shack exploding, miners were bound to leave. However, at the rate people were coming west, Ramon knew Mr. Dalton would have a full complement of miners again in no time.

Sipping his beer, Ramon noticed a calendar hanging beside the big mirror. He had two more years before his term as sheriff was up. Ramon wondered whether he would bother to run for re-election. Shaking his head, he wondered if he would even stick around Socorro. He'd heard his cousin had a nice little place down south by Palomas Hot Springs. Maybe he'd go there.

Without bothering to finish the beer, Ramon dropped a coin on the bar and stepped back out into the night.

The next day, Ray Hillerman burst through the door, stopping just before he collided with the sheriff's desk. He put his hands down on his knees and just breathed for a few minutes before he finally stood upright. "Sheriff, there's something strange going on at the San Miguel Church."

Ramon sat back and folded his arms. "What's going on?"

Ray dropped into a chair next to the desk. "There's a crowd gathering and they're collecting enough firewood to set a forest on fire."

"They're probably just gathering for a fiesta of some kind." He sounded skeptical of his own words. It wasn't even ten in the morning. "Did you say firewood?"

"I guess they could be getting ready to roast a pig up there." Ray shrugged. "But they didn't look like they was in a celebrating mood and one of them was Mr. Dalton."

"Maybe I'd better take a walk up there, just to see what's going on." The sheriff stood up and stepped over to the door. "If it's a party, maybe I can wrangle myself an invitation." He reached over and grabbed his hat from a nail on the wall.

Going outside, Ramon patted his horse's nose, then turned and walked toward the church. San Miguel was said to be the oldest church in New Mexico, even older than the mission of the same name in Santa Fe. Whether or not it was, the building wasn't much to look at. It was a plain brown adobe, just two stories tall with two small bell towers on either side of the portcullis. On one side of the church was a courtyard. As Ramon approached, he heard voices from the courtyard and they didn't sound happy.

The sheriff's instincts told him to be cautious, even though he couldn't think of any reason he should fear approaching a church. Instead of walking up to the courtyard's gate, he stepped around to the back of the church. There he found a couple of crates. He stood on one and found he could look into the courtyard. There, tied to a stake in the middle of the courtyard, was Fatemeh. Stacked around her ankles was enough wood to start a bonfire.

Mrs. Chavez stood in front of Fatemeh, listing off many of the so-called offenses she had cited to the sheriff over a week before. "She never goes to church. She always wears black..." *and she's a good scapegoat for the problems at your mine*, thought the sheriff as he caught sight of Mr. Dalton. Ramon quickly scanned the rest of the people gathered. There weren't all that many, really, only about fifteen. Even so, it was more than he could deal with all by himself, especially since many of them were grumbling and nodding agreement with every word Mrs. Chavez said.

What worried Ramon most was that Mr. Dalton's brother-in-law, Bishop Ramirez, stood to one side holding a torch. The sheriff wasn't sure he had time to run off and get help. His suspicions were confirmed when Mrs. Chavez finished her rant and the bishop started walking forward. "Based on the testimony, I understand that you have familiars, that you have contempt for the Church and for God-fearing men," he looked at his brother-in-law at that moment. "I have no choice but to declare that you are a witch and a consort of Satan. We must cleanse this evil from our midst."

Ramon thought if he'd been Fatemeh, he would have been scared, but she just stared at the bishop. She looked confused and uncertain of what she had done wrong, but not repentant. She looked around the wall, then whistled, like she did the night the sheriff first met her.

Ramon caught sight of a movement from one wall. An owl lifted off from its perch and swooped down at the bishop. It fluttered around in his face, causing him to drop the torch at his feet. Instead of lighting the wood piled around Fatemeh's feet, it ignited the bishop's long robes. The owl flew away and the bishop screamed.

Ramon scrambled over the top of the wall and dropped

into the courtyard. The group panicked and several tried to push their way through the gate. Father Esteban appeared, pushing his way through the escaping mob.

"What's going on?" asked the young priest, completely baffled by the scene.

Ramon pointed to the bishop. "He needs help." Father Esteban ran to the bishop while the sheriff ran to Fatemeh, drew his Bowie knife, and cut the ropes that held her to the post.

The sheriff was leading her to the wall when Mrs. Chavez stepped into their path. "The witch is getting away!" she shouted, but no one listened. Most of the mob had gone and Father Esteban was too busy helping the bishop.

Ramon drew his gun and pointed it at Mrs. Chavez's nose. "I don't want to shoot a woman, but if there's a witch that's going to die here today, it's you, not Fatemeh."

Mrs. Chavez swallowed hard and stepped aside. Ramon led Fatemeh to the wall and hunched down. She climbed on his back and pulled herself on top. Once there, she held her hand down to the sheriff. He took it and she helped him scramble to the top of the wall. Together they dropped to the ground on the other side. They ran past several buildings until they were well out of sight of the church.

Fatemeh and Ramon took a few minutes to rest and finally he looked into her green eyes. She smiled and said, "Thank you for saving me."

"I'm only doing my duty, ma'am," he said. He started walking her back to her house. "I recommend you clear on out of here," he said after a few minutes of silence. "When the bishop recovers he's not going to be too happy."

She nodded and was silent for a moment. "Can't you maintain the law and protect me?" she asked.

Ramon chewed his lower lip and thought about that question. "I wish I could," he said. "Thing is, around these parts, the Catholic Church is more feared than this." He pointed to the tin star that hung from his shirt.

"I thought there was freedom of religion in this country," she said wistfully.

"There is," Ramon said adamantly, then added, "just some people don't know it yet."

"Where should I go?" They reached her little adobe and she looked down toward the river.

The sheriff shrugged. "You might follow the river south to Las Cruces and Mesilla. It's more agricultural down there. They might take more kindly to your ways about being in harmony with the land."

"What about you?"

"I suppose I'll have to leave, too. I'm an elected official. Mr. Dalton and Bishop Ramirez will probably get me removed from office."

"Are there Catholics down in the South?"

Ramon nodded. "Fortunately, though, I think most Catholics are more like Father Esteban than Bishop Ramirez."

"Perhaps you should come with me," she said, "and help me avoid making more enemies." Those sharp green eyes of hers pleaded with the sheriff more strongly than words. If he really believed she was a witch, he would have said she was working her magic on him. Maybe she was. Ramon looked down at the river and considered his options. He could stay and try to sort things out—maybe finish out his term as sheriff—but then what?

"Do you have room in your wagon for a bachelor's few belongings?" he asked.

# CHAPTER TWO
## ELECTRIC KACHINAS

His name was Legion.

For millennia, the nanite swarm that was his current form explored galaxies and visited planets populated by thousands of races. He hadn't always been this way. Many centuries ago he had another name on a planet now nothing more than dust, gradually drifting outward from the exhausted core of a dead star. On that world, he'd possessed a mortal body. The thing called Legion remembered that world, and remembered his old body, and also the first computer he lived in, but he knew such memories meant little in the face of his immortal existence.

Unconstrained by a mortal lifetime or the distance he could travel, Legion gathered information about everything he came across. The universe contained so much variety that if he grew bored in one location, he simply moved on to another.

Eventually, he found his way to a small cluster containing two spiral galaxies and several dwarf galaxies. While ambling through one of the spirals, he came across a middle-aged yellow star that supported a handful of planets in stable orbits.

Legion was especially interested in the problem of intelligence. How did it evolve? What was its purpose? In all of his travels, he had yet to find a satisfactory answer. This humble solar system looked like one that could nurture life.

As he approached one of the inner, rocky worlds of this system, Legion grew excited. The planet contained large bodies of water broken up by landmasses, not unlike the world where he evolved. As he drifted closer, he saw straight lines cut into the ground and regular, geometric patterns of growing things.

Not only was there life on this world, but there was life that altered its landscape. That indicated intelligence. Legion decided on a closer look.

On the world, he found corporeal beings, similar to the creature he once was. Legion realized these beings might be at the perfect stage to help him answer a few of his questions about the purpose of intelligence. They had developed agriculture and industry. However, they still appeared primitive. All the devices he saw could have been built by hand or through the use of rudimentary machines. The creatures of this planet appeared to be on a path to become as intelligent as he was, yet they were still primitive enough he might be able to glean some understanding of how that intelligence came about.

He sought out an intelligent being so he could study its neural structure and attempt to interpret its thoughts with minimal interference or detection. Because of that, he chose to seek out a being in a sparsely inhabited area. He found a river valley he hoped would serve his purpose.

It was windy in the valley and Legion allowed his component parts to ride the air currents. The wind came in gusts, propelling him some distance, but then quieting, allowing him to regroup and scan his surroundings. He passed what appeared to be a military fortification near the river and then he saw ruins of much older habitations. Walking among the ruins was a lone creature, who looked around with interest.

The being was perfect. He was clearly the same type of creature who had altered the landscape. Moreover, the creature was alone. If Legion affected the creature adversely, detection was unlikely.

Before the next gust of wind, Legion drifted over to the creature.

The being took a deep breath and some of the components entered its nasal passages. Those components traveled into the being's lungs and ultimately into the bloodstream where they were carried to the brain, scanning and transmitting information as they went. Other components scanned the ruins and still others, further down the river valley, analyzed patterns of technological development and settlement, then compared that information to data collected from other worlds.

Alberto Mendez belonged to a team of men installing telegraph lines between Santa Fe and El Paso. The team consisted of carpenters, electricians, linesmen, post hole diggers and even lumberjacks. Mendez helped to wire up the electrical equipment at each of the telegraph stops. They had arrived at Fort McRae that afternoon and would begin installing the telegraph station in the morning. The soldiers at the fort told him about some Indian ruins nearby and he decided he would take a hike and have a look before settling in for supper and a night's sleep.

Despite his Spanish name, Mendez was an Indian from the pueblo of Tortugas. His ancestors used to live in the pueblos around Fort McRae. They used to be called the Piro.

In 1598, a group of Spaniards emerged from the harsh desert south of the ruins led by a man named Juan de Oñate. The Piro provided food and water to the dying men. The pueblo was a city as grand as anything the Europeans had in Mexico and it was the site of America's first Thanksgiving. Despite that, the pueblo would be abandoned within the year. Over 250 years of wind and rain had all but erased the pueblo's existence.

Mendez put his hands on his hips and looked around at the low walls that surrounded him—sad reminders of the grand pueblo that used to stand in this place.

He took a deep breath and let it out slowly. A few minutes later, as he continued along the path, strange words formed in his mind. They weren't English, Spanish or even the few words of Piro that were still known, but somehow he understood them just the same—or at least some of them.

*"...DNA analysis confirms this being is a descendent of creatures that inhabited this site 278 planetary years before..."*

Somehow Mendez knew that meant he was, in fact, a descendent of the people who once inhabited the pueblo ruins where he now stood.

*"...archeological evidence, along with memories from this being, suggests two waves of invasion..."*

After the Spaniards left the Piro Pueblo, they went north and enslaved the other peoples they encountered. Not wanting to incur the wrath of the Spaniards, the Piro refused to join when the other pueblos revolted. Like Oñate and his men, the Piro were driven south, toward El Paso del Norte. Shunned by their own people and abandoned by the Spaniards, the Piro were just as much victims of the invasion as the northern pueblos.

Now, there was another group of invaders forcing Indians from their homes. This time the invaders came from the east. Mendez looked over his shoulder at Fort McRae.

"...*topological and technological analysis indicates a 97% probability this area will be the site of a hydroelectric facility within the next century...*"

A picture formed in Mendez's mind of a great wall being built on the Rio Grande. The mighty river would be trapped and the valley where he stood would be flooded, all for the benefit of the newest wave of invaders.

Alberto Mendez did not have to think too hard to know where the images were coming from. He was on the land of his ancestors. The wind—a mighty elemental force—whipped through his hair. He must be in the presence of an elemental spirit. His people called such spirits kachinas. Alberto Mendez believed this kachina had selected him for a mission.

Ramon Morales was bone-weary when he finally saw Fort McRae on the opposite side of the Rio Grande. The landscape around the fort was more barren than around Socorro. It was as though the land near the river could not drink enough to grow vegetation. The mountains that bordered the Rio Grande Valley were covered in scrub brush instead of trees and seemed less friendly than they did further north.

Washes ran down from the mountains and cut through the flatlands of the valley, but did not actually carry any water this time of year. They left the land looking like a cracked and dried husk. Ramon wondered, not for the first time, if fleeing south had been such a good idea.

He took off his hat and wiped gritty sweat from his brow. It had been a long time since he'd spent the better part of a day on horseback. At least it wasn't windy like it had been a couple of days before.

Fatemeh Karimi, who rode in a wagon next to him, also looked bedraggled. Her black dress was coated in a fine layer of dust. Rivulets of sweat etched dirty streaks down Fatemeh's skin. Strands of wiry, black hair jutted out here and there. "Maybe we should go up to the fort and see if they'll put us up for the night," Fatemeh said.

"Nah." Ramon shook his head. "We've only got a couple more miles until we get to Palomas Hot Springs. My cousin Eduardo has a small hacienda there. He can put us up and we can get a hot bath."

"That sounds wonderful." Fatemeh's smile lit up her face and her green eyes sparkled.

Ramon's heart leapt at the sight of her renewed energy, but a hollow feeling soon formed in the pit of his stomach. He'd just thrown away his job as sheriff of Socorro to help her and yet he didn't know whether she would stay with him once they reached Las Cruces. He still didn't know whether she honestly liked him, or if she was merely using him as a protector and guide until they reached their destination.

At last, they topped a rise and could see Palomas Hot Springs. It really wasn't a town as most people would think of one. It was more like a wide spot in the road before entering a bad stretch of desert called Jornada del Muerto—the journey of death. There were a couple of rooming houses, a livery stable and a few meager haciendas. They all traded with the fort a few miles north. There were no stores, saloons or other establishments in Palomas Hot Springs.

What really drew people to the area were the hot springs themselves. The Apaches and the pueblo people considered it a holy place and neutral territory where they could trade. Medicine men would use the curative power of the hot springs to heal warriors after a battle. Anglos and Spanish folk were welcome to trade there, too, and the Indians didn't seem to mind the few settlements.

The austere scenery around the area certainly gave it the feeling of a holy place. Sheer cliffs of multi-colored rock walled in the barren valley and there was a dramatic butte, shaped a little like an elephant, near the river itself.

As Fatemeh and Ramon rode into Palomas Hot Springs, they caught sight of an Indian sitting on a blanket in the shade of an overhang. He had a wooden crate overflowing with wood and other odds and ends that looked like they could be springs or rolls of wire and tubing of some sort. Surrounding the Indian were little wooden dolls. He seemed to be whittling one of them.

Fatemeh pulled on the reins and stopped the wagon. Ramon tried to motion that they should continue on. He was tired and wanted to get to his cousin's before dark. He really didn't want to sit around while Fatemeh bartered with an Indian.

Either she didn't see Ramon's gesticulating or she didn't care. She climbed off the wagon's seat and stood before the Indian. He looked up as if noticing her for the first time. Gasping, he reached out as if to collect up the dolls. Ramon rolled his eyes and brought his horse to a stop. After climbing off, he wrapped the horse's reins around a nearby hitching post.

"These are kachina dolls, aren't they?" asked Fatemeh. "I didn't know any Pueblo Indians this far south made them."

"All pueblos respect the kachinas," said the Indian, looking around nervously, as though trying to find an escape.

"May I see one?" Fatemeh reached for the nearest doll.

The Indian waved his hands. "They are sacred."

Fatemeh knelt and nodded, solemnly. "I know they are. That's why I'm interested." As she took hold of the kachina doll, her eyes went wide and she gasped. She quickly released the doll and brought herself to her feet. "What was that?!"

"The kachinas are displeased," said the Indian. Ramon watched as he carefully reached out, took a doll by its head and hefted it into the box. The little wooden doll was apparently heavier than it looked at first sight. "First the Spanish came and caused this land to be taken from my people. Now the Anglos are coming and taking it from the Spanish. When will it stop?" He hefted another doll into the box. "Mark my words, great flood waters will come and destroy the land."

"I'm neither Spanish nor Anglo," said Fatemeh. "I'm Persian."

"Perhaps your people will be the next wave of invaders."

The Indian grabbed the last kachina doll. "You must face the truth of the kachina's displeasure and leave, or you will face consequences. Mark my words." The Indian stood, gathered up his blanket and placed it in the box. With a heave he picked up the box and started waddling down the road.

Fatemeh looked at Ramon with wide eyes.

"What happened when you grabbed that doll?"

"It's hard to describe," she said with a shrug. "It was a tingle like my hand fell asleep, but it was also like a bite." She climbed back up on her wagon.

Ramon's brow creased as he considered what might have caused the sensation Fatemeh described, but nothing came to mind. Too tired, hungry, and saddle sore to consider the matter further, he gathered the reins and mounted his horse. Besides, Eduardo might already know something about this Indian and his kachina dolls.

A few minutes later, Ramon and Fatemeh found themselves in front of Eduardo's small adobe hacienda. Eduardo came outside and greeted them with a warm smile. He looked much like Ramon would without glasses. He was a little taller, thinner, and—if one were to judge by the girls who fawned over him when he was younger—more handsome.

Ramon led his horse to a watering trough, then helped Fatemeh unhitch her two horses. Once the animals were tended, Eduardo ushered Ramon and Fatemeh into the kitchen, all the time casting sly glances between them. The former sheriff did his best to explain the events of the past two weeks in Socorro.

"Ah, Búho." Eduardo winked. "I always knew your desire to do the right thing would get you in trouble with someone."

"All I ask tonight is a meal and a couple of rooms," Ramon said.

"And a hot bath," interjected Fatemeh.

"Of course." Eduardo grinned. "Alicia is making a big caldo de rez this afternoon. You may stay as long as you like. This is a place to rest and recover before moving on."

"So, Ed, why haven't you moved on?"

He held his arms out wide. "I haven't finished resting and recovering!"

Later that evening, Eduardo's wife Alicia prepared a beautiful supper for Ramon and Fatemeh. Alicia was a little shorter than Ramon and wore her hair tied back in a neat bun. Ramon noticed she was a little heavier than when he'd last seen her. In her clean, blue dress, she looked a lot like his aunt. Her appearance was a stark contrast to Fatemeh's now-wild hair, rumpled black dress and fiery green eyes. As they ate, Ramon thought about how he had tried to catch Alicia's eye when they were younger, but she pursued Eduardo instead, as though she had been under his spell. Casting a glance toward Fatemeh, Ramon felt drawn to her, but he was concerned she didn't reciprocate his feelings.

After supper, Fatemeh decided it was time to have a bath. A short walk behind Eduardo's house was a place where water bubbled up from the ground. Eduardo had stacked rocks around the spring to give the bather some privacy. While Fatemeh availed herself of the natural spring, Ramon went to his room to unpack a few things. Finally he took a towel from a dresser drawer and found a bench just outside the backdoor to wait for Fatemeh to finish. The sun was setting and the rocks had taken on a deep red hue. There was enough of a chill breeze that a dip in the hot spring would feel very good to a hot and dusty traveler.

Ramon looked up and saw Fatemeh as she stepped from the rock enclosure. She wore a clean, modest black dress, but it clung to her skin because of the moisture. Her feminine curves were very apparent. Ramon watched, mesmerized as she stepped over and sat down next to him.

"You should close your mouth," she said. "There are mosquitoes."

Ramon quickly apologized, but she laughed lightly without any hint of mockery and told him not to worry about it.

Ramon took a deep breath, and then looked her in the eye. "Fatemeh, there's something I want..."

Eduardo stepped around the corner carrying an armload of firewood. "When you guys came into town, did you see that Indian with the kachina dolls?"

"Yes." Ramon nodded. "I wanted to ask about him."

Eduardo let the firewood tumble to his feet. Ramon stood

and helped him neatly stack it behind the backdoor. "He showed up about the time a group of telegraph workers arrived at Fort McRae. He keeps moving around with that big box of his." He looked over his shoulder. "He's camped out a little ways down from the house. I wish I could find out what he keeps in that box."

"So do I." Fatemeh whistled a few short notes. Ramon looked up and noticed the silhouette of a burrowing owl perched atop the rock enclosure around the hot spring. She whistled again and the owl did a little dance and then flew from the wall to the ground near Fatemeh's feet. "I might even have a way to distract him so we can find out."

A short time later, Ramon found himself hunkered down behind a watering trough in front of Eduardo's house watching the Indian work beside his campfire. He asked Eduardo why they couldn't wait until the Indian was asleep and just sneak a peek in his box.

"He never sleeps as far as I can tell," whispered Ramon's cousin.

The little owl Fatemeh summoned flew over and perched on the edge of the Indian's box. The Indian shooed it away, but the owl returned and started pecking around in the box. The Indian shooed at it again, but this time the owl had something in its beak. When the Indian noticed, he scooted after the owl.

Ramon ran to the box and grabbed one of the kachina dolls—careful not to touch anything other than the head, as he'd seen the Indian do earlier. The thing was a lot heavier than Ramon expected from a little wooden doll. He hauled it back to his hiding place behind the water trough. He looked up in time to see the Indian return to the campfire, holding something that looked like a wire. The Indian dropped the wire back in the box. The owl returned to the box and looked as if he was going to dig for the wire again when Fatemeh whistled. The owl's head turned, seeking the sound's source. It did its little dance and then flew away.

Once the owl was gone, the Indian returned to his work.

Ramon grabbed the kachina doll by the head and carried it inside where he found Fatemeh, Eduardo and Alicia already gathered at the table. In the light of the kitchen lamp Ramon could see a piece of metal sticking out of each side of the doll. "What are these?" He reached for one of the metal pieces. "Careful." Fatemeh batted his finger away. "I think I grabbed those when I touched the doll before."

Being careful not to touch the two pieces of metal, Eduardo picked up the kachina doll and examined it closely. There was something round and metal on the bottom. He set the doll down and reached for it, but Alicia stopped him. "We don't know what it'll do," she said.

"What's for certain is that there's something inside the thing," Ramon said. Before someone could say anything else, Ramon reached out, grabbed the doll by the head and brought it down hard on the table. Fatemeh gasped in shock. The soft wood of the doll shattered, revealing a metal cylinder inside. The two pieces of metal that stuck out the side of the doll were connected to the cylinder by copper wire. "What the hell?" asked Ramon.

"I'm not positive," said Fatemeh, "but I think that's a dry cell battery."

"Of course!" said Eduardo. "They use them in the telegraph equipment."

"That Indian must be loco," declared Alicia. "Why would he put batteries inside kachina dolls?"

"Maybe he wants people to believe kachina spirits really inhabit the dolls," Fatemeh said. "It almost convinced me when I grabbed one and it felt like it was alive."

Ramon shook his head. Things didn't add up. "If he's trying to scare people with his dolls, why does he pack them up and run away whenever someone comes near?" The former sheriff stepped out the front door. The Indian's campfire was out and he was nowhere to be seen. Ramon took off his glasses and rubbed the bridge of his nose as he considered the questions that ran through his mind. The Indian must want to power something with the batteries in the kachina dolls, but what? He hadn't seen anything besides dolls and wires in the box. The only thing he knew of in the area that required electric power was the telegraph, but then why hide the batteries in kachina dolls?

The door creaked open behind him. Fatemeh stepped up next to Ramon, so close he could feel the heat of her skin. He put his glasses back on and swallowed hard as he tried to turn his mind from the problem of the Indian to the questions he had about the nature of their relationship. He took a deep breath and formed a question.

Just as he was about to reach out and take Fatemeh's hand, Eduardo appeared in the doorway. "Where'd that Indian go?"

Ramon blinked a few times and sighed. "It's getting late, Cuz. I think I'm going to go have my bath and call it a night."

The dip in the hot spring after a long day of riding let Ramon sleep very well, but he still woke up sore the next morning. He dragged himself out of bed, washed his face in the basin of water that was in the room and dressed. Ramon could smell coffee and something else, a blending of chocolate and cinnamon he hadn't smelled in many years. He followed the smells and sat down at the kitchen table. Alicia placed a bowl of chocolate and cinnamon-spiced atole in front of Ramon along with a cup of coffee. "I haven't had atole since I was a kid," he said as he dug in. "I'm not going to want to leave."

Fatemeh stepped into the kitchen. "Is there any reason to leave right away?" She offered to help Alicia, who instead told her to sit and then placed a bowl of atole in front of her.

"Well, I don't want to wear out Eduardo and Alicia's hospitality."

"Don't worry about that, Búho," said Eduardo as he entered the kitchen. "I already told you, you are welcome to stay as long as you'd like. Besides, they're having a big shindig up at Fort McRae this afternoon."

"What's the occasion?" Ramon inclined his head.

Eduardo leaned forward. "They're testing the telegraph."

Alicia turned around, wide-eyed. "That's exciting."

Fatemeh smiled. "It sounds fascinating. I'd like to go."

Ramon turned to his bowl of atole so he wouldn't have

to face her. It didn't matter whether he was a bodyguard or a suitor. She hadn't asked what he wanted to do, or even what he advised, and it stung his pride. He wasn't certain whether she noticed his silence or if it was just good manners, but she finally asked, "What would you like to do, Ramon?"

Ramon took another bite of atole and let the chocolate and cinnamon dance on his tongue a moment. He thought about his saddle-sore backside and how good another dip in the hot spring would feel. Finally he took a sip of coffee to wash down the atole. "Yeah, I'm game for a trip to the fort."

That afternoon, Ramon, Fatemeh, Eduardo and Alicia rode north and then crossed the river to Fort McRae. Like many forts in the West, it wasn't purely a military installation. It also served as a trading post and stopping point for travelers on the road between El Paso and Santa Fe. The installation was a series of adobe buildings hunkered behind a wall. Just inside the gate was a dusty courtyard that could be used as an assembly point or parade ground of sorts. At the center of the courtyard, a brass band played. Several of their notes went flat, but no one seemed to mind.

Next to the band, several people gathered around a canopy. From the distance, Ramon couldn't make out what they were looking at, but he guessed that would be the place the telegraph was set up. The arrival of the telegraph meant the fort could send dispatches, wire for supplies, or receive news from around the country. Ramon presumed that after the ceremony, the telegraph would be moved inside one of the buildings.

Big pots of steaming food stood at one side of the courtyard. Ramon detected the earthy smell of corn mixed with chile. Perhaps someone was steaming tamales, cooking posole, or both. Despite his breakfast of atole, Ramon's stomach rumbled.

Fatemeh turned toward the other side of the courtyard where several people had games set up. Ramon watched as a boy pitched a ball toward some bottles and missed. Next to the stacked bottles, there was a dartboard set up on the fort's outer wall. An Indian came up and paid a penny. His first dart hit the bull's eye and the man running the game produced a string of glass beads. The Indian scowled at the beads, but took them anyway.

Ramon heard a round fired from a six-gun. "They must have a shooting range set up. Let's go see." The former sheriff wasn't confident in his ability to throw a ball or a dart, but he knew he could win a prize at a shooting competition.

As Ramon tried to follow the sound of gunfire, he tripped and fell flat on his face. Fatemeh helped him to his feet as he cursed about not seeing the thing he fell over. That's when Ramon realized that what he tripped over was very hard to see—a pair of wires partially buried in the dust. He looked a question at Fatemeh. She shrugged.

The former sheriff wasn't a half-bad tracker, so he turned his attention to the ground and followed the hidden wires to find out where they went. Fatemeh followed. They soon found themselves facing the canopy where the telegraph key was on display.

"Maybe the wires you tripped over are how they connected the telegraph to the outside lines," Fatemeh said.

Ramon shook his head and pointed to a pair of wires that ran from the telegraph to a pole just inside the fort's outer wall. He turned and followed the wires back the other direction. The wires led well away from the main activity and ran parallel to a row of identical adobe structures. Ramon assumed they must be the barracks.

Eventually, the wires disappeared under the dirt, but unless they turned, they went to a door that was guarded by two men who looked at once stern and disappointed that they were not taking part in the festivities. A sign on the door read: "Dangerous! Explosives!"

Without thinking too much about it, Ramon stepped up to one of the guards. "Hello, I'm Sheriff Ramon Morales of Socorro County and I've just seen something suspicious." Ramon figured there was no way for the guard to know he was no longer sheriff and his gut told him something was very wrong. The possible danger outweighed any scruples he had about lying. "Is there a reason there would be telegraph wires running into this building?"

The guard looked at him dumbfounded. "No, sir," he said. "No reason that I can think of."

"Do you mind opening the door and letting me have a

look inside?"

The first guard looked to his companion and they both shrugged. One of the guards stood right next to Ramon while the other opened the door. Inside, as Ramon expected, was a stockpile of dynamite and blasting powder. However, what really surprised him were the kachina dolls stacked all around— one connected to a pair of copper wires that came up from the ground. The other dolls were connected to the first by still more wires.

"That doesn't look normal, does it?" Ramon asked.

Both guards shook their heads.

Ramon looked at Fatemeh. "I think we better find the guys who installed the telegraph and ask them what this is all about."

They ran back to the telegraph pavilion. A few high-ranking officers and some other men had gathered. Ramon figured those other men must be some of the telegraph crew. He caught his breath and said, "Do you know you've got some extra wires coming out of the key?"

One of the men, who wasn't in uniform, looked at Ramon like he was wasting his time. "What extra wires?"

The former sheriff stepped forward and lifted the covering from the table where the telegraph key sat. The man knelt down and blinked at the wires. He looked up. "Harvey, there should only be one ground wire," he said. "Why are there two down here?"

"That's because I changed the wiring, Mr. Hinkley." The strange Indian had suddenly appeared next to the table. "The truth has been revealed by the kachinas. The invaders keep coming and coming. Now, the time has come to face the consequences."

The man called Mr. Hinkley shook his head. "Alberto, where have you been? We've been looking all over for you. What are you talking about? Truth? Consequences?"

Alberto reached out. "It is time for the consequences."

"Stop him!" Ramon called. "He's got the telegraph key wired up to the dynamite—some kind of detonator or something."

The soldiers, though confused about everything happening at once, reacted to the former sheriff's authoritative voice.

They grabbed the Indian, but he struggled. Fatemeh whistled and Ramon wondered if she'd seen Eduardo and Alicia and was trying to warn them to get away. Ramon rushed around the table to try to help the soldiers—to calm things down enough so he could explain what was going on.

Alberto broke free and pushed the telegraph key. Ramon closed his eyes and winced but nothing happened. When he opened his eyes, he saw a little burrowing owl perched on the table. It had plucked one of the power supply wires off the key and still held it in its mouth. It dropped the wire and flew off.

One of the officers summoned more soldiers and Alberto was taken away for questioning. The fort's commander, Major Johnson, stepped up and introduced himself. Ramon led Major Johnson and Mr. Hinkley back to the dynamite shack to show them what he'd discovered. On the way, Hinkley explained that Alberto Mendez was part of their crew. He'd gone missing the day they arrived at Fort McRae and no one was quite sure what had happened to him.

Major Johnson whistled when he saw kachina dolls stacked around the dynamite. "That's quite a detonator setup he had."

Mr. Hinkley pointed out that another set of wires ran toward the armory.

"He could have blown up the entire fort," said the major.

"And himself, too," Hinkley said. "He must have really gone loony in the head."

Ramon saw that as a good time to make his exit. The soldiers had the evidence they needed and could question Alberto Mendez further. Ramon didn't want to stick around so they could find out he wasn't still sheriff of Socorro County.

Ramon made his way back to the pavilion, where he found Fatemeh leaning against a nearby building.

"Thanks for calling that little hooty owl," he said. "He saved all of our lives."

"What makes you think I can summon owls?" she asked with a cagey smile.

Ramon took her hands in his and brought her close.

Just then, Eduardo showed up. "Where have you two been? I've been looking all over for you! One of the vendors has empanadas!"

Ramon ignored him and kissed Fatemeh anyway.

Over the millennia, Legion had known a few creatures that could sense the communications among the component nanites of his swarm. This was the first time he'd seen such a creature react so badly to the data and pictures the nanites sent.

Several of his component parts argued he should have terminated connection to avoid interference. However, most of his components were fascinated by the being's way of relating the physical world to an unseen spiritual realm. Legion sensed these humans did hold answers to the meaning of life that had eluded him before. Moreover, he couldn't dismiss the possibility the human called Alberto Mendez had simply been unstable. Observing the humans called Fatemeh Karimi and Ramon Morales further bolstered his supposition more rational humans existed.

Legion decided he would try to communicate with another human before giving up on the species. Before making the attempt, he would spend time observing the humans and their activities from a distance to gain more clues about their behavior. At the very least, these humans weren't boring.

# CHAPTER THREE
## THE CLOCKWORK LOBO

Fatemeh Karimi and Ramon Morales rode toward Mesilla, New Mexico on a pleasantly warm and clear spring afternoon. Ramon was atop his horse and Fatemeh drove the colorful wagon that held the herbs, roots, and infusions she used in her work as a healer. Just as they got close enough to town to hear the bells of the San Albino church, they came upon a sign and the main road veered away from Mesilla itself. "Horses aren't allowed on the streets of Mesilla," read Ramon. "We have to leave them at the Mesilla Park."

Weary from the long ride, Fatemeh simply nodded and urged her horses forward along the road that led to the liveries that served the largest town in the region. A short time later, they spent more of their precious money than they would have liked stabling their horses and storing Fatemeh's wagon.

Ramon carefully counted the money they had left. "I think we may have just enough for four or five nights at a modest hotel or a boarding house. After that, we're going to have to find some more money."

"Right now, all I want is a bath and soft bed. We'll worry about money tomorrow. In a town the size of Mesilla, I'm sure it'll be easy to find people who need the services of a curandera."

"Hopefully you'll have better luck here than in Socorro." Ramon gathered up his saddlebags and slung a rifle over his shoulder while Fatemeh packed what she needed into a satchel she wore on her back. Together they set off toward the center of town. "Just try not to anger any of the farmers or ranchers in the area and we should be fine."

"I would like to think farmers and ranchers are more in

tune with their surroundings than miners who rip minerals from the earth."

"One would hope," said Ramon. As they walked toward the town square, he looked at the shops and saloons, wondering if he would be able to find work. He looked down a side street and caught sight of the Mesilla Town Marshal's office. Ramon knew he would make a good deputy. However, if word of his sudden departure from Socorro had reached this far south, he could find himself inside a cell rather than guarding one. In the end, he decided to stay clear of the marshal's office until he had established himself as a good citizen of Mesilla.

They reached the town square and made their way around it, looking at the businesses and also seeing what lay down the side streets. At one corner of the square was a large building called the Corn Exchange Hotel, but it was tucked right between the courthouse and a saloon. Ramon and Fatemeh looked at each other and decided to continue their search without going inside.

A little further on, they spotted a respectable-looking rooming house down one of the side streets. It was a square, two-story adobe building with a wooden front porch and a carved sign proclaiming, "Castillo's—Rooms for Rent." Pots of flowers adorned the porch's railings and a string of drying chilies hung alongside the door. Ramon led the way to the building.

As they approached, he noticed a sign tacked to one of the porch's posts, apparently placed there by one of the local ranchers. "Five-dollar reward for each lobo carcass," it read.

"The ranchers must be having wolf problems," Ramon said aloud. A flash of teeth, claws and fur crossed his memory and he frowned as he subconsciously rubbed old scars on his elbow, hidden by his shirt.

"That's terrible." Fatemeh sneered at the sign. "It's not the wolves' fault cattle are easy prey."

"Five dollars would get us rooms for another night—it would be another bath." Ramon continued to rub his arm. He inclined his head toward the gun at his back. "I'm a pretty fair shot. Maybe I can collect some of that bounty."

Fatemeh's eyes grew wide. "How dare you, Ramon! How could you even consider hunting wolves? I could never sleep in a bed that was paid for with such a bounty." Her cheeks were flushed, both from the sun and her rising anger.

Ramon took a deep breath and let it out slowly, trying to release the memory of long-ago pain. Suddenly aware he was rubbing his arm, he stopped and held out his hands. "I'm sorry, Fatemeh, I should have known better." ...*than to say anything.* He left the last part unspoken.

"That's right, Ramon Morales. There will be no more talk of hunting wolves." She hitched her satchel more firmly onto her shoulder, then stormed through the door.

Ramon sighed and took one last look at the poster before he followed her in. Inside the door was a small room with a wooden counter. Behind it, keys were hung on brass hooks. Two green-upholstered chairs sat against a wood-paneled wall. Red tile covered the floor. One door led to a dining room and another led to a sitting room. Ramon thought it looked like a pleasant place to stay and hoped they would be able to afford even one night in this place.

A balding man with a bushy mustache and a blue, silk vest appeared at the sitting room door. "I'm Castillo. May I help you, Señor?"

Ramon nodded. "I hope so. We'd like to rent two rooms."

Mr. Castillo smiled and quoted a price.

Ramon swallowed hard, but remembered the poster on the porch. "We'll take it."

Fatemeh tugged at Ramon's sleeve. "We can't afford that for more than two nights," she whispered

"I know, but it'll give us a place to stay while we look around." He placed his saddlebags on the counter, so he could retrieve money to pay Mr. Castillo.

Later, while Fatemeh soaked in a bath, Ramon went to the sitting room. The room held a couch and four chairs, arranged so the occupants could speak to one another. The smell of cigar smoke clung to the chairs' upholstery. A piano sat in one corner and there was a fireplace. Mr. Castillo pounded a nail into the wall. He reached down and retrieved a wooden clock. After hanging it, he inserted a key into a hole on the face and wound it. The clock began ticking and the gears within purred gently.

Ramon cleared his throat. "I was curious, who posted that sign on the porch?"

Mr. Castillo turned around. "Warren Shedd posted that sign. He owns the San Augustin Ranch up out of Las Cruces." He pointed toward the sheer, rocky Organ Mountains to the northeast. "He runs cattle all around the base of the mountains, but those lobos come down and snatch the calves. It's a real problem for him."

Ramon thanked him for his time and soon afterward met Fatemeh for a very good supper of steak and beans prepared by Mrs. Castillo. Tired as she was, Fatemeh decided to go to bed right after supper. Ramon followed her upstairs and went into his own room. He was tired, too, but didn't go to sleep. Instead, he opened his pocket watch and waited for an hour to go by. Ramon quietly slipped out of the room and walked back toward the Mesilla Park and his horse. He rode toward the Organ Mountains. As the land rose, he found a grove of trees and a small stream that offered a good view of the valley beyond. Cattle grazed in the grass nearby. It seemed a good place to camp and watch for wolves.

Ramon found a hidden spot in a ring of rocks just at the edge of the little grove. There, he laid out his bedroll. Opening his rifle, he aimed the barrel toward the moon and checked that there wasn't too much powder buildup, then loaded a shell into the barrel so he'd be ready to fire without delay. He was determined to shoot a wolf, but tired as he was, he fell asleep instead.

He dreamed of a time when he was a child, running through a field on his way home from school. He saw two wolf pups wrestling with each other in the tall grass. Nearby, a mother wolf watched him. The young Ramon thought they were cute and wondered if he could pet the pups. Remembering his dad's warnings to stay away from wild animals, he decided he should give them a wide berth. Just then, he felt a sharp pain and heard a loud snap.

He woke suddenly and realized the snap was a nearby twig. There was another sound as well—a strange whirring and buzzing, not unlike the soft sounds that came from Mr. Castillo's clock.

Slowly, he reached for his rifle and turned toward the grove. The moon was high and there were deep shadows amongst the trees. His throat was parched and he wished he had time to take a drink from his canteen. However, he soon spotted movement. A lobo stepped from the shadows and strode confidently toward the cattle down the hill.

Ramon tried to swallow, but no saliva would come to his mouth. He thought he detected a flash of movement behind him, and quickly looked around. Not seeing anything amongst the rocks and deep shadows, he turned his attention back to the strange lobo that walked so brazenly in plain sight. Ramon thought a wolf would have been more cautious when stalking prey, but he was glad for its erect stance, and slow, steady stride. It was an easy target. He carefully aimed his gun at the wolf.

Just as Ramon started to squeeze the trigger, someone pushed the gun. His shot went wide, missing the lobo. Ramon cursed and turned, finding himself facing Fatemeh's angry glare. "What are you doing out here? That animal doesn't deserve to be shot just so you can have a few dollars."

"It's not about…" Ramon shook his head. Fatemeh would not understand. "We really could use the money." He looked down, avoiding her gaze.

She sighed. "I know, but there are other ways."

Ramon looked at the lobo. The gunshot had not spooked it. It strutted through the grove, ignoring its surroundings. It didn't even seem to notice the strange clicking and whirring sounds—Ramon looked around, trying to figure out where they were coming from. When he looked back at the wolf, he saw it was headed straight for a rock. Surely it would turn before it got there, but no. It walked right into the rock and the most amazing thing happened. There was a bright flash of light accompanied by a loud popping. The top of the wolf's head flew off and its body toppled over sideways.

"What the hell?" Ramon scrambled out from his hiding place. Fatemeh followed close behind.

He reached the wolf and peered inside its head, expecting to find a bloody mess. Instead, the head was mostly empty and separated into two compartments. At the back of one of the compartments was a small, glass photographic plate. The other compartment held the charred remains of some kind of powder. The wolf's eyes were lenses with black metal just behind them. Ramon reached in and felt around, then dragged the wolf's body out into the moonlight where he could see better. It was much heavier than a wolf would be, as though most of the body was made from metal rather than skin or bones.

Fatemeh looked inside. "It's like a camera."

Ramon nodded. "There's some kind of spring-loaded mechanism that lowers these metal contraptions just behind the eyes." He pushed on a rod inside the wolf's head and sure enough the metal plates lowered, which would, in turn, expose the glass plate at the back of the head to light—except that the plate had already been exposed when the top of the head was blown off.

"But what caused that bright flash of light we saw?"

"Flash powder," said a voice from the trees.

Ramon and Fatemeh looked up as a figure strode out into the moonlight. He wore a tailored jacket with matching pants. His vest was red silk and he wore a cravat around his neck. For a guy out in the woods, he was immaculate. "I see you found my lobo." Then he looked closer. "Its head blew off again. That's very disappointing."

"Who are you?" asked Fatemeh.

"Pardon my ill manners. I am Professor M.K. Maravilla of the Pontifical and Royal University of Mexico." He bowed and kissed Fatemeh's hand.

Fatemeh stood and dusted off her full, black skirt. "I am Fatemeh Karimi and this is my friend, Ramon Morales."

Ramon stood up and extended his hand toward the professor, whose grip was somewhat light for the former sheriff's taste. "I thought the Mexican Government closed down the university."

"Ah, but they did," said Maravilla with an air of sadness. He tugged on his elegant trousers as he squatted near the strange wolf with a camera in its head. "That is why I had to carry my researches north. I have been studying the Mexican Gray Wolf, trying to understand its behavior. I have been hoping to photograph wolves in the wild, see what they see when no people are around."

Ramon's eyes narrowed. The word maravilla was Spanish for marvel or wonder. "Is 'Maravilla' your real name?"

Maravilla snorted. "My name is as 'real' as yours, sir." Then the corner of his mouth turned upward. "Although I'll concede that it might not be the name I was born with. Under the circumstances, I believe a pseudonym is...prudent."

Ramon pursed his lips and nodded. "So, what exactly is this contraption?"

The professor reached over and opened a small, concealed hatch on the wolf's side. Inside were gears and pistons. "This machine is the result of years of work. I had the help of a taxidermist who preserved the skin of a wolf—one that died of natural causes, I might add." He made a point of nodding toward Fatemeh. "The insides were built by a clockmaker and a photographer in Mexico City."

Maravilla examined the insides of the strange clockwork lobo for a few minutes, then clapped his hands in delight. "Ah, but it has successfully taken some photographs." He pointed to the head. "You see, it holds several of these small glass plates. I can set the clockworks in the lobo to take photos at different intervals. Each time a photo is taken, the plate is released into this compartment here." He pointed to a door between the wolf's shoulders.

"What's the other compartment in the wolf's head?" asked Fatemeh.

"A most ingenious invention," declared the professor. "It is a reusable flash that allows the camera to work in dark places and take short exposures." He shook his head. "But, as you can see, sometimes too much powder is released and boom!" He sighed and then stood. "What is it you two are doing out here at this late hour?" he asked at last.

"Camping," said Ramon.

"Trying to find a way to keep the wolves from killing the cattle," said Fatemeh at almost the same moment.

"Ah, you're out to shoot lobos and collect the bounty," said Maravilla, a little sadly.

"No!" said Fatemeh with a sudden shake of her head. "No, the wolves are only killing cattle because they're easy prey. If we can get the wolves to seek out their natural prey—deer and rabbits—order will be restored and the ranchers won't have need of a bounty."

"That is possible," said Maravilla, looking up.

Maravilla and Fatemeh moved over to the ring of rocks where Ramon had set up his campsite and continued their conversation. Ramon moved toward the grove of trees and gathered up some twigs and fallen branches. He thought about a wolf's jaws clamping down on his arm when he was a child— about being dragged. As he brought the wood back toward the campsite he saw Fatemeh and the fancy Professor Maravilla sitting awfully close together. She was gazing into the professor's eyes as their passionate conversation continued about the wolves. Ramon set about building a fire. Once it was going, he made a point of sitting on the other side of Fatemeh, as close as he could, but not so close that she would strike him with her arms as she spoke.

"It would be wonderful if we could introduce the wolves to their natural prey," said Maravilla. "The only problem is, if the wolves can't find easier prey than cattle, how can we?"

"That is easily solved," said Fatemeh. She looked around the area and then moved a short ways off, towards the stump of a tree that had been felled by lightning. She made several short, sharp whistles and then listened quietly. She whistled again. A few minutes later, a little burrowing owl flew down and alighted on the tree stump. It chirped and whistled three times, then bowed to Fatemeh. She returned the almost courtly bow and whistled again. The owl gave several short, sharp chirps.

Professor Maravilla watched, his mouth agape. He turned to Ramon and whispered, "Is she really speaking to that owl?"

"I believe she is," Ramon said almost reverently.

"She is truly a singular woman," said Professor Maravilla. He straightened his silk vest, then ran his fingers over his petite, immaculately trimmed mustache, pushing any errant hairs in line.

The little owl flew off and Fatemeh turned back to the men. "About two and a half miles from here there's a rabbit warren that's getting overpopulated with the spring. The wolves haven't discovered it yet, but I think they could be led there."

"That would, indeed, be good prey for the lobos," said Maravilla, standing. He reached out and took Fatemeh's hand. "But tell me, good lady, how do you know this? Did you really speak to that owl?"

"Owls don't speak. They chirp and whistle," said Fatemeh. She pulled her hand back from Maravilla's, but not before giving it a gentle squeeze. Ramon pursed his lips. She moved closer to the fire and held out her hands, warming them. She looked at Ramon and then looked at Professor Maravilla. "Can you repair your clockwork lobo by tomorrow night?"

"If I could have a little assistance in the afternoon," said Maravilla with a slight bow at the waist. He gave Ramon and Fatemeh directions to his lodgings.

"Good," said Fatemeh. "We'll see you tomorrow at two. I have a plan." She looked at Ramon. "Now help me douse this fire. There are perfectly good beds waiting for us in Mesilla and I for one am very tired."

Ramon slept in late the next day. He missed breakfast and Fatemeh had already gone out without leaving a note. Her plans had been to learn about the local doctors and curanderas—see if she could find one she could help. Barring that, she planned to find somewhere she could park her wagon and proffer her services, much as she had done in Socorro. Ramon worried she had gone to seek out Professor Maravilla. He looked down at his own trousers and shirt, shabby from the time on the road. Professor Maravilla certainly cut a more striking figure and it was clear he was interested in her.

Fatemeh and Ramon had shared a few romantic moments. He was definitely under her spell, but feared his own quiet personality might be giving the wrong impression. Ramon worried she might not think he was sufficiently interested in her. He wondered if M.K. Maravilla would be able to steal her away from him. They certainly seemed to have similar interests and they were able to talk at length on the subject of lobos. Ramon rubbed his arm and thought about his own encounter with a wolf when he was young. He shook his head and tried to think about something else.

Ramon's thoughts returned to Fatemeh. That gave him pause. He couldn't deny he was falling in love with her. However, she was a Bahá'í—a religion from Persia he had never heard of before meeting her. He was a not-so-devout Catholic boy who didn't know whether he believed enough to ask her to convert to his religion, but still feared being damned forever if he converted to hers. If their love grew, could he ask such a woman to marry him?

Ramon wiped his sweaty palms on the bedspread, dressed, and then went over to the General Store where he found some tortillas he could afford. After eating two of the tortillas, he took the rest back to his room and then asked the boarding house's owner if he knew whether anyone around town was looking for hired hands.

"What are you good at?" asked Mr. Castillo, eyeing Ramon carefully.

Ramon took a deep breath and let it out slowly as he thought back. Before he was sheriff of Socorro, he had been a deputy. Before that, he had been a hand on his uncle's farm. "I'm a hard worker," he said at last. "I'm a good rider and I know something about law."

"Do you have a degree?" asked Mr. Castillo.

Ramon shook his head.

"You might talk to Thomas Bull. He used to own the San Augustin Ranch," suggested Mr. Castillo. "He still owns some land up near the mountains. He's usually looking for hired hands—especially now that the spring roundup is approaching. He also has some office jobs here in town." He gave Ramon directions to Mr. Bull's office. Ramon thanked Mr. Castillo and went to find Mr. Bull.

Mr. Bull turned out to be friendly, but a bit distracted. He struck Ramon as a man with a lot of irons in the fire, so to speak. Not only did he own a ranch, but he also owned several businesses around Mesilla and Las Cruces. He told Ramon to report to the ranch foreman the next day and if the foreman approved, Ramon could help with the roundup.

That could lead to more work.

Ramon felt like he was walking on air as he started back to the boarding house.

As he passed the apothecary, he heard a shout. "What are you? Some kind of a bruja?"

Without thinking about it, Ramon drew his six-gun and ran to the door. Inside, a man with a beet-red face held up a finger at Fatemeh, who stood with her hands on her hips. "What's going on here?" asked Ramon. Even without a star pinned to his shirt, he knew his voice and the gun carried the authority of a peace officer.

"That ... that ... woman ... is calling me a cheat!"

"No," said Fatemeh with an edge to her voice, "I said that some of these so-called elixirs and patent medicines do no good." She looked at Ramon. "I told him I could make herbal remedies for him that would actually cure people but would cost him half as much. That's when he started yelling and calling me a witch."

"I do not cheat my customers," said the man forcefully. He grabbed a bottle and held it up. "This tonic is guaranteed to cure the common cold."

Ramon holstered his gun, then reached out and took the bottle. Pulling out the stopper, he took a whiff. The smell of the alcohol was so strong that it almost knocked him over. "That'll make you feel better all right," he said.

"There is no cure for the common cold," insisted Fatemeh. "But there are herbal remedies that can relieve the symptoms until you get better." She opened her mouth to continue, but Ramon held up his hand, cutting her off.

He placed the bottle on the counter and took Fatemeh by the elbow, leading her toward the door.

"Thanks, Deputy," called the man from the counter. "I appreciate your help. That bruja is bad for business."

Ramon turned on his heel and strode back to the counter. He grabbed the clerk by the collar and pulled him close. "Listen, Señor, you may not like the lady, but you damn well better not call her a witch again in my hearing. Comprende?"

"Understood," said the man, nodding quickly.

Ramon let go of his shirt and turned around. "Let's get out

of here. It's about time to meet the professor."

Fatemeh nodded and the two left together.

From the way he dressed, Ramon expected the professor would be staying in a fine hotel. Instead, as Ramon and Fatemeh followed the professor's directions, they found themselves walking into a very poor part of town. They passed a long building where several women leaned out of upstairs windows, wearing a lot of make-up and not much else that Ramon could tell. Fatemeh hurried him along until they found the professor's lodgings—a run-down adobe rooming house. The owner showed them to Maravilla's room.

The professor met them at the door. "I must apologize for the humility of my domicile," said the professor. "However, since I have resumed—how shall I say—unfunded research, I must make every dollar stretch as far as I can." He motioned for Ramon and Fatemeh to step inside the room.

There was a simple cot. The lobo was on the floor with several hatches open, exposing the inner clockwork mechanism. Blankets had been hung in one corner of the room, making the already tiny space much more cramped. The professor stepped toward the hanging blankets. "This is my darkroom," he explained. "The photos from last night should be ready. Let's see what I got." He brought out two delicate glass photographs. "Nothing on this one but a field." He shrugged and tossed it onto the bed. Then he looked at the other and smiled broadly. "Look, wolves!"

He handed the photograph to Fatemeh.

"Very good." She passed the photo to Ramon. He could just make out some shapes that looked a little like dogs or wolves. The whole photograph was rather blurred and Ramon really couldn't tell what the professor was so excited about.

Ramon felt a hand on his shoulder and he jerked, nearly dropping the photograph. He looked up and saw a worried frown on Fatemeh's face. "There's anger in your eyes," she said.

"What?" Ramon set the photograph down on the bed next to the other one.

"You said it yourself last night, it's not about the money," she said slowly. "You really hate wolves. I can see it in the way you look at the photograph."

Ramon grabbed his arm and quickly stepped out of the room and onto the boarding house's unpainted, creaking porch. A few minutes later, Fatemeh appeared at his side. She put her hand on his arm. "It's okay," she said. "I just want to understand. Why do you hate the wolves?"

Ramon stood there for a long time, looking out into the street. Finally, he took a deep breath and let it out slowly. "When I was ten, I was walking home from school. I saw a mama wolf and her pups. I knew enough to stay away from them. I kept her in sight and I tried to edge around where she was so I could get where I was going. Then suddenly, another wolf grabbed me from behind and dragged me several feet. Finally, it let me go and I ran away home. I thought I was going to die." Ramon rolled up his shirtsleeve and showed Fatemeh the scars on his right arm where the wolf had latched on. "They were afraid I was going to lose the arm. Fortunately, it never got infected and it finally healed."

"You must have been attacked by the she-wolf's mate," said Fatemeh knowingly.

"That's what I always figured." Ramon nodded. "However, I could never figure out why he attacked me."

"He did it for the same reason you grabbed the apothecary. He thought you were threatening his pups and his mate." She stepped around and looked Ramon in the eye. "That wolf could have easily killed a small boy, but he didn't. He just dragged you away from his family. He gave you a stern warning."

The professor appeared at the door. "I just took out the next set of photos. One of them is really stunning. Come and see." He disappeared again.

"Look," said Fatemeh, "I understand if you don't want to help. It's okay. I'm very sorry about what happened." She smiled, and then went back inside.

Ramon stood on the rooming house's porch for a long time. He thought about going back to the Castillos' and waiting for Fatemeh, but something in her words rang true. Also, even though he had grown to hate wolves, Fatemeh still didn't hate him. Ramon found he couldn't walk away from that. Finally, he went back inside. There, he found Fatemeh kneeling on the floor next to Professor Maravilla. She was holding the clockwork lobo still, while he carefully filled one side of the head with fresh flash powder and then replaced the top of its head. She pointed to the bed. "Take a look at the professor's most recent photo. I think you'll find it interesting."

Ramon picked up the small glass plate. It was a photo of a wolf and its den. Nearby was an owl. Ramon blinked at the photo. "That wolf is in an owl burrow, isn't it?"

"And the wolf did not eat the owl," finished Maravilla, standing up and wiping his hands together. "I think the wolf and the owl share the burrow."

"That's ... remarkable," Ramon said at last.

"That's why I'm doing this," said Maravilla pointing to the clockwork lobo. He took out his pocket watch. "I think it's nearly time to go."

A short time later, Fatemeh and Ramon rode out to the grove near the mountains. Professor Maravilla had remained behind in his room to make a few adjustments to the clockwork lobo, but had arrived before them. He had spruced up since Ramon and Fatemeh last saw him and, if anything, he was dressed more elegantly than the day before. His jacket was decorated in gold braid and his vest was made of fine silk brocade. His boots were polished to perfection, shining in the afternoon light. The clockwork lobo stood nearby. Maravilla helped Fatemeh dismount while Ramon led both of the horses to a nearby tree and tied off their reins.

After a short discussion, Professor Maravilla opened a hatch on the side of the clockwork lobo and wound a key. After closing the hatch, the animal started walking toward the wolves he had photographed the day before. The professor, Ramon and Fatemeh followed the clockwork lobo for a time. As they topped a rise, Ramon saw movement in the distance. He held up his hand and they stopped, allowing the clockwork lobo to continue on.

Professor Maravilla retrieved a small, collapsing telescope from one of his pockets and extended it. He scanned the area where Ramon had seen movement. "Ah ha!"

Placing his arm around Fatemeh's shoulders, he handed her the telescope and pointed. Ramon restrained an urge to challenge the professor to a fight right there. Instead, he tried to look where the professor was pointing. Ramon thought he could see wolves milling around. The clockwork lobo was heading right for them. Fatemeh shrugged off Maravilla and took the telescope. She smiled at what she saw and then handed the telescope to Ramon.

Ramon looked through the telescope and could make out four lobos—two adults and two pups. The pups were rolling around cavorting with each other. One of the adults noticed the clockwork lobo as it approached. Ramon couldn't quite make out details through the telescope, but it looked like its hackles were up, preparing to challenge the intruder.

Ramon handed the telescope back to Fatemeh, who, in turn, handed it to Maravilla. "Now this is interesting," said the professor. "I wonder what will happen if they attack my clockwork creation."

"I don't think they will," said Fatemeh.

As Maravilla continued to watch, his mouth dropped open. "Would you look at that?" He handed the telescope to Fatemeh. Acting as though she either knew what she would see or wasn't interested, she handed the telescope directly to Ramon.

Ramon looked through and discovered a little burrowing owl perched atop the clockwork lobo's head. It stood there, riding on the machine like an Indian Raja might ride atop an elephant. The other wolves eyed the sight warily. As the clockwork creature passed, the pups followed, curious about the strange new wolf in their presence. Keeping an eye on the pups, the parents followed at a bit of a distance. Ramon handed the telescope back to Maravilla and the three of them made their way down the hill, doing their best to keep the wolves in sight for a time.

"They're heading in the direction of the rabbits," said Fatemeh.

"That's very good," echoed Maravilla.

"So, why is it fine for the wolves to kill rabbits and I can't kill the wolves?" Ramon asked, a bit confused.

"It's natural for wolves to kill and eat rabbits. Besides if the wolves don't kill and eat some of the rabbits, there will soon be too many. They would eat all of the grass and that would create problems for the ranchers," explained Fatemeh.

"So, in a way, we're helping the ranchers by not killing the wolves," Ramon said.

Fatemeh smiled at Ramon.

"What happens if the clockwork lobo walks right past the rabbits?" asked Ramon.

"That won't be a problem," said Maravilla. "I don't think the wolves will pass up a feast—besides, the clockwork lobo will likely wind down before much longer."

"What happens if he winds down before they get to the rabbits?" pressed Ramon.

"Why do you think the owl is along for the ride?" Fatemeh asked.

They continued walking. Indeed, they soon found the clockwork lobo on its side in the grass. Professor Maravilla stood it up and brushed the grass off. He then took out his telescope, handed it to Fatemeh and pointed. She looked briefly and handed it to Ramon. The owl was on the ground, acting like it had a broken wing—a trick they use when trying to distract predators from their young. When the wolves got a little too close, the owl would fly off in the direction of the rabbits. Curious as they were, the wolves continued to follow the owl.

"They'll find the rabbits soon, and then they'll forget about our friend, the owl," said Fatemeh, satisfied. "Our work here is done." The gloom of twilight was beginning to settle on the land. "I think it's getting about time to get back to the boarding house." She took Ramon's hand. "After all, you have work tomorrow and I still need to find a job."

Professor Maravilla stepped up, took Fatemeh's hand and kissed it again. "It was a pleasure. I hope we will meet again."

"I'm sure we will," said Fatemeh.

"Where will you go now?" Ramon asked.

"Me? I abjure all roofs, and choose to wage against the enmity o' the air; to be a comrade with the wolf and owl."

"Shakespeare?" asked Fatemeh.

"King Lear, Act II, scene 4," affirmed Maravilla. With that, the professor shook Ramon's hand and then bent down and opened the hatch on the side of his lobo, preparing to wind it up. The automaton was really too heavy to carry, so he undoubtedly would let it walk ahead of him—wherever it was they were going.

Ramon's hands were thrust down in his pockets and his head hung low as he and Fatemeh hiked back toward the horses.

"Why so glum?" asked Fatemeh. "Are you disappointed we found a way to save the wolves?"

Ramon thought about that for a moment, then shook his head. "No. I can't say I've learned to like wolves, but I think I understand them a bit better. I don't actually hate them anymore."

"Then what is it?"

"I suppose I'm worried you might find someone you like better than me."

"What, Professor Maravilla?" asked Fatemeh. "A man like that stands out too much." She ran her hand down the brown sleeve of Ramon's coat and then across the white shirt—colors not unlike an owl's plumage. "You are much more in tune with your environment."

Ramon pulled her close and kissed her. Releasing her before his glasses fogged up too much, they made their way to the horses and rode off toward the lights of Mesilla.

# CHAPTER FOUR
## DAY OF THE DEAD

Two weeks after their arrival in Mesilla, Fatemeh Karimi and Ramon Morales were in the sitting room of the Castillos' boarding house. Fatemeh read quietly by the light of an oil lamp while Mrs. Castillo played the piano. Despite the cheerful music, Ramon sat forward with his hands in his lap, his brow furrowed. Fatemeh marked her place in the book with a ribbon and took Ramon's hand. "What's the matter?"

Ramon flashed a grin, then shook his head. "Oh, nothing. I was just thinking I should go to Mass tomorrow."

"Would you mind if I came along?"

Ramon shifted uncomfortably. "Well ... I've never been to this church, and I don't know how well they'd take to someone asking questions...."

Fatemeh laughed lightly. "Don't worry, I won't embarrass you."

"I didn't say ... I mean..."

She put her finger to his lips, silencing him. "You see. That's the thing Bishop Ramirez in Socorro never understood. Like you, I believe in Jesus Christ."

"You do?" Ramon inclined his head, confused. "Then, you mean to tell me you're really a Christian?"

"No," she said with forced patience. "I'm Bahá'í. I follow the teachings of Bahá'u'lláh."

"Bah ... who?" Ramon's eyebrows came together.

"Bahá'u'lláh. He's a teacher and the one who God made manifest."

Ramon sat back and narrowed his gaze. "It sounds like you're saying he's the second coming of Christ."

Mrs. Castillo hit a sharp note. Ramon and Fatemeh looked

up. The landlady blushed, cleared her throat, and then began playing again.

Fatemeh pursed her lips and nodded. "I hadn't really thought about it that way, but his teachings are an interpretation of God's will for this age."

Ramon stood and walked over to the fireplace, making a show of studying some knickknacks on the mantel. Fatemeh set her book aside and went over to him. "What's the matter, Ramon?"

He took off his glasses and made a show of inspecting them for a moment. "This Bahá'í religion really does sound kind of dangerous."

"It's the practitioners of your religion who tried to burn me at the stake."

Ramon sighed. "You're right, but it's what I've believed my whole life."

She took his hand and looked around at the Castillos' sitting room. "This is a nice comfortable place. Maybe we should stay here for a while. I could go to Mass with you and learn more about Catholicism. In the meantime, I can teach you more about the Bahá'í Faith. What do you say?"

"I think I like that idea." Ramon squeezed her hand and kissed her on the cheek.

The next day, Ramon and Fatemeh rose and walked around the corner to the town square. San Albino Church dominated the north side of the square. Its façade looked as though it would be more at home in the French countryside than in New Mexico Territory. The church's entryway consisted of a single tower topped by a wood-shingled steeple. Within the tower, bells rang, calling the faithful to Mass.

Inside, the church reminded Ramon of San Miguel in Socorro. Whitewashed adobe walls surrounded wooden pews. Statues of saints stood in alcoves along the walls. Fatemeh's brow creased. "I thought Christians were opposed to idolatry."

Ramon frowned. "We are." He led her to an open place at a pew and sat down while he tried to think how to explain. "We don't exactly worship the statues. It's more like we use them to remind us of the stories of the saints."

"Ah, I see." Fatemeh then put her hands together, looked

toward each of the saints and gave a short bow from her seat.

Ramon inclined his head. "What are you doing?"

"Showing respect to the saints represented by those images."

Just then, the congregation stood and began chanting a song. Ramon looked around and saw an altar boy carrying a cross followed by the priest. Looking across the way, Ramon saw the apothecary Fatemeh had confronted on their second day in town. His eyes were narrowed and he was looking straight at Fatemeh.

Through the course of the service, Fatemeh sat in rapt attention. Occasionally she would lean over and ask Ramon what was being said or the meaning of some prayer. He was embarrassed to admit he didn't know all the Latin being spoken. She frowned. "Bahá'u'lláh teaches us to investigate the scriptures ourselves, so we know what they say."

Ramon put his fingers to his lips to indicate she shouldn't speak so loudly, but silently he thought there was wisdom in her words. When time came for the Eucharist, Ramon stood, but indicated Fatemeh should remain seated. He knew some churches didn't approve of communion with non-Christians.

After Mass was complete, the priest strode to the rear of the sanctuary and the congregation began to file out. The apothecary crossed the aisle and glared at Fatemeh. "I'm surprised to see you here. I noticed you didn't partake of the Eucharist."

Fatemeh opened her mouth to respond, but the sound of the priest clearing his throat cut through the murmur of the crowd. Ramon, Fatemeh and the apothecary all turned. "Mr. Candelaria," said the priest. "All are welcome in God's house. You know that."

"Yes, Father Duran." The apothecary nodded toward the priest and then departed, but not before casting one more sidelong glance at Fatemeh.

As spring progressed into summer, Ramon and Fatemeh became more settled in the Castillos' boarding house. Ramon's job kept him at the ranch for long hours. In the meantime,

Fatemeh learned Mr. Castillo suffered from arthritis. Standing and working around the house for long hours was extremely painful to him. Fatemeh went to her wagon and mixed some herbs into a poultice he could rub on his joints at night. Within a few weeks, he felt better and began spreading the word about her skills as a curandera. He also gave them an improved rate on their rooms.

One night, Fatemeh finished dinner at the Castillos' boarding house and looked up with a sigh. Ramon was not back from work at the ranch. Looking over to the calendar, she saw it was nearly the end of October. Hardly able to believe so much time had passed, she patted her lips with a napkin. She stood and took her plates to the kitchen, and then went upstairs. The sun had set about a half hour before and shadows filled her room. Fatemeh lit two lamps, then sat down and pulled off her shoes. She looked forward to the next chapter of the novel she'd purchased two days before—*From the Earth to the Moon* by Jules Verne. Just as she picked up the book, there was a knock at the door. Thinking it was Ramon, she put the book down and said, "Come in."

Instead of Ramon, a short woman wearing a hooded cloak stepped through the door. "I am sorry to intrude," said the woman. "Are you Fatemeh Karimi?"

"I am." Fatemeh stood and gestured for the woman to take the room's other chair.

The woman pushed back the hood of her cloak. Black hair framed pale skin. "My name is Mercedes Rodriguez," she said. "I have heard you are a curandera."

Fatemeh inclined her head. "What can I do to help?"

The woman sat and looked at her hands. "I don't really know where to begin. I have not been well for many years. I am very sensitive to sunlight and sometimes I suffer serious stomach pain." She lowered her voice, almost as though she was afraid to continue. "There are times I can't think straight and I start to feel very anxious. When I've gone to doctors or the apothecary, they treat me like I'm some kind of monster. I just want something to help."

"Why do they think you're a monster?" Fatemeh's brow creased.

"They say I have a problem with the blood." Mercedes looked up into Fatemeh's eyes. "They say I'm like a vampire."

Fatemeh took a deep breath and let it out slowly. She knew all too well what it was like to be misunderstood. She retrieved a jar from the large carpetbag beside the bed, and then pulled out three more jars and a small cloth pouch. She poured leaves and flower petals from three of the jars into the pouch. "When you start to feel anxious, make a tea from this mixture." Opening the fourth jar, she counted out five leaves. "These are coca leaves from South America. Chew on one when the pain becomes too much to bear. However, it may increase your sense of anxiety, so have some of the tea ready."

"Thank you, Miss Karimi." Mercedes left a coin on the table next to Fatemeh's book.

"Come back if you have any more problems, or if these don't help." Fatemeh handed the leaves and the cloth bag to Mercedes.

"Mercy smiles upon you," she said. She pulled the cloak's hood up over her head. Fatemeh opened the door for Mercedes and watched as she walked down the hall. Sighing, she wondered how scientific men such as doctors and apothecaries could believe in vampires. She closed the door and went back to the bed to repack the carpetbag.

The next morning, a man named Luther Duncan, wearing a bowler hat and pinstripe suit, eyed the wanted posters tacked to a wooden board outside the Mesilla Town Marshal's office. A reporter for the *Mesilla News*, Duncan was always on the lookout for a good story. He already had a great one lined up. A friend back in Washington, D.C. wired to tell him the Russian military attaché was traveling to California and would pass through Mesilla on the train in a few days' time. Duncan planned to be on hand to interview the foreign dignitary. However, there were issues of the paper to fill before the general's arrival.

One of the wanted posters caught Duncan's eye. It showed a man with a round but stern face and owlish glasses named

Ramon Morales. According to the poster, Morales was wanted for assaulting the Bishop of Socorro and for abandoning his duly elected job as Socorro County Sheriff. Duncan inclined his head and studied the picture. He took out a pad of paper and a pencil and jotted down some notes.

One of the deputies stepped out of the building. "Can I help you, Mr. Duncan?"

Duncan nodded thoughtfully. "What can you tell me about this Ramon Morales?"

"Don't know much," said the deputy. "We just got the wanted poster today. Apparently, he tried to burn down the San Miguel Church in Socorro and when he didn't succeed, he ran away with his girlfriend."

"Really!" Duncan lifted his eyebrows. "Any idea where he went?"

The deputy shook his head. "No idea, but we're keeping an eye out for him. He might well come through here. Lots of work at the ranches, so he might try to blend in."

"Either that, or he might come this way for the train. He might be long gone."

"That's always possible," agreed the deputy.

"Thank you for your time." Duncan made a few more notes, then folded up the paper and put it in his pocket. The deputy tipped his hat and continued on his way. Duncan looked at the picture of Ramon Morales one more time and then decided it was time visit his friend Warren Shedd, who owned the San Augustin Ranch.

Fatemeh awoke to the aroma of baking bread. She dressed quickly and made her way downstairs. She found Ramon in the dining room of the Castillos' boarding house, already eating breakfast. "Where were you last night?" she asked, hands on her hips. "I was worried."

"You were?" Ramon quickly blinked back a look of surprise and smiled. "Sorry, we had a long day. When we were finished, the rest of the boys asked if I would go to the saloon with them."

"You know I don't like saloons." Fatemeh sat down at the table.

Ramon nodded and took a bite of his bacon. "That's why I didn't come back here first."

Fatemeh scowled at him as Mrs. Castillo stepped into the room, carrying a bunch of flowers. "Ah, Fatemeh dear, I see you're awake. I'll get you some breakfast straight away." She placed the flowers into a vase and carefully arranged them.

"Thank you," said Fatemeh. "By the way, the bread you're baking smells wonderful."

"Gracias. It's pan de muerto. I'm making it for supper." With that, Mrs. Castillo turned and disappeared into the kitchen.

Fatemeh was beginning to pick up a little Spanish. "Did I understand her right? Pan de muerto?"

"You did." Ramon pushed his glasses up on his nose. "It means bread of the dead."

Fatemeh's eyes widened. "She's kidding, right?"

Ramon shook his head. "Not at all. It's Diá de los Muertos—The Day of the Dead. People go out to the cemetery and set up altars to their loved ones, sing songs, and play games. We didn't celebrate it much up in Socorro, but I've heard it's a big to-do down here in Mesilla." Ramon pulled out his pocket watch and looked at it. "Tell you what, after I'm finished with work today, I'll meet you back here for supper, then I'll take you out to the cemetery so you can see."

Fatemeh smiled just as Mrs. Castillo returned carrying a breakfast plate. "I'd like that. It sounds interesting."

"In the meantime," said Mrs. Castillo, "I'll show you the altar I'm building for my mother and father." She set the plate down in front of Fatemeh.

Ramon wiped his lips with a napkin. He reached out and gently squeezed Fatemeh's hand, then left for work.

Luther Duncan eased into a chair at the Palacio Saloon and ordered dinner. He was saddle sore from riding much of the day. After seeing the wanted poster, he rode out to Warren Shedd's ranch, only to learn the rancher was working out on the range. He climbed back on his horse and finally found Shedd an hour later. Unfortunately, he wasn't much help. Shedd couldn't remember hiring anyone named Ramon Morales. "You might ask Thomas Bull, though. I heard he hired some new ranch hands back in the spring." With that, Duncan rode back to town.

Duncan had better luck when he returned to Mesilla. "Yes, I did hire a man named Morales," said Thomas Bull.

"Did Mr. Morales come from Socorro?"

"I'm afraid I don't recall."

"Did he have a round face and little round spectacles?"

Bull nodded thoughtfully. "I believe he did." The rancher leaned forward. "Is Morales in some kind of trouble, Mr. Duncan?"

"I hate to say too much until I get all the facts, but it sounds like he might have an interesting story to tell."

Bull didn't know where Morales lived, but sent him to speak to the ranch foreman. With a sigh, Duncan returned to his horse and rode out to Bull's ranch. He found the foreman and learned that Ramon Morales lived at the Castillos' boarding house.

Luther Duncan ate quickly and drank a beer, hoping the alcohol would alleviate some of the pain in his backside. He looked out the window and sighed. It was getting dark and he wasn't sure he would be able to learn anything more about Ramon Morales before morning. Still, he thought it was worth taking a walk over to the Castillos' boarding house, just in case.

The boarding house was only four blocks from the saloon. Duncan leaned against a tree across the street and lit a cigar. One of the upstairs lamps went out and a short time later, a man and a woman stepped out. Even in the waning light, Duncan saw the woman had black hair and olive skin. However, she didn't appear to be of Mexican descent like her companion. The man seemed to have a difficult time taking his eyes from the woman, as though he was under her spell. Duncan grinned around the cigar when he saw the man had little round glasses. He decided to follow them.

Ramon Morales and his companion walked down the road, toward the cemetery at the edge of town. Gentle guitar music wafted through the air as someone played a familiar ballad. Duncan nodded to himself, realizing it was Diá de los Muertos. There would be a handful of people at the cemetery. He could blend in and observe the couple without being too obvious.

Morales and his companion only took a few steps past the cemetery gates. They stopped and Morales spoke to the woman and pointed to the altars set up at some of the nearby graves. She knelt down and took a closer look at one.

Realizing he could not follow them in without being seen, Duncan cut to the left and climbed over the rock wall. He nearly fell over a cloaked woman kneeling at an ancient grave marker. The woman stood suddenly. "What are you doing here?" she said.

"Pardon me." Duncan stood and dusted himself off. "I'm sorry to intrude." He looked down at the grave marker. It was worn rock with words run together in Spanish and a date sometime in the 1500s. The name on the marker was Reynaldo Rodriguez. The reporter realized the woman must be Mercedes Rodriguez, who was said to have been from a very old family. There were even rumors Mercedes was some kind of vampire. The reporter wanted to interview her, but this wasn't the time. He tipped his hat and moved over to a nearby pine tree.

One group of nanites from the swarm called Legion followed the river called the Rio Grande north. The other group followed the river south. Both swarms cataloged flora, fauna and geology as they traveled. Many of the forms were compelling, but none were quite as interesting as the intelligent beings called humans.

Each of the nanite swarms discovered human population centers around the same time. Both population centers had the usual infrastructure intelligent beings set up for themselves—dwellings, places to obtain food, educational facilities and ritual centers of various sorts. However, as the swarms exchanged information, Legion realized the focus of each population center was somewhat different. The swarm in the north observed humans digging into the planet, extracting rocks and minerals for industrial purposes. Meanwhile, the southern swarm saw humans engaged primarily in agriculture. The focus of each population center seemed logical given the geological and climatic conditions in the respective areas.

In addition to their agricultural activities, a number of humans in the south seemed to be preparing for a ritual. Many were gathering items together. They seemed to be creating altars of some kind. At first, Legion assumed they were getting ready for a mass tribute to some agricultural deity. However, each altar was different. They contained representations of other humans along with items that seemed of little or no consequence. Legion searched many millennia of databanks accumulated on millions of worlds and determined the humans must be engaged in some kind of ancestor worship. Although he had observed primitives doing the same before, something seemed different about the ceremony these humans were preparing. If Legion understood human emotions from his contact with Alberto Mendez, then these humans were happy, not sad as many intelligent beings are when thinking about members of their own species who had already died. He found this fascinating.

The alien swarm observed one particular human in the southern population center. He moved from place to place asking questions and recording his observations on a primitive recording device. Legion realized contact with such an inquisitive human could provide unique insights into the humans of the south and the interesting ritual they were preparing. Legion entered the human's mind.

Fatemeh sniffed the marigolds adorning one of the altars and ran her fingers along a flute that belonged to a man named Amarante de la O. She stood up from the altar. "This Day of the Dead is a very lovely tradition," she said with a sigh. She looked around. "Do you have any idea who that man was, who was following us?"

"What man?" asked Ramon.

Someone screamed nearby. The soft guitar rhythms

stopped. Ramon, Fatemeh and several other people at the cemetery ran over to investigate. They found a man on the ground, clutching his head. "I hear voices...hundreds of voices," groaned the man.

"It's that reporter, Luther Duncan," said the man holding the guitar.

Duncan muttered strange phrases. "Contact established... Ritual referred to as Day of the Dead...Human of note: Alexander Gorloff..." The pitch of his voice rose and fell. It sounded as though Duncan were speaking in several different voices.

"What's he saying?" Ramon leaned down so he could hear better.

Someone pulled Ramon away. "Stay back! That man's possessed." Ramon turned and saw the apothecary, Mr. Candelaria. Sweat beaded on the man's forehead, despite the chill air.

"What?" Fatemeh looked at the apothecary and blinked, then looked down at Duncan. "He's having a seizure of some kind. Maybe I can help him."

"You can't," growled Candelaria. "She's to blame." He pointed at Mercedes Rodriguez, who stood nearby, toying with a ring on her finger and glancing around, as though looking for a means of escape.

Ramon felt the tension escalating. It reminded him of being in a barroom just before a brawl broke out. Subconsciously he let his hand drift toward his hip, where a gun rode when he was on the range, but he had taken it off before coming to the cemetery. Realizing he had no recourse to a weapon he swallowed and mentally cast about for the right words to defuse the situation before it got out of hand.

"See if you can get her out of here." Fatemeh's voice was barely a whisper. "I'll try to help this man."

Ramon nodded. Casually as possible, he moved over, next to Mercedes Rodriguez. "I think I should escort you home before this crowd gets any ideas."

"I think they already have some ideas, and I don't really like them." There was a tremor in Mercedes's voice.

Together, Ramon and Mercedes moved toward the cemetery's gate. The apothecary and two other men stepped into their path. "Where do you think you're going?"

"I'm walking this lady home." Ramon's voice held more authority and confidence than he felt. "She doesn't look well."

"I would like her to answer for what she's done." Candelaria glared at Mercedes.

"Done?" Ramon looked at the reporter on the ground. "That man is sick and he needs help. He's only getting sicker while you're standing in my way. I suggest you go help my friend get him inside. Once he's there, call a doctor. Maybe you have something in your shop that will help."

"He needs an exorcism. We need to get Father Duran," said Candelaria.

"Then maybe you should go get him instead of standing in my way," said Ramon through gritted teeth.

The two men behind the apothecary looked uncertainly at one another. One of them went over to where Fatemeh was kneeling on the ground. Another person from the crowd also joined them. The two men picked up the reporter and moved toward the cemetery gates. Fatemeh followed.

"Mercedes Rodriguez consorts with the devil," said Candelaria. "She must have been summoning demons when the reporter stumbled upon her. They've possessed him."

Duncan looked toward them. His eyes narrowed. "Ramon Morales: Subject of interest."

Ramon shook his head and wondered if he heard that correctly. Two people in the crowd knew Ramon and studied him with puzzled expressions. "I think we better get out of here." With that, he took Mercedes's hand. The two quickly pushed past Candelaria and ran toward the cemetery gate. Fatemeh and the men carrying Duncan moved toward a nearby house, in the opposite direction.

Ramon looked at Mercedes. "Where do you live?"

"On Calle de Guadalupe, near the Corn Exchange Hotel."

Ramon nodded and moved that direction. However, when they reached Calle de Santa Ana, he pushed her behind a shrubbery that lined an adobe wall. She gasped in surprise, but Ramon covered her mouth. He pointed as Candelaria and three other men walked past.

"Where'd they go?" asked one of the men. "I lost sight of them."

"They must be heading to the vampire's house," said the apothecary. "They can't be far ahead." They continued down the street.

Once they were out of sight, Ramon led Mercedes from behind the shrubbery and quietly went the other direction.

One of the men who carried Luther Duncan lived in a house near the cemetery. They took the reporter inside and laid him on a divan in the main room. The man who owned the house introduced himself as Oscar Sanchez. "Should I call a doctor?" he asked.

"Give me a minute. I think I can help." Fatemeh looked into Luther Duncan's eyes and listened to his rambling. He sat up and took her hands. Although his grip was firm, it did not feel like the uncontrolled clenching that would accompany a seizure. "Mr. Duncan, can you hear me?"

He nodded. "I can hear you." His voice changed. "Alexander Gorloff arriving by train…"

Fatemeh inclined her head. "Who is Alexander Gorloff?"

Duncan shook his head, as though fighting something. "Military attaché from Russia to America," he grunted. "Plan to interview…"

"You said you heard voices in your head?"

Duncan's mouth moved, as though he was struggling to find words. "It's like I'm hearing hundreds of questions all at one time," he said after a moment. "It's like I'm giving answers whether I want to or not and I don't have to speak."

Fatemeh squeezed Duncan's hand, then helped him lay down on the divan again. As a Bahá'í, she didn't believe in literal demons. However, she had heard about a French surgeon named Étienne Eugène Azam who had written a monograph on the subject of a woman with multiple personalities. He had used hypnotism to calm the mind and separate out the personalities. Fatemeh wasn't versed in hypnotism, but she had some herbs that could calm the mind. She stood and looked at Mr. Sanchez. "Do you have some bourbon, honey, and a teapot?"

Sanchez nodded.

"I think I have something back at my room that can help. I'll go get it. In the meantime start boiling some water." She looked back at Duncan. Even if this wasn't a case of multiple personalities, she suspected something that would relax Duncan would help considerably. Still, there was always a chance she could do more harm than good if she was wrong. She turned to the other man who helped them carry Duncan to the house. "Go get the doctor. It would be a good idea if he was close at hand."

The man nodded and Fatemeh left the house.

Ramon led Mercedes into the brightly lit Palacio Saloon. He stopped by the bar and ordered a beer for himself. "Can I buy you something?"

"Just water for me."

The bartender delivered the drinks. Ramon and Mercedes made their way to a table near the back. "This hardly seems a good place to hide." Mercedes looked at all the people sitting at tables and at the bar. It seemed as though people were entering and leaving almost constantly.

"I doubt this is the first place someone would think of looking for a wayward…what did he call you again?"

"Vampire." She said it as though it was a dirty word.

"What? Like those creatures from the dime novels that drink the blood of the living?" Although tales of shape-shifters, witches, and vengeful ghosts were a common part of Ramon's upbringing, vampire stories were only recently imported with settlers from back East.

Mercedes nodded.

Ramon drank from his beer. "Why would he call you that?"

Mercedes told Ramon about her blood condition and explained that she had sought Fatemeh's help. "People have always been nervous around me because I'm never out in the daylight. I have lived by myself ever since my husband died."

The former sheriff studied the woman and thought she seemed awfully young to be a widow, but he knew from experience life could be cruel. He'd seen several young men killed and maimed in mine accidents around Socorro. There had even been several close calls while he worked on Thomas Bull's ranch.

"What I don't understand," said Mercedes, "is why Mr. Candelaria got so angry and blamed me for the reporter's condition."

Ramon snorted. "When the reporter started speaking in all those strange voices, he got scared. I could see it in his eyes. When men get scared, they try to find something they can attack. Sometimes it's easier than trying to fix what actually went wrong."

"Is that what Fatemeh will try to do? Fix what's wrong with Mr. Duncan?"

"If she can, she will."

"What will we do?"

"Wait right here for a while. Hopefully, with a little time, Candelaria will simmer down and Mr. Duncan will be better. Then we can sort things out."

"What if Mr. Candelaria doesn't simmer down?"

Ramon took in a deep breath and let it out slowly. After a moment, he picked up the beer and took another drink. "Let me think on that."

When Fatemeh returned to Mr. Sanchez's house, she was surprised to find the living room full of people. The doctor knelt by the divan, listening to Luther Duncan's heart with a stethoscope. Mr. Candelaria was there, making the sign of the cross. Duncan still muttered incoherently. Fatemeh found Oscar Sanchez and took him aside. "Did you boil that water?"

He nodded and led Fatemeh to the little kitchen. She poured the water into a mug and added some bourbon. Then she pulled the cork from a small vial she had in a pouch at her waist and added a green liquid to the brew. She stirred the mixture, then summoned her resolve and returned to the living room.

"Doctor, I think I have something that can help," she said.

The old doctor looked up. "You're that Persian curandera I've heard about, aren't you?"

Fatemeh shrugged. "I guess I am."

"Some of my patients have told me good things about you," said the doctor. "If you think you can help, be my guest."

The apothecary stepped forward and grabbed Fatemeh's arm. "She consorts with witches and vampires. Don't let her near the reporter with that vile brew."

The doctor put his hand on the apothecary's shoulder. "Please, Mr. Candelaria, let her give this a try. Do you have anything in your shop that would help?"

The question seemed to give Candelaria pause. Finally, he shook his head.

"If Miss Karimi's herbs don't work, you can summon Father Duran to exorcise the demon—presuming that's what's wrong with this man." The doctor patted Candelaria on the shoulder.

The apothecary frowned, but let go of Fatemeh's arm.

She knelt next to Luther Duncan and helped him sit up. She handed him the cup and told him to drink. He sipped the warm liquid. His breathing relaxed and the torrent of words slowed to a murmur and finally stopped. His half-lidded gaze darted from person to person in the room.

Legion tried to learn more from the man called Luther Duncan, but the human's brain cells began to go quiet. The woman called Fatemeh Karimi had given him chemicals that distorted and slowed the reporter's thought patterns. It grew increasingly difficult to extract any useful information. Legion considered the information he had acquired. The human called Alexander Gorloff sounded rather interesting. He was a liaison between governments and might provide much insight into human behavior. Observing the room through Duncan's eyes, Legion concluded he had made a mistake by entering the reporter's mind while he was awake and in a public place. The reporter had drawn attention to himself and Legion's presence might have been exposed if not for the apothecary—Mr. Candelaria— who invented an excuse to explain Duncan's rambling. Legion would regroup, wait for Gorloff, and follow him. When the man went to sleep, Legion could enter and quietly integrate with his brain cells. He had learned humans sometimes spoke in their sleep. Satisfied with the plan, Legion departed Luther Duncan.

The reporter smiled. "Thank you, Miss Karimi. The voices ... they're gone."

"I'm glad to hear that." Fatemeh patted Duncan's hand, then stood. She took a step and then looked around. "How did you know my name?"

He tapped his forehead. "The voices..." His eyelids fluttered and he lay back.

Fatemeh knelt down beside the divan. "Earlier, you mentioned Ramon." Her voice was a sharp whisper. "What do you know about him?"

"I've been following you two." His words were slurred. "He's wanted up in Socorro..." Duncan's eyes fluttered closed. A moment later, he began to snore.

The doctor helped Fatemeh to her feet. "He looks a lot better. What was in that tea you gave him?"

Fatemeh blinked and stammered for a moment, trying to focus on what the doctor had asked. "Oh, the tea...it's an herb I brought with me from my homeland. It relaxes the mind. I thought it would help."

"It certainly seems to have done the job. He said the voices were gone. I think that counts as a cure in my book." The doctor cast a meaningful glance at Mr. Candelaria.

The apothecary folded his arms and narrowed his gaze at Fatemeh. "A potion to drive out demons. It seems suspiciously like witchcraft to me."

"Balderdash!" The doctor stepped over and put his arm around Candelaria's shoulders. "Luther Duncan was just suffering from overwork. I'm afraid you're pushing yourself toward the same end. You should get some rest."

Candelaria pursed his lips and remained silent for a moment. "Perhaps you're right, but I still sense evil was at work here in some form." He strode across the room, retrieved a coat from the rack next to the door and stalked out into the night.

Fatemeh handed the teacup back to Mr. Sanchez. "If there's anything else I can do for Mr. Duncan, let me know, but I think he just needs a little rest now."

"I think you may be right," said the doctor.

Without acknowledging the doctor, Fatemeh stepped through the door bound for the marshal's office near the downtown plaza.

Ramon yawned, then looked at his watch. "It's getting late. I think it may be safe to walk you home, now. Hopefully those people who chased us out of the cemetery have gone to bed."

Mercedes nodded. "For Mercy's sake, I hope so."

Ramon thought she looked surprisingly wide awake for the hour. Perhaps it was her sensitivity to sunlight. The former sheriff suspected she might be used to keeping later hours than he did. They stood and started for the door.

Fatemeh burst into the saloon. "There you are!" She pointed at Ramon.

Several laughs and catcalls sounded from the drunks around her. Ramon led her outside. "I was just about to walk Miss Rodriguez home and return to the boarding house."

"Yes, I think she'll be fine now." Fatemeh cast an apologetic glance toward Mercedes. "Mr. Candelaria seems to have lost interest in vampires. Now he's concerned about the witches in town." She grimaced and pointed to herself.

"Don't tell me it's time for us to clear out of town again. Just when I was getting to like it here." Ramon snorted a laugh, but cut it short when he saw the look on Fatemeh's face.

They walked Mercedes back to her house and bid her good night. Ramon turned around and started toward the Castillos' boarding house, but realized Fatemeh wasn't following. He looked around and saw she was stalking off toward the center of town. He ran to catch up with her. "What's going on?"

"You've got to see this," said Fatemeh. She led him to the marshal's office and pointed to the wanted poster on the wall. "Luther Duncan *was* following us before he collapsed and started hearing voices."

Ramon read the wanted poster by the soft light of the moon and shook his head. "I was afraid they might decide to track me down. I'd just hoped this was far enough away." He put his hands in his pockets. "I'm sorry, Fatemeh."

Her frown softened into a gentle smile. She reached out and touched his shoulder. "What are you sorry for? Saving me?"

"I'm sorry we have to run again." He hugged her.

"Let's get a good night's sleep, Ramon. We'll get going in the morning." Hand in hand, Ramon and Fatemeh walked back to the boarding house.

# CHAPTER FIVE
## THE TRIAL

The next morning, Ramon met Fatemeh at the breakfast table. Mrs. Castillo carefully folded the newspaper she was reading, set it aside, then left to get breakfast. A few minutes later, she returned carrying plates piled high with flapjacks and a ham steak apiece. "We'd like to settle our bill, Mrs. Castillo," said Ramon.

She nodded as she set one of the plates in front of him. "I'm sorry to hear that. It's been so good to have you here." She placed the other plate in front of Fatemeh. "May I ask where you're going?"

"Uh…" He hadn't discussed the question with Fatemeh yet. He took off his glasses and made a show of inspecting them.

"California." Fatemeh's tone was matter of fact. "There are good opportunities there." She cast a meaningful glance at Ramon.

He nodded and replaced his glasses. "After all, with winter coming on, Mr. Bull doesn't need as much help at the ranch. I need to find something more permanent."

"We will certainly miss you." With that, Mrs. Castillo left the room.

"So, where *are* we going?" Ramon looked at Fatemeh over the top of his glasses.

"Don't you like California?" She removed the ham steak from her plate and deposited it on Ramon's. Then she took one of his flapjacks. It had become a habit.

"I don't know." Ramon cut the first piece of ham. "I've never been to California…"

He popped a piece of ham into his mouth just as Mrs. Castillo returned from the kitchen carrying a pot of coffee. She poured a cup for Ramon and then one for Fatemeh. With a sad smile, she disappeared again.

"Doesn't it make sense?" Fatemeh spread some preserves on each of the flapjacks. "There are a lot of people in California. I would think it would be easy to blend in."

Ramon nodded. "But why not Texas or Kansas?"

"I've heard the people in California come from all over the world—from China, Spain, Russia—anywhere you could think of. Doesn't it excite you to consider the possibilities?"

Ramon took another bite of ham and shrugged. "We could find that further east. What about New York City or Boston?"

Fatemeh laughed lightly. Ramon frowned and concentrated on his food. After a moment, she reached across the table and touched his hand. He looked up and saw her smiling pleasantly. "I've been to New York. You wouldn't like it. There are far too many people."

Ramon took a deep breath and let it out slowly. "I feel like you know so much about the world and I've hardly been anywhere."

"Well, we're going to fix that, aren't we?" Fatemeh took a bite of one of her flapjacks.

Ramon inclined his head. "You've been running a long time, haven't you?"

Her smile turned wistful and she nodded. "Being here through the summer has been nice. I'd like to settle down somewhere."

Ramon swallowed hard, then took a drink of coffee. "Do you want to settle down with me?"

She looked up. "I have grown comfortable with you."

Ramon shook his head. "That's not exactly the answer I was looking for."

"I know." She looked down for a moment. "I love you and the prospect of marriage pleases me, but I think we still need to learn a little more about each other before we decide to take that...most sacred step."

Ramon's breath caught as she looked up and he found himself gazing into her earnest, green eyes. "If I was to ask you to marry me, what is required in your faith?"

Fatemeh chewed her lower lip for a time. Ramon thought

she was contemplating the question longer than necessary. "We would need to seek our parents' approval," she said at last. "If they granted us permission, we would be free to marry."

Ramon's shoulders slumped. "My father is dead and it seems we're getting farther and farther away from my mother in Estancia."

Fatemeh wiped her lips with a napkin, then stood and stepped around the table to Ramon. "We are even farther away from my father and mother. They're back in Persia." She stopped short, as though she had more to say. After a moment, she added, "I don't think this is our most insurmountable challenge, though."

"I've been afraid to make a commitment to you because of your beliefs, but last night, I finally realized that you're already committed to me." Ramon gathered Fatemeh into his arms. "Let me show you I'm no longer afraid." He pulled her close and kissed her.

A throat cleared from the sitting room doorway. Ramon and Fatemeh looked around. They saw Mr. Castillo next to the doorframe. "I'm sorry to interrupt, but there's a man here to see you, Mr. Morales." He stepped through the door and held it open. A stocky man with a thick, handlebar mustache stepped into the dining room.

A star was pinned to the man's black jacket. "Sorry to intrude, ma'am." He tipped his hat to Fatemeh, then turned his attention to Ramon. "I'm Mariano Barela, Sheriff of Doña Ana County and Deputy Marshal of Mesilla. Please come with me, Mr. Morales. You're under arrest."

Ramon glanced from one side of the room to the other, as he sought options and a possible escape. His arm twitched as he instinctively reached toward a gun that wasn't on his belt. Sheriff Barela's hand was already on the grip of his pistol. His gaze did not waver from Ramon. Finally, Ramon held up his hands, resigned that there was nothing he could do.

"Where are you taking him?" Fatemeh's voice had risen an octave. Ramon saw a mix of anger and fear on her face. Her cheeks flushed pink.

"Just over to the county jail, ma'am." Barela stepped around Ramon and put his hand in the center of his back, nudging him gently toward the door.

"I'll go with you," she declared.

Barela shook his head. "Ma'am, it would be better if you remained here."

Ramon looked down at his feet, then back up into Fatemeh's eyes. "Fatemeh … corazón … I think we should do what the sheriff says. He's the law here."

Fatemeh's lips tightened into a line. She nodded sharply.

As the sheriff led Ramon out of the room, he saw Mrs. Castillo put her hand on Fatemeh's shoulder. "I'm sure everything will be fine."

Ramon heard Fatemeh's answer as he was led through the front hall. Her words were clipped—angry, yet thoughtful. "The sheriff is the law and Bahá'u'lláh instructs us to obey the law. I will do so, but that doesn't mean I can't take action."

Fatemeh stormed into the offices of the *Mesilla News*. She saw a clerk wearing an apron setting type on a printing press. "Where can I find Luther Duncan?"

The clerk pointed across the room. Fatemeh marched past him and banged on the door.

"Come in."

She threw the door open and saw Duncan sitting behind a desk working on a strange machine. Fatemeh was curious in spite of her anger and stepped around the desk to get a better look at the unfamiliar device.

"It's called a typewriter," he said. "I'm still getting the hang of it." He pointed to messy handwriting on one of several sheets of paper. Then, he lifted another sheet with neat text that looked as though it had been printed. "It makes my notes a lot easier to read. Mike—you probably saw him out in the other room—doesn't make as many mistakes when he sets my stories into type if I write them using this machine." Duncan sat back and indicated the chair opposite the desk. "What can I do for you, Miss Karimi?"

Fatemeh remained standing. "Did you turn Ramon into the Marshal's Office?"

Duncan blinked back surprise. "No, ma'am. I slept in late, then hurried right to the office so I could work on this story. I was out pretty much all day yesterday, so I'm behind schedule."

"Oh." Fatemeh felt that someone had thrown water on the flames of her anger. She moved around to the chair. "Ramon was arrested this morning. Who do you suppose turned him in? Could it have been the apothecary, Mr. Candelaria?"

Duncan sighed and sat forward. "Who knows? I gather you've been in town some time. I'm sure lots of people know you. It could have been anyone who saw the wanted poster."

Fatemeh wrung her hands. "What's going to happen now? In my country, when arrests are made, people go away for a long time and even die. It's why I came to the United States." She looked up and saw Duncan's gaze soften in apparent sympathy.

"There will be a trial where a group of Mr. Morales's peers will decide if he really committed the crimes he's accused of. If they find him guilty, most likely he'll spend some time in jail."

"How much time?"

Duncan pursed his lips. "For the crime of assault, no more than a few years."

"A few years!" Fatemeh sprang to her feet. "That's terrible. What can we do?"

The reporter snorted. "Do? Nothing really. We need to wait and see what happens at the trial."

"Where will they hold the trial?" Fatemeh asked in a resigned tone.

"That's hard to say." Duncan shrugged. "Normally you're tried in the town where you're accused. However, since Ramon was a sheriff, I'm sure a lot of people in Socorro have strong feelings about him. They may hold the trial somewhere else so they can get a jury of twelve impartial people."

"If they don't have the trial in Socorro, where would it be?"

Duncan shook his head. "I'm not really sure, but it could be here. The district judge is in town. It might be easier for him to hold the trial now than put it off."

Fatemeh nodded and turned to leave.

"Miss Karimi."

She paused in the doorway, but did not face Duncan.

"I owe you a debt of gratitude. If there's anything I can do to help, let me know."

She nodded and stepped from the room, pulling the door closed behind her.

Two days later, Luther Duncan paced the rail platform waiting for the Southern Pacific to make its brief stop. He would only have about half an hour to interview the Russian military attaché before the train continued westward. Duncan paused and listened. All he heard were the sounds of wagons rumbling through the Mesilla Park and the chirping of birds in nearby trees. He looked at his watch. Five more minutes before the train was scheduled to arrive.

During his ninth sojourn across the platform, his sensitive ears picked up a telltale low-frequency whine from the tracks. Before long, the train's whistle blew. Duncan took a deep breath and let it out slowly. The train would soon be at the station. He took out his notepad and pencil. The reporter watched in awe as the black locomotive rumbled past him. Its pistons turned the mighty wheels in a syncopated rhythm and smoke churned from the stack, almost obscuring the train's line of cars. The locomotive's brakes squealed as it slowed. Even though he had seen the sight numerous times, he was still impressed by the machine's power. At last, the train came to a stop.

A man from the station pushed past Duncan on his way to the mail car. People emerged from the train and milled about on the platform, getting some fresh air and stretching their legs. At last, the reporter sighted his quarry. A man with a thick, black beard, wearing an elaborate uniform with gold epaulets stepped from a private car near the back of the train. He retrieved a cigar from his pocket and lit it. He looked toward the rugged Organ Mountains and sneered.

Duncan swallowed, then strode up to the man. "Excuse me. Are you General Gorloff?"

The bearded man evaluated Duncan as though he was something distasteful found on the bottom of his shoe. He took a leisurely draw on the cigar and then nodded slightly. "I am."

Duncan introduced himself. "I'm a reporter for the *Mesilla News*. I was wondering if I could ask you a few questions." He held out his hand.

The Russian military attaché studied the proffered hand for a moment. Finally, he reached out and gave it one firm shake, then put his hands behind his back. "I do not have much time. I think we will be leaving soon." He cast a meaningful glance back toward the train.

"Yes, sir." Duncan opened his notebook. "It's rare for us to have such a distinguished visitor here in Mesilla. What brings you out west?"

"I am traveling to Call Ranch in California. Russian citizens live on that land. They have been there for forty years and they do not want to move. The rancher, George Call, wants the land for his cows."

"Why are there Russian citizens on Mr. Call's ranch?"

Gorloff removed the cigar from his mouth and snorted, releasing a billow of smoke. Duncan was reminded of the locomotive. "That used to be Fort Ross." He made the statement as though it should explain everything.

Duncan's brow furrowed as he searched his memory. "Wasn't Fort Ross built by the Russian American Company?"

"It was." Gorloff nodded sharply. "A few of our people stayed behind. They are old and do not want to leave. Mr. Call called California's governor for help. The governor wired President Grant." The general shrugged. "The President—he asked me to help."

"Why you? This seems a strange job for the Russian military attaché."

"Perhaps, but our new ambassador, Nicholas Shishkin, has just arrived in Washington," explained Gorloff. "President Grant has known me for many years, even before my own short term as ambassador. We are both military men with similar tastes." Gorloff held his cigar aloft. "I believe he felt comfortable asking this favor."

"Do you think you can help?"

Gorloff shook his head and sighed. "This is no matter for ambassadors or generals, but I can speak their language. I will see what I can do." He looked around. "At least it gives me an excuse to see your American West again." The general smiled for the first time since the interview began. "It is ... a marvelous place."

"You like the West, then?"

"When Grand Duke Alexis came to this country four years ago, we came west to hunt buffalo with Generals Custer and Sheridan and Buffalo Bill Cody."

Duncan looked up, his eyes wide. "That must have been some hunting trip."

"It was. I demonstrated Smith and Wesson revolvers to the Grand Duke. He was most impressed—"

The general was interrupted by the conductor's cry of "All aboard!"

"You will excuse me." Gorloff turned back toward his private car.

"Thank you for your time," called Duncan. He continued jotting notes on his pad, satisfied with the interview. Finally, he put the notepad and pencil back in his pocket and turned to leave. As he passed by the station's ticket office, he caught sight of the calendar. Ramon Morales's trial was scheduled to begin the next day. At the Marshal's Office, he'd learned Judge Bristol decided to hold the trial in Mesilla because he was afraid Ramon wouldn't get a fair trial in Socorro where everyone knew him. On one hand, Duncan was pleased, since that would provide material for yet another good article. However, the reporter's smile was wistful. His pleasure at the prospect of a good story was tempered by his concern for Miss Karimi. The trial would no doubt be a harrowing experience for her, and he did not want to see his new friend hurt.

All of Legion's component parts gathered near the train station at Mesilla. The nanite swarm observed Luther Duncan as he paced the platform. The swarm was fascinated by the train when it finally arrived. Components of the swarm entered the locomotive and began making a thorough study. It was a primitive, yet powerful mechanism. Legion himself was a living intelligence uploaded into a machine. Seeing the humans and the locomotive together sent a surge of excitement through the swarm. It was like seeing two disparate lines of his family together, long before they merged into one.

Despite his interest in the locomotive, the swarm was still focused on finding General Gorloff. Most of Legion's component nanites continued to observe Luther Duncan. Eventually, Duncan approached another human. Legion monitored the conversation and determined the human was, in fact, the military attaché. After a few minutes of conversation, Gorloff turned and entered one of the units pulled by the locomotive.

Legion followed Gorloff into living quarters aboard the train and watched as he settled into a chair. The swarm found a place near the ceiling and scanned the quarters while he waited. Comparing the scans to the data recorded from Luther Duncan and Alberto Mendez, Legion believed most humans would consider this so-called private car rather opulent. This data served to reinforce Legion's belief Alexander Gorloff was a man of power.

A short time after the train began moving, an elderly human entered the general's compartment and poured liquid from a closed container into an open one. A few of Legion's components investigated and determined the liquid was a mix of alcohol, water and fruit sugars. Searching through the information garnered from Mendez and Duncan, the swarm believed the liquid was called brandy. Gorloff drank three of Legion's component nanites with the brandy, but they floated quietly in his digestive system, not wanting to draw attention.

Eventually, the light in the general's compartment grew dim. He stood and disappeared behind a door. While he was gone, the elderly man who had poured the brandy appeared and turned back the covers of a bed, then left again. When Gorloff emerged a few minutes later, he wore lighter weight clothing than he had before. He slipped under the covers of the bed and, after a few minutes, he began to snore. Legion moved toward the general.

Alexander Gorloff thought he heard voices. His eyes fluttered open and he felt the rumbling of the train. He looked around, searching the darkness, but didn't see anyone. Finally, his eyes drifted shut. A short time later, the general had the most remarkable dream.

He found himself in a vast white space, surrounded by a swarm of some strange species of insect. They neither landed on him nor bit him, but he heard soft whispering voices as though they were speaking to one another. He plucked one out of the air and looked at it. It was soft and malleable, but he could not squish it like an insect. It flew away from him and joined its comrades.

"We are called Legion," came a velvety voice speaking Russian.

"Where are you?"

"All around you."

"You're the insects?" Gorloff raised his eyebrows.

"We are a swarm, but we are not insects. We have come to learn about your world."

"My ... world? Where are you from?"

"We are from a distant island of stars." The scene around him changed. At first, Gorloff thought the room had become black and the swarm was now white, but then he realized he was looking at the night sky. However, when he looked at his feet, he realized he was not standing on a surface. Instead, he was floating, carried by the swarm, which swathed him like a blanket. The swarm carried him through the sea of night to a great whirlpool of stars. "This is where we came from."

Legion then carried the general back through the sea of stars. Finally, Gorloff saw a blue-green ball that floated in the void. In the distance he saw the sun, but it looked strange floating in a sea of black, instead of hanging in a blue sky. The blue-green ball unfolded and Gorloff realized he was standing in the white room again, looking at a remarkably detailed map of the world. Light whispers continued in the background—so many voices, but so soft, it was almost a white noise. The general was aware of questions being asked and suggestions being made very gently, as though Legion didn't want to break something delicate.

Gorloff found himself studying the Russian Empire and the United States. As he did so, Legion helped him to understand things about their relationship he had never known before. The memory of Alaska's sale to the United States came to the forefront of his mind. He remembered the land as a potential target should Great Britain renew its hostility toward Russia. As a strategist, the Russian general had agreed the sale of the land to the United States was necessary. However, Legion showed him there was great wealth in Alaska he had not known about. Not only were there great gold deposits, but there was oil, which was vitally important to machinery. Alaska's sale to the United States had been accomplished less than a decade before, but after Legion's revelations Gorloff began to wonder if it was a mistake.

The military attaché shook his head, trying to clear his thoughts. "This is a crazy dream." His tone was harsh. "America is our friend."

The swarm appeared at Gorloff's side. Its whispers were more audible to him now. "Analyzing political and economic structures of countries called the United States of America and the Russian Empire. Recent war in the United States will have lasting effects on the population, including increased economic stress in certain sectors. There is a 90% likelihood that such stress will result in an uprising by the labor class to improve their well-being. This movement will likely spread around the world..."

The voices continued. Although Gorloff did not understand all the words, he followed the meaning surprisingly well. He began to have a vision within his dream. He saw workers rising up in Russia and toppling his beloved Czar. In spite of that, Russia grew even more powerful. America also increased its might. Eventually, a time came when the two countries were directly in conflict. He saw a future where Russia and the United States of America developed horrible weapons—weapons that could murder every man, woman, and child in the world. Finally, Gorloff had a vision of a charred and blackened Earth, floating dead in space.

"This is terrible." Gorloff put his hands to his head. "I cannot let this happen."

Legion's soft murmurings changed and the general saw a new vision. This time the Civil War ended differently and America was permanently cleaved in two. In the world that resulted, neither the Union nor the Confederacy would ever become a dominant world power. The labor class of the United States would not rise up in the same way and there was a chance the Czar could keep his power, especially if he made conditions better for Russia's laborers.

General Alexander Gorloff saw a future where Russia was the strongest country in the world.

"The only problem," said Legion, who sensed the general's thoughts, "is that machines will become increasingly important. Although Russia has resources, they may not be sufficient to power the machines necessary to obtain dominance."

Gorloff's attention went back to Alaska. He thought about the American Civil War and how it almost divided the country. Looking at the map in front of him, a plan began to form.

"Can you help me?"

The swarm grew agitated. "We only wish to gain information. We are not interested in interfering with this planet."

"Help me, and I will introduce you to Russia's greatest minds. You will learn from them and they will learn from you."

"Your proposition is most interesting."

Fatemeh Karimi nervously entered Mesilla's courthouse. She wasn't certain what to expect. The courtroom was a simple affair. There were a few benches facing a wooden barrier with a gate in the center. Fatemeh was not surprised to see Luther Duncan sitting in the first row. She *was* surprised to see some sympathetic faces in the audience, including Mr. and Mrs. Castillo and Thomas Bull. Also in the audience was another somewhat familiar face—Ramon's former deputy, Ray Hillerman. Fatemeh would have been glad for the company of Mercy Rodriguez, but suspected she was absent because of her sensitivity to sunlight. Behind the barrier was an ornately carved desk. A big chair stood behind the desk and another one sat to its side. Two tables with chairs faced the desk and two empty rows of benches sat to the side of the room. Fatemeh sat next to the Castillos.

A few minutes after Fatemeh arrived, a group of twelve men were ushered in by one of Mesilla's Deputy Marshals. They sat on the benches at the side of the room. Soon after they arrived, Sheriff Mariano Barela led Ramon into the room. Fatemeh gasped when she saw him. His arms were handcuffed behind his back. His white shirt was disheveled and sweat-stained. His round glasses hung askew on his face, threatening to topple to the ground. It looked as though he hadn't shaved since his arrest. Barela and Ramon sat down at one of the tables. Fatemeh stood, but Mrs. Castillo grabbed her arm and indicated she should sit quietly.

For the better part of fifteen minutes, an uncomfortable silence filled the room, broken only by an occasional muffled cough. Finally, a door opened and another man with a star entered the room. Mrs. Castillo leaned over and whispered that he was the court bailiff.

"The Territorial District Court of New Mexico is now in session, the Honorable Judge Bristol presiding. All rise," declared the bailiff. Fatemeh watched as everyone around her stood. She quickly did the same.

A man in black robes entered the room and sat at the large, wooden desk. "You may be seated," he said. He shuffled through some papers while everyone resumed their seats. The judge took time to read two papers he singled out from the rest. He had gray hair and a long, gray mustache that made him look like he was always frowning. After a moment, he looked at Ramon. "Ramon Morales, you are accused of assaulting the Bishop of Socorro and it says here that afterwards, you abandoned your duly elected duties as Sheriff of Socorro. How do you plead, sir?"

Ramon stood up and his arm twitched, as though he was going to reach up and adjust his glasses. "I'm not guilty of assaulting the bishop, Your Honor. However, I do plead guilty to abandoning my job."

"Well, that makes things a little easier," said the judge. Fatemeh thought she saw the corner of his mouth turn up in a smirk. "Come have a seat." The judge indicated the chair next to his desk.

Ramon moved around the table and stood in front of the judge. Sheriff Barela followed him and unlocked the handcuffs. Ramon rubbed his wrists and then straightened his glasses.

The bailiff stepped up, holding a Bible. "Do you swear to tell the truth, the whole truth, and nothing but the truth, so help you God?"

Ramon looked at the Bible for a moment, then cast a quick glance toward Fatemeh. Finally, he put his hand on the Bible. "I do." He sat down next to the judge.

"Mr. Morales, I have an affidavit here from Bishop Ramirez that says you interrupted a ceremony at the San Miguel Church. You grabbed a torch and you lit his robes on fire. I'd like you to tell us what happened in your own words."

Ramon swallowed. "Well, Your Honor, Bishop Ramirez had decided to take the law into his own hands. There was a new curandera in town who objected to his brother-in-law's mining interests. The bishop decided to burn Fatemeh—the curandera—at the stake as a heretic."

The judge laughed outright, even though he still seemed to be frowning. "Do you expect me to believe that? It sounds like something out of the Salem Witch Trials, not something from the Nineteenth Century."

"Your Honor, I swore to tell the truth," said Ramon. "When I tried to stop him, the torch he was going to use to light the pyre fell. It lit the bishop's robes on fire."

Fatemeh stood up in her seat. "That's exactly what happened," she declared.

Mrs. Castillo reached up and pulled her back to the seat as the judge banged a little hammer on the desk. "I'll have order in this court." He pointed the hammer toward Fatemeh. "What is your name, young woman?"

"Fatemeh Karimi," she said. "I'm the…curandera."

The judge nodded. "You agree with Mr. Morales's testimony?"

"I do, Your Honor." Fatemeh nodded emphatically.

The judge looked over at Ramon. "She your girlfriend?"

Ramon smiled sheepishly. "Yes, Your Honor. She is."

"So tell me," said the judge, his brow creased, "if the

bishop was going to burn this young lady—who seems quite taken with you, by the way—why didn't you arrest him and charge him with attempted murder?"

Fatemeh felt her cheeks grow warm at the judge's words. Ramon shifted uncomfortably in the chair. "The bishop is popular, Your Honor. His brother-in-law owns one of the major businesses in Socorro. I was afraid I might have a riot on my hands."

"You took an oath to uphold the law, Mr. Morales. Whether your story is accurate, or Bishop Ramirez's, I don't take kindly to what you've told me. You either committed a crime, then fled the scene, or you witnessed a crime and didn't pursue it. Do I understand that correctly?"

Ramon looked down at his hands folded in his lap. "Yes, Your Honor. You do."

"You may step down," said the judge. As Ramon stood, Sheriff Barela approached and put the handcuffs back around his wrists and led him to the table. The judge then turned and asked Ray Hillerman to take the seat next to him. Once Hillerman was sworn in, the judge turned to him. "Mr. Hillerman, I gather you're the new acting Sheriff of Socorro. What can you tell us about the day Mr. Morales is accused of assaulting the bishop?"

Hillerman shifted in his seat and he looked from Ramon to the judge. "I saw a lot of riled up people carrying wood to the San Miguel Church. I reported that to the sheriff."

"Did you accompany Mr. Morales to the church?"

"No, Your Honor. I stayed behind at the office."

"So, you didn't actually see the events transpire at the church?"

"No, Your Honor."

"What did you think was happening?"

"I'm not rightly sure." Hillerman's brow creased as he remembered the day in question. "I thought it could be something like a barbecue, but like I said, the people seemed awfully riled up. I figured some kind of trouble was brewing."

"Do you have any reason to doubt Mr. Morales's story?"

"No, Your Honor. A lot of people around Socorro still talk about Miss Fatemeh like she's some kind of witch. I think they're glad she's gone. Others miss her, though. She helped a lot of people, too."

"What about Mr. Morales? Are people glad he's gone?"

Ray Hillerman smiled and shrugged. "I don't know about most people, but I sure miss having the sheriff around. I wish he hadn't left, but if I were in his shoes, I mighta done just what he did."

"You may step down." The judge turned to the jury. "We've already heard Mr. Morales plead guilty to the charge of abandoning his duties in Socorro. All I need from you is a decision about whether or not he really assaulted the bishop." He handed some papers to the bailiff who passed them to one of the men in the jury. "That's the affidavit from the bishop and you've heard Mr. Morales's side of the story. The bailiff will take you to chambers where you can deliberate. Let him know when you've reached a decision." The judged banged his gavel on the desk.

"All rise," called the bailiff. Everyone stood as the judge left the courtroom.

Luther Duncan walked over to Fatemeh and the Castillos. "Well, that was about the briefest trial I've ever seen."

"What do you think's going on?" asked Mr. Castillo.

Thomas Bull came over. "I've heard a little about Randolph Dalton. He doesn't like it when other people get the better of him."

"That's right," Hillerman said. "I wasn't going to press charges against the sheriff, but Mr. Dalton and the bishop kept after me for the last six months. I didn't have any choice."

Fatemeh excused herself and went up to the rail. "Ramon, I'm so sorry," she said.

Ramon looked around. His glasses had slipped down his nose again. "I'm not. The last few months have been the happiest I've ever had. I'd gladly do it all over again, even if I knew the price was jail."

Fatemeh pushed his glasses back up on his nose and kissed him. She stepped back. "Where will they send you?"

"Probably up to the territorial prison in Santa Fe."

"Will I be able to come and visit?"

"I hope you will," said Ramon with a wan smile.

They were interrupted when one of the deputy marshals led the jury back into the room. Luther Duncan eyed them, his head inclined, as he went back to his place and opened his notebook. "That was quick," he muttered as he passed Fatemeh.

"All rise," called the bailiff.

The judge entered and took his seat at the big desk. "You may be seated," he said. He looked over to the jury. "I understand you've reached a verdict?"

One of the men in the jury stood. "We have, Your Honor. We find Mr. Ramon Morales not guilty of assaulting Bishop Ramirez."

Fatemeh let out a sigh of relief and Ramon smiled. The judge nodded and indicated the juror should be seated. He made some notes and then looked up at Ramon. "Please stand, Mr. Morales."

Ramon stood up.

"The jury has found you not guilty of the crime of assault, but you have pleaded guilty to abandoning your duties as Sheriff of Socorro. I sentence you to five years in the Socorro County Jail." He banged his wooden hammer on the desk. "Sheriff Hillerman, you will take the prisoner in your custody."

The bailiff called for everyone to rise once again as the judge left the courtroom. Hillerman and Ramon looked uncomfortably at one another. "I'm sorry, Ramon, I'll do what I can to keep an eye out for you," said Hillerman.

"I know you will," said Ramon, but Fatemeh heard a certain hopelessness in his words.

"What do you mean?" asked Fatemeh. "Ramon, I thought you said they would take you to Santa Fe."

"That's what I thought they would do…"

Mariano Barela stepped between Ramon and Fatemeh. "Ma'am, I'm going to have to ask you to leave the courtroom."

"But Sheriff Barela…" she started to protest.

"Please, leave now," said Barela firmly.

Fatemeh nodded, a tear running down her cheek. She blew a kiss toward Ramon and turned away. Outside the courthouse, she found Luther Duncan, Thomas Bull, and the Castillos.

"I don't like what's happened here today," said Thomas

Bull. "Not one little bit. Ramon Morales is a good man."

"Why are they sending him to Socorro?" Duncan shook his head. "Unless the county jail up there is a lot bigger than the one down here in Doña Ana County, it's not equipped to hold anyone for five years. They should have sent him to the Territorial Prison."

Bull let out a sigh. "He's not being punished for leaving his job as sheriff. He's being punished for defying Randolph Dalton and his brother-in-law, Bishop Ramirez. That's why the trial was such a rush job. Once the judge got the guilty plea, he didn't need to waste any more time."

"Do you think he was paid off?" asked Duncan.

Bull shrugged. "Doesn't matter. No judge wants to spend more time on a trial than he needs to. Maybe he was paid off; maybe he just didn't want to sit around all day. The result's the same."

"That may be true," interjected Fatemeh. "But why does it matter whether he's a prisoner in Socorro or Santa Fe? He'll still be locked up for five years."

Frowning, Bull put his hands in his pockets. "In my opinion he'll be lucky if he lasts five years in Socorro. I'm guessing Dalton wants him there so he can make an example of him."

Fatemeh shook her head. "Can't good men like Ray Hillerman protect him?"

"My dear," said Mr. Castillo. "I'm afraid Mr. Bull may be right. Ray Hillerman can try to keep an eye on Ramon, but he can't watch the jail all the time. If Mr. Dalton is as powerful as people seem to think he is, I'm sure it would be all too easy for him to arrange for Ramon to have an 'accident'."

Fatemeh's eyes widened. Mrs. Castillo wrapped her arm around Fatemeh's shoulders.

"We've got to do something," said Fatemeh. "Whether he's guilty of a crime or not, Ramon shouldn't die because he defied a powerful man."

"I agree," said Bull, "but I'm not sure what we can do."

Luther Duncan chewed on his lower lip and looked to the west. "I think I may know someone who can help."

# CHAPTER SIX
## KID ANTRIM

Fatemeh Karimi tossed and turned under the blankets of her bed in the Castillos' rooming house. Several times, she opened her eyes to the darkened room. Luther Duncan promised to meet her soon after sunrise. He indicated he knew someone who could help get Ramon out of jail. She thought he might have been referring to an attorney or perhaps another judge, but when she asked him about it, he was rather evasive. She suspected his plan to get Ramon out of jail did not lie along legal channels.

Sighing, Fatemeh fluffed up her pillow, rolled onto her back and stared at the darkened ceiling. She thought about Ramon at the trial—unshaven with his glasses askew. It broke her heart to think about him that way and a tear trickled into her hair. She wiped it away, wondering how a man could affect her so.

Back in Persia, Mohammedan women submitted themselves to their husbands. Only five years before, her family had been inquiring among their network of friends and acquaintances about a suitable husband for her. Fatemeh shuddered at the memory and pulled the blankets up around her neck. She had no desire to subject herself to a man she did not know. Around that time, she heard the words of Bahá'u'lláh. His teachings that men and women were equal appealed greatly to her. Over time, she learned more of the Bahá'í Faith and eventually converted, much to her parents' dismay.

Staring at the ceiling, she realized that what attracted her to Ramon was how he really did seem to treat her as an equal—more so than any other man she had ever known. He spoke to her as a friend, not as an inferior or potential property. Not only did he treat her as an equal, he seemed to listen to everyone around him. It was almost as though he was Bahá'í, but didn't know it yet. She smiled at that thought.

Lying there in the dark, her thoughts turned to Bishop Ramirez and the people he'd sent to abduct her in Socorro. She thought about them tying her to a post and how the ropes cut into her wrists and ankles. Her thoughts moved to memories of her friend, Nava, who had been strangled by religious leaders who considered her a heretic. Another tear fell as she thought about the people who watched, unwilling and afraid to help. When something similar nearly happened to her, Ramon had not been afraid. Now that Ramon was in trouble, she had to be courageous as well. She would listen to Luther Duncan's plan and, unless she could think of something better, she would do her part to rescue Ramon. Even though she hoped the plan was legal, Ramon's imprisonment in Socorro was not just. She would break the law to get him out, if that was required.

Wan light began filtering in through the window, bathing the ceiling in a soft glow. Fatemeh arose from the bed and went to the window. A small, burrowing owl stood outside the window on the porch's roof. She pushed the window open as quietly as possible and whistled lightly at the owl. It turned its head and looked at her, then moved from one foot to the other.

"I don't know if you can help me or not," she said. "Be ready."

The owl bobbed up and down, then took to the air, and flew toward the horizon.

Later that morning, Fatemeh rode next to Luther Duncan. They were heading northwest, toward the mining town of Silver City. She left her wagon at the livery stable in the Mesilla Park along with one of her horses. She patted the horse she left behind on the nose and promised to return before long. The horse she rode trotted along contentedly, apparently happy to be on the trail and not confined to a stable. The landscape was flat and barren, dotted by scrub brush, prickly pear cactus, and tall, spindly ocotillos. In the summer, the heat would be unbearable on the trail, but it was November and a light breeze cooled the air. Mountains stood in the distance against a vivid, blue sky.

"Can you tell me who we're looking for in Silver City?"

asked Fatemeh.

"I've been hearing about a new deputy sheriff up there named Dan Tucker," said Duncan. "I'm hoping he'll be willing to help us out. If he can't, maybe he knows someone who can."

Fatemeh breathed a sigh of relief. She was pleased to hear they weren't seeking help from an outlaw. As they continued to ride and she thought more about the situation, her brow creased. "What makes you think this Dan Tucker will help us?"

"According to what I've read, people think Sheriff White-hill was crazy to hire Tucker." Duncan looked toward Fatemeh. "It's rumored he was involved in some trouble up in Colorado."

"If that's true, why exactly did Sheriff Whitehill hire him?" Fatemeh's brow creased.

"Whitehill likes him because he has a strong sense of justice." Duncan turned to face the trail again. He was silent for a time, apparently gathering his thoughts. "I suppose you could say he's more interested in doing the right thing than following the letter of the law. He's the one person I can think of who would listen to your story impartially and have any chance of helping."

"That seems like a real long shot." Fatemeh shook her head. "And, it seems like we're going far out of our way to talk to this man who may or may not help us."

"I know." Duncan pursed his lips. "But do you know anyone in Mesilla or Las Cruces that could help?"

Fatemeh drew in a deep breath and let it out slowly. She thought about the ranch hands who had worked with Ramon. They all seemed friendly, but she couldn't imagine any of them risking their lives to get Ramon out of jail. Her thoughts turned to Ramon's cousin Eduardo in Palomas Hot Springs. He would help if he could, but Fatemeh wasn't certain what skills he had. Finally she looked at Duncan. "I'm afraid you're right. We need someone who knows what they're doing. Still, I would feel better if the person we were entrusting our story to wasn't a complete stranger."

Duncan nodded, then looked at the sun in the sky and the mountains in the distance. "We better step up the pace. We still have quite a ride ahead of us." He prodded his horse into a canter with Fatemeh following close behind.

Ramon awoke to the sound of the deputy sheriff shoving a plate of flapjacks and a cup of coffee under the bars of his jail cell in Mesilla. Sunlight already streamed through the windows. He rubbed his eyes, then sat up and retrieved the plate. The flapjacks were cold and there were none of Mrs. Castillo's delicious preserves to sweeten them. He rolled one of the flapjacks and chewed it half-heartedly. The coffee was bitter, but at least it was hot.

Once Ramon finished with his rather lackluster meal, Deputy Barela opened the cell and ordered him to hold his arms out. The deputy cuffed his hands, then led him outside. They walked through the streets, toward the Mesilla Park. As they walked, Ramon looked around, wondering if Fatemeh would be there to see him off. He didn't see her anywhere. As he passed the street with the Castillos' rooming house, he wondered what she was doing. Was she enjoying a good breakfast? Was she worried about him? Was she making her own plans for the future?

An old coach, probably retired from one of the stage lines, was waiting at the Mesilla Park. Deputy Barela gave Ramon's shoulder a slight shove. Awkwardly, he grabbed the handle with his cuffed hands and pulled himself into the coach.

Inside was Ray Hillerman. Once Ramon was seated across from him, Hillerman banged on the coach's roof. The driver snapped the reins and the horses took off down the road. The way the coach rattled and thumped, causing him to bounce on the wooden seat, Ramon felt his suspicions were confirmed. The coach was old and its springs were shot.

As the coach made its way northward, Ramon's thoughts returned to Fatemeh. She enchanted him like no other woman had. When he was a teenager, girls laughed at him because of his glasses and because he was short. His father taught him how to use guns to hunt and defend himself, but also instilled in him a sense of right and wrong and taught him to respect the law of the land. Respecting their new country—the United States of America—Ramon's father had joined the Union Army in 1861. He died less than a year later, killed at the Battle of Glorietta Pass outside of Santa Fe. Despite that, Ramon continued to respect the law and eventually became a deputy sheriff. A few years later, he was elected Sheriff of Socorro. Through all of that, Ramon sensed women respected him. A few even batted their eyes at him when they said "hello" in the morning, but none of them seemed all that seriously interested in him.

Fatemeh was the first woman he really felt he could talk to. She indicated she was interested in considering marriage. Yet, she was not even there to see him off. As he bounced on the hard wooden seat of the coach, he wondered if their love had merely been an illusion. If he lived through his sentence in Socorro, he wondered if he would ever see her again.

It was late when Luther Duncan and Fatemeh Karimi arrived in Silver City. They found a hotel and obtained rooms for the night. Both slept late into the next day. After breakfast they asked directions to the sheriff's office. It was only a few buildings away from the hotel.

As they approached the sheriff's office, they saw a tall, clean-shaven man enter the building. He gripped the arm of a scrawny kid. Fatemeh figured the kid couldn't be much older than fifteen. The teenager limped and winced.

Fatemeh and Duncan looked at each other, then continued toward the sheriff's office. Duncan opened the door for Fatemeh. When she entered, she saw the tall man opening the jail cell at the back of office. He shoved the kid inside and slammed the door shut, then turned the key in the lock.

Turning around, the tall man removed his hat. "What can I do for you, ma'am?"

"We're looking for Dan Tucker," said Fatemeh.

"Well, you found him," said the tall man. "I'm Tucker."

Fatemeh tried to place his accent. "You're from Canada, aren't you?"

Tucker chuckled. "Very good, ma'am. Most people around here seem to think I'm a Southerner." He made his way over to a desk and indicated a pair of chairs. "Now tell me, how can I help you?"

Fatemeh introduced herself and Luther Duncan. Duncan tipped his bowler hat and sat down.

"A friend of mine is in trouble," explained Fatemeh. "His name is Ramon Morales and he used to be Sheriff of Socorro."

Tucker nodded knowingly. "I've heard of Búho Morales. He seems like a good man. I was really surprised when Sheriff Whitehill got a wanted poster for him a couple weeks ago. I never figured he was the kind of man that would assault a bishop."

"That's not the way it happened," interjected Duncan. "The bishop was hosting a lynching party and Fatemeh here was the guest of honor. Morales put a stop to it."

*It was more like a barbecue than a lynching,* thought Fatemeh. However, she decided Duncan's explanation took less time. "Ramon was tried two days ago in Mesilla and the jury found him not guilty of assaulting the bishop. He acknowledges he was wrong to leave his duties as sheriff, and he's willing to serve his time, but they're taking him to jail in Socorro."

"And you're afraid that it's now Búho's turn to be guest of honor at a lynching party, is that it?" Tucker leaned back in his chair and put his feet up on the desk.

A derisive laugh came from the jail cell. "And you've come to ol' Dangerous Dan for help? That's a real hoot."

"You shut up." Tucker pointed his finger at the cell.

"Come make me!" called the cocky teenager.

Tucker shook his head.

"Who's your prisoner?" Duncan looked toward the cell.

"Calls himself Kid Antrim." Tucker chuckled to himself. "He's been making a real pain in the ass of himself over at Fort Grant in Arizona." He blushed and tipped his hat at Fatemeh. "Pardon my language, ma'am. They say he keeps stealing their supplies out from under them. His mother lives here in Silver City and I finally caught him this morning."

"You wouldn't o' caught me if it wasn't for this ankle," grumbled the kid.

Fatemeh stood and stepped over to the cell. "What happened to your ankle?"

"Sprained it, hopping onto a horse." The kid looked as his

feet, apparently embarrassed at the notion of being clumsy.

"A horse he stole." The deputy sheriff scratched the back of his head. "I'm taking him back to Arizona tomorrow so he can stand trial at the fort. Even if I wanted to, I'm not sure there's anything I could do to help Búho Morales. What you need is a good attorney and a judge sympathetic to your case, not a deputy sheriff like me—no matter how much I admire his reputation."

"Whacha really need is someone to break him outta jail," said the kid.

Fatemeh ignored the comment and returned to her seat at Tucker's desk.

"Is there anyone you know that could help us?" Duncan leaned forward.

Tucker dropped his feet back to the floor. "Not around here. You might try Albert Fountain in Mesilla. I hear he's pretty good with difficult cases."

Fatemeh looked at Duncan with narrowed eyes. He gave an apologetic shrug. She redirected her gaze to the deputy sheriff. "I'm sorry we've bothered you, Mr. Tucker."

"No bother at all, ma'am." Tucker smiled faintly. "May I ask what the bishop was going to lynch you for?"

"His brother-in-law, Randolph Dalton, accused me of running off his miners. I was a better curandera than the ones in his parish..." She began counting off items on her fingers.

Tucker held up his hand and smiled. "I get the idea. If you'll excuse my language again, you were a pain in his ass."

Fatemeh grinned at that. "I think that about sums it up." She looked toward the cell. "I wonder if you would allow me to treat the young man's sprained ankle?"

Tucker shrugged. "It would sure make getting him to Arizona a lot easier if he could walk on his own two feet."

Fatemeh nodded, then stood and left the sheriff's office. She tried to think if there was anything else she could say to persuade Dan Tucker to help them out. It was clear he admired Ramon's good reputation as a lawman. However, he was right. They needed a lawyer to get Ramon out of jail, not a deputy sheriff. She approached her horse and patted it on the nose, then went to her saddlebag and retrieved a bottle and some bandages. A few minutes later, she returned to the sheriff's office.

She took the chair from in front of Dan Tucker's desk, placed it in front of the jail cell and sat down. "I have something to help your sprain," she said.

"Much obliged, but these things heal themselves with time." Kid Antrim looked at the bottle suspiciously.

"This will help. I promise."

Kid Antrim limped over to the bars. Gingerly, he pulled off his boot, then stuck his foot through. Fatemeh uncorked the bottle and the kid quickly pulled his foot back. "What in the name of Hell is that?" he cried, wrinkling his nose.

"Horse liniment. It's the best thing I know for sprains."

"I ain't no horse."

"Stick your foot back through the bars."

He complied and she massaged his ankle with the liniment. Then, she wrapped his ankle snugly with the bandages.

"Hey, that feels better already."

"Sure you don't want to help me get him over to Arizona?" asked Tucker. "He listens to you better than he listens to me."

"I would consider it, if you could help me with my problem." Fatemeh put the cork back in the bottle of horse liniment.

The deputy sheriff scratched the back of his head, as though giving it serious thought. "The problem is I just don't see any way I can help you, short of breaking Morales out of jail. If I really thought he'd been wronged, I might even help you do that, but from what you tell me, he admitted he was guilty of running away from his duties. It sounds like he may be facing a bad situation in Socorro, but how do I know what you're telling me is true?"

"You don't."

"If you can think of any way to help, send word to me at the *Mesilla News*," offered Duncan.

"I'll do that." Tucker stood from the desk and showed the visitors to the door.

That evening, Fatemeh and Duncan ate dinner at the hotel. Afterwards, they planned to get some sleep and ride back to Mesilla the next day.

"So tell me, Mr. Duncan, why exactly did we ride all the

way out here, when we could have just spoken to this Albert Fountain back in Mesilla?"

Duncan sighed. "Albert Fountain is a very high-powered attorney. I thought his services would be more than you could afford."

Fatemeh looked down at her plate and stirred the food around with her fork. "I suppose you're right." She looked back up into Duncan's eyes. "So what exactly are we going to do?"

Just then, the hotel door flew open and the scrawny fifteen-year-old kid from the sheriff's office appeared. He slammed the door behind him and looked around. Seeing Fatemeh and Duncan he made for the table.

"What are you doing here?" Duncan's eyes were wide.

"My ankle felt better, so I broke out of jail." The kid smiled. "I didn't feel like waiting around to go back to Arizona, so I thought I'd come here and see if I could help you all."

"We don't need your help." Duncan made a shooing motion.

"I think you do," said the kid.

"Why do you want to help us?" Fatemeh turned so she faced the kid.

The kid's grin broadened. "Dangerous Dan said you were a pain in the ass. That makes you my kind of people!" A moment later, his expression turned serious and his gaze fell to Fatemeh. "More than that, though, you helped me. I appreciate it."

"Not many people have seen fit to help you, have they?" Fatemeh reached out and took the kid's hand.

He shook his head.

"What's your name?" asked Fatemeh. "I presume it isn't really 'Kid Antrim'."

"My name's Billy ... Billy McCarty."

"How do you think you can help us?" Luther Duncan sat back and folded his arms across his chest.

"I can get your friend outta jail."

"And how exactly would you do that?"

Billy pulled his hand back from Fatemeh's and held his arms wide, as though his presence there should be all the explanation required. "I've been getting in and out of Fort Grant for the better part of a year without being caught. Plus, I got myself out of jail with a sprained ankle."

"Maybe you can help." Fatemeh stood. "However, I think we'd better get moving soon. It won't be long before Sheriff Whitehill or Dan Tucker come looking for you."

Billy jumped to his feet and winced when he landed on the sprained ankle. His grimace quickly dissolved into a fresh smile. "My thoughts exactly."

Luther Duncan shook his head. "I don't know if I like this."

When they left Silver City the next day, Fatemeh was surprised they rode to the northwest, further into the mountains and away from both Socorro and Mesilla.

"It'll be harder for ol' Dangerous Dan to track us," explained Billy. "We'll circle around and come back to Socorro from the west."

"Won't that give Tucker time to warn people in Socorro about us?" asked Duncan.

"First off, he'll be more concerned about me than you two," said Billy. "I don't think he'll consider it a possibility that I'm helping you. He'll waste time checking at my ma's place, then checking over at Fort Grant. That'll give us lots of time to get ahead of him. Even if he does think I might be helping you all, he'll either be behind us on the trail, or he'll ride into Mesilla and then go up through Jornada del Muerto. Either way, he'll take as long or longer getting to Socorro than we will."

"He could always send a wire from Mesilla." Duncan appeared dubious.

"Do you think any telegram he could send would give people in Socorro a good enough description they'd spot me out of a crowd?"

"All I can say is that I hope you're right," grumbled Duncan.

General Alexander Gorloff stood outside a meeting hall in Windsor, California, just a few miles away from Call Ranch. He took a deep breath, inhaling the pine scent. He admired the tall trees that surrounded the area. He was reminded of the forests of his homeland and smiled at the thought this territory would soon be part of Russia if all went according to plan. He loved the American West and understood his kinsmen who had chosen to call it home.

He turned around and entered the meeting hall. It was a simple log structure with benches on either side of a central aisle. At the front of the room was a podium. He estimated three dozen people occupied the benches. Of them, about a dozen had gray hair and wrinkled skin. These were the older people who stayed behind when the Russians left Fort Ross thirty years before. The younger people in the room were probably their children, many of whom likely felt they had claims on their parents' land, but actually lived in Windsor or other nearby towns. It was also possible one or two of those present were, in fact, George Call's men, there to see what Gorloff said to the settlers.

Call might have spies, but Gorloff did too. The general felt his spies were superior to any the rancher might send to the meeting. He still didn't fully understand the creature called Legion, but he could feel it in the back of his mind. A part of him worried he was going crazy and he was imagining the voices he heard. However, he proposed to put that idea to the test during this meeting. He knew Legion somehow understood him, even when he did not speak aloud.

*Seek out the Russians that are here,* he thought. *Ignore any that are not my kinsmen.*

"*What if they react poorly to our presence in their thoughts?*" asked Legion.

*Don't overwhelm them with images,* thought Gorloff. *Just listen to what I say and let them picture it in their minds.* Gorloff felt Legion's agreement to this course of action.

The general reached the podium and introduced himself to those assembled—in Russian. He continued speaking in his native language. "I am told George Call has occupied Fort Ross and has purchased the surrounding land. He does not recognize your claims."

Many of those gathered in the room nodded their assent.

"I tell you, there is no hope George Call will relent his claim," said Gorloff, sternly.

There were many shocked murmurs around the room. One of the old men stood up. "Can't you negotiate with Mr. Call?" he asked in Russian.

"The time for negotiation has ended," growled Gorloff. "However, I do not feel you need to relinquish your land to George Call. This land is rightfully yours. It was claimed by the Russian Empire and it must stay in the empire's hands, not in the hands of the Americans."

A younger man stood. "Our people relinquished their claim to this land thirty years ago. How can we expect help from Mother Russia?"

"It was a mistake for Russia to leave." Gorloff folded his arms across his chest and looked from the young man's eyes into the eyes of the older man next to him. Legion informed Gorloff that the old man was the young man's father. "Many of you in this room came to this land to help strengthen the empire. You stayed because you fell in love with the land, but now new settlers refuse to recognize your claim. Is that right?"

Most of the people gathered nodded agreement. Some had blank stares, as though they didn't understand the words.

Gorloff paced in front of the hall. "Those who came from Russia sought to build a future for their children in this new land. They sought to leave houses and farms their children could inherit, but now a rancher seeks to take that away." The general stopped and turned, facing those assembled. "You must be prepared to fight for what belongs to you. I tell you, Russia will reclaim this land and it will be yours."

There were more nods and murmurs of agreement.

"This young country of America has shown it is fragile and weak." Gorloff returned to the podium. "The War Between the States was just a sample of the divisiveness this country is capable of. Such disarray must be reined in by the strong hand of the Russian Empire. I have a plan and will present it to the Czar." He stepped around the podium and addressed the people in an intimate tone. "I need a half dozen volunteers to travel with me to Russia. People who know this area and are capable of leading Russian forces to drive men like George Call off our land."

Seconds ticked by while those assembled looked on in silence. For a moment, the general was afraid the people in the room would turn on him for presenting his plan. Perhaps this Legion was only part of his imagination after all.

Then one of the young men raised a hand. "How do you propose to invade America with only a half dozen men?" he asked.

"I need you as advisors. I need you to help me..." He considered his words carefully. These men would carry Legion with them back to Russia, allowing him to build popular support for his plan. "I need you to help me spread the word among our people about how we can accomplish our goals. I need Russians passionate about America. If successful, we will return with the might of the Russian army."

The young man nodded. "I am with you, General Gorloff."

Soon another young man stood, volunteering to go with the general. A moment later, several more stood.

The general smiled as he listened to Legion's report about which of the men assembled would be most effective helping him when he returned to Russia and which would, in fact, make the best generals.

One of the older men stood. "God bless you, General Gorloff. My people are descended from the Tartars of Central Russia. My grandfather used to tell me stories of how the holy men could assume the form of owls to drive out evil." The old man swallowed, as though afraid to continue, but finally gathered resolve. "I can see owls driving the evil out of this land."

Gorloff nodded somberly. He wasn't certain about owls, but Legion had shown him how Russia could build mighty ships that traveled by air. There was nothing in America that could stop such power. The general picked the men who would accompany him back to Russia.

Fatemeh paced back and forth on the porch of a hotel in the small town of Magdalena. The town rested in mountainous country thirty-five miles west of Socorro. Duncan and Billy had ridden ahead the day before to find out where Ramon was being held. They figured if she was spotted, people like Randolph

Dalton and Bishop Ramirez would know something was up. Dark clouds were forming in the brilliant blue sky and the chill air was turning downright cold. Fatemeh thought she smelled moisture on the breeze.

As the sun settled on the horizon, Duncan and Billy rode up to the hotel. They climbed off their horses and hitched them to the post in front of the porch. "He's all right," said Duncan. "He's being held at the sheriff's office. I was able to get in and talk to him."

"The thing I didn't like were the people who watched you go in and talk to him," said Billy.

"I didn't see anyone watching me." Duncan's eyebrows came together, apparently perplexed.

"I think they were miners." Billy shook his head, then looked into Fatemeh's eyes. "They wore dirty clothes and no hats. They were sitting on benches across the street."

"What's strange about miners in Socorro?" Duncan's gaze narrowed further.

"What would miners be doing out on the street in the middle of the day?" Billy shot back.

"I see your point," said Fatemeh. "I gather we'll need to move fast."

Billy nodded. "There's no way we can get back there before morning. Let's get some grub and rest up. We'll ride out tomorrow afternoon."

Fatemeh swallowed hard, then gathered her resolve and nodded.

Snow flurries gently wafted around them as Duncan, Billy and Fatemeh rode into Socorro the next day. It was ten o'clock at night when they arrived. With no moonlight, the streets were mostly dark. A few gaslights cast a ghostly glow over the streets. They rode past the light of a boisterous saloon on the town square. Billy looked at the saloon and nodded, seemingly satisfied. The sheriff's office was on a road that led away from the town square, a short distance from the saloon.

They hitched their horses a few doors down from the sheriff's office, then made their way back to the side of the building and huddled in the shadows.

"What do we do now?" asked Fatemeh.

"We wait." Billy removed his gun from his holster, held it by the barrel, and crouched quietly near a window. He seemed to be listening. The only thing Fatemeh heard was the noise from the saloon.

After about half an hour, there was shouting from the direction of the saloon and some loud noises. Fatemeh could just make out Billy's smile. He jumped to his feet and smashed the window of the sheriff's office. Fatemeh nodded when she understood Billy's plan. Anyone hearing the sound of glass breaking would attribute it to the fight at the saloon. Carefully, Billy reached through the broken window, found the latch, then lifted the window. He climbed through. Fatemeh and Duncan followed, being careful not to cut themselves on the broken glass.

The office was dark. Luther Duncan retrieved a box of matches from his pocket and lit one of the oil lamps. Holding it up, he caught his breath. The jail cell was empty.

"He was here yesterday," said Duncan. "Where did he go?"

"They took him somewhere." Billy looked over at Fatemeh. "But where?"

Fatemeh looked down at one of the desks. She picked up a scrap of paper and shuddered. "It has one word. 'Mine'."

"If that's related to Ramon at all, it could mean anything." Duncan stepped around and held the lantern closer to the paper. "It could be Dalton saying Ramon 'is mine.' It could mean take him to a mine."

"I think it's both," said Fatemeh. "We need to go to Dalton's mine." She thought about the miners scattered on the ground after the explosion in the dynamite shack.

"Makes sense to me. A mine's a good place to have an accident. Especially one where you don't want people identifying the body," said Billy.

"I hope you're right." Duncan blew out the flame and started to set the lantern down, but Fatemeh stopped him.

"Bring the lantern along, we may need it." Fatemeh took a second lantern from one of the other desks.

As they left through the front door, Fatemeh hoped they had guessed right. The ride to Dalton's mine would take time. If Ramon had been taken somewhere else, he could be dead by the time they found him—*if* they found him. However, they didn't dare split up. If they did find Ramon, they would need to be together to have any hope of rescuing him and there wasn't time to seek out and recruit other people who might be friendly to Ramon.

An hour later, Fatemeh, Duncan, and Billy rode up to the entrance of the Dalton mine. Two horses were already hitched nearby. The remains of the destroyed dynamite shack had been cleared away. A light dusting of snow was beginning to settle on the ground. Billy climbed off his horse, took one of the lanterns and lit it. He looked around for a moment, then pointed at some footprints. "Two horses, three men," he said.

"Where did they go?" asked Fatemeh.

Billy looked over to the mine entrance. "In there."

Fatemeh and Duncan each lit their lanterns and followed Billy into the mine. Billy followed the fresh tracks several yards into the cave before the ground became too rocky to see footprints. He held up his hand and stood quietly, barely breathing, apparently listening.

As they stood there, Fatemeh thought she heard something. There was a crack followed by a wet thud. A voice cried out. Fatemeh pushed ahead of Billy and followed the sound. About a hundred yards further into the mine, they came to a junction. Two tunnels led in different directions.

"Which way do we go?" asked Duncan in a whisper.

"Hey, what's that owl doing here?" Billy pointed to a burrowing owl, perched on a mine cart.

"He probably came in out of the cold to hunt," said Fatemeh. "Lots of bugs and mice in here, I'm sure." She whistled lightly at the owl. The owl danced from one foot to the other, then looked toward one of the tunnels. It looked back at Fatemeh, chirped and then flew off in the opposite direction. She turned her head to Duncan. "You just need to ask directions." She moved toward the tunnel the owl had glanced at.

"You mean to tell me that owl told you which direction to go?" Duncan sounded incredulous.

"No, the owl just chirped and looked this way. He didn't like something down here. My best guess is people and noise." She proceeded down the tunnel.

After a short distance, she caught sight of a soft glow. Then she heard harsh words, "Get up, Morales, or have you had enough?"

"I think he's had enough," said another voice. "Boss doesn't want him dead until he gets a chance to talk to him, tomorrow."

Fatemeh ran ahead. The tunnel opened into a small chamber. She gasped at the sight that met her. Two large miners hovered over a figure huddled on the dirt floor of the mine. There was blood in a small pool near the figure's head. A pair of broken and twisted glasses sat some distance away. "Get away from him!" called Fatemeh.

The two men whirled. A slow grin formed on one of their faces. "Well, what do we have here?"

"A whole lotta trouble." Billy appeared at Fatemeh's side, his gun drawn. Duncan came up behind them a moment later.

"What I see is one skinny boy who'll probably piss himself if that gun makes a loud bang, a city slicker, and a pretty woman ripe for plucking." The miner took a step forward. "Young man, hand me that gun before you hurt yourself."

Billy's gaze was like steel. "Don't come any closer, asshole."

"What'd you call me?" said the miner, with a sneer.

"I called you an asshole," said Billy. "But I shoulda called you dead, cuz that's what you'll be if you don't stop."

The miner took another step. There was a blast and blood splattered from the miner's gut as he fell backward.

"No!" Fatemeh whirled on Billy. "We didn't come here to kill."

He aimed his gun at the other miner and turned his icy gaze toward Fatemeh. "It was him or me, and it was clear they aimed to kill your friend, if he ain't already dead." Billy looked back at the other miner. "Get away from Morales, now."

The second miner held up his hands and backed toward the wall.

Fatemeh darted into the chamber and knelt down next to Ramon. One eye was swollen shut and a trail of blood came from his nose and mouth. His good eye fluttered open. "Am I dreaming?" he muttered.

"We need to get out of here." Fatemeh helped Ramon to his feet. He wobbled unsteadily. She looked up at Duncan. "Give me a hand!"

Duncan rushed to their side. Together, the three moved toward Billy.

"Take my horse," said Billy. "If they catch you, they can't call you a horse thief and hang you."

"What about you?" asked Fatemeh.

"I think there's another horse I can use." His grin sent a chill up Fatemeh's spine.

"That's not what I meant," she said through gritted teeth.

"They've already got reason to hang me." Billy's gaze remained fixed on the miner. "Now, get outta here."

"Whatever you do, don't kill the other miner." Fatemeh moved forward again.

"Why not?" Billy's icy tone had become one of genuine curiosity.

"Because all life is sacred, even the bottom feeders." With that, she and Duncan helped Ramon to the mine's entrance. With a little help, Ramon was able to climb onto Billy's horse. The three rode away from the mine without waiting for Kid Antrim.

"So, where are we going now?" asked Duncan.

Fatemeh looked over at Ramon, slumped over Billy's horse. "What we need is a place for Ramon to rest and recover. I think I know just the place." She pulled on the reins, turning the horse southward toward Palomas Hot Springs.

# CHAPTER SEVEN
## THE FOLLY OF LIBERATION

Alexander Gorloff watched as the California coastline re-
ceded into the distance. He was bound for Russia aboard
a steamship, along with the six volunteers from Windsor. The general pulled his coat tight to guard against the chill,
autumn air. Winter would be fully upon them by the time they
reached the Imperial Palace at St. Petersburg. He nodded to
himself, pleased at the prospect of a stronger Russian Empire
in the new year.

Gorloff felt Legion, restless in the back of his mind. The
general tried to shrug off the sensation, but when it wouldn't
go away, he moved toward the ship's bow and looked off into
the gray-green expanse of the ocean. When the general focused
his attention on the alien, he could make out words. *"We are not
entirely sanguine about your thoughts of world domination."*

"I thought you agreed the empire's invasion of the United States was a 'noble experiment.' You hoped that by taking
action, you could stabilize the human race and avert the catastrophe that would result if two major powers were allowed
to develop on this planet." Gorloff spoke aloud, finding it easier
to focus his thoughts than if he remained silent.

*"Correction: it is a noble experiment to bring stability to the
human race and hopefully avert a catastrophe that* could *result."*
Although Legion spoke in the general's mind, he thought he
detected a certain irritability in the words. *"While it is highly
probable the human race will destroy itself along with most life on this
planet if no action is taken, it is hardly a foregone conclusion."*

The general lit a cigar, tossed the match overboard, and
took a puff. "I still do not understand the problem."

*"You promised to introduce us to the great minds of the human
race,"* said Legion. Behind the statement, the general thought

he caught a second set of words. The alien was examining the effects of nicotine on his body and brain. Gorloff liked what he heard about nicotine improving the efficiency of something called neurotransmitters, but didn't like the information about the smoke's effects on his lungs and heart.

The general closed his eyes and returned his focus to the primary conversation. "I will be introducing you to great minds. I'll be introducing you to generals, strategists and even the Czar himself."

*"We have shown you that you will need machines to accomplish the task of stabilizing the human race. Your thoughts do not contain specific plans of meeting with the scientists and engineers that could bring your plan to fruition."*

Gorloff smoked the cigar in silence while looking out at the ocean. "I still do not understand. The generals and strategists who we will speak to will instruct the scientists and engineers to build the things we need."

*"Perhaps that is true,"* said Legion. *"However, to assure the success of this plan, we feel it is important to communicate with key scientists and engineers directly."* Legion paused as though thinking. When Legion first entered Gorloff's mind, the general sensed he heard most of the alien's thoughts. As time went by, he began to suspect Legion was becoming better able to select which thoughts he heard and which were hidden. *"It is evident humans place little value on scientific inquiry. It is one thing that places your species in danger."*

Gorloff shook his head, still confused. "Of course we value science. Discussions of scientific discovery are in vogue among the elite. We build universities and fund experiments…"

*"It is a good beginning, but as you say, their work is discussed by the elite. They are not elite themselves. Scientists are not leaders in your society."*

"They rarely seem interested."

*"It would be interesting to find out why that is so."*

"Are you doing all right, General Gorloff?"

The general whirled, startled by the strange voice that interrupted his conversation with the alien. He faced the ship's captain, whose brow was furrowed in apparent concern.

"You look agitated." The captain placed his hands behind

his back and moved up next to the general.

"I'm doing fine," said Gorloff. "Just running through a... speech I have to give when we get home."

The captain nodded as though he understood, but the concerned look never quite left his face. "If you do need anything, please don't hesitate to let me know." He looked out over the ocean. "I'm hoping for a smooth crossing."

"So am I." Gorloff tossed the remains of his cigar overboard and made his way back to his cabin.

Fatemeh, Ramon and Luther Duncan arrived in Palomas Hot Springs just as the sun was setting. Eduardo and Alicia Morales were sitting together on the porch. As the horses approached, Eduardo shot to his feet and rushed toward them. Alicia followed close behind.

"Búho! What happened?" called Eduardo as he came alongside the horse.

"I think Randolph Dalton wanted to send a message to anyone who might think about interfering with his mining operation." Duncan lifted his bowler hat, nodded to Alicia, and introduced himself. "I write for the *Mesilla News*."

Eduardo eased Ramon off the horse while Alicia took the reins and led it back to the stables. Duncan and Fatemeh followed her. Once the horses were tended, the three went inside. They found Eduardo cleaning Ramon's cuts and scrapes with iodine. Ramon winced each time the cloth was applied, but hardly moved otherwise.

"How is he doing?" asked Fatemeh. She sat at the table on the other side of Ramon from Eduardo.

"They beat him badly," said Eduardo, "but I don't think they broke any bones. He'll be good as new with a few days resting up and visiting the hot springs."

Duncan shook his head and took another seat at the table. "I don't think they have a few days."

"What do you mean?" asked Alicia, who was placing logs into the kitchen's wood stove.

"We were with a kid named Billy McCarty," explained

Duncan. "He shot and killed one of Dalton's men. There's sure to be a posse riding out before long."

"Ay!" Eduardo gritted his teeth. "You really got into a mess this time, Búho."

"What really annoys me is that they broke my glasses." Ramon's comment was barely audible through his swollen lips.

"That, I might be able to help you with." Eduardo went into the living room. Fatemeh heard him rummaging through some drawers. After a moment, he returned, holding a pair of glasses. "Remember how Aunt Sofia used to have me carry a pair of your glasses with us to school? That way I'd have a pair if you broke one."

Ramon took the glasses and gingerly slipped them on. He squinted through the lenses. "They're a bit small and things look kinda blurry."

"Well, they're the ones you wore almost fifteen years ago. You're lucky I kept them." Eduardo smiled. "Better than nothing, eh?"

"Thanks, cousin." Ramon started to smile, but then winced in pain.

Fatemeh wrung her hands. "Well, I think the next order of business is what to do now? Ramon was willing to serve time for leaving his job in Socorro, but surely he doesn't deserve to die."

"No one here agrees with that more than I do," said Ramon. "Even I can't believe Randolph Dalton would be this cruel." He took a deep breath and let it out slowly. "We were planning to go west—to California. I think that's still the best plan—if we can get there."

Duncan stood and walked over to the window, peering out into the dark as though expecting to see a posse ride into the valley at any minute. "The fastest way would be by train and the closest station is Mesilla. The problem is they'll probably expect you to go that way."

"Then we should go north to Santa Fe," said Eduardo. "That way you can take the Denver and Rio Grande into Colorado and pick up the Central Pacific into California."

"But you'll have to ride back through Socorro to get to Santa Fe." Duncan scratched his head.

Eduardo nodded. "We'll have to cut around Socorro. I'm thinking out East and behind the Manzanos."

"Up through Torreon, then behind the Sandias through Madrid and Cerillos to Santa Fe." Ramon pursed his lips. "It just might work—if we get going soon."

"There's only one problem." Alicia stood from the wood stove. "Do you think they might have trackers who could follow the trail here? If so, wouldn't they simply turn around and be on your trail again?"

"Hard to say," said Ramon. "Juan Gomez used to be pretty good trailing people."

Duncan turned around and faced the table. "I'll ride south to Mesilla." All heads turned to face him. "I need to get back there anyway. It might, at least, confuse them."

"I'll go with you," said Alicia. "They'll be looking for two horses. I can stay down in Mesilla. Eduardo can ride down and meet me when Ramon and Fatemeh are safely on the train in Santa Fe."

"There is one other problem," interjected Fatemeh. "My wagon with all my herbs and supplies—it's still in Mesilla. I have a horse down there as well."

"We'll bring them back here when we come home," said Alicia. "Once you're settled in California, let us know and we'll bring them out to you."

"I'll help with any costs," offered Duncan.

Fatemeh shook her head. "I couldn't ask you—"

"You haven't asked us," said Alicia. "We're volunteering."

Duncan took a step toward the table. "Besides, I have a feeling you saved my life back in Las Cruces. I owe you."

"Sounds like we have a plan." Eduardo stood. "We should get our supplies packed, get a couple hours of sleep, and then set out."

"What about the posse?" asked Duncan.

Ramon shook his head. "I'm guessing it'll take a few hours for them to get a posse together. We have some time."

Eduardo sighed. "Still, one of us should keep watch, just in case."

Ramon pulled himself to his feet. "What can I do to help?"

Fatemeh stood and helped support Ramon. "I think you

need some time in the hot spring followed by a little sleep. We can handle the packing."

She led him out back to the enclosure that surrounded the spring bubbling behind Eduardo's house. Just as they reached the door, Ramon paused.

"I think I can manage from here." He took a step and nearly fell over.

"Let me help you into the water," said Fatemeh.

Ramon's blush was just visible in the light from the house. "Are you sure that's proper? We could get Eduardo...or Duncan."

Fatemeh sighed. " I'm a healer. It won't embarrass me to undress you down to your skivvies. Second, we've talked about marriage. I would like to see you naked one of these days."

Ramon's blush deepened, but he also smiled. "Will you return the favor?"

Fatemeh inclined her head. "Perhaps...when you're feeling better. For now, my main concern is getting you to a point where you feel good enough to ride. Without that, we won't have a 'later.'" She placed her arm around his waist and they moved toward the enclosure's door.

Once inside the enclosure, Ramon held up his hand.

"What is it this time?" she asked.

"Thank you for coming to get me." Ramon leaned over and kissed her gently, then winced slightly in pain.

Fatemeh led Ramon into the enclosure and helped him undress and get into the water. She then returned to the house where she helped gather supplies for the journey northward. Satisfied they had everything they needed, Fatemeh returned to the enclosure, carrying a towel and some clean clothes. She found Ramon dozing in the hot spring. Kneeling down beside him, she touched him gently on the shoulder.

Ramon's eyes fluttered. "Ah ... corazón. Time to get out already?"

She smiled briefly at being called corazón—the Spanish word for heart. She helped him out of the water, then turned her back while he dried himself and dressed. Once finished she helped him up to the house and under the covers of a bed. She took the bed in the room across the hall. Without even bothering to turn back the covers, she lay on top in her clothes. She tossed and turned and finally dozed briefly just as Alicia came in to tell her it was time to go.

Bleary eyed, she climbed out of bed. Ramon's bed was empty, already made. She clambered down the stairs and found him sitting at the kitchen table sipping coffee. His face was still swollen, but he looked much better. She helped herself to some coffee. Alicia came downstairs a moment later and shooed them outside to where Eduardo was waiting with two horses. Duncan was already saddled up. Alicia made her rounds of the house, making sure the fires were out and the animals secure.

Fatemeh helped Ramon mount his horse. Once done, she turned and saw Alicia approach. Eduardo took his wife into his arms. "Be careful. We don't know whether these are lawmen or hired thugs on our tail. The latter might not care if you two don't exactly meet the description of the people they're looking for."

Alicia nodded, then kissed Eduardo. A moment later, they separated and Fatemeh, Eduardo and Alicia mounted their horses. They rode away from the hacienda just as the sun came over the horizon.

The ride northward was hard, and largely silent. They took a route over broad flat land, dotted with scrub. A range of mountains stood between them and Socorro. Dark clouds billowed over the countryside. During the ride, Fatemeh and Eduardo scanned the surrounding countryside, looking for signs of pursuit. When they camped, they took turns watching for approaching riders at night. After the first day, Ramon felt well enough to take a turn on watch.

As the days wore on, they passed one range of mountains and approached a second more closely. The dusty, scrub-covered flatland gave way to undulating, grassy hills and valleys dusted with snow. Each time they descended into a valley, Fatemeh worried an ambush would be waiting when they crested the next hill. Her worry increased as the terrain became even more rugged and the occasional pine and aspen sprung from the ground.

At one point, the trail led them through a narrow canyon lined with snow-covered wooden shacks. An icy wind blew, intensified by the canyon walls. "Do we have to go through there?" asked Fatemeh.

"It's just a little mining town called Madrid," explained Ramon.

Fatemeh pursed her lips. "I think I've had enough of little mining towns."

Ramon laughed. "Madrid means we're getting close to Santa Fe. After this, we should be home free."

"I wish I could be as certain as you are." Fatemeh gathered her resolve and followed the two men through the narrow canyon. She relaxed somewhat when she saw an owl crouched in the eaves of one of the buildings, sheltered from the cold. It opened its eyes and looked at her, giving silent reassurance that nothing was amiss in the village.

That night, they camped at the base of a sheer cliff on rocks blown clear of snow by the wind. The natural rock pillars reminded Fatemeh of Egyptian gods carved into the mountainside watching over them.

The next day, they rode into the small town of Lamy, just a few miles from Santa Fe. The depot was located there because New Mexico's capital city was just too high and rugged for the railroad. Once there, they dismounted, tended to their horses, and bought train tickets. The train wouldn't arrive for a few hours, so they went to a nearby restaurant and ordered lunch. Fatemeh looked around nervously at the people, trying to see if she recognized anyone familiar from Socorro.

"You've hardly touched your food," said Ramon.

Fatemeh smiled nervously and pushed the plate aside. "I'm afraid I'm not very hungry."

After lunch, they returned to the train station. Fatemeh paced the platform, patting her arms, warding off the cold until the train finally arrived an hour later. She jumped when its whistle sounded. Ramon tried to suppress a laugh and she shrugged and gave him an embarrassed smile. Both Fatemeh and Ramon embraced Eduardo, then climbed onto the train and found seats.

Even before the train lurched out of the station, Fatemeh's head fell against Ramon's shoulder and she began softly snoring.

Alexander Gorloff admired the view of the Winter Palace in St. Petersburg. Unlike many other European palaces that looked like old fortresses or fairy tale castles, the Czar's Winter Palace was a great, sprawling mansion. It seemed a fitting place from which to rule much of the industrialized world. It was early evening, but already dark. Gas lamps illuminated the palace and the snow around it, giving the building a magical quality.

In fact, the whole city of St. Petersburg seemed energized. A new year was about to dawn and the Russian Orthodox Christmas would come a week later. Gorloff rubbed his hands together in anticipation and walked toward the palace.

The journey from San Francisco had been a long one, and Gorloff was pleased to be home. The general and his supporters had landed in Vladivostok at the end of November and had taken the train to St. Petersburg. Once in the city, Gorloff made appointments with several old Army friends and introduced them to his new generals. With Legion's help, he tentatively broached his plans for American conquest.

General Mikhail Dragomirov's reaction was typical. "Tensions with Turkey are high right now. However, I do not relish the thought of going to war with the Ottoman Empire. If turning our attention to the Americas will save the Czar and the world, I'm all for it." At that point, Dragomirov placed his hand on Gorloff's shoulder. "But the Czar considers America a friend. He will not be swayed easily."

Gorloff nodded knowingly to that statement. In the meantime, with each new appointment and introduction, Legion was spreading out, piece by piece and gently bringing dreams to the Russian military and political elite. At first, Gorloff was concerned Legion might spread himself too thin, but the alien assured him he could create new components as needed. After two weeks in St. Petersburg, Gorloff was ready to seek an audience with the Czar.

The general was greeted at the door of the Winter Palace. An attendant took his hat and coat and led him into a sitting room. After only half an hour, he was taken to the palace's

Amber Room. The Czar sat behind a desk. His hair was cut short and great muttonchops came down to meet an impressive, bushy mustache, meticulously waxed on the ends.

The general knelt in front of the monarch.

Czar Alexander II smiled and stood. "How good to see you, Alexander Petrovich. It has been too long." He held out his hand and indicated the general should rise and be seated.

Gorloff stood and moved to a chair across from the Czar. "Thank you, Your Highness."

The Czar opened a gold-inlaid box on his desk. "Would you care for a cigar?"

"You honor me." The general reached into the box and took a cigar, but did not light it. He waited for the Czar to retrieve his own cigar first and return to his seat. While doing so, the general took a moment to admire the room's walls. Large sections of amber had been cut, polished, fitted together, and accented with gold trim. A servant, who had been standing unobtrusively in a corner of the room came forward and lit the Czar's cigar and then the general's.

"I have to admit, I'm surprised to see you, although I'm glad," said the Czar. "I think perhaps you have anticipated that I plan to reassign you to London."

"Again, you do me great honor, Your Highness." Gorloff nodded in deference. "I do wish to speak of change, even though I did not anticipate your specific plans."

The Czar pursed his lips and seemed to consider the remark. "Interesting. Go on, Alexander Petrovich."

"Almost fifteen years ago, you took one of the bravest steps of any Czar in the history of Russia and freed the serfs. For that you will always be remembered."

The Czar sighed. "Alas, I fear that has not gone as well as I would have liked."

Gorloff nodded sympathetically. "Two years later, Abraham Lincoln in America followed your example and freed the slaves in his great country." Silently, Gorloff told Legion it was time to enter the Czar's mind and quietly build visions. "Lincoln's plan did not go as expected either."

"Indeed." The Czar's striking blue eyes darted from side to side. "The result was a nearly catastrophic war and Mr. Lincoln was the last casualty." Gorloff knew there had already been assassination attempts on the Czar's life as well.

"I admire Your Highness's intentions, but I have come to say there is a certain folly in liberating slaves and serfs. I respectfully submit that you and President Lincoln have set the world on a dangerous path. One which not only could result in the destruction of Russia, but in the destruction of the entire world."

Czar Alexander's eyebrows came together and he opened his mouth to speak. However, he quickly turned and looked to the side as though hearing a voice from an unseen source. His eyes drifted to the corner of the room and seemed to glaze over. His hand, holding the cigar, hovered over a stack of papers. Gorloff gently extracted the cigar and set it into an ashtray. The servant in the corner of the room looked from the Czar to Gorloff, trying to understand what had happened. Just as he took a step toward the desk, the Czar blinked and focused his attention on the general.

"I see what you mean, Alexander Petrovich. The world is clearly in danger. What do you propose we do about it?"

Gorloff nodded somberly. "Russia used to have claims to much of America—Alaska, of course, but also Oregon, California and the Washington Territory. I submit that selling Alaska to the United States was a mistake and moreover, we have a legitimate claim on the western regions of America."

The Czar leaned forward and brought his hand to his mouth and blinked in surprise when he saw the cigar was not there. He retrieved the cigar, took a puff, and then sat back. "Let us suppose that is true. Why should we attack the United States of America? They have been our fast friend for many years."

"They have, but I submit that will not always be true."

The Czar set his cigar on the ashtray just as his eyes glazed over again. After a moment he looked up. "I see what you mean. In less than a hundred years, they are likely to become our greatest rival."

"Indeed," said Gorloff. "We must act to preserve our empire, while America is still recovering from its own Civil War."

"I believe you are correct." The Czar blinked and frowned,

as though uncertain how exactly he understood. "However, I'm afraid a war in America could tie up our troops for many years and could leave us defenseless in the west. You have, no doubt, heard about the tensions with the Ottoman Empire."

"*The scientists and the engineers,*" came Legion's voice from the back of Gorloff's mind. "*New technology is the key to success.*"

Gorloff felt the hairs on the back of his neck prickle at Legion's prompting. "I have brought men familiar with America. Those men are working with Russia's top generals and strategists. They will help me in my cause." The general paused and inhaled smoke from the cigar. He exhaled the smoke with a sigh and gave into Legion's prompting. "Also, we will need new technology. It is the key to success."

A smile appeared, underlining the Czar's great mustache. "Go to the university. Speak to Mendeleev."

"Mendeleev is a chemist, isn't he? Developed something called the periodic table. How can he help?"

"I think you will find Mendeleev has many skills that could prove useful in your cause, General." The Czar snapped his fingers and ordered the servant to bring vodka. When it arrived, the Czar held up his glass. "To the Russian-American Empire!"

Ramon and Fatemeh arrived in San Francisco just before Christmas. Ramon hoped Eduardo didn't have any problems as he rode back south to Palomas Hot Springs. The train journey allowed Ramon ample time to sleep and recover from his injuries. The swelling and bruises were mostly gone when they arrived in California. He kept pulling off his glasses and adjusting them, trying to get them to sit comfortably on his face. When he did wear them, he squinted, trying to bring things into focus. He looked forward to finding an optometrist.

They arrived in San Francisco in the middle of the day. The skies were cloudy. Wan light filtered to the ground. Stepping out of the train station, Ramon caught sight of a hotel. The two gathered their meager belongings and crossed the busy street, then entered the hotel lobby. Ramon rang the bell at the front desk.

A clerk came out from a back room and eyed the couple warily. "May I help you?"

"We'd like a room for the night," said Ramon.

"Sorry, we don't have any rooms."

Ramon's eyebrows came together. "The sign in the window said 'vacancy.'"

The clerk looked toward the window, then back at Ramon. "I'm sorry, I should clarify. We don't have any rooms for Mexicans."

Ramon and Fatemeh looked at each other. "I'm not Mexican," he said. "I'm an American citizen. My dad even fought for the Union Army."

"I'm not Mexican either," declared Fatemeh. "I'm from Persia."

"I don't care if you're from Timbuktu." The clerk sneered. "You both have brown skin. You'll need to find another hotel."

"Begging your pardon," said Fatemeh, "but your skin is somewhat brown, too. Ours is just a little darker than yours."

Ramon put his hand on Fatemeh's forearm, indicating it was time to let him do the talking. "Is there any place in town we *can* stay?"

"You might try the Mission District. Go out the front door, turn right, follow the tracks about ten blocks south and cross to the other side." The clerk turned his back on the two and acted busy, examining the mail slots.

Ramon gathered his satchel and threw it over his shoulder. "Are we just going to stand for that?" asked Fatemeh.

Ramon sighed and did his best to adjust his glasses. "I don't like it, corazón, but I'm too tired to cause trouble. Maybe this Mission District will be a bit friendlier."

The two stepped out of the hotel and followed the clerk's instructions. Both of them looked in awe at the sheer number of mortar and brick buildings that surrounded them. The streets were lined with horses and carriages darting around one another. A carriage sped down the street and hit a puddle, sending horse manure and mud toward Fatemeh. Ramon pulled her away just in time.

"Kind of makes you long for laws that keep horses out of the streets," said Ramon.

"That's true. Still, it's not quite as bad as New York City," observed Fatemeh.

They found a hotel on Valencia Street. This one, with its cracked white stucco exterior, seemed much more run down than the pristine red brick hotel across from the railroad tracks. However, the clerk was amenable to letting them rent rooms. When he quoted a price, though, Ramon's breath caught. He took Fatemeh aside. "We only have enough money to stay here a week if we each have separate rooms...and I need to get new glasses."

A brief smile lit Fatemeh's face. "The money would last longer if we only get one room."

Ramon's mouth fell open. "Fatemeh!"

"Just sign the register Mr. and Mrs. Morales." Fatemeh's tone was matter-of-fact. "Ask for a room with two beds, though."

Ramon opened his mouth to protest, but finally swallowed and turned back to the clerk. He paid for one room with two beds and then the two carried their belongings up to the room.

General Alexander Gorloff strode down a corridor at St. Petersburg University and knocked on a door.

"Come in," called a distracted voice on the other side.

The general opened the door and was astonished to see a desk surrounded by books, some open, others closed—all in some kind of disarray. The desk itself was covered by papers. On the wall was a black chalkboard covered in incomprehensible scribbles that—as far as the general could tell—were some combination of hieroglyphs and a foreign language. None of this astonished the general as much as the man who sat behind the desk. His head was covered with a wild mop of gray-streaked, black hair. A bushy beard hid most of the man's face.

The general introduced himself. "You are Mendeleev?"

"Yes, yes," said the scientist, impatiently without rising from his chair. "What can I do for you, General?"

The general turned and closed the door. "I wish to discuss a matter of some secrecy that is important to our Czar."

At this, Mendeleev turned his attention fully to Gorloff.

"Go on."

"In my duties as military attaché to the United States of America, it has come to my attention that the young country poses a threat to the Russian Empire."

Mendeleev scowled. "This does not surprise me. It is a country of cowboys and loose cannons who have no respect for intellectual pursuits. The country has been around for a century and I cannot name one decent university or important literary work that has come from there."

"I have heard some critics speak highly of a novel called *Moby-Dick*," ventured the general.

The scientist waved his hand as though subjected to a bad smell. "A long-winded book about a madman hunting a whale? It has no value. Poe showed some promise, but he was obviously influenced by the French."

"Obviously," muttered the general in agreement. He sat down and decided to steer the conversation back to the topic at hand. "While in America, I also learned there are vast reserves of gold and oil in Alaska," continued Gorloff.

Mendeleev's disdainful frown turned into a smug grin—although the general had some difficulty telling that through the thick beard. "I knew it was a mistake for the Czar to sell Alaska."

"America poses a threat to Russia and the stability of the whole world," declared the general. "I ask you, as a patriot, will you come to the aid of our country?"

"I am loyal to the Czar, General Gorloff. He has a good heart. He showed that when he freed the serfs. Ask what you will." Mendeleev folded his arms across his chest, his eyes intent.

"We need a way to move quickly to the United States without being stopped by their navy," explained the general. "We also need a way to deploy troops and heavy artillery across large sections of western North America."

Mendeleev nodded and thought for several minutes. His head fell forward and for a moment, the general thought the scientist had fallen asleep. Just as he was leaning forward to tap Mendeleev on the shoulder, the scientist leapt to his feet and erased a section of the chalkboard. He drew a large ovoid shape.

Next, he added boxes with something like ship propellers attached. Underneath, he drew a bigger box. "Imagine if you will, a ship of the air," said Mendeleev, pointing at his drawing. "We build a steel frame. Inside will be great bags that we fill with a gas that's lighter than air—say hydrogen." He pointed to the boxes and propellers. "Light as it will be, small steam engines can be deployed to move it through the air. Underneath, like a balloon's gondola, is a pilothouse. Within the steel frame structure, we can place troops, artillery, whatever you like."

The general stared at the drawing wide-eyed. "Will such a thing really work?"

"I have been working on the problem of such a craft for the past few years." As Mendeleev spoke, he continued sketching on the board, showing the airship from underneath. "The only thing that has kept me from building it is funding. If the Czar is serious about having such a war machine, I believe I can design it and we can build a small fleet."

"This year?" Gorloff shook his head in wonder.

"If enough resources are dedicated to the problem." Mendeleev stepped aside. The silhouette of an owl adorned his new sketch.

"Why do you adorn your airship with an owl?"

"My ancestors are Kalmyk, General Gorloff. A story has been passed down through the generations that an owl saved Ghengis Khan's life. To us, owls have long been talismans of great power. These ships will be like great owls, expanding the Russian empire. We will guide the Americans to a more civilized age."

Gorloff nodded satisfied. "Begin work designing these ships. Send word to the palace and let us know what materials and personnel you need. We will make sure they are sent." The general reached out and shook Mendeleev's hand. "It was a delight meeting you, Professor Mendeleev."

"The pleasure was mine."

Back out in the hall, the general heard Legion in the back of his mind. *What a fascinating individual.*

"You did well." Gorloff's voice was barely above a whisper. He didn't want to attract attention as he walked down the hall. "It seems Professor Mendeleev responded quite well to the visions you showed him."

"*We showed Professor Mendeleev no visions.*"

"What?!" The general shouted, then looked around quickly to make sure that no one had heard him. "What do you mean you showed him no visions?"

"*We didn't need to. Those were Mendeleev's own ideas.*"

Gorloff felt his knees go weak. He trusted in Mendeleev's plan because he felt that Legion had been guiding him. "Are such airships really possible?"

"*They are,*" said Legion. "*Do not fear, part of me will enter Professor Mendeleev's dreams tonight and we will guide him to make sure his plans are sound.*"

Reassured, the general continued on his way.

Ramon returned to the room he shared with Fatemeh late on Christmas Eve. Fatemeh noticed he wore a new pair of glasses. Like his old pair, they were round and gave his face an owlish appearance. He held his hands behind his back. Fatemeh stood and wrapped her arms around Ramon, but was surprised when he didn't return the embrace. "What's the matter?"

"Nothing." Ramon's voice held a sly edge.

"It looks like you were successful in finding new glasses."

Ramon smiled. "Yes, these are even better than the old ones." He shrugged. "The optometrist thinks my eyes have been getting a little worse."

"That's too bad." Fatemeh returned to her chair.

"However, I did have enough money left over to get you something." He brought his arms out from behind his back. In his hand was a narrow box, about eight inches long. "Merry Christmas!" Just then he pulled the box back. "Do Bahá'ís celebrate Christmas?"

"Not normally," said Fatemeh, "but as I've said, we respect the teachings of Jesus. I'm happy to celebrate his birth with you, Ramon." She held out her hand and Ramon handed her the box. She opened it and saw a necklace. Adorning it was a hand-carved wooden bead in the shape of an owl.

"I bought the necklace. I carved the owl myself, though."

"It's very sweet." Fatemeh smiled and put the necklace on. She stood and kissed Ramon, but held his hands as they parted. "How is our money doing?"

"I think I can find a job, but it's not going to pay much," admitted Ramon. "We could stay here about six more days and I could keep looking, or we could move on."

"I like the idea of moving on." Fatemeh returned to her chair. "I really didn't like the reception we had on our first day and it's loud here, even late at night." She looked out the window at a saloon across the street.

"Where would you like to go?"

She pulled out a map and set it on the small table between the room's two chairs. "What do you know about Los Angeles?"

"It's a small town. There's some farms and some industrial work." Ramon shrugged.

"What does Los Angeles mean?"

"It means 'belonging to the angels,' The name's short for something like town of the queen of angels."

"Sounds lovely. Can we leave tomorrow?"

Ramon laughed. "Tomorrow's Christmas. I doubt the trains are even running. What about the next day?"

"That sounds perfect." Fatemeh put her hand to the new necklace. "I'm afraid I didn't get you a present. What else do people do on Christmas?"

"We sing songs." Ramon sat in the empty chair next to Fatemeh.

"Teach me a Christmas song worthy of the angels, Ramon."

# CHAPTER EIGHT
## THE PIRATES OF BAJA

Ramon stepped up to the door of a shack near the waterfront in San Pedro, California. The sign over the door read "Southern Pacific Railroad." The railroad had just finished its line into Los Angeles and was now pouring money into the port so it could compete with Central Pacific's rail and shipping interests in Northern California. Ramon was tired after spending the day talking to numerous foremen and supervisors. Three of them said they might have work for him next week and that he should check back. All of them suggested he should talk to Bryan Burke at the railroad office. Ramon rapped on the shack's door.

"Come in," came a voice from the other side.

Ramon entered the shack and was greeted by a tall, lanky, balding man with a sly but affable smile. "Mr. Burke?" asked Ramon.

"That's me." Burke indicated a seat in front of the desk. "What can I do for you?"

Ramon introduced himself, then turned and closed the door. "I'm new in Los Angeles and I'm looking for a job."

Burke nodded and sat down behind the desk. He steepled his fingers under his nose. "What kind of experience do you have, Mr. Morales?"

"Most recently I was a ranch hand in Mesilla, New Mexico." He sat down opposite Mr. Burke. "I've done a lot of repair work on corrals and barns. I'm good with a hammer and a saw."

Burke frowned. "What other experience do you have?"

Ramon chewed his lower lip, debating how much to tell the railroad man. He didn't want to lose a potential job because someone asked for references and found out he was a wanted man. Finally, he took a deep breath and let it out slowly. "I was a sheriff in New Mexico territory." He settled on the truth without too many specifics.

Burke's eyes widened. "Really? Are you a fast draw?"

Ramon pursed his lips and shrugged. "I'm pretty good."

"Can you show me?"

Ramon chuckled. "I'm afraid I don't have a gun. I didn't think I'd need it for construction work."

"No worries, my boy." Burke walked over to a cabinet in the corner of the room. He retrieved a gun belt and handed it to Ramon. "It's a Navy Colt. Sometimes people try to steal supplies. It can come in handy around here."

Ramon took the belt and strapped it around his waist. He had to admit it felt good to have a gun on his hip again. "Are you looking for a security guard?"

Burke's brow furrowed. "Something like that." He stepped back and held out his hand. "Let me see that draw."

"I'm a little out of practice. Give me a minute to get the feel of this rig."

"Take your time."

As Burke returned to the desk, Ramon drew the Colt and evaluated its weight. He slipped it into the holster and drew it a couple of times, getting the feel of the metal against leather. Finally he took a stance and pictured Randolph Dalton at the other end of the room. He narrowed his eyes, reached for the gun, and aimed it.

"I'm impressed," admitted Burke. "Are you as accurate as you are fast?"

"Yeah, I'm pretty good."

"Let's see." Burke opened the shack's rear door. They walked out onto the wooden pier. At the end of the pier, a target was set up.

"Do you do a lot of target practice, Mr. Burke?"

"Let's just say I'm looking for some highly qualified men for a job I have in mind." He indicated the target. "Let's see how you do." He retrieved three rounds of ammunition from his coat pocket and handed them to Ramon.

Ramon placed the cartridges into the revolver and snapped it shut. Holstering the gun, he took a careful stance and evaluated the target. He drew quickly and fired all three rounds into the bull's eye.

Burke nodded. "I think you might do nicely, Mr. Morales. Come inside and let's discuss this job I have in mind."

"You've been hired to do what?" Fatemeh stood with her hands on her hips.

"Apparently a group of pirates have been harassing ships leaving the Port of Los Angeles. Southern Pacific Railroad wants it stopped." Ramon shrugged. "They offered to pay me a year's wages for a few weeks' work."

"A lot of good that will do if you get killed." Fatemeh shook her head. She walked over to the window of the hotel room they shared and looked out at the white-washed walls of the surrounding buildings.

"These pirates haven't killed anyone." Ramon stepped up behind her. "Apparently they disable the ships, subdue the crew and steal most of the cargo, then leave."

Fatemeh turned around, her brow furrowed. "How do these pirates disable the ships? Do they fire cannons?"

Ramon shook his head. "Mr. Burke was a little unclear about that. All he said was the pirates somehow break the rudder. Didn't sound like cannon fire to me."

Fatemeh dropped into a chair with a deep frown. "I still don't like it. It seems like there are a lot of ways you could get hurt."

Ramon moved to the chair next to hers. "There were a lot of ways I could get hurt when I was sheriff of Socorro." He sat down and met her eyes. "This isn't the job I was looking for, but I think it's a lucky break. We're out of money, but he's already paid me enough to buy a new gun, rent the room for another month, and I should even have enough left over for you to stock up on some new supplies."

Fatemeh sighed. "You know how I feel about taking lives— any lives. Even if these people are pirates, I would not be happy if I found out you killed one of them."

Ramon looked down at his hands, then back up into Fatemeh's eyes. "I know, corazón. But, if what Mr. Burke says is right, I don't think I'll have to fire a shot. These pirates aren't used to encountering resistance. Our ship is the *Stockton*. It's under the command of an experienced Navy captain named Mercer. Our goal is to round up these pirates and bring them to port for trial." He held out his hands. "For me, that sounds like pretty easy work for a year's wages."

Fatemeh closed her eyes and considered what Ramon had told her. She tried to think how pirates could disable a ship without firing a shot. "I presume they'll be careful to make sure the crew of this *Stockton* is trustworthy."

"I would think so. They would need to know they could rely on the crew."

"It seems like the easiest way to disable a ship without firing a shot is to have a spy aboard." Fatemeh inclined her head. "How do you know the pirates will even attack if everyone aboard the ship is loyal?"

"I guess that's a chance we'll have to take." Ramon shrugged.

"Will this Mr. Burke pay you if you don't capture the pirates?"

Ramon looked down at his hands again, but did not lift his eyes. "He says they've been spreading the word the *Stockton* is carrying a valuable cargo. He's pretty certain the pirates will strike."

"Pretty certain, Ramon?"

She saw Ramon's Adam's apple move as he swallowed hard. "I'll get to keep the money we've already been paid, even if we don't meet pirates."

Fatemeh nodded. "At least that's something." She stood and looked out the window again. "Be safe, Ramon. I'll say a prayer of protection for you." As she spoke, she considered there might be a more direct way to look out for the man she loved.

Ramon stood by the rail of the *Stockton*, looking out at the vast expanse of ocean. Having grown up in New Mexico, he had never seen so much water in his life. He'd been afraid he might feel seasick, but the gentle rolling of the ship didn't bother him at all. The calm seas had been no worse than riding on a horse or in a train. However, the unbroken seascape all around did make him feel somewhat claustrophobic. He was all too aware he stood on the deck of a small ship surrounded by many people.

Still, he felt somewhat relieved to have some time away from Fatemeh. He felt a prickle of guilt at that thought—he did love her, after all. However, he was still glad to have some time alone with his own thoughts, to think about the events of the past few months and evaluate their relationship. The voyage gave him some time to consider whether he was ready to settle down and spend the rest of his life with her.

He turned his attention to the afterdeck and saw Captain Mercer watching the horizon. The stout man wore a blue Navy coat and black captain's cap. His cheeks were covered by gray, bristly sideburns. Standing behind the captain was the lanky form of Bryan Burke. Ramon's own concerns about the voyage had been put at ease when he saw the railroad man would accompany them. Ramon doubted Burke would put himself into more danger than necessary to protect the railroad's interests.

Black smoke poured from a single stack amidships. A steam engine below decks turned the two paddle wheels—one on each side of the ship. The ship also sported three masts. Ramon didn't know much about ships, but assumed sails could be deployed from the spars if the engine broke down. Lookouts stood in crow's nests at the top of each of the masts.

The boatswain appeared on the *Stockton's* afterdeck and blew his shrill whistle. The first watch of the day was over. A man pushed past Ramon and began climbing up the lines next to him. Ramon looked up, glad he was spared that duty. He noticed the man climbing down from the crow's nest didn't seem as dexterous as the man going up. The one coming down took his time and his foot reached around and searched for the ropes below more than other sailors. Finally, the sailor reached the deck. He started to move past Ramon just as the ship lurched and the two bumped into each other.

"Sorry," apologized the sailor in a surprisingly familiar high-pitched voice.

Ramon looked up and blinked at the quickly retreating, olive-skinned sailor. He noticed long black hair tied back and tucked under the shirt collar. Ramon rushed forward and blocked the sailor's path. His mouth dropped open when he realized he was looking into familiar green eyes. "Fatemeh?"

Her cheeks flushed red and she grinned sheepishly. "Hi, Ramon."

"What are you doing here?" Ramon looked up and saw that several sailors were beginning to take notice. He took her by the arm and led her back to where he'd been standing by the ship's rail.

"I wanted to come along and make sure you stayed safe." She shrugged. "Also, it allows us to make a little extra money from this voyage."

"How in the world did you get hired as a sailor?"

"When I came to America from Persia, some of the men showed me how to handle sails and climb the rigging into the crow's nests." She inclined her head. "I'm not as good as all the men on the ship, but I'm good enough that I was able to get a rating as an able seaman."

Ramon opened his mouth to say more, but was interrupted when one of the lookouts shouted from above. "Ship off the port bow!"

Looking up, Ramon saw the captain open a telescope and begin scanning the horizon. He turned around and thought he could make out a black cloud in the distance. He realized he must be seeing smoke from another ship.

"Is there something between us and the other ship?" Fatemeh pointed toward the smoke on the horizon.

Ramon tried to see where she was pointing. After a moment, he caught sight of white, roiling water, like a ship's wake moving rapidly toward them. However, he couldn't see any signs of a ship or a boat. "What's going on? Is it an invisible ship or something?"

"I don't think so. Look closer."

Ramon held up his hand to shield his eyes from the sun. There was something dark, very low to the water—maybe just below the surface of the water—generating the wake. "Maybe it's a whale or a dolphin."

"If it's a whale, it's the fastest one I've ever seen."

Ramon nodded. "I'd better go tell the captain." He ran back to ship's stern and climbed the ladder to the afterdeck where Mr. Burke towered over Captain Mercer.

"The ship is definitely coming toward us," said the captain, peering through the telescope.

"Do you think it's the pirates?" asked Burke.

The captain grunted. "We'll soon see."

"Captain," called Ramon as he stepped up to the two men, "there's something between us and that ship, down in the water and approaching fast." He pointed.

The captain turned his telescope toward the place where Ramon pointed. "What the blazes?"

Burke inclined his head. "There's steam coming from the water's surface."

Ramon looked around again. The dark shape in the water was closer and he could see white clouds of vapor billowing just over the water.

The captain gritted his teeth and slammed his telescope shut. "If I didn't know better, I'd say that's a submersible, like the *Hunley* back in the war." He turned toward his first officer. "Beat to quarters, action stations."

The mate nodded and stepped forward calling out, "Action stations!"

A boy—Ramon guessed he must be about thirteen years old—rushed to a locker near the ship's stern. He opened it and retrieved a drum and two sticks. He began beating out a martial rhythm. Armed crewmen rushed out from below decks and lined the rails. Ramon caught sight of Fatemeh near one of the masts. He climbed down from the afterdeck and went to her. "You better get below decks."

Before she could respond, there was a loud crash and the ship listed over to the side. Looking up, Ramon noticed the portside paddle wheel no longer turned. There was a cry of "All stop!" from the afterdeck. With both wheels stopped, the ship settled upright in the water. Ramon rushed to the rail and saw the dark shape in the water pulling back. It turned and made a wide arc toward the ship's stern. Ramon drew his revolver and fired two shots. Both made a loud clang and a whistle as they hit the metal of the thing in the water and ricocheted.

Ramon rushed back to the ship's stern and ascended the ladder. Just as he reached the top, there was another crash. He nearly toppled back down, but held on. The man at the ship's wheel cursed. "They've broken the rudder. We've lost helm control!"

Ramon stepped up next to the captain. The other ship was nearly upon them. He could just make out the ship's name, *Tiburón*—Spanish for shark.

"With no helm and no engines, we're sitting ducks," said the captain. He turned to the first mate. "Prepare to repel boarders."

The first mate bellowed out the order. Ramon felt the level of tension on the ship increase. He drew his revolver, snapped open the cylinder, and replaced the two cartridges he'd already fired.

As the *Tiburón* came alongside, men on the other ship hurled grappling hooks on ropes and grabbed onto the *Stockton's* rails. Ramon took careful aim and picked off one of the men on the other ship. The rest of the pirates ducked below the rail with curses and a few exclamations of surprise. Ramon's brow creased as he began to wonder just how experienced these pirates actually were.

Orders were shouted and three of the pirates leapt to their feet, wielding six-guns. The captain, Burke and Ramon all hit the deck as a hail of bullets flew over their heads. When they looked up, pirates were swinging across from the *Tiburón* to the *Stockton*. Some of the *Stockton's* men fired at the pirates. Two of the buccaneers were hit and fell from the lines, but others landed on the decks. In the close quarters of the ship's decks, the pirates drew knives and flailed them at the men. Others simply waded in with their fists. Ramon went to the afterdeck rail and tried to get a clear shot. He saw one lone pirate and fired, cutting him down, but others turned their attention toward him.

"Uh oh," said Ramon. He ducked as one of the pirates pulled a revolver and fired up at him. By the time he lifted his head, he saw pirates swarming over the afterdeck. Two pirates rushed forward and grabbed the captain's arms. Ramon tried to raise his pistol, but another pirate knocked it from his grip. He put up his hands.

Below, two pirates lowered a rope ladder over the side of the ship. Ramon saw the black shape of the strange submarine craft come to the surface. A hatch popped open on the top and a man emerged. As the man climbed the ladder, Ramon noticed that he seemed strangely out of place, wearing the attire of a gentleman. He wore a white shirt and a bright blue silk vest. Around his neck was a black cravat. The only anachronisms were the denim pants common to sailors and a black hat similar to the one Captain Mercer wore.

"Well, it would seem this ship wasn't all we were led to believe," said the man who had appeared from the submersible. He turned and ascended the ladder to the afterdeck. "Who's in charge here?"

"I am Captain John Mercer of the USS *Stockton.*" The captain struggled in the grip of the pirates who held him. "I demand you release my ship."

"You are not in a position to demand anything." The dapper pirate waved his hand. "I'm guessing this ship is not carrying the silver and gold I expected to find heading for China. However, I see quite a fine cargo of ammunition. That would do nicely in exchange for your life, Captain."

With a nod of his head, the pirate captain sent members of his crew below decks to see what they could find. A moment after they left, a pirate led one of the *Stockton's* crew up the ladder. Ramon's breath caught and a knot formed in his stomach when he saw it was Fatemeh. Her shirt had been ripped and he could discern the soft swell of her breast.

"Ah, it would seem the *Stockton* transports other things of value besides ammunition," said the pirate captain with undisguised delight.

"No!!" shouted Ramon. The back of his head exploded with pain and everything went black.

Fatemeh was taken aboard the *Tiburón* and locked in a small,

but nicely appointed cabin. There was a bed—more comfortable than the hammock she had aboard the *Stockton*. There were
some books on the shelf. She took one and leafed through the
pages. It was written in Spanish. On the cabin's small desk was
a locked box. She picked it up and found it was rather heavy
and rattled. Looking around, she saw a trunk. Opening it, she
found shirts and pants. She removed her shirt, torn in the scuf-
fle with the pirate crew, and put on one of the shirts she found.

Opening the cabin's window, she saw she was on the opposite side of the pirate ship from the *Stockton*. She lay down
on the bed and listened to the sounds of the pirates scuffling
on the deck above and outside her door. She tried to discern
exactly what they were doing. Loud bumps and thumps came
from different parts of the ship and she could imagine cargo
being secured. She wondered if the submersible was stowed
aboard the ship or traveled alongside.

The engines soon fired up and she thought the ship moved.
Kneeling on the bed, she craned her head as far out of the window as she could and saw the *Stockton* receding in the distance.
She hoped Ramon was going to be okay—he had taken a nasty
blow to the back of the head. She lay back on the bed, chewed
her lower lip, and wondered what was going to happen next.

The sky was darkening when someone rapped at the door.
A key rattled in the lock and a sailor in a torn and bloodstained
shirt looked in. He said something in Spanish and gestured
with his hand. She gathered she was supposed to follow and it
appeared he was being polite rather than demanding.

Fatemeh followed the sailor to a cabin at the ship's stern.
He opened the door. Inside, a table was laid out with a sumptu-
ous meal. There was meat in a rich, brown sauce, a cauldron of
soup, a bowl with beans, and a basket that appeared filled with
tortillas. The ship's captain sat at the head of the table. He stood
and held out a chair. "I am Captain Onofre Cisneros. Welcome
to the *Tiburón*."

"Thank you." Fatemeh entered the cabin and the sailor
closed the door behind her.

"Do you like your cabin?"

"I do, thank you." Fatemeh sat in the chair held by the
captain. "I hope I'm not putting its owner to any discomfort."

The captain returned to his seat at the head of the table. "I'm afraid he won't be needing it again. The cabin belonged to my first mate and he was killed today." He looked down at his lap and sniffed. He took a deep breath and blew it out, then looked up again.

"I'm sorry for your loss."

The captain shrugged, then reached out for a flask of wine. "I suppose it's expected when you engage in piracy." He poured a glass of wine for Fatemeh and then one for himself.

"You suppose?" Fatemeh's gaze narrowed. "From what I was told, you've been menacing ships for quite some time."

Captain Cisneros laughed outright. "Is that what you were told?"

Fatemeh sat back and thought about what she had seen. The pirates were not well armed. They only had a few knives and pistols. "You weren't expecting the kind of resistance you met on the *Stockton,* were you?"

"I should have known better." Captain Cisneros lifted the glass and took a drink. "After taking two ships easily, I should have expected heavier resistance with the third."

"You've only taken two ships?" When the captain didn't answer, Fatemeh lifted her own glass and took a drink. She nodded appreciatively. "I don't normally drink alcohol, but this wine is quite good."

"It is made from grapes that grow near my home in Ensenada." Cisneros reached out and spooned some of the meat in brown sauce onto his plate. "Try the chicken molé. My cook outdoes himself."

Fatemeh took the dish and served herself.

Cisneros leaned forward. "What else have you been told about me and my pirates?"

"Only that you somehow disable ships without firing a shot."

"Nothing about the submersible?"

"No."

The captain's eyebrows came together. He looked down at his plate and shook his head. Fatemeh sensed that Cisneros was frustrated.

"These raids ... they're not really about piracy, or even

gold, are they?" Cisneros remained silent, so Fatemeh ventured another guess. "You're trying to get attention for your submarine craft, aren't you?"

Cisneros retrieved a tortilla, then took a sip of the wine. "Ten years ago—when Emperor Maximillian was on the throne—I owned a gold mine in Sonora. I had a number of wealthy French investors and I did quite well for myself." He took a bite of the chicken in molé sauce and took another sip of wine. "However, Mexican resistance to the French proved too costly and they finally withdrew. I was afraid my mine would be seized by President Juárez's soldiers, so I took what money I could and fled to Ensenada." He took a bite of his tortilla. "I always loved the sea."

Fatemeh took a tentative taste of the chicken molé. Her first impression was chocolate, then hot spices danced on her tongue. She washed it down with a sip of wine. "So you turned to piracy to make a living?"

The captain pursed his lips and shook his head. "Not really. You see, when I still had the mine, I came across plans for a submarine vessel from Spain called the *Ictíneo*. It was built by an inventor named Narcís Monturiol i Estarrol. Even before I was a mine owner, I was an engineer. Estarrol's plans fascinated me and I wondered if I could improve on his design. I hoped I could sell it to the Mexican Navy. However, by the time I finished the craft, President Tejada wasn't interested."

Fatemeh nodded. "From what I've heard about submarine boats, they're rather dangerous aren't they? The *Hunley* was lost with all hands during the American Civil War." Her stomach rumbled and she took a portion of beans.

"The *Hunley* was a poor design. The men only had the air aboard that was there when they closed the hatches." The captain shook his head. "Estarrol solved that problem by inventing a chemical reaction steam engine. My *Legado* uses the same type of engine. Fuel rods create a chemical reaction that heats the water. Oxygen is released as the fuel rods are used up. You can stay under water as long as you have fuel."

"*Legado?*" asked Fatemeh around a forkful of beans.

"That's the name of my submarine vessel. The English

word is legacy." The captain took another sip of wine. "Anyway, when the Mexican government refused to buy the *Legado*, I was left with no money. I had to find a way to recoup my investment."

"But why piracy?" Fatemeh narrowed her gaze.

"To get attention," said Cisneros. "I had hoped word of my boat would make it to the owners of the ships I attacked, or even President Grant himself. That's why I ordered my men not to kill the crews of the ships. I hoped someone would seek out the creator of the submarine to learn more about it."

"You didn't think they would hunt you down?"

Cisneros snorted. "Again, that's why I left the crews alive. I thought people would be more curious than angry."

The captain and Fatemeh ate in silence for a time. Finally, Fatemeh paused and pointed her fork at the captain. "Would you be able to use your submersible to repair ships?"

Cisneros sat back and wiped his lips with a napkin. "I suppose so, Estarrol imagined he could use the *Ictíneo* to rescue divers."

"Scientists might also pay to use such a craft to explore the ocean." Fatemeh leaned forward. "Is Ensenada a good port?"

"It could be, with some development."

"You've raided two gold ships at this point. Have you made back your investment in the *Legado*?"

The captain nodded. "Very close."

"I think you see piracy isn't going to get you the attention you want. Maybe you should find a better way to make people aware of your submersible. Perhaps Ensenada could be developed into a port to rival Los Angeles or even San Francisco. The *Legado* could be used to make repairs more efficiently than they could be made at other ports."

The captain placed his napkin on the table and stood. He walked to the windows at the back of the cabin and looked out toward the night sky. "The only problem is that I'm now a wanted man. I suspect the captain of the *Stockton* would like nothing more than to see me swinging from the yardarm of his ship."

Fatemeh sighed. She didn't approve of Captain Cisneros's decision to pursue piracy, but he had avoided killing. He was a good engineer. "Perhaps we could speak to Captain Mercer and Mr. Burke aboard the *Stockton*. If they would drop the charges against you, would you give up piracy?"

"Do you think they would listen?" The captain's eyes remained locked on the darkened ocean outside his window.

Fatemeh chewed her lower lip. "To be honest, I'm not sure."

"Why would you suggest this?" The captain turned his head. "Even though I've only attacked three ships, I'm still a pirate and I have taken you hostage. Even if we succeed, how do you know I would not simply return to piracy?"

Fatemeh nodded. "Your actions speak louder than words, sir. You could have chosen to lock me in your brig, rape me, or even kill me. You could have used the *Legado* to sink the *Stockton*. Instead, you merely disabled her and you've left the crews you've come across alive. You would rather get rich selling the plans for the *Legado* than stealing gold."

Cisneros looked down at his feet but did not say a word. Turning, he went to the door and summoned one of the sailors. The sailor escorted Fatemeh back to the first mate's cabin. She heard him turn the key in the lock. Sitting on the bunk, she wondered what the captain would decide.

"Ship approaching!"

Ramon was lying in his hammock aboard the *Stockton* when he heard the call from on deck. The *Stockton* had been adrift for two days and he wondered how long it would be before they were rescued. He rolled out of the hammock and as soon as his feet hit the deck, his head began to throb anew. He closed his eyes until the pain subsided just a bit, then made his way outside.

In the distance, Ramon saw the smoke from a ship's steam engine. He climbed the ladder to the afterdeck and stood next to Captain Mercer and Mr. Burke. The captain scanned the approaching ship with his telescope. After a moment, he snapped it shut. "I'll be damned if it's not the *Tiburón*."

"Why would she come back?" asked Burke. "They already

took everything we have of value."

"There are a few things that fancy-pants pirate could still take and I'll be damned if I let him have them." The captain stormed off the afterdeck, leaving Ramon alone with Burke.

As the *Tiburón* approached, Ramon noticed that she flew a white flag from the stern. He hadn't noticed if there had been a flag there before.

Burke watched the ship through his own telescope. "They're launching a boat."

Ramon picked up the captain's abandoned telescope and looked toward the *Tiburón*. His heart skipped a beat when he realized one of the people in the boat was Fatemeh. The others were the dandy captain and two of his sailors. Before long, they were approaching the *Stockton's* side.

Just then, Captain Mercer appeared on deck wielding a Navy Colt revolver. Ramon realized he must have had it hidden in his cabin and the pirates missed it when they were cleaning out the ship's store of weapons and ammunition. The captain took aim and fired at the boat. The shot went wide and there was a splash of water next to the boat. Seeing the danger to Fatemeh, Ramon launched himself down the ladder and tackled the captain.

"This is mutiny," growled Mercer.

"They're under a white flag and Fatemeh is aboard that boat," countered Ramon.

The captain pushed Ramon off and made a grab for the revolver. Ramon kicked it further out of reach. "She was aboard under false pretenses," said Mercer. "As far as I'm concerned, she can hang with the damned pirates."

As he spoke, Bryan Burke descended the ladder and picked up the captain's revolver. "Just so, I would like to hear what they have to say. As Mr. Morales points out, they're under a white flag."

The captain sneered. "Very well."

He motioned for two of the crewmembers to lower a rope ladder over the side. Once the boat from the *Tiburón* came alongside, the pirate captain and Fatemeh climbed aboard. The pirate bowed to Captain Mercer. "I have come to offer assistance to you and your vessel. Furthermore, if you agree not to pursue me, I will cease my raids on American vessels."

"The only thing I'm interested in is your unconditional surrender!" shouted Captain Mercer.

Burke's eyes narrowed. "Are you really willing to give up your raids on our ships? Why the change of heart?"

Fatemeh swallowed. "The captain realizes piracy isn't as profitable as he once thought."

Mercer turned toward Burke. "Don't trust them. They're pirates. She came aboard under false pretenses. She's probably a spy for him."

"She is no spy," interjected Ramon. "I would trust her with my life."

"All I want is to see these pirates hang!" Mercer's face was beet red.

"You forget your place, Captain Mercer." Burke's voice was calm. "This is not a Navy ship. This ship is under contract to the Southern Pacific Railroad and I'll decide what is in the best interests of the mission."

"I am captain of this ship," growled Mercer through gritted teeth.

"Not anymore." Burke motioned for the first officer. "Mr. Reed. You're in command. Please escort Captain Mercer below and then join us on deck."

Reed saluted. "Yes, sir." He called for two of the sailors to help him.

"I will not stand for this," Mercer shouted as the men led him below decks. "I will be calling a maritime board of inquiry!"

Burke looked to Captain Cisneros once the door closed on the captain's shouting. "What can you do to help us?"

The pirate captain smiled. "I would like to offer the services of my submersible, the *Legado*. I believe we can use it to repair the damage to the *Stockton*."

Burke nodded approvingly. "I would like to see that. If it works out, would you be interested in licensing your patent to Southern Pacific Railroad?"

"We could certainly discuss that." Cisneros smiled and looked to Fatemeh.

She winked at the pirate. "See, this is a far better way to get attention for your craft and a far better application than naval warfare."

Burke and Cisneros shook hands. As Mr. Reed came out on deck again, Burke's expression turned hard. "Although I am interested in your submersible, I must warn you, if I agree to this and then find you've returned to your ways of piracy. I will not stop the next captain I send to hunt you down." He cast a meaningful glance at Reed.

Cisneros nodded. "I understand."

With that, Burke followed Reed up the ladder to the afterdeck.

Cisneros looked at Fatemeh. "You've given me new hope. What can I ever do to repay you?"

Fatemeh looked from Cisneros to Ramon, then she looked back to the *Tiburón*. "I do have something in mind."

Ramon sat in a small seat looking out through windows in the *Legado's* side. He had never imagined there were so many varieties and colors of fish. The submersible dove deeper and they moved along the floor of the Pacific. The former sheriff of Socorro, New Mexico marveled at the sight of the corals and forests of undersea plants that swayed in the currents. He looked to the seat opposite him and smiled at Fatemeh, who was similarly enraptured by the sights visible through the windows. Captain Cisneros stood at the helm. His head disappeared into a small pillbox-shaped protrusion that rose above the submarine's hull with a window facing forward.

Ramon turned and peered out at the ocean again. Although the submarine was smaller than the *Stockton*, Ramon no longer felt claustrophobic. Instead, he felt like he was seeing the future, and he could see no limits to the possibilities.

# CHAPTER NINE
## OIL AND THE FUTURE

R amon Morales was in something of a daze as he walked hand-in-hand with Fatemeh Karimi to the pay office at the Port of Los Angeles in San Pedro. His mind was still filled with visions of the wonders they had seen while under the ocean aboard Onofre Cisneros's submersible, the *Legado*. After dealing with Randolph Dalton in Socorro and being turned away from a hotel room in San Francisco, Ramon had worried about a grim future. Now he began to see a glimmer of hope and he wondered what else would be in store for his life with the amazing woman whose hand he held.

They arrived at the pay office and Ramon handed the clerk a note written out by Bryan Burke just before they had left the USS *Stockton*. The clerk went to the safe and brought out a stack of twenty-dollar bills. He counted out two hundred dollars and passed the stack over to Ramon. Fatemeh handed the clerk her pay voucher while Ramon counted the money himself. His brow furrowed. "This can't be right," he said.

The clerk looked up and blinked at Ramon. "I'm sorry?"

"Mr. Burke promised me four hundred dollars for this expedition."

"That's not what it says here." The clerk handed the pay slip back to Ramon.

Ramon gritted his teeth as he read the voucher carefully for the first time. He had been in such a daze since riding on the submarine boat that he really hadn't paid attention when the railroad man wrote out the voucher. Indeed, it was only written for two hundred dollars. "There must be some mistake." He turned to Fatemeh, who only received fifty dollars.

She shrugged. "I was only promised fifty dollars as an able seaman."

"And pretty good wages, too, I might add," said the clerk, who didn't bat an eye that he'd just paid able seaman's wages to a woman.

"Hang on," said Ramon. "I'll be right back." He shoved the money in his pocket and stormed out of the pay office. A few minutes later, he was knocking on the door of the shack the railroad man used for an office.

Bryan Burke fumbled at the door for a moment before opening it. "Ah, Mr. Morales. What can I do for you?" One of Burke's arms was already in a sleeve of his coat, the other side hung loose. He reached around and slipped the coat fully on.

Ramon held up the pay slip. "There must be some mistake. You promised me four hundred dollars if we stopped the pirate raids. I only received two hundred."

Burke inclined his head and looked down toward his feet. "No mistake, I'm afraid." He took two steps back toward his desk. "You see, the contract specified that we had to be certain the pirate raids were stopped for good. To my mind that means we would have had to bring Captain Cisneros to trial. Since that didn't happen and since he still has his ship, we really have no guarantee he won't raid us again."

Ramon blinked at Burke. "But, he agreed to sell you his submarine design..."

"Yes," said Burke slowly, "and that's extra money we'll have to pay out." The railroad man put his hands behind his back and looked up at Ramon. "Thing is, I'm not really sure your skills as a marksman even contributed to stopping Onofre Cisneros and his pirate crew." He shook his head. "Don't get me wrong, I appreciate the risk you took coming along on the mission. However, I think we were very generous paying you two hundred dollars under the circumstances. I just don't think full payment is justified, either."

Ramon's shoulders slumped forward and he let out a sigh that sounded like air escaping from a balloon.

Burke put his hand on Ramon's shoulder. "You see, I have to justify to my employers what I paid out based on what actually happened."

Ramon nodded slowly. "I see your point, Mr. Burke." He grinned wistfully. "It's still a lot of money and I do appreciate it."

The railroad man's smile was genuinely charming. "I'm glad to hear it, my boy." He turned Ramon toward the door. "Listen, if you need a reference for another job, I'll be happy to provide one. Now, if you'll excuse me, Mr. Morales, I need to check a few things and get home myself. I haven't seen my wife for several days and she'll be worried."

Ramon felt the whoosh of air as the door closed quickly behind him. He trudged back to the pay office, where he found Fatemeh waiting for him.

"Is everything okay?" she asked.

"Fine." The word came out like a heavy sigh. "I just misunderstood the terms of the contract." He brightened a little. "But hey, it's still two hundred dollars. That will last us until I can find regular work."

"I'm happy, Ramon." Fatemeh wrapped her arms around the former sheriff and kissed him. "Let's find some dinner and then hire a buggy home."

Despite his smile and forced optimism, Ramon didn't have much appetite and found himself worried a little more about the future. True, he had nearly six month's pay in his pocket, but he was still disappointed that it was less than he had hoped for. He hoped he could find work before the money ran out again and worried that despite Mr. Burke's smile, his promise of a reference might not be as helpful as it would have been if he had brought the pirates to justice.

They found a restaurant a short distance from the dockyard and ordered dinner. When it arrived, Ramon picked at his meal while Fatemeh talked about what they had seen in their short undersea voyage. Finally she stopped and looked at him. "Are you sure you're okay?"

He forced another smile. "Yeah, just a little tired, I guess."

Fatemeh nodded. "We should call it an early night."

He saw the concern apparent in her eyes. Reaching across the table, he took her hand and felt a strength he really hadn't noticed before. Perhaps it came from climbing the ropes on the *Stockton,* but somehow he knew there was more to it—there was an inner strength to Fatemeh Karimi that he valued more than anything. His breath caught and his appetite returned. They finished the meal in silence, then found a horse and buggy that would take them to the hotel room they shared.

Half an hour later, they stepped across the threshold. Ramon lit a match on the striker by the door and touched it to an oil lamp's wick. Fatemeh closed the door and moved close. He turned around and took her in his arms. They kissed deeply. As they did, his hands on her back inched their way lower. She didn't stop him. In fact, her own hands removed his vest, then she reached down and unbuckled his belt.

A moment later, they were sitting next to each other, on the bed. He suckled her earlobe then kissed her neck while she unbuttoned his shirt. He looked up, breathless. "Fatemeh, I love you, but…"

She put her finger to his lips. "We have been on the run for so long. Even in Mesilla as we were getting to know each other, we were on the run from poverty. Maybe we only have eight months' wages between the two of us, but we're not running anymore and we're together. I love you, Ramon. I want you."

Ramon took off his glasses, then kissed her again. He reached around and unfastened the clasps on the back of Fatemeh's dress.

An hour later, Ramon and Fatemeh lay in bed naked, wrapped in each other's arms. "The time has come," said Fatemeh, "to ask what we are together."

Ramon smiled. "What we are, is amazing. Look at all the things we've done—stopped pirates, saved Luther Duncan and Mercedes Rodriguez, kept Alberto Mendez from blowing up Fort McRae…"

Fatemeh placed her finger lightly on Ramon's lips. "I know, but what I mean is, what are we during the quiet times? What are we together when we aren't dealing with a crisis? We lived in Mesilla for six months. I built a reputation as a curandera while you went off to work at the ranch and we only saw each other occasionally."

Ramon sat up in bed and frowned. "Are you asking whether I've decided to convert to your Bahá'í faith?" He retrieved his glasses from the nightstand and slipped them on.

"I would be delighted if you were willing to do that." Fatemeh sat up, pulling the sheet around herself. Ramon found himself thinking the modesty was at once strange given their newfound intimacy, yet very much in keeping with Fatemeh's personality. "Actually, I'm asking something more fundamental. What are your plans with your life, Ramon Morales? What are your goals?"

Ramon reached out and took Fatemeh's hand. "Now more than ever, I want to marry you, corazón. I will do whatever it takes..."

"I think you need to find yourself, Ramon."

He laughed and put his hand on his chest. "I'm right here, Fatemeh!"

She smiled in spite of herself. "I don't mean that. I mean how do you envision the world in twenty years? What will your place in it be?"

Ramon took a deep breath and let it out slowly. "I guess I really haven't thought about that." He blinked twice, then looked into Fatemeh's vivid, green eyes. "How do you see the world in twenty years?"

"I picture a world where we humans finally see ourselves as more similar than different, where we have come together to work on common goals." Fatemeh pushed the sheet aside and Ramon couldn't help but feel his eyes drawn to the luscious curve of her buttocks or the smooth, brown skin of her back as she stepped over to her bag. She bent down and retrieved the copy of Jules Verne's *From the Earth to the Moon* she had been carrying and turned around. Ramon's breath caught as he took in the sight of her holding the book. She was bare to him, physically and emotionally, and he couldn't help but feel a little overwhelmed. "I see a world where humans are working together toward a common goal. Maybe it's reaching for the moon and the stars. Maybe it's working to fix all the problems of the world—all the hunger and the sickness, ending all the wars."

"Is it even possible?" Ramon looked down at his hands, his voice soft, barely audible.

She set the book down and returned to the bed. Lifting the

sheets, she crawled in and pulled Ramon close. "That's what you need to answer for yourself."

"If I do that, will your parents give us permission to marry?" Ramon looked up, hopeful.

"I have a confession to make." Fatemeh's cheeks flushed pink. "My parents are Mohammedan. They have disowned me. I don't think their permission could ever be obtained."

Ramon's eyebrows came together. "Then what's preventing us from getting married now?"

"I need to know your answer to my question…and I would like to meet your mother and get her approval."

Ramon nodded and sighed. "And until that happens…"

"I think it might be best if we had separate rooms again." She reached over and kissed him on the forehead. "I love you, but I need to know if you really are the person I can spend the rest of my life with. I love the way your body feels, Ramon, but I don't want to let those fleeting pleasures dictate a commitment."

Ramon inclined his head and frowned. He saw the wisdom of her words, even if he didn't completely like it. "Then I suppose I should go get my things together."

"Not just this instant, my friend." She sought his mouth and kissed him deeply.

The Czar had given General Alexander Gorloff and his recruits from America a wing of the Mikhailovsky Castle to use while they planned their invasion of America. The castle served as the army's main engineering school and seemed a good base from which to plot out a whole new kind of warfare.

Sharing the wing was a Navy Captain, Stepan Osipovich Makarov. He had already made a name for himself advocating new military technologies. The admiralty decided he should command the first airship to invade America. Makarov divided his time between Mikhailovsky Castle and St. Petersburg University. At the university, he studied aeronautics with Dmitri Mendeleev. At Mikhailovsky Castle, he did his best to formulate a new kind of naval strategy that operated from the air rather than the ocean. Like all of Gorloff's men, he was guided in his endeavors by the alien, Legion.

Gorloff stood in a room of Mikhailovsky Castle, studying a map of North America. He was flanked by Makarov and one of the Russians from America, Peter Berestetski. They had decided that Denver was their primary objective. From there, they could capture the United States Mint and effectively cut off the western United States from the eastern half. The question was, how to get there?

"I suggest we take a northern route." Makarov pointed to the Bering Strait and indicated a path along the Aleutian Islands. "We could drop some men in Alaska, go back out to sea and follow the Canadian coast, then come ashore again near Seattle." He pointed to a logging camp in Washington Territory that was growing into a thriving town.

Gorloff nodded. "Yes. Seattle is the largest town in the northwestern United States. It would be a good place to deploy troops either northward into Alaska or southward to San Francisco or Denver. The town would be easy to take and control." He walked over to a table, retrieved a cigar from a box, and offered another to the captain.

Makarov declined the cigar and turned back to the map, indicating a southeasterly course from Seattle to Denver. "From Puget Sound, we could make a fairly easy crossing of the Rockies in Montana Territory and then drop down to Colorado. There is very little population in those northern territories. We would be unhindered in our advance."

Berestetski's attention had been on the map the whole time. He shook his head. "That route will be time consuming. Why not bring the airship ashore at San Francisco? Much of the American Navy's Pacific Fleet is stationed there. We could attack them and destroy their ships, cutting off support from the west. Then we could take a more direct course overland to Denver."

Gorloff frowned and lit the cigar as Makarov gave voice to his thoughts. "Once we get to Denver, the navy won't be our biggest threat. We'll have to worry about the army already stationed there and in the surrounding areas. We can't afford to waste munitions in a coastal battle that's not necessary to our objective. Also, that will be a hazardous place to cross the Rockies, they are at their highest on the straight-line path." He pointed to another mountain range in California. "Not to mention the Sierra Nevadas."

"Agreed." Gorloff took a puff of the cigar. "San Francisco should be our target *after* we've secured Denver." The general chewed on the cigar, concerned about Peter Berestetski's inexperience. The general also found he had a difficult time trusting the man who called himself by the Anglicized form of Piotr and did not use a patronymic.

*"Be tolerant,"* cautioned Legion from the back of Gorloff's mind. *"If you are successful in your invasion, young Peter represents the future."*

*What do you mean?* Gorloff thought his question silently while continuing to smoke the cigar.

*"He is both American and Russian. He is a vision of the new empire you hope to create."* Even though Legion's voice was not audible, Gorloff felt the alien was irritated at having to explain something it felt was trivial.

*I am more worried about his naiveté.* Gorloff's lips pursed around the cigar.

*"His suggestion is not without merit,"* countered Legion. *"If the airship comes ashore near Seattle as proposed and takes the city, there is a ninety-two percent chance the army in Denver will be alerted before your arrival. If you attack San Francisco first, there is a thirty-four percent chance you would succeed in cutting off military lines of communication long enough to arrive at Denver before anyone expected you. The high mountain crossing is not without risk, but it is possible."*

Gorloff looked from Berestetski to Makorov, then took a few steps away from the map. *So, does this mean you think we should follow young Berestetski's advice?*

*"Not at all,"* said Legion. *"Even though it is quite likely the army in Denver will be alerted if you take Seattle first, it is unlikely enough people will understand your intention and form a defense in time. More than likely, they will assume you plan to attack a target further east."*

The general's silent conversation with Legion was cut short by an insistent rapping on the door. Gorloff removed the cigar from his mouth. "Come in," he called.

A man in the uniform of an imperial courier stepped through the door and saluted the general. "I have a message from the Czar."

Gorloff placed the cigar in his mouth, returned the salute, and held out his hand. The courier promptly handed over the letter, then spun on his heel and left. Gorloff read the message silently.

"What does it say?" asked the impetuous Berestetski.

"The Czar would like to review the two airships under construction." Gorloff spoke around the cigar. *I hope Mendeleev is making good progress,* he thought.

*"We believe the Czar will be suitably impressed,"* said Legion.

The general frowned and hoped Legion was correct.

Ramon woke with the sunrise. He looked over and saw Fatemeh lying in bed, still asleep. He couldn't help but think how beautiful she was and how lucky he was to have found a woman who loved him in return. He was determined to do everything in his power to make their relationship a permanent one.

Quietly, he pushed the sheets back and climbed out of bed. He slipped on his clothes and left the room. He missed the Castillos' rooming house in Mesilla where he could just slip downstairs for a quick breakfast. Fortunately, there was a small café just a few doors away from the hotel. At the street corner, a boy was selling newspapers. Ramon bought one of the papers and slipped into the café.

A waitress came by and poured him a cup of coffee while he stared at the headlines. He was somewhat surprised the paper contained no news of the *Stockton's* successful mission, stopping pirates off the coast of California. Beyond that, he really didn't pay attention to the headlines. Instead, it occurred to him Fatemeh recently revealed a side of herself he hadn't noticed before. She joined the *Stockton's* crew without telling him. She had concealed the fact her parents were Mohammedan and she really didn't talk to them anymore. Even though he still reveled in the glow of the previous night, he found himself wondering what else she hadn't told him. He was somewhat disappointed Fatemeh wanted separate rooms again, but she had made it clear further intimacy was not out of the question and he actually liked the idea of having some space to think things through before he finally committed to the relationship.

Ramon's thoughts were interrupted when the waitress came by and took his order. He mumbled something about eggs over easy and sausage—an extravagance he couldn't have afforded before the *Stockton*, but didn't seem so bad with money in his pocket.

Thoughts of money brought his attention back to the reason he bought the newspaper in the first place. Before the waitress retreated to the kitchen, he borrowed a pencil, then turned to the want ads at the back of the paper. He circled a couple of job ads that looked promising.

Soon, his breakfast arrived and as Ramon ate his eggs and sausage, he looked at the newspaper's headlines again. There were stories of armed robberies and bar fights. It reminded him of his days as Sheriff of Socorro and contrasted so much from what he had seen during his brief underwater voyage aboard the *Legado*.

No wonder Fatemeh wondered who they would be during the quiet times.

A different article caught Ramon's attention. A company called Star Oil had just opened a refinery in the nearby town of Newhall and they were looking for new employees. In the last year he had seen example after example of how machines were making a new future—everything from wonders like M.K. Maravilla's clockwork lobo and Onofre Cisneros's submersible to more mundane things like locomotives and steamships. Oil was the future. The Star Oil refinery held not only the promise of steady work, but it was a place where he could see the future being built. He folded up the paper, finished his breakfast, and strode back to the hotel room.

Ramon found Fatemeh sitting on the bed, mostly dressed. "Could you help me with the clasps on the back of my dress?"

"It'll be my pleasure, corazón." Ramon sat down behind her and felt a renewed thrill being so close to her and couldn't help caressing her back just as he finished doing up the clasps.

"I think I may have found a place to look for work."

Fatemeh looked at him expectantly.

"Star Oil has a new refinery up in the town of Newhall, just north of Los Angeles. They're looking for workers." Ramon's smile betrayed a certain pride at his discovery.

Fatemeh frowned. "Is an oil refinery really all that different from Mr. Dalton and his mines? Instead of digging into the Earth, these people draw out the Earth's blood through their wells."

Ramon looked into Fatemeh's eyes. "Corazón, you've asked me to look to the future. In the last year, we have seen many marvels, you and I. Almost all of them need oil to run. Oil may not be the future all by itself, but it certainly is part of the future. Is there really a better place to work, while answering your question about who we are during the quiet times?"

Fatemeh swallowed and then blinked. A moment later, her eyes met Ramon's again, but she stayed silent.

"Besides, Newhall is a small, quiet town. I suspect you'd have an easier time working as a curandera there than you would in the heart of the city." Ramon took her hand.

She was silent for a long time and Ramon wondered what was going on in her mind. Finally she nodded. "All right. Let's go see if you can find a job in Newhall."

General Alexander Gorloff rode in a gilded carriage with Czar Alexander II along the waterfront in St. Petersburg. The carriage stopped in front of a building that rivaled the Winter Palace in size. General Gorloff knew it had been built to construct warships, but had been given over to Dmitri Mendeleev and the airship project. Two soldiers standing guard by the main door snapped to attention as the carriage approached. Professor Mendeleev appeared from inside just as the carriage pulled to a stop. As a guard opened the carriage door, the professor bowed low. General Gorloff noted that even though Mendeleev wore fine clothes, they appeared rumpled and disheveled, as though he had been working in them for many hours.

The Czar approached the scientist and held out his hand,

indicating he should rise. Mendeleev seemed to hesitate for a moment, then stood.

"You honor us with your presence," said Mendeleev.

"General Gorloff has told me spectacular things about this project," said the Czar. "I am naturally curious."

Mendeleev led the way into the giant building. As they crossed the threshold, the Czar of all the Russias gasped at the sight before him. He stood facing two mighty, cigar-shaped vessels. Each vessel was longer than the biggest warship in the Czar's navy. The vessel to the Czar's left was covered with a light-colored fabric. On the bottom, at the bow, was painted a great owl, its wings and talons outstretched, as though ready to strike at its prey. At the back of the airship were great tail fins. The Russian flag had been painted prominently and proudly.

A cacophony of sound from hammers, torches, and men shouting assaulted the Czar's ears. However, silence quickly fell starting at the front of the building and working its way to the rear, as though some unheard signal had been relayed along the building's length.

The Czar took a few steps toward the nearly completed airship and pointed to a compartment that hung from the bottom of the hull, enclosed in glass. "What is the purpose of that structure?" he asked.

"That is the airship's bridge, where the captain and his officers direct its flight," explained Mendeleev.

"And those hatches behind the bridge?" The Czar pointed to a series of doorways that lined the bottom of the airship.

"From the air, we can use them to drop bombs," said General Gorloff. "When the airship comes near the ground, they can be used to deploy our troops rapidly."

The Czar nodded approvingly and walked between the two airships. The workers who surrounded each of the airships stood at attention. As they walked, Alexander Gorloff could just discern a slight faltering in the emperor's step, as though his knees felt weak at the grand sight before him. The Czar's eyes darted between the nearly completed airship and the one on the right that did not yet have its outer skin. A bare skeleton of steel girders enclosed great, flaccid bags. Underneath the bags were two decks that spanned the length of the vessel. Crew quarters, a great mess hall, and storage areas could all be seen through the superstructure.

The Czar's eyebrows came together. "This whole structure will be lighter than air?"

Mendeleev nodded. "It will be, Your Majesty, once the bags inside are filled with hydrogen gas."

"They will be like balloons, floating on the wind," said the emperor. "How will their flight be directed?"

"By steam engines," said the professor. He pointed to the nearly completed airship. Two engines were visible. They hung from the side with propellers facing aft.

"How will you shovel coal out to those engines when the ship is in the air?"

"We don't. These steam engines burn oil fed into the burner from a pipeline. Given the explosive nature of hydrogen gas, it is best if the engines are kept well separate from the interior of the ship."

The Czar pursed his lips. "You have thought this out well."

The professor bowed. "You do me great honor, Your Majesty..."

Czar Alexander held up his hand. "However, couldn't the explosive nature of hydrogen be a weakness in the design?"

"No doubt it would be," interjected Gorloff, "if the enemy had airships of their own, or ordnance that could fire skyward at these ships. However they do not."

The emperor nodded, seemingly satisfied by the answer. "It seems these engines must use a lot of oil to run."

Gorloff looked briefly toward Mendeleev just as an answer formed in the back of his mind. "We have enough oil for the invasion. We will have more than enough to replace it once we own Alaska and California again."

Czar Alexander folded his arms and a grin slowly appeared. His eyes roved slowly from one airship to the other. "The future of the Russian Empire looks very bright, gentlemen. You have done well." He strode from the building with General Gorloff following close behind.

A month later, Ramon walked to work from the rooming house in Newhall to the Star Oil Refinery. Spring was coming early to the mountains around Los Angeles and wildflowers bloomed beside the road. Once again, Ramon had a room across the hall from Fatemeh, and he made a point to meet her for dinner and spend time with her each day. The day before, they sent a telegram to Eduardo and Alicia, asking them to bring Fatemeh's wagon out to California as soon as the weather permitted.

True to his word, Bryan Burke had provided a stellar reference for Ramon. The former sheriff now found he had a comfortable job as a clerk, processing shipment orders from the refinery. Ramon stopped off at the refinery's mailroom and picked up a sheaf of papers, then went to his small office.

Once there, he sat down behind a small, tidy wooden desk and began sorting through the morning's orders. A large number of the orders came from either the Southern Pacific or Atlantic and Pacific Railroads. Other orders came from the steamship companies operating out of San Pedro and San Francisco. However, the vast majority of the orders came from the United States Navy.

Ramon took in a deep breath and let it out slowly. He had come to Star Oil to see the future. Although he enjoyed his new, quiet job very much, he was afraid he was seeing more of the future than he bargained for—a future dominated by war and profiteering.

He came upon a purchase order that brought a smile to his face. The postmark was from Flagstaff in the Arizona Territory. A short letter accompanied the order: "I am a professor conducting experiments at the Grand Canyon. I need oil for my research. Upon receipt of the order, I will wire funds to the account directed." The letter was signed in big, bold script: M.K. Maravilla.

Ramon looked toward the window and found himself wondering what kind of mechanical wonder the professor was working on. Was it another clockwork lobo, or something else? He also found himself wondering whether the professor could really afford to pay for the oil he requested. Still, he was only looking to buy a single five-gallon drum. Ramon decided to approve the order. If Maravilla did not pay, he would simply not approve any future orders. Ramon then finished going through the stack and tallied the orders and the shipping locations. He left the office, took the information to his supervisor, and retrieved the rest of the work he needed to do for the day.

When Ramon returned to the office, he was surprised to see Fatemeh in one of the room's two small chairs. "It's a pleasure to see you this morning, corazón. What brings you here?"

Fatemeh stood and put her arms around Ramon. As best as he could, Ramon set the papers down on the desk, then returned the embrace.

"I just received an answer from Eduardo," said Fatemeh, taking a step backward.

Ramon moved around the desk. "That's great news! When will he and Alicia be out?"

"They're not coming out to California," said Fatemeh. "They want us to return to Palomas Hot Springs. Apparently, there's trouble at Fort McRae."

# CHAPTER TEN
## THE BREAKDOWN

"What kind of trouble?" Ramon's eyebrows came together.

Fatemeh read the telegram. "It says, 'Major Johnson at Fort McRae requests urgent assistance, stop. Supplies from Lincoln County disrupted, stop. The Major asked for you and Fatima personally.' He spelled my name wrong..." She scowled.

"Never mind that," said Ramon with a wave of his hand. "Go on."

"'Please come at once.' That's the end of the telegram."

Ramon sighed and dropped into the chair behind his desk and looked outside. "Lincoln County...that's a real mess. From what I understand there's been trouble brewing between some of the ranchers. One side or the other has probably found some hired guns to disrupt shipments."

Fatemeh sat down in the chair across the desk from Ramon. "So, why would he ask for our help? When I was in Silver City, Dan Tucker was helping the soldiers at Fort Grant. Couldn't the major get help from one of the local sheriffs?"

Ramon smiled at the mention of Dangerous Dan Tucker. "He's a good man." The former sheriff pursed his lips and thought. "Lincoln County's sheriff is a man named Brady. He's pretty tight with one of the big ranchers—a businessman named Murphy. Could be he's mixed up in what's going on somehow."

"Like Sheriff Hillerman and Randolph Dalton."

"Possibly, or it could just be a problem of the county's size. Lincoln County is huge." Ramon pushed his glasses back on the bridge of his nose. "Either way, Major Johnson might not get much help from the law out that way and he really doesn't have the authority to investigate on his own."

"So he wants someone he can trust—someone who helped him before."

"That's the way it seems." Ramon folded his arms and nodded.

They sat in silence for a time. When Fatemeh didn't say anything, Ramon started sorting out the papers he'd brought with him, getting his work lined up for the day. It was easy work that wouldn't get him shot at, and yet somehow rather dull work. He wondered briefly whether he could be a clerk forever, or even very long. A part of him wanted to go back and investigate the trouble at Fort McRae, but he also heard a warning voice in the back of his mind. The two sets of thoughts warred with each other and kept him from answering right away.

"I think we should go," said Fatemeh after a few minutes.

Ramon looked up and blinked. "You can't be serious." The statement came from both the warning voice and from his perception of what Fatemeh would want.

"They've asked for our help. Do you think we can help them?" pressed Fatemeh.

Ramon set down a sheaf of papers and sat back. "Look, if I went back to New Mexico, there's a very good chance I'd get caught by Randolph Dalton's men again and be right back where you found me in that mine." He turned and looked out at the pine trees through the window. "Besides, you wanted to find out who we are together during the quiet times. We really haven't been able to do that."

Fatemeh smiled. "Yes, Ramon, but does it matter who we are together in the quiet times if we can't show courage when our family and friends call on us to help?" When Ramon continued looking out the window, she leaned forward and put her hand on his forearm. "Besides, even if Major Johnson can't investigate, don't you think the U.S. Army could keep you from falling into Dalton's hands if they didn't want you there?"

Ramon turned and looked into Fatemeh's eyes. "That's probably true, but what if the telegram really isn't from Eduardo? What if it's some kind of ruse from Dalton?"

"How would Dalton have any idea where to find you?"

Ramon shuddered. "I hate to think about that."

"If Dalton's men somehow found out from Eduardo and Alicia where we are, don't we still need to go—to help them?"

Ramon nodded slowly. "As always, you're right on all counts, corazón." He looked wistfully out at the trees again. "I was beginning to like it here."

"So was I," she said. "But you know what? If we go back, maybe once we sort everything out, we can go to Estancia and meet your mother. We can find out what she thinks of me."

"I have no doubt my mother would think you're just as much of a pain in the ass as I think you are." Ramon shook his head.

"That's what Dangerous Dan Tucker said about me," said Fatemeh with a grin. "I think I'll take it as a compliment."

Ramon snorted, but smiled. "Why don't you go check on train prices and find the quickest way for us to get back to New Mexico? I'll get done what I can here and then talk to my boss and see if I can take leave this soon, or if I'm just going to have to quit."

"Whatever the answer, I'm sure it's God's will for us." Fatemeh walked around the desk and kissed him.

"God's will always seemed easier when I went to Mass and heard it in Latin."

"Of course. When it was in Latin, you didn't understand what God was saying."

"Leave time! You want leave time?" Ramon's supervisor, Jacob Kelly, was red-faced. "You've only been working here three weeks!"

"Hasn't my work been good?" asked Ramon, taken aback by his supervisor's reaction.

Kelly scowled at him. "It's been fine, but I can't believe you'd expect me to give you leave this soon, especially when you can't tell me what it's for." He shook his head. "I should have known better than hire a Mexican, no matter how good your references were."

Ramon straightened at those words. "I am not a Mexican, I'm an American citizen. My dad died keeping the Union together."

"Well, you sure can't tell it by the color of your skin or that accent of yours." The cruel words seemed incongruous coming from the scarecrow of a man wearing half-moon spectacles.

"In that case, I'll be cleaning out my desk," growled Ramon. "I won't bother coming back."

"You owe us two weeks' notice, Mr. Morales."

"I don't owe the likes of you nothing!" Ramon turned around and stormed toward his office, snatching a satchel from a hook as he passed. When he entered, he tossed his few personal belongings into the satchel. Once he was finished, he looked up and saw Jacob Kelly in the doorway.

"What's so important that you have to leave right now anyway, Morales? Can't you at least tell me something?"

"Our government has asked for my help," spat Ramon. "That would be the United States Government, I might add. Good day." He pushed past Jacob Kelly and strode down the street to the rooming house where he lived.

Going upstairs, he found Fatemeh in her room. Her lone satchel was packed. She smiled when she saw Ramon, but the smile melted when she saw his expression. "Things didn't go well, did they?"

Ramon shook his head and dropped onto the bed next to Fatemeh's bag. "It seems I can't help anyone these days without pissing off someone else. I'm getting tired of it."

Fatemeh sat next to him. She put her arm around his shoulders. "Are you having second thoughts about going?"

"Not at all." Ramon turned toward Fatemeh, but looked down at the bed coverings. "It's just that I find myself wondering more and more about why you came here. Don't get me wrong, I'm glad you came." He glanced up for a moment, then looked down at his hands again. "But is America really better than Persia?"

Ramon had a hard time reading Fatemeh's shallow smile. It seemed at once a little sad and a little wistful. "Is anyplace really better than any other place? I fled Persia because if I stayed, I'd likely die, but I would like to go back one day and at least visit. I'd like to see if I could heal some old wounds. I am a curandera after all."

"I would like to go with you, if you went back."

"And for that reason, I'm glad I came to America," said Fatemeh. "America is far from perfect, but there are many people here who realize that and are working to make things better." She lifted his chin and Ramon found himself looking into her earnest, green eyes. "You're one of those people who wants to make things better." She gave him a deep kiss.

When they parted, he nodded. "I think we may be finding out who we are during the quiet times, even when things are crazy, eh, corazón?"

Fatemeh smiled, then looked at a clock on the wall. "Speaking of crazy, you should get packed. I spoke to the man at the telegraph office. He said if we can get to Union Station this afternoon, we can catch the Atlantic and Pacific into Albuquerque. There's a stagecoach passing through in half an hour, heading that direction."

"Did you send a telegram to Eduardo?" Ramon started toward the door.

"I did. I'm hoping we'll have an answer when we get back to the office."

Like Fatemeh, Ramon didn't have many belongings to pack. They had yet to buy many clothes since their arrival in Newhall. A few minutes later, with their satchels over their shoulders, Ramon and Fatemeh went to the lobby, checked out, and walked to the telegraph office.

The man behind the counter wore a green visor, suspenders and no jacket. His sleeves were rolled up past his elbows. "Ah, good to see you, Miss Karimi. I just received an answer to your telegram." He handed her a slip of paper.

She read it and handed it to Ramon. He set down his satchel and read the slip of paper, nodding approvingly. "The major must be serious about needing our help. Sounds like he'll be sending some men to meet us."

Fatemeh turned toward the clerk. "Did we make it in time for the stage?"

"Just," said the clerk, looking out the window. "It's rolling up right now."

As they stepped outside, Ramon saw Jacob Kelly from the

refinery running toward them. Ramon's gut clenched. Gathering his wits, he paid the stagecoach driver and hurriedly handed up his satchel along with Fatemeh's. Kelly approached just as Ramon and Fatemeh were climbing aboard the coach. He was out of breath.

"Good, I caught you," said Ramon's former supervisor as he gulped for air.

"I think we've said everything that needs saying," said Ramon, sharply.

"I just received a telegram over at the refinery from a Major Johnson in New Mexico Territory. I wanted to catch you before you left so I could apologize for the way I acted. You're welcome back when you've finished your business for the army."

Ramon's mouth fell open for a moment, but he quickly closed it and swallowed. He stepped out of the coach and held out his hand. "Thank you, Mr. Kelly."

Kelly returned the handshake.

"Mr. Kelly, I appreciate that you came out here once you heard from Fort McRae, but I think you need to understand that you can't tell a patriotic American by the color of his skin."

Kelly frowned, but tipped his hat. "Good words and I'll certainly give it some thought."

"You do that." Ramon stepped back into the coach and closed the door. With a lurch, the stagecoach took off down the street.

Ramon turned and looked at Fatemeh. "I still don't like how he jumped to conclusions or acted like an ass, but maybe you're right. Maybe people here can learn and improve themselves."

"I only hope that can become true everywhere."

The next day, after breakfast in the train's dining car, Ramon and Fatemeh returned to their seats in the coach car. She watched the scenery for a while—mostly flat, barren countryside—then leaned her head on Ramon's shoulder. It was strong and somehow being next to him was growing more comfortable as time passed. Different as their backgrounds were, they were also a lot alike. With those thoughts in her mind, she drifted off to sleep.

Not long after, or so it seemed to her, there was a sudden lurch and she fell forward, hitting her head on the seat in front of her. Blinking a few times, she saw Ramon was rubbing his head. Apparently, whatever happened had also caught him off guard.

The terrain had changed outside. Instead of barren countryside, they were in more forested country. Moreover, the train had stopped moving. "What happened?" Fatemeh managed at last.

"I'm not sure. We both dozed off." Ramon put his glasses back on. He looked outside, then he took out his pocket watch and studied it for a moment. "It's about ten in the morning. We must be pretty close to Flagstaff."

Similar conversations started up around the coach car as people wondered where they were and what was going on. A few minutes went by and then a door opened at one end of the coach. The conductor entered and cleared his throat. "Ladies and gentlemen, it appears the locomotive threw one of its piston rods. We're going to have to get some materials out here to fix the damage. At this point, I'm not sure how long it's going to take. At a minimum, we'll be here until tomorrow. I'm afraid though, it'll be more like two days before we're under way again."

There was collective grumbling up and down the car. The conductor held up his hands. "We'll get you to your destination as soon as possible, even if we have to bring another locomotive out from Los Angeles or Albuquerque, but even that will take more than a day. The good news is that Flagstaff is only five miles away. We'll put you up in a hotel there until we have some news. Pack up your belongings and meet me at the side of the car in fifteen minutes." With that, the conductor started making his way through the car and the grumbling resumed.

Ramon stopped the conductor as he passed. "Excuse me, sir. How far is the Grand Canyon from Flagstaff?"

"Thinking about visiting while we're stopped?"

"If there's time,"

The conductor shrugged. "It's about sixty miles northwest

of here. I bet you could make it up and back before we're ready to go again if you rent a couple of horses in town."

"Thanks." Ramon let the conductor go on his way.

"Do you have something in mind?" Fatemeh yawned, then did her best to straighten her hair.

Ramon retrieved their satchels from the overhead luggage rack, taking his time before answering. "I've heard the Grand Canyon's really spectacular. I thought since we're stuck here for a little while, it might be kind of interesting to see it."

Fatemeh inclined her head. "I'd like to, but don't you think we should stay close to the others in case the train is ready to go sooner than expected? The major's expecting us in New Mexico, after all."

Ramon tossed his satchel over his shoulder and stepped aside so Fatemeh could enter the aisle. She grabbed her satchel and the two clambered out of the rail coach and met with the other people gathered alongside the train. The conductor and his assistants counted the people assembled. Apparently satisfied everyone was accounted for, they began the five-mile walk to Flagstaff.

The air was cold as they walked and a dusting of snow covered the ground. Fatemeh retrieved a coat from her satchel and buttoned it up. "I think a nice warm hotel room will feel really good after this walk."

Ramon frowned. "Then I take it you don't want to go to the canyon."

Fatemeh shrugged. "It seems like we could come back at a better time of year." She studied him for a moment and found his expression unreadable. "So, why all the interest in the canyon?"

Ramon remained silent for a time. "Just before you came into my office yesterday morning, I discovered Professor Maravilla is doing some work at the Grand Canyon. I thought it might be interesting to see what he's up to."

Fatemeh's eyes widened. "That would be interesting to see." For a moment, Ramon's lips turned down and she thought she might have hurt him with her enthusiasm. "I didn't get the impression you cared much for Professor Maravilla," she observed.

"I can't rightly say he's my favorite person," agreed Ramon. "I'm not even sure we'd be able to find him—the canyon's a big place, after all—but the professor is one of the people I've met who seems interested in building the future. I'd kind of like to see what he's up to if we're able. I don't know what will happen when we get to New Mexico. It might prove to be something easy to sort out or we might get into a big mess. Either way, getting another glimpse of the future might just get me through the coming days."

"What if we don't find him?"

He shrugged. "From everything I've heard, the canyon's a beautiful place. It could be an inspirational side trip whether we find the professor or not."

Fatemeh smiled. "In that case, let's go. What's the worst thing that'll happen? They'll get the train fixed and we'll have to wait for the next one."

"Another day or two won't hurt the major."

Looking up, they realized they'd fallen behind the group marching toward Flagstaff. They stepped up the pace to catch up.

It was a brisk, but clear day in St. Petersburg, Russia. A mooring tower had been erected on top of the building where Russia's new airships were being constructed. One of the airships was now complete and tethered to the mooring tower. It swayed gently back and forth in the cold breeze that blew in from the Baltic Sea.

General Gorloff followed Czar Alexander up a tall ladder toward the mooring assembly. The general was surprised that the Czar was such a nimble man—able to climb the ladder in the great fur coat that protected him from the biting wind. Gorloff himself had to pause twice to catch his breath and then hurry to catch up.

Already at the top were two sailors. Both of them bowed when the Czar arrived. One presented Alexander with a bottle of champagne and the other handed him a megaphone. Turning around, Gorloff saw a gathering of workers and the idle curious in the street below. The general felt his heart pounding hard in his chest despite Legion's reassurance the structure they occupied was quite sound and it was unlikely they would fall.

*Unlikely?* asked Gorloff silently.

*"An accident is never impossible,"* said Legion within the general's mind. *"However, it is highly improbable."*

*Somehow, I don't feel very reassured.* The general swallowed and put on a brave face, waving to those assembled with one hand, while holding onto the railing that surrounded the mooring assembly with the other.

The Czar raised the megaphone to his mouth. Eschewing the traditional Psalm 107, Alexander chose to quote from Psalm 8. "What is man, that thou art mindful of him? And the son of man, that thou visitest him? For thou hast made him a little lower than the angels, and hast crowned him with glory and honour. Thou madest him to have dominion over the works of thy hands; thou hast put all things under his feet: All sheep and oxen, yea, and the beasts of the field; The fowl of the air, and the fish of the sea, and whatsoever passeth through the paths of the seas. O Lord our Lord, how excellent is thy name in all the earth!" The Czar paused for a moment. "Thus we dedicate this first ship of the air, this ship that will give us dominion over all the things of the Earth, in the sea, *and* in the air." The Czar smashed the champagne bottle on the airship's metal mooring ring. "I christen thee *Czar Nicholas* in honor of my father." The Czar retreated toward the railing.

The two sailors detached the mooring clamp and gave the great airship a shove. Gorloff shook his head, amazed two people could move such a great craft with such a humble motion.

The ship drifted backward for a time, eerily silent. Finally, the two portside motors kicked on and the tail rudder moved. The *Czar Nicholas* drifted in a long, slow arc out over the gulf. Gorloff could just make out men in the gondola, hanging under the airship. He knew Mendeleev would be there with them, overseeing the first flight.

There was a rumbling and a roar of voices from the street below as the crowd made its way to the waterfront to watch the airship make a long, slow circle over the Gulf of Finland.

The workers cheered their creation on. Gorloff simply nodded to himself. *It seems too beautiful to be an engine of destruction,* he thought.

"*It was never our intention to help you build an engine of destruction,*" said Legion. "*Our goal was to create a vehicle that would help you unite your world and prevent needless destruction.*"

Gorloff frowned, but nodded. *It seems a fitting craft for that. Let us pray we have been successful, then.*

It was nearly sunset when Ramon and Fatemeh came to the edge of a stand of trees and found themselves looking out over the great fissure in the Earth known as the Grand Canyon. Ramon's breath caught as he craned his neck first one way and then the other, trying to gauge the canyon's extent. He climbed off the horse, then helped Fatemeh down. Her hand was trembling. Ramon wasn't sure whether that was because of the cold or because she too was nearly overwhelmed by the sight.

Together, they walked toward the edge and peered into the canyon. They saw layers of red, yellow, gray and almost green rock. From where they stood, they could not see the river down at the bottom. Little tree-covered buttes jutted out into the canyon some distance below.

"Just think," said Fatemeh, "the Colorado River, which we can't even see, cut all this with a little patience and persistence."

"I'm glad I came, corazón," said Ramon, quietly. "Whether we find Professor Maravilla or not, I have glimpsed beauty and grandeur and yes, I now know what patience and persistence can accomplish. The future can be a better place." Standing up straight, Ramon briskly rubbed his arms. "It's getting cold. We should find a place to camp and start a fire."

"I couldn't agree more," said Fatemeh. They climbed back on the horses they'd rented in Flagstaff. While in town, they'd also purchased a small tent and several blankets.

As they rode, Ramon had a hard time keeping his eyes from the canyon. Every time he looked, he saw something new in the shape of the rocks and the colors. The ever-changing light of the setting sun altered the way things looked almost constantly. Over the canyon, a few birds swooped around, hunting in the fading light. Something glinted on the other side of the canyon. Ramon brought his horse to a stop. Fatemeh noticed and brought her horse alongside Ramon's.

"What's the matter?" she asked. "This still seems a bit too rocky a place to camp."

Ramon shook his head. "I thought I saw something, flying over the canyon."

"What? The birds?"

"No, something else." He tried to catch sight of it again. A moment later, he saw another glint and pointed. "There! Did you see it?"

"It's like something metal." Fatemeh's eyebrows came together. "Could it just be a white or gray bird?"

"I don't think so," said Ramon. He continued to point. "I thought those were thin clouds over there, but now I'm not sure. It looks like smoke or steam."

Ramon caught sight of the glint again and worked to hold onto it. It looked like a bird and it made a slow turn in their direction. At that moment, Ramon wished he had a pair of binoculars or a telescope.

"It's like an owl," said Fatemeh, looking the same direction as Ramon. She clutched the owl necklace he'd carved for her. "Only it's the biggest owl I've ever seen."

Ramon nodded. She was right. The great bird had the shape of an owl. Mostly it was gliding on the air currents, but occasionally it would flap its wings and there would be a little puff of smoke or steam from it. The strange owl flew away some distance, then slowly banked in the air and came back toward them.

This time, when it approached, Ramon could see better. It wasn't really a bird, it was a machine of some sort, but its frame was in the shape of an owl. Within the frame was a man sitting at a set of controls. He seemed as interested in Ramon and Fatemeh as they were in him. He made another long arc in the sky and then flew back in the direction he was originally heading.

The sun sat on the horizon and long shadows were beginning to obscure the landscape. Fortunately, it was near full moon and the sky wouldn't go completely dark. Ramon spurred his horse onward in the direction the owl-like machine had gone.

After about two miles, the sun was fully below the horizon and the twilight gloom had enveloped the landscape. Ramon shook his head. "It's no use. I don't think we'll ever find out who or what that was."

"Why don't we find a place to camp? We can look again tomorrow," suggested Fatemeh.

Ramon pursed his lips and nodded. He turned toward the trees and tried to discern a likely place to set up their tent. Just as he thought he saw a place, a voice cried out. "Hello there!"

Ramon and Fatemeh turned their horses and saw a man standing near the rim of the canyon waving to them. He held a lantern, placing him in silhouette. He held it up and studied them. "Madre de Dios, it *is* you!"

"Professor Maravilla?" ventured Fatemeh.

"Yes, yes!" said the man, lowering the lamp. Ramon could see the man in the black trousers and red silk vest. The only thing that appeared different than the last time they'd seen him were a pair of goggles adorning his head. "How remarkable to see you here."

"Actually, we were looking for you," said Ramon as he climbed off the horse.

"Really? How did you know I was here?"

Ramon explained about the order he'd seen while working at the refinery in Newhall and then about the train breakdown.

"It is wonderful to see you again!" The professor looked from Ramon to Fatemeh. "But, you must be getting cold. I have set up crude, but comfortable lodgings in a cave not far from here. I believe you'll find it much warmer."

"That would be wonderful," Fatemeh said through chattering teeth.

Professor Maravilla led them to the edge of the canyon and showed them a place where they could leave the horses for the night. He helped unload their supplies and then took them to a trail that went a short ways into the canyon. There, they found the wide mouth of a cave. Sitting in its entrance, illuminated by oil lamps, was something that looked like a half-complete sculpture of an owl. The professor removed the goggles from his forehead and hung them from a rock.

The "owl" was made of some kind of lightweight metal. Covering the wings and tail was a fabric of some sort. The rest of the framework was open to the air. In the center of the cage was a seat and a set of controls. Right behind the seat was the smallest steam engine Ramon had ever seen. Rods connected the engine to the wings. Another set of rods connected the tail to some kind of wheel mounted at the controls.

"This is remarkable," exclaimed Fatemeh.

"Why thank you," said Maravilla with a slight bow. "It was our time together outside of Mesilla that gave me the idea for this craft."

"Really?"

"Indeed. After the things I observed, my attention turned from studying wolves to trying to understand owls. I wanted to see how they fly, how they hunt. What better way than by becoming an owl myself?"

"What's more," said Ramon, wide-eyed, "you've invented a flying machine."

The professor dismissed the words with a wave of the hand, then led them further into the cave where he had some rudimentary furniture and a wood stove. Looking up, Ramon saw the smoke from the stove was carried in a pipe that ran along the cave's ceiling to the entrance. "I'm afraid it's not a very practical flying machine," said Maravilla. "It only carries one person and not very far. The engine is so small I can't carry much fuel. It's basically only good for my research."

"Even so," said Ramon, "it seems like you could patent the idea and make a small fortune."

"Wouldn't that let you carry on your research in comfort?" asked Fatemeh.

"My dear lady, I once had comforts aplenty." Professor Maravilla took out a sack of potatoes and a knife. Sitting down, he began slicing them into an iron pot. Ramon and Fatemeh followed his lead and sat down near the stove. Ramon held up his hands, feeling the delightful warmth.

The professor continued speaking while he retrieved carrots and onions and sliced them into the pot as well. "Although I admit I miss those comforts, I have never learned as much as I have since I gave all of that up and became a vagabond of sorts, studying the things I want to study and doing the things I'd like." He paused and pointed with the knife. "Do you think the regents at the Pontifical and Royal University of Mexico would have granted me money to build a flying machine?"

Fatemeh shook her head.

"So tell us more about the owl," prompted Ramon.

Maravilla placed the stew pot on the wood stove. "Really it's not that different from the clockwork lobo you saw. The challenge was making it big and light enough to carry a person. The owls were my inspiration and, as you can see, that's the morphology I chose for my creation. However, I came to the canyon so I could study the largest birds in this part of the world—the great condors. I watched how they moved their wings and tails and created a motor and steering mechanism that would do the same."

"That's absolutely remarkable." Fatemeh leaned forward with her chin on her hand.

Several months before, Ramon would have been jealous. He now realized she was not pining for the professor, but captivated with the idea. He had to admit, he felt much the same way.

"Enough about me," said the professor. "Tell me what you have been up to since I saw you last—and tell me more about this train breakdown. Maybe there's something I can do to help and repay your approving the barrel of oil for me, Mr. Morales."

Professor Maravilla stood beside the Atlantic and Pacific locomotive wiping his hands on a rag. His sleeves were rolled up and his jacket and waistcoat hung on a nearby tree branch. With help from the engineer, fireman, conductor and Ramon, he had remounted the thrown piston rod and made repairs to the piston and valve assemblies.

The engineer and fireman climbed into the cab and the others stood back. A fire was stoked while Maravilla retrieved his finery from the tree. Soon he looked as immaculate as ever. After about thirty minutes, the engineer opened the throttle.

The train lurched forward and lumbered down the track about a quarter mile. Maravilla, Ramon, Fatemeh and the conductor ran to catch up.

Once alongside the locomotive again, they saw the engineer leaning his head out of the cab. "Professor Maravilla, you are a mechanical genius. I thought we were going to need a whole new piston and rod assembly out here."

The professor nodded gravely. "The repairs I made won't last. You'll still need to make that repair, but now you can do it in the Albuquerque yards where it'll be a lot easier."

"That is true," said the conductor. "Once we get back into Flag we'll wire ahead and make sure things are good to go. How much do we owe you, professor?"

The professor started to protest, but Ramon suggested a sum of money.

The conductor nodded. "That seems most equitable. Let me get it from the pay box."

Maravilla looked at Ramon. "I appreciate the gesture, Mr. Morales, but I was happy to do the work as a favor to you and Miss Karimi."

"The amount I quoted will pay for that barrel of oil that's being shipped out here—plus a little to help with your research." He smiled and put his hand on the professor's arm. "Call it a 'thank you' for giving me a glimpse of the future."

The professor bowed at the waist. "You are most welcome, Mr. Morales."

The conductor returned and handed a small roll of bills to the professor, then looked around. "All aboard!"

Fatemeh and Ramon gathered up their satchels and clambered aboard the coach car. The conductor looked at the professor. "Can we give you a lift back to Flagstaff? It seems the least we can do."

"That is most appreciated, but I brought my own transportation."

As the train moved forward toward Flagstaff, Ramon and Fatemeh watched out the window and saw a clockwork owl lift off from the trees with a puff of steam, and wing its way back toward the Grand Canyon.

# CHAPTER ELEVEN
## LINCOLN COUNTY WAR

Feelings of warmth and dread battled with each other as Ramon looked through the train's window at the deep blue sky outlining Albuquerque's adobe buildings. It was good to be in familiar surroundings, but it was also a little frightening to be so close to Socorro again. Swallowing hard, he retrieved his bag and made his way to the platform. He was glad for Fatemeh's company, but worried for her safety as well.

He was relieved when he stepped out of the train and saw two blue-coated soldiers. One of them stepped forward. "Mr. Morales?"

"I'm Ramon Morales."

"Sergeant Bill Forrest." The soldier held out his hand and Ramon clasped it. "My partner's Corporal Jesse Lorenzo."

The man tipped his hat toward Fatemeh. "*Jesús* Lorenzo," amended the soldier with a Spanish accent. "The sergeant calls me Jesse because he thinks it's sacrilegious to call me Jeezus."

"Pleased to meet you, Jesús," said Fatemeh, pronouncing the soldier's name as he had.

"We best get going." Bill Forrest looked around a little uncomfortably. "We have about three long days of riding ahead of us to get to the fort." He started making his way toward a team of horses hitched to a covered wagon.

"Will we be stopping in Socorro?" asked Ramon.

"We'll be passing through, but you'll be in the wagon," explained Corporal Lorenzo. "Major Johnson explained the situation to us. He sent us with the wagon to pick up some supplies here in Albuquerque. We have camping gear as well. We don't want to take a chance Randolph Dalton or his men will see you as we pass through."

Ramon swallowed hard. "What can you tell us about the trouble in Lincoln County?"

"I think it would be best if we let the major fill you in," said Forrest. He held out his arm and helped Fatemeh climb into the back of the wagon. Ramon tossed in his bag, then clambered up after her. A few minutes later, Forrest and Lorenzo climbed up onto the buckboard at the front of the wagon and they started the journey southward.

The ride south was free of incident. Still, Ramon breathed a sigh of relief as they pulled through the gates of the small fort on the Rio Grande. Sergeant Forrest brought the wagon to a stop in front of the fort's small trading post. Corporal Lorenzo hopped down from the buckboard and went to the back to help Fatemeh out of the wagon. Ramon followed awkwardly and rubbed his sore backside.

Fort McRae was quieter than the last time they were there. Two Indians had blankets with goods set out in front of the trading post. A soldier hurried through the compound on some errand. Over at the parade ground, some soldiers were organized in a diamond pattern. One threw a ball toward another who held a thin club.

"What's going on over there?" asked Fatemeh.

"Looks like some of the men are playing a game of baseball," explained Lorenzo.

"Baseball?" Ramon's eyebrows came together.

"Yeah, some of the soldiers from back East have been teaching us. It's kind of fun. If there's time, maybe you can join us for a game."

Ramon nodded thoughtfully. "I'd like that."

Sergeant Forrest made his way around the wagon. "The major would like to see you right away." He pointed in the direction of the commander's office.

Corporal Lorenzo led the way and Ramon and Fatemeh followed. A few minutes later, they found themselves standing in front of a wooden door. Lorenzo knocked and they heard a muffled "come in" from the other side.

Stepping inside, Ramon and Fatemeh blinked in the comparative darkness of the office. Major Johnson stood up from behind his desk. "Good to see you." He looked toward Lorenzo. "I want you and Sergeant Forrest to oversee the unloading of the supplies, then come on back. I'll want your reports."

The corporal saluted, then walked out, leaving Ramon and Fatemeh alone with the major. Johnson indicated two chairs in front of his desk, then sat down.

Ramon sat and placed his bag beside him. The chair was hardwood, but contoured and much more comfortable than sitting on crates in the back of the covered wagon. Fatemeh sat down next to him.

"Thank you for coming," said the major. "I wasn't sure you would after I heard about the trouble in Socorro."

Ramon inclined his head. "I'm a little surprised you asked for our help."

Major Johnson smiled and sat back. His blue eyes seemed to twinkle in the faint light coming in through the room's one window. "You saved this installation, Mr. Morales and I'm grateful for that. You demonstrated powers of observation that eluded my men." The major sat forward and stroked his long, brown mustache. "It's true I became concerned when the wanted posters were delivered, but I spoke to Sheriff Hillerman in Socorro and I got the impression there was more to the story than meets the eye. Because of that, I spoke to your cousin Eduardo in Palomas Hot Springs. He's well respected in these parts and told me what really happened." The major shook his head. "I haven't had any dealings with Randolph Dalton, but I've known enough men like him to believe your side of the story."

Ramon nodded, satisfied. "So, if we help you, you think you can get my name cleared?"

The major cleared his throat and folded his arms. "I'm working on that."

Fatemeh inclined her head. "Your answer doesn't inspire a lot of confidence."

"It's the most honest one I can give."

"So, what exactly do you want us to do?" asked Ramon.

The major let out a breath and his shoulders relaxed. Ramon sensed relief that he was asked a question he could answer. "Most of the forts in New Mexico Territory buy their beef from L.G. Murphy and Company in Lincoln County."

Ramon nodded. "I know. Murphy's a rancher and a business owner out that way. His store is the only source of feed for the whole county."

"The problem is a gang of rustlers has been ambushing Murphy's men each time they try to bring the cattle over to this part of the state," explained the major.

Ramon leaned forward and his eyebrows came together. "That seems like Sheriff Brady's problem."

The major pursed his lips and shook his head. "It's happening in Socorro County, outside his jurisdiction. Sheriff Hillerman up in Socorro hasn't been responsive to my requests for help. He says he can't spare the deputies."

Ramon sighed, disappointed his former deputy would give such a poor excuse. When he was sheriff, he knew all too well how important it was to help out the forts in the county. They were often the only places ranchers and farmers had to trade their goods in such a sparsely populated territory. It sounded to Ramon that Hillerman had just decided he didn't want to face the danger represented by a band of rustlers. "So, where exactly are the rustlers striking?" he asked, deciding to keep the conversation focused on the business at hand, rather than saying anything bad about his former deputy.

The major took in a deep breath and let it out slowly. "To be honest, I'm not sure. I'd like you to ride over to Lincoln with Sergeant Forrest and Corporal Lorenzo. The three of you will escort the cowboys back."

"I could do that."

"What about me?" asked Fatemeh.

Ramon inclined his head. "This sounds like dangerous work. Cowboys and rustlers…I think it might be best if you stayed here at the fort."

"We'd be happy to make room for you," offered the major helpfully.

"Or you could stay with Eduardo and Alicia," said Ramon.

Fatemeh narrowed her gaze and scowled at Ramon. "Is it really any more dangerous than facing pirates at sea or someone hell-bent on destroying Fort McRae?"

Ramon shifted uncomfortably. "I suppose not."

"I'm going with you, Ramon."

Someone knocked at the door. Major Johnson tried to suppress a smile, apparently thankful for the interruption. "Come in." He stood.

Forrest and Lorenzo entered and saluted. The major returned the salute and told the soldiers to stand at ease. He turned his attention back to Ramon and Fatemeh. "Take a couple of days to freshen up and visit with your cousin." He turned to the soldiers. "You men will take that time to gather the supplies you need. You'll accompany Mr. Morales and Miss Karimi to Lincoln, where you'll meet with Mr. Murphy and make arrangements to come back with the cattle coming this direction."

"Yes, sir." The sergeant and corporal snapped a salute.

Ramon looked at Fatemeh. "I hope you know what you're doing, corazón. You'd be a lot more comfortable at Eduardo and Alicia's."

"Wherever you go, I go," said Fatemeh, firmly.

Randolph Dalton sat in his office in Socorro, reviewing reports from the last week. He had a full complement of miners again and production was finally back at the level he wanted. It had taken longer than he expected after the dynamite shack exploded and scared off so many of his men. Of course, they had been further spooked by that Persian woman who spouted off about the Earth striking back when it's hurt. That kind of talk was especially dangerous around the Mexicans and Indians he liked to employ for low wages. He thought she would be a simple problem to deal with.

Dalton lay down the sheaf of papers and opened the ledger. He thumbed through the records—months of the lowest profits he had seen since coming to Socorro. Indeed, the Persian woman's words were bad enough. They drove off workers, who went home and talked to their families. That made it difficult to recruit new miners. However, that wasn't the worst problem.

What really galled him was that Ramon Morales rescued her. The sheriff had questioned his power and authority. That made Dalton look bad and kept buyers away. He turned to the most recent entries of the ledger. Production levels might be up, but sales were still down.

To make matters worse, he had Morales—had him in his grip—and yet the former sheriff had managed to get away. One loyal man was dead. Another was crippled. Morales cost him money and made him look weak. Even Sheriff Hillerman wasn't listening to him like he once did. Dalton realized he held a page of the ledger tightly in his grasp. He let go, then did his best to smooth out the page. Once Ramon Morales was dead, everything would be fine again.

Dalton pulled out his pocket watch. The day was almost over. He looked forward to going home and having a nice meal. He gathered his papers, stood, and took them to the filing cabinet.

When he turned around, he saw the door was open. Silhouetted in the afternoon light was a thin stranger. A coachman's hat, like an Englishman might wear, adorned the stranger's head. "I hear you have a problem and you're looking for the best way to solve it."

The voice belonged to a woman.

Dalton laughed and looked the figure up and down. Indeed, he now noticed she wore a skirt. He stopped laughing when he realized she pointed a gun in his direction. "So, what can the likes of you do for me?"

A gunshot shattered the air and exploded in the wall just above Dalton's filing cabinet.

"I don't take kindly to being laughed at."

She took a step further into the office and Dalton could discern a businesslike coldness in her gaze that he saw in few men. Certainly she seemed more determined than the likes of Sheriff Ray Hillerman or even those miners he'd paid to do in Ramon Morales. Dalton's lips turned up in a grim smile. "Perhaps we do have some business to discuss. Why don't you have a seat and we'll talk things over, shall we?"

A week later, Ramon, Fatemeh, Sergeant Forrest and Corporal Lorenzo rode into Lincoln. The town was in high country on forested land and Fatemeh was struck by certain similarities to Newhall, California. Like Newhall, there were few buildings. One of the biggest was a long two-story structure with a sign identifying it as the Lincoln County Courthouse. Another large building had a sign that simply proclaimed, "General Store."

The riders hitched their horses outside the store. When they entered, a young man behind the counter eyed them suspiciously. "Can I help you?" he said.

Ramon tipped his hat. "We're from Fort McRae. May we have a word with Mr. Murphy, please?"

The young man frowned, then took in the sight of the two soldiers. "I'll go get him." He left through a door behind the counter.

Fatemeh looked around at all the items in the store. It was an impressive selection for such a small town. The store was dominated by farming supplies, but there was a section for clothing and another for food. She took a look at some women's dresses hanging on a rack. Lifting one of the sleeves, she caught sight of a price tag and whistled.

Ramon stepped up beside her. "Do you like it?"

"Not at that price. There were nicer dresses for less in Los Angeles."

Ramon shrugged. "Sometimes things cost a bit more in small towns like this, because of how much it takes to get it here."

"This much more?" She showed him the price tag.

Ramon caught his breath. "I see what you mean."

A throat cleared behind them. They turned around and saw a thin man with a goatee and slicked-back hair. "My name is Lawrence Murphy. I understand you were looking for me."

"Yes, sir," said Ramon. "Major Johnson at Fort McRae sent us."

"Come to my office." Murphy led Ramon and Fatemeh toward the same door the clerk had exited through. On their way, Ramon caught Forrest's and Lorenzo's attention and signaled that they should follow. A moment later, they all found themselves in a lavish office that rivaled anything Fatemeh had ever seen. It was certainly nicer than Major Johnson's office, featuring fine brass lamps and a marble fireplace. Looking toward the floor, her eyes went wide as she recognized a Persian rug.

Ramon and Fatemeh took seats across from Murphy, while the soldiers sat on a couch at the back of the room. Murphy sat in a high-backed leather chair behind an ornately carved oak desk. "I presume Major Johnson has told you all about the problems we've had with rustlers."

"That's why I'm here," said Ramon. "I'm … familiar with the area, as are these gentlemen." He indicated the soldiers at the back of the room. "The major would like us to ride with your men and see what we can do to assure the cattle get to the fort."

Murphy frowned. "And the lady?"

Fatemeh opened her mouth as though to speak, but Ramon cut her off. "The lady cooks for us. She's also a curandera." When Murphy looked perplexed at the word, Ramon explained further. "She's a healer—a doctor. If there's gunplay, she can help."

Murphy nodded thoughtfully. "I'd heard there were some women doctors. Didn't hear about no Mexican women doctors."

"I'm not Mexican," said Fatemeh before Ramon could interrupt. "I'm Persian—like the rug you walk on."

Murphy scowled, but before he said anything, Forrest raised his hand. "Sir, perhaps you can show us where most of the attacks occur."

The storeowner nodded. He opened a drawer in his desk and brought a map out. He laid it across the top of the desk. The two soldiers stood and approached. Murphy pointed to a pass between mountain ranges labeled Sierra Sacramentos and Sierra Oscuras. "My men usually camp at the outlet of the pass, before crossing into the Valley of Fire."

"The Valley of Fire?" asked Fatemeh wide-eyed. She pictured a literal, flaming valley.

"It's a valley of jagged red and black rock," explained Ramon. "Very treacherous country."

"They say one of the mountains in the area used to be a

volcano," continued Lorenzo. "The red rock is lava that hardened."

"I'm surprised you bring the cattle through there," said Fatemeh. "Isn't there an easier way?"

"Not without going over a hundred miles out of our way." Apparently Murphy was unfazed Fatemeh asked the question. "We've looked at other routes, but we'd be just as vulnerable to rustlers—or Indians—going another route."

"When will you send the next shipment?" asked Forrest.

Murphy picked up the map and began rolling it up. "Now that you're here, I can get the men to round up some cattle and send them along any time. Give me a day to get everything arranged."

"Two mornings from now, then?" asked Ramon.

"I'll have the boarding house put you up until then. Don't worry about the price," said Murphy. "I'll pick up the tab."

"That's mighty kind of you," said Ramon.

Fatemeh looked around the office one more time. She admired the leather-bound books and two golden goblets on the mantle of the fireplace. *If anyone can afford it, it's L.G. Murphy,* she thought.

As Billy McCarty rode through Lincoln, he caught sight of four people leaving Lawrence Murphy's general store. He thought he recognized the woman as Fatemeh Karimi, the woman who had once helped him with a sprained ankle and who he in turn helped by rescuing her boyfriend. He wondered if the short, tough-looking guy with owl-like glasses could be the boyfriend. He hadn't looked so tough when they pulled him broken and bleeding from a mine near Socorro.

He might have ridden over and said something, but the sight of two soldiers stopped him from getting too close. If there were soldiers at Murphy's, that could only mean one thing. They were likely to try taking some more cattle to one of the forts soon. Billy lowered his hat and rode on.

A short time later, he came to a shack that sat on John Tunstall's land. He climbed off his horse and led it to a water trough. Then he gathered some tin cans from the shack's porch and carried them over to a nearby fence where he lined them up. As he stepped away from the fence, three shots rang out. Looking around, he saw that the cans were all down.

Looking up again, he saw a woman on horseback with her gun drawn. She smiled at Billy, then holstered her six-gun. She tipped her strange flat-topped hat. "I hear there are some strangers of interest here in Lincoln County. What can you tell me about them?"

Fatemeh rather enjoyed the first part of the ride from Lincoln toward the pass between the Sierra Sacramentos and the Sierra Oscuras. The smell of pine pervaded the fresh air. Four cowboys and two dogs accompanied the twenty-five head of cattle L.G. Murphy sent toward Fort McRae. Not all of the cattle would be left at the fort near Palomas Hot Springs. If they made it that far, some of the cattle would be herded up river to Fort Craig.

Fatemeh sensed the cowboys felt awkward around her. They were used to going on these kinds of rides without any women along. However, it seemed to help she was "attached" to Ramon. The cowboys were all respectful toward her, but she did catch them ribbing Ramon a few times about having his lady friend along. He not only seemed to shrug it off, but something in the way his lips turned up even when he was being teased, indicated he enjoyed it. She considered that and decided she liked that about him.

About five miles out from Lincoln, the terrain changed. The pines thinned out and the landscape was dominated by low-lying scrub brush. Fatemeh knew that would be the case, but she sighed anyway, wishing they could spend a little more time among the trees.

Finally, after about eighteen miles, they stopped and made camp at the summit of the pass between the Sierra Sacramentos and the Sierra Oscuras. They had been climbing and descending all day. Fatemeh wasn't sure whether they were higher or lower than Lincoln, but from the campsite, she could look down and see the Valley of Fire spread out below them, like a dark red scar cut into the surrounding brown landscape.

After tending to the cattle, the cowboys set up the bedrolls around a campfire. Ramon and the two soldiers lay their bedrolls near the cowboys, then Ramon came back and helped Fatemeh set up a small tent so she could have some privacy. In many ways, she would have liked to have shared in their company, but appreciated having a place to sleep without having prying eyes on her. She and Ramon cooked a simple stew for the men. Although she had been annoyed Ramon told Murphy she was a cook, she was pleased to see he shared some of the burden of his own lie.

After dinner, the cowboy named Frank pulled out a guitar and strummed slowly. Fatemeh sat next to Ramon and held his hand, humming along with the music. The dogs, Duke and Maxmillian, trotted over and lay down by the fire. After a time, Frank stopped playing, and reached down, scratching Duke's ear.

"May I see the guitar?" asked Fatemeh.

"You certainly may." Frank stood and handed the instrument to her.

She strummed softly and after a moment began to sing in Persian. When she was finished, the men around the campfire clapped. "That was beautiful," said Frank.

"What did the words mean?" asked Sergeant Forrest.

"They're words of the Persian teacher Bahá'u'lláh," said Fatemeh. "'The well-being of mankind, its peace and security are unattainable unless and until its unity is firmly established. You are the leaves of one branch and the fruits of one tree.'"

"A beautiful thought," said Corporal Lorenzo. "I hope that will be true one day."

"I believe it's true now," said Fatemeh.

A black cowboy named Ezra shook his head. "It sounds good, but I think it may be wishful thinking."

"It'll never happen, if we don't make a few wishes," said Fatemeh with a soft smile.

Frank took the guitar back and looked up at the stars. "Well, wishful thinking won't get these cattle to Fort McRae. I think we'd better turn in for the night and get some sleep so we can move them along tomorrow."

The cowboys muttered good night. Ramon gave Fatemeh a discreet kiss and said, "I love you."

She stood and went to the tent. Once inside, she crawled into her bedroll and lay there for some time, wishing she could see the stars, and wishing for the warmth and the camaraderie of the fire. She sighed and rolled over, but still could not drop off to sleep. After a time, she thought she heard faint hoots over the occasional low moo from the cattle. Curious, she climbed out of the tent. The men were all sound asleep.

Following the sound, Fatemeh came to a short pine tree that seemed to cling tenaciously to the desert sand. In its branches was a spotted owl. It turned its head nearly 180 degrees, looked her in the eye, and made six urgent hoots. Then the owl hopped toward an outer branch and flew off toward Lincoln.

Fatemeh sighed and walked back to the camp. She knelt down next to Ramon's bedroll and shook him slightly. "Huh… what's going on?"

She hushed him and bent close to his ear. "There are six men riding a short distance behind us. They don't have a camp fire, but they're there."

Ramon sat up. "How do you know that?"

"You were expecting an ambush. Looks like the rustlers have set one up just as we expected." With that, Fatemeh made her way back to the tent.

The next morning, the men gathered their supplies while Ramon and Fatemeh made a simple breakfast of oatmeal and coffee. They were leading the cattle down the trail by eight in the morning. The ride was easier on the second day, since they traveled entirely downhill.

Ramon kept a wary eye out. He shared Fatemeh's warning with the soldiers but kept it from the cowboys. He didn't know how Fatemeh knew there were six men following them. Although he trusted her information, he didn't understand how she learned it. The cowboys might press him for answers he couldn't give.

It was late afternoon when they came upon the first of the jutting red rocks that filled the so-called Valley of Fire. A tank had been set up to catch runoff from the pass and the men tended their horses and let the cattle graze on the scrubby grass that grew in the tank's vicinity. They would wait until the next day to traverse the barren Valley of Fire. They wanted the horses and cattle well fed and watered before they set out.

While Ramon and Fatemeh broke out the cooking supplies, Sergeant Forrest, Corporal Lorenzo and the cowboys scouted the area looking for places where they could take cover in case they were attacked. Satisfied they had a plan, the soldiers and the cowboys settled in by the campfire to await dinner.

"After dinner, do you think you could grace us with another song, Miss Fatemeh?" asked Lorenzo.

Fatemeh grinned and opened her mouth to answer, but was interrupted by the thundering sound of hooves from the trail behind them.

Neither Forrest nor Ramon waited to see who was coming. They hurried the cowboys and Fatemeh toward the rocks. Based on Fatemeh's warning the night before, they knew the rustlers would be coming down the trail and all eyes and guns were focused in that direction.

Just as they came into sight, Forrest announced, "There are six of them."

Ramon was thankful that no one questioned the sergeant. Perhaps they just assumed he had really good eyesight. A moment later, the rustlers shot their guns into the air, spooking the horses. The cattle followed suit, and began tromping their way toward the south, between the mountains and the Valley of Fire.

Taking careful aim at the lead rider, Ramon fired his rifle. He missed the rider and got the horse. The horse crumpled in a shower of dust and pebbles, leaving the rider sprawled on the ground. Three of the other horses reared and the rustlers struggled to get their mounts under control.

One of them took aim and fired. A bullet sent fragments of basalt flying near Ramon's head and he ducked down.

"Ramon!" shouted Fatemeh.

"Quiet, corazón!" Ramon whispered harshly.

The soldiers and cowboys took the opportunity to get a good aim at the rest of the rustlers and fired. They dropped two of the rustlers. Fatemeh hunkered down and covered her eyes. Ramon knew she didn't lack courage, but she hated the waste of life.

The remaining three rustlers, realizing they were out-gunned and out-positioned, turned their mounts and rode back up the trail.

Without the provocation of gunfire, the horses and cattle slowed somewhat, but continued in the direction they'd been going. Frank sent Maximillian and Duke after them. The dogs ran off. Their presence seemed to calm the horses and cattle. The animals slowed to a gentle trot. Frank then sent two of his men to catch the horses and begin rounding up the cattle.

Ramon cautiously peeked out from the rocks, then went over to the fallen rustlers. One man was dead, shot through the chest. One horse lay on the ground, trying to raise itself on a leg shattered by Ramon's bullet. The cowboy named Ezra came up and fired a bullet through the horse's head, putting the animal out of its misery. The horse's rider sat up and made a grab for his pistol, but realized it had fallen from its holster. He leapt for the weapon, but Ramon pointed his rifle and fired between the reaching arm and the gun. "The next shot goes through you, stranger."

The fallen man looked up and Ramon realized he was just a boy in his teens.

"Billy McCarty?" asked Fatemeh. She ran toward the boy.

"Fatemeh," said the boy. "I thought I'd seen you in Lincoln."

"You know him?" asked Ramon.

"He helped Luther Duncan and me rescue you in Socorro." Fatemeh rushed to the boy's side and knelt beside him. "Are you hurt?"

"Only my pride," said the boy called Billy.

Frank pointed his six-gun at Billy. "Why you're Billy the Kid," he said. "I should plug you where you sit, you no good rustler and horse thief."

Fatemeh stood up between Frank and Billy. "You'll do no such thing."

Frank's eyes narrowed. "Why are you protecting that no-account, Miss Fatemeh?"

Ramon stepped close and put his hand on top of Frank's gun. "Put the gun away. She's right. I'd like to question him, find out what's been going on."

Frank shook his head. "I guess you're within your rights, but I want nothing to do with him." He holstered the gun and turned his attention to the cattle that had run off.

"Miss Fatemeh, this man's hurt real bad," Lorenzo called. "Maybe you should come see what you can do for him."

Fatemeh looked from Billy to Ramon, then went over to the other fallen man. Ramon grabbed Billy the Kid by the collar and hoisted him to his feet. "What's all this about, son?"

"Why should I tell you anything?" said Billy with a sneer.

"Because you're a no-good rustler and a horse thief and I just saved your life," answered Ramon.

"My life ain't worth spit if you take me in," said Billy. "I'd rather you shoot me down here than take me in to a judge that'll hang me."

Ramon shook his head. "Fatemeh says you helped save my life. If that's true, I've repaid my debt." He looked around and made sure the cowboys were out of earshot. "However, I'm in no hurry to turn you in to anyone in this county. I don't think the law has much more love for me than they do for you. I'm just here to make sure the cattle get to the fort."

Billy snorted. "You wanna know something? L.G. Murphy is stealing from those soldiers just as surely as my boss is."

Fatemeh stepped up. "Ramon, that other man is hurt very badly. I've helped him as much as I can, but we should get him to a hospital."

Ramon looked back toward Lincoln, then out toward the Valley of Fire. "The nearest doctor would be at Fort McRae." He turned back to Billy. "Son, you're going to ride with us."

"Why should I ride with you?" asked Billy.

Ramon shrugged. "I only see one other option, you walk back to Lincoln. I'm guessing those cowboys will be headed back that way before you can get there on foot."

Billy thought for a moment. "You make a very good point, sir. I'll ride with you."

Riding ahead of the cowboys, Ramon, Fatemeh and Billy made good time getting back to Fort McRae, even carrying a wounded man on a makeshift travois. The cowboys had been worried about encountering more rustlers, so Forrest and Lorenzo stayed behind. On the way to the fort, Billy McCarty explained how L.G. Murphy and his partner James Dolan controlled all the feed prices in Lincoln County. Murphy was able to charge a lower price for his cattle than other ranchers—including Billy's employer, John Tunstall. However, Murphy's prices to the army were still more than they needed to be.

"Murphy sounds like a man possessed of much greed," said Fatemeh.

"That still doesn't make Tunstall's approach right," Ramon said. "There ought to be a better way to compete with Murphy than rustling his cattle. That doesn't just hurt Murphy's business, it hurts the forts and all the people of the territory."

"Well, if you figure out a better way, Mr. Morales, you let me know," grumbled Billy.

Soon after, they arrived at Fort McRae and discovered that the normally quiet installation was alive with activity. Cavalrymen were checking rifles and horses. Cannons and artillery shells were being readied for action.

Ramon, Fatemeh, and Billy took the wounded rustler—a man named Dick Brewer—to the base infirmary. Once their business was finished, they stepped back into the light and saw Major Johnson crossing the compound. Ramon waved him down.

Johnson turned and eyed Ramon hard. "What are you doing back, Morales? Where are Sergeant Forrest and Corporal Lorenzo? Where are my cows?"

Ramon held up his hands. "They're on their way, sir. We stopped the rustlers. One of them was wounded, so we rode ahead."

"He could have died for all I care. They better be back soon or there's going to be hell to pay," said the major.

"If you don't mind, sir," interjected Ramon. "What exactly's going on?"

The major shook his head. "I almost don't believe it myself, but we've received word that the Russians have attacked Sitka, the capital of Alaska. Apparently they brought the troops in using giant balloons."

"Balloons?" asked Fatemeh.

"I guess you could call them airships," said the major. "We're not sure where they're going to strike next, but we're getting ready, in case we're called upon. Now, if you'll excuse me, I have duties to attend to." He took a few steps away, then turned. "That beef had better be here soon! I don't want soldiers fighting on empty stomachs." With that, the major continued on, and disappeared into one of the buildings.

Billy whistled. "Wow! Airships? That's some serious shit!"

"Yeah," said Ramon. "And if those airships turn south and attack here, we're going to need soldiers ready to take action. Do you think you can persuade John Tunstall to stop interfering with the beef shipments?"

Billy shook his head. "I don't know if he'll listen to the likes of me."

Fatemeh put her hand on Billy's arm. "You've seen what's happening here. You've got to try."

Billy took a breath and then let it out with a snort. "Didn't you once call me a bottom feeder? I can't imagine anyone— even my boss—thinking more highly of me than that."

Fatemeh stared into Billy's eyes. "I may have called you that, but it's only true as long as you let it be true. You can make yourself better, Billy McCarty. You can choose to keep being a rustler and keep being a bottom feeder, or you can choose to help these men and be a hero. What will it be?"

Billy swallowed, then forced himself to take his eyes from Fatemeh's gaze. He looked around at all the activity, then nodded. "I'll do my best, Fatemeh. I'll do it for you."

She let go of his arm and Billy took a step, but turned around. "Mr. Morales—I have to warn you. You may have something worse than Russian airships to deal with soon."

Ramon inclined his head. "What would that be, son?"

"Randolph Dalton in Socorro's hired himself a bounty hunter to get you. She's a woman, but she's the best shot I've ever met. Her name's Larissa Crimson."

"If she's such a dangerous bounty hunter, why didn't she strike earlier?"

Billy shook his head. "My best guess is she's waiting for you to be on your own, away from all these soldiers. I suspect she isn't far away."

"Thanks for the warning, Billy," said Fatemeh.

Ramon reached out and shook Billy's hand. "Good luck, son. We'll keep an eye out for this Larissa Crimson."

Billy tipped his hat, then turned and mounted his horse. Ramon put his arm around Fatemeh and watched him ride into the distance, hoping he would be successful and wondering when he would encounter the bounty hunter.

# CHAPTER TWELVE
## THE SHADOW OF THE OWLS

General Alexander Gorloff rode in the gondola of the dirigible *Czar Nicholas*. Standing near the front, he watched as they flew over the islands of Puget Sound on their way to Seattle and Tacoma. The sky was gray, but the clouds were high and the air smooth. He hoped taking over these cities would prove as easy as the flight.

The light resistance they met so far had surprised many aboard the dirigible. However, Gorloff knew few soldiers were stationed in the northwestern most reaches of the United States. The Indians in these areas were, for the most part, friendly and did not cause as much trouble as the Apaches or the Commanches further south. There had been one major confrontation between white settlers and Indians in Seattle, which had been dealt with by a ship dispatched from San Francisco. By the time a ship from San Francisco arrived in Puget Sound, Gorloff believed his airships would already have control of Denver.

Gorloff finally spotted Seattle. It clung to the coastline tenaciously, as though it were afraid it would fall off.

*"That is an apt analogy,"* said Legion from the back of Gorloff's mind.

*What do you mean?* asked the general silently.

*"We have been making a thorough study of human records,"* said Legion. *"Seattle has been subject to occasional flooding. Based on our experiences with similar cities on other worlds, we expect the city will be moved further inland, over the course of the coming decades."*

Gorloff thought that sounded reasonable, but the observation did not affect their immediate plans, so he pushed it to the back of his mind and studied the coastline. He wished he could smoke a cigar. It would help his concentration, but smoking had been banned on the dirigible to avoid causing any sparks that would ignite the hydrogen keeping them aloft.

Captain Makarov stepped up next to Gorloff and studied the coastline. "A lot of short buildings all clustered close together," he observed. "That makes landing in the city difficult. Inland, the terrain gets rather rugged."

"What about landing at the waterfront?" suggested the general.

The captain nodded. "That's what I was thinking. It would work if we can find a pier without any ships docked. It'll be something of a challenge to unload the men, because we won't be moored. We'll just have to hover as close as we can to the pier and let them descend by ladder."

"They've trained for it," said Gorloff. "I trust you'll find the most suitable landing place."

The captain nodded and retrieved a telescope. He studied the coastline in detail. Finally, he pointed. "Two piers side by side. It's as close to perfect for the two ships as we're liable to get."

*Do you concur?* Gorloff asked Legion.

"*Of course,*" replied the strange alien presence. "*The captain has already consulted with us on the matter.*"

Gorloff tended to forget Legion continued to speak to everyone he had come in contact with—not just him. On one hand, the general was thankful for that. It meant the crew and the soldiers took the best possible actions most of the time. On the other hand, Gorloff didn't like everyone aboard having access to the same information he did.

"*Why should this worry you?*" asked Legion. "*Information should be freely available to all.*"

*Information is power,* thought Gorloff. *It is about delineating control.*

"*Why should any one person need power if you all have a common objective?*" Legion asked the question in apparent innocence.

*That would be anarchy.* Gorloff frowned, so disgusted he almost said the words aloud.

Thankfully, Legion remained quiet after that.

Captain Makarov called out commands into a speaking tube and the general watched as they approached the pier and drifted down. Through the window, he could see their sister ship, the *Czarina Marie*, drifting toward the neighboring pier.

The general went to the back of the gondola and climbed a ladder that led up into the massive superstructure of the ship. He walked along a gangway, through a bulkhead door, and continued toward the rear of the crew compartment. There, he came to a staging theater. One hundred men were there, checking their equipment and preparing for the landing. Peter Berestetski—now wearing the uniform of a colonel—saluted the general. Gorloff returned the salute.

"We are coming in near Seattle's waterfront. Are your men ready for the landing?"

"They are," reported Beretetski. "Legion has shown us the location of City Hall based on archived maps. We will head directly there and report when it's under our control."

Again Gorloff felt both grateful and annoyed Legion provided information so freely. "Very good," he said. "I'll watch operations from the gondola." He turned to leave, but paused. "Be careful. It will be a tricky landing."

"Legion has informed us of that, sir," said the colonel.

Gorloff pursed his lips, thrust his hands behind his back and strode back to the gondola at the front of the ship. As he descended the ladder, he heard Captain Makarov giving the orders to open the hatches and lower the ladders. Gorloff stepped toward one of the windows and watched as the troops made their way down the swinging rope ladders onto the pier. The soldiers were all nimble as they climbed down and dropped to the slick wooden pier. Not one of them made a misstep or had to be helped by a colleague. The general felt a swelling of pride at their ability.

*"We provide motor feedback to the men, helping them coordinate their eyes, arms and legs,"* explained Legion. *"Are you still sorry we provide information to all?"*

*I am grateful for this aspect of your help,* Gorloff admitted reluctantly.

The general saw the soldiers march past the waterfront marketplace and up into the streets of the city. As they marched, Legion kept Gorloff informed of their progress. The general had to admit this was an aspect of Legion's involvement he also liked.

In other battles he'd overseen, he had to wait for runners from the front line to give him information. Now he knew the vendors and shop owners on the waterfront were merely confused by the sight of the airships and the men landing on the pier.

Further into the city, some of the people considered whether they should resist the soldiers they saw marching through the streets. However, the soldiers' trim black coats with silver buttons were not entirely unlike the coats worn by U.S. Army soldiers. It would seem many people wondered if the soldiers wandering through the streets were simply Americans.

Half an hour after the soldiers left, Legion informed Gorloff they had taken City Hall. The general nodded satisfaction and then made his way back to the main hatchway. Despite his size and age, he found he descended the ladder just as deftly as the soldiers.

"Have I become more agile, or are you helping me?" asked Gorloff aloud.

*"We are helping you just as we helped the soldiers,"* affirmed Legion.

"I am grateful, old friend."

There was a flutter, like laughter from the back of Gorloff's mind. *"We appreciate the sentiment, but we have known you for the merest instant of our existence. We are glad you consider us friends, but we are hardly long acquaintances in our opinion."*

"Be that as it may," said Gorloff. "I do find myself wondering why you didn't help me up the mooring post in St. Petersburg."

*"Ah, but we did help you then,"* said Legion.

With a grunt, the general strode toward the marketplace. When he judged he was a safe distance from the airship, he retrieved a cigar and lit it, savoring the taste and the smell.

An old Indian woman wearing a headscarf and voluminous skirts rose from behind a table. She shuffled over to Gorloff on unsteady legs and eyed him suspiciously. "What is going on here? What are these great balloons adorned with owls?"

"We are Russians, old woman, and we are claiming what is rightfully ours." He dismissed her with a wave. "Now tend to your wares, we mean you no harm."

She opened her mouth to say more, but was interrupted

when one of the Russian soldiers approached and saluted Gorloff. "Sir, we have taken City Hall. Would you care to accompany us as we raise our flag?"

Gorloff took a puff on the cigar and nodded. He followed the young soldier through the streets of the small northwestern city.

"*The woman is following us,*" reported Legion. "*She is keeping a discreet distance and remaining in the shadows, but we sense her presence.*"

*What matter is she to us?* asked Gorloff silently.

"*She is one of the indigenous people of North America. Some of our components are in her mind, listening to her thoughts. She sees herself as part of the ruling clan of this area.*"

Gorloff shook his head. *That doesn't matter. The Indians no longer control this land. They have already been subjugated by the white man.*

"*White man?*" asked Legion. "*We have come across that designation. An interesting distinction as you are all descended from common ancestors and all of your skin tones are merely controlled by the amount of brown pigmentation in your cells.*"

"Nonsense!" growled Gorloff around the cigar.

The soldier escorting the general looked around. "I beg your pardon, sir?"

"Nothing," said the general. "It's not important."

Finally, the soldier and general arrived at Seattle's city hall. It was an unpretentious building constructed of wood from the surrounding lumber mills. Noting the general's arrival, Colonel Berestetski ordered the lowering of the American flag.

A balding man with a bushy white beard stood nearby. "What's going on here? This is outrageous! Who's in charge?" His words had a distinct German accent.

Gorloff stepped up to the man. Legion informed him the man was Seattle's mayor, Bailey Gatzert. "Mr. Gatzert, I assure you there is no danger. We are bringing the western half of America under the fold of the Russian Empire in order to preserve future generations."

"That is the most ridiculous thing I have ever heard!" cried Gatzert.

Gorloff instructed Legion to enter the mayor's mind. Legion replied he was already there, working his way to a point where he could present images without inspiring the madness he had during his early encounters with humans.

Three of the soldiers carried simple instruments—a violin, a viola, and a set of drums. They brought them out as a soldier removed the American flag and then attached the Russian flag to the line. Colonel Berestetski ordered the raising of the Russian flag. The soldiers with instruments played "God Save the Czar."

Gorloff flicked the ash off his cigar, placed the remainder in his pocket, then saluted as the flag reached the top of the mast. Once the ceremony was complete, Gorloff looked around at Mayor Gatzert. The mayor had relaxed and was nodding. A slight smile appeared on his face. "I see what you mean. We don't dare let the world stay on the destructive course it was on."

The general reached out his hand and Mayor Gatzert shook it. "It is not our intention to interfere with the running of your city. We merely need a place to billet four dozen soldiers."

"That can certainly be arranged," said the mayor.

*"The Native American woman has retreated,"* said Legion in the back of Gorloff's mind.

Gorloff shook his head. *That is of no importance to me.*

Stepping through the gates of Fort McRae, Ramon was pleased to see a dozen cows in a pen. The beef had been delivered as promised. He pressed onward to the base commander's office and knocked on the door. A moment later, he heard a muffled "come in." The former sheriff stepped through the door and saw Major Johnson staring out the room's lone window with his hands behind his back. Ramon cleared his throat.

"Ah, Mr. Morales," said Johnson, looking over his shoulder.

"I see the cowboys made it here with the livestock and have moved on." Ramon removed his hat and stood awkwardly holding it. He wasn't quite sure whether he was invited in to sit or if he should stay where he was. "I think you'll find there won't be any more interference with the cattle drives this direction."

"That last part remains to be seen, but I'm hopeful you're right." The major turned around and faced Ramon. "What can I do for you?"

"You promised to help me clear my name in Socorro." Ramon's grip on the brim of his hat tightened. "I was wondering if we could look into that."

The major sighed and shook his head. "I'm sorry to say that's gone plumb out of my mind." He sat behind his desk and indicated that Ramon should also take a seat. "Fact of the matter is, even in the best of times, what I promised isn't easy. Now with these Russian airships getting closer, I'm not sure what I can do for you. I think we're going to receive marching orders any day now."

"Has something new happened?" Ramon's own problems were forgotten in the wake of the major's concern.

The major nodded. "The Russians have taken Seattle and Tacoma up in Washington Territory without a single shot fired." He held up a telegram. "I don't know whether the people up there were just too scared to act or what. They left a contingent and the airships were last seen moving to the southwest. That means they may become our problem real soon." The major took in a deep breath and let it out slowly. "I'm sorry, Ramon. I'm not sure if there's anything I can do to help you until this crisis has passed."

Ramon closed his eyes. After a moment he opened them, then set his hat on his head. "Is there anything I can do to help you, Major?"

The major's smile was sad. "Let me think on that."

Standing, Ramon tipped his hat. "I'll be at Eduardo's if you need me."

The major stood and shook Ramon's hand. "Thanks and I'll let you know if things change and I can help more."

Ramon went back to the fort's gate and retrieved his horse. Climbing on, he rode to Palomas Hot Springs. At Eduardo's, he led the horse around back to the stables and brushed it down while it munched on fresh hay. Giving the horse a final pat, he left the stable, went in the house, and hung his hat by the door.

Inside, Fatemeh was sweeping the floor. "Any luck at the fort?"

Ramon shook his head and dropped into a chair. "No. The major's been too preoccupied with the Russian airships. Apparently they landed troops in Seattle and Tacoma and they're making their way to the southwest."

Fatemeh leaned the broom against the wall and sat down next to Ramon. "What do you think this means?"

"I don't know." He took Fatemeh's hand. "I figure we have three choices. We can stay here and wait out the crisis or we can go to Estancia and spend some time at my mom's. It's so far away from everything we might be safe there."

"What's the third choice?" asked Fatemeh.

"We could go back to California. I could get my old job back."

She shook her head. "I can't say I'm happy about going back to California. It seems like everywhere we went, we ran into some kind of prejudice. Even Mr. Kelly assumed you weren't honorable just because of the color of your skin."

Ramon sighed. "The problem with staying here is that Dalton or his people are likely to catch up with me sometime soon."

"We've been here at Eduardo's over a week and we haven't seen any sign of this Larissa Crimson person. If she were out there, she would have struck by now."

"You think Billy's warning was exaggerated?" Ramon's eyebrows came together.

"I don't know what to think." She moved her chair closer. "All I know is that events seem to be moving out of our control."

Ramon found himself looking into Fatemeh's irresistible green eyes. Just as he leaned in to kiss her, the door opened. Eduardo stood there, holding a newspaper.

"Stagecoach just came through. I picked up a copy of the *Mesilla Valley News*. Your friend Luther Duncan has a story about those Russian airships." Eduardo laid the paper on the table.

Fatemeh picked it up and read the article on the front page. "It says here, Chief Seattle's daughter Angeline saw the whole thing. The Russians marched right up to City Hall without firing a shot and raised their flag. Mayor Gatzert protested at first, but then his countenance suddenly became calm and he welcomed the invaders."

Ramon sat back and folded his arms. "That makes no sense. Where were the police? Aren't there any soldiers up in Washington Territory?"

"There aren't as many forts up there as there are down here," said Eduardo. "I don't know about the police."

Ramon took off his glasses and rubbed the bridge of his nose. "I think I need some fresh air. I'm going for a walk."

"Do you want me to come with you?" asked Fatemeh.

"No, I'll just be a few minutes." Ramon put on his glasses, stood, then retrieved his hat from beside the door and stepped outside. He looked around at the colorful rocks near Eduardo's home and the sparse buildings. A few high, thin clouds were spread across the deep, blue sky like a gauzy shroud. He took a deep breath. He didn't want to leave New Mexico again if he could help it. His only fear about going to Estancia was concern he would get there and find his mother really didn't like Fatemeh after all. He wasn't sure what he would do then. Would Fatemeh agree to marry him without her approval? Did that even matter knowing Fatemeh's own parents wouldn't give their approval?

Ramon shook his head and stepped off the porch. As Fatemeh said, events seemed outside their control and he was having a hard time knowing the right thing to do.

Just as he turned, he heard someone cock a six-gun's hammer. He looked up and found himself facing a woman with a flat-topped coachman's hat pointing a gun at his chest.

"Come with me real peaceable like."

"Larissa Crimson, I presume," said Ramon.

She tipped her hat with her free hand.

Fatemeh stood so she could finish the sweeping. As she grabbed the broom, she glanced out the window. A woman pointed a gun at Ramon. She spoke a few words to him, then led him away. Silently, Fatemeh summoned Eduardo to the window.

"Do you suppose it could be that bounty hunter?" he whispered.

"Who else could it be?"

"What can we do? If we go out there, she's liable to shoot him."

"We need help." She looked out the window again. Ramon and the woman had disappeared from view. Grinding her teeth, Fatemeh turned and led the way through the house to the back. They retrieved a pair of horses from the stable and rode to the front of the house. Just as they reached the road, they saw the woman ride by on the seat of a modified English hansom cab. She tipped her hat and snapped the reins. The woman's cab shot off in a cloud of dust.

"Ramon must be in that buggy," said Eduardo. "Do we go after her?"

"What would we do if we caught her? Neither of us is armed." She shook her head. "There's only one thing we can do. We need to go to Fort McRae and ask for Major Johnson's help." Fatemeh snapped her own reins and took the most direct overland route to the fort. Eduardo followed close behind.

When they arrived at the fort half an hour later, they saw men in the courtyard forming up in ranks. A guard standing beside the open gate challenged them. "Who goes there?"

Eduardo and Fatemeh drew up their reins and brought the horses to a stop. "I'm Fatemeh Karimi. I have urgent business with Major Johnson."

"I'm under strict orders to let no one into the fort, ma'am." The guard stood a little straighter, but kept his rifle in front of his chest. "Sorry."

Eduardo leaned over, as though trying to get a better look at the activity in the courtyard. "What's going on?"

"I'm afraid I can't say, sir."

Just then, Fatemeh caught sight of the major. Undaunted by the guard's gun, she snapped the reins on her horse and darted forward. "Major Johnson!" she called.

"Ma'am, halt!" called the guard from the gate.

The major held up his hand. "Miss Karimi, I have no time for a social call. I've just received orders. We're marching to Denver."

"Right now?" Fatemeh climbed down from the horse and looked into Johnson's eyes. "Major, Ramon has just been captured by a bounty hunter. You told him you'd keep him safe. What can you do about it?"

The major looked to the ground and shook his head. "Nothing, I'm afraid. It's too bad. Mr. Morales is a good man. I could really use him..." The major turned and took two steps away, but paused. Fatemeh thought he must be recalling where he was going before she had interrupted him.

Spitting a word in Persian that would have made her Mohammedan parents blush, Fatemeh put her foot in the horse's stirrup.

Major Johnson turned around. "Bounty hunter, you say?"

Fatemeh looked over the horse's saddle at the major and nodded.

Larissa Crimson was making good time on her way back to Socorro. She was pleased with the prospect of the reward she would receive for Ramon Morales, and also content he hadn't put up a fight. Of course, she got the drop on him while he was unarmed. The problem was, the more she learned about Morales, the more she began to question whether she was actually doing a just service by taking him to Randolph Dalton.

According to Dalton, Ramon ran away from his duties as Sheriff of Socorro. That certainly seemed worthy of bringing a man in for justice. However, Billy McCarty told her Morales left the job because Dalton and his people tried to kill Morales's girlfriend—the Persian woman he traveled with. The only thing Dalton said about the Persian woman was that she was a troublemaker who caused problems at one of the mines he owned. Larissa knew Billy McCarty was not the most trustworthy person around, but according to him, Dalton hired men to beat Morales to death and Morales's girlfriend helped Billy in a time of need.

Larissa sighed. She really wasn't sure what to believe. The truth seemed complicated and she'd be glad to get her money from Dalton and be done with the whole affair.

She decided to plan for nightfall. There was no way she could drive her coach all the way from Palomas Hot Springs to Socorro in one day. Where could she make camp? The coach was modified to be enclosed. Morales was locked inside, and she'd provided a chamber pot, some water and a good supply of food. He'd be fine. She'd sleep just a short time to make his confinement as brief as possible.

Larissa reached the bottom of a small canyon called La Cañada Alamosa. In flood times, it fed runoff from the nearby mountains into the Rio Grande. Fortunately it was dry and she crossed with no trouble, but from the swearing she heard in the coach, she guessed Morales had been jostled out of his seat. As she started up the other side of the canyon, a dozen horses crossed over the ridgeline ahead.

Larissa soon found herself surrounded by army soldiers. Their leader wore the oak leaves of a major on his collar. "Are you the bounty hunter called Larissa Crimson?" he asked.

"What if I am?" she retorted.

"If you are, I'm willing to pay the bounty on the man you've taken into custody."

Larissa thought about that. On one hand, it would save her a hard two-day journey. On the other, she really didn't like developing the reputation as the kind of bounty hunter who didn't complete a job. "I'm supposed to take him to the sheriff in Socorro."

"He's also wanted by the United States Army," said the major. "There's a wartime emergency in process and my jurisdiction trumps local authorities."

Larissa Crimson inclined her head. She hadn't heard anything about a wartime emergency and didn't believe the army ever took precedence over local jurisdiction where a civilian was concerned. Even so, she still harbored doubts about whether Morales really was justified in leaving his job or not. The major was conveniently providing her with a reasonable excuse to turn her prisoner over right then rather than take him all the way to Socorro.

"I've been promised a bounty of one-thousand dollars," said Larissa. "Can you match that?"

The major's mouth dropped open. A moment later, he

swallowed and his stone-faced demeanor returned. "I can pay you twelve-hundred dollars for your prisoner," he said. "But you'll have to bring him back to the fort and I'll pay you there."

Larissa Crimson nodded. "You've just persuaded me to turn my prisoner over to you."

"Very good," said the major. "Let's get riding."

He signaled for his men to form up while Larissa turned her wagon around. There was more swearing as they went back across the wash and then finally Morales called from inside, "What the hell's going on out there?"

Larissa opened a small hatch in the roof. "You found someone to pay your bounty. We're on our way to Fort McRae."

Fatemeh was pacing in front of Major Johnson's office when she saw the major and his men ride through the gate followed by the bounty hunter and her hansom cab. The men who had been gathered for their march had been dismissed to get a little rest, but their gear still littered the ground. She started to walk toward the major and the coach, but Eduardo stood up from the chair he occupied on the major's porch and put his hand on Fatemeh's shoulder. "Let them take care of whatever business they're doing."

One of the major's men dismounted and ran to the paymaster's office. He arrived a short time later and handed a roll of bills to the bounty hunter. She counted the bills carefully, then climbed down from the seat and unlocked the coach's door. Ramon, looking sweaty and disheveled, clambered out of the coach.

Fatemeh couldn't restrain herself any longer. She ran to Ramon and grabbed him in a tight embrace.

The bounty hunter flashed a slight grin as she closed the coach's door. She climbed back on the hansom cab's seat and rode away.

Major Johnson climbed down from his horse and approached Ramon and Fatemeh. Ramon held out his hand, but the major kept his arms behind his back. "Mr. Morales, I'm grateful you came to New Mexico at some personal peril to help us deal with our difficult supply situation. However, I have now spent over a year's salary on you with no proof we will receive further shipments. Furthermore, through no fault of your own admittedly, that proof is not likely to come for some time."

Ramon lowered his hand. "I am grateful for your help and I appreciate all the money you've spent, but I came back because you promised you would help clear my name. That hasn't happened yet."

The major cleared his throat. "I know and I'm afraid circumstances will prevent it for a time. Nevertheless, it occurs to me I could use your advice in the difficult times we face. It also occurs to me I'd have an easier time clearing your name if you had a service record. Can I persuade you to join my regiment, at least for the duration of the current crisis?"

Fatemeh stepped between the two men. "Ramon, you don't have to do this."

The major shook his head. "No, you don't have to do this, but you won't have my protection if you stay and there are liable to be other bounty hunters."

Ramon nodded, but again Fatemeh was the one who spoke up. "Major, you didn't prevent Ramon from being taken by the bounty hunter."

The major's jaw tightened as though his patience was taxed nearly to the limit. "Ma'am, you two elected to stay at Palomas Hot Springs. That limited what I could do. Also, I just spent a very large sum of money keeping Mr. Morales out of the hands of the authorities in Socorro, thus putting my own career on the line. I will not stand here and be accused of asking for something while doing nothing in return."

Fatemeh opened her mouth to speak, but Ramon put his hand on her elbow. "He's right, corazón. There's no good answer here. Going with the major, maybe I can help. My father served the United States when New Mexico became a territory. Now it's my turn." He looked at the major. "Sign me up."

This time Major Johnson held out his hand and Ramon shook it. He inclined his head toward the quartermaster's office. "Go check out a uniform and a weapon, Private Morales, then come out here and form up with the rest of the men. We'll be marching within the hour."

Ramon stood straight and saluted. The major returned the salute, then spun on his heel and walked away with a captain who hovered nearby. Ramon turned and pulled Fatemeh into his arms.

"I don't want you to go," she said into his shoulder.

"I don't really want to go either, but it feels like the right thing to do. I'll be back as soon as I can." He turned his head and looked into her eyes. They kissed deeply for a time, then pulled apart.

"Giant airships with the strength to take over a town like Seattle," mused Fatemeh. "Do you really think the Army has the power to combat something like that?"

"I really don't know, but if not the army, then who?"

A soldier blew on a bugle and men emerged from the fort's barracks. Ramon swallowed and gave Fatemeh another quick kiss. "I'd better get going."

Fatemeh watched Ramon stride toward the quartermaster's office. She sensed someone standing nearby. Looking over her shoulder, she saw Eduardo. He stepped close and put his arm around Fatemeh's shoulder. "He'll be back."

Fatemeh sighed and nodded. "I hope you're right."

Together, they went back to their horses, climbed on, and rode through the gates of Fort McRae.

As they rode, Fatemeh thought of soldiers and how vulnerable they would be to airships flying over them. The word airship evoked images of a wallowing behemoth floating among the clouds, able to destroy anything below it at will. It seemed to her, the only way to tackle such a problem would be if soldiers could fly through the air, especially if they could maneuver faster and better than the lumbering airships she pictured. Fatemeh remembered Professor Maravilla and his mechanical owl. *What if there were several owls and what if there were people to fly them?*

As Fatemeh remembered the owl, she looked up and saw Larissa Crimson and her hansom cab in the road ahead. Several thoughts went through Fatemeh's mind. After a moment, she looked over at Eduardo. "I'd like to talk to her." With that, Fatemeh snapped her reins and the horse darted forward.

"Fatemeh!" called Eduardo from behind her.

Fatemeh soon found herself alongside Larissa Crimson. The bounty hunter looked over and tipped her hat. "You're Ramon Morales's girlfriend, aren't you?"

"I am," said Fatemeh tightly. "Why did you do it? Why did you hunt down Ramon and sell him to the highest bidder?"

Larissa inclined her head and then looked forward. "I'm a bounty hunter because I believe in justice."

"Then why not apply for a job as a peace officer?" asked Fatemeh.

Larissa laughed loud and long. Finally, wiping a tear from her eye she looked over at Fatemeh. "You're serious, aren't you?" The bounty hunter shook her head. "No one hires a woman to be a peace officer."

"Why do they hire you to be a bounty hunter, then?"

"If I bring in my quarry, no one has a choice but to pay me."

Fatemeh sighed. Eduardo finally caught up. He looked at the two women, but remained silent. Finally, Fatemeh looked at Larissa again. "Have you heard about the airships that invaded Seattle?"

Larissa nodded. "The soldiers told me a little as we rode to the fort. Sounds like bad business."

Fatemeh looked from Larissa to Eduardo. "I don't think the army stands a chance against them, no matter how many men they send against these things."

"But what else can be done?" asked Eduardo.

"I have an idea, but I'm going to need help. I need to round up some men and some equipment, then I need to get to the Grand Canyon. We need to work fast so our force can meet up with those airships before it's too late."

Eduardo shook his head. "I don't know..."

"Is there anything in it for me?" asked Larissa.

"I'm looking to see justice done, Miss Crimson," said Fatemeh. "And, you'll get a glimpse of the future. In my mind, it's a future where you can do whatever job you're good at, whether you're a man or a woman and no matter the color of your skin."

Larissa Crimson pursed her lips and nodded. "I like the sound of that. Count me in."

Fatemeh looked over at Eduardo. He shook his head. "I think you're both loco, but I'll do what I can to help my cousin. You can count me in as well."

They came up over the rise and saw Palomas Hot Springs below them. "Very good," said Fatemeh. "Then it's time to make some plans."

# CHAPTER THIRTEEN
## PIRATES, GUNSLINGERS, AND CLOCKWORK OWLS

The next morning, Fatemeh, Eduardo, and Larissa readied their horses for the journey northward to Albuquerque. Once there, they would catch the train to Flagstaff. Larissa stored her hansom cab in Eduardo and Alicia's stable. It would cost too much to store it in Albuquerque or take it to Flagstaff with them.

Once Fatemeh was satisfied her horse, Husniyah, was ready to go, she stepped into the kitchen. There, she found Alicia preparing food for the journey. "How are you doing?" asked Fatemeh.

Alicia's smile was thin—not quite forced, but not altogether happy, either. "I'm well. Are you nearly ready to go?" She collected some beef jerky from a tin, placed it in a cloth satchel, and set it with the rest of the food.

"We are." Fatemeh stepped close to Alicia. "Do you wish you were going with us?"

Alicia sighed and shook her head. Her smile became more genuine. "No, not really. I'm not a fighter and someone needs to tend to the animals."

"You're worried about Eduardo, though, aren't you?"

Alicia's smile faded and she nodded. "I'm worried about all of you. Isn't it enough the army must fight this war against these airships? Why must you, Ramon, and Eduardo go as well? Eduardo's no more a fighter than I am."

"Ramon felt he had no better choice. Me?" Fatemeh shrugged. "I'm a healer. This invasion feels wrong, like the invasion of a disease in the body. I'm going to help Ramon, but I'm also going to heal. If I'm right, maybe I can save more lives than are lost."

"What about Eduardo?"

"You'll have to ask him," said Fatemeh.

Eduardo stuck his head through the door. "We'd better get moving soon if we want to make the most of the day."

Fatemeh gathered up an armload of the supplies and walked past Eduardo. "I think your wife would like a few minutes before we go."

Eduardo blinked twice, then went into the kitchen, closing the door behind him. Fatemeh handed some of the food up to Larissa and packed the rest into her own saddlebags.

"It just occurred to me," said Fatemeh, climbing onto Husniyah, "your name is Crimson and yet I've never seen you wear any red."

Larissa climbed onto her horse. "I'm a bounty hunter. That would be like wearing a target. I'll stick to dark colors, thank you very much." She looked around. "Where's Eduardo?"

"He'll be out in a moment."

A few minutes later, Eduardo and Alicia came out of the house. Both wore somber expressions. They packed the rest of the food into Eduardo's saddlebags, then Eduardo turned and brought Alicia into a tight embrace. "We'll be back. I promise," he said.

"You better be," she said. "I love you, Eduardo Morales. Don't ever forget that."

With a smile, he climbed onto his horse. Fatemeh snapped her reins and the three horses moved northward together. Eduardo turned around, holding his hand up until the homestead was out of sight.

Half an hour into their journey they came to Fort McRae. The fort seemed strangely silent with the majority of the soldiers gone. Fatemeh rode up to the guard on duty. "Could we still send a telegram from here?"

The guard tipped his hat. "By all means."

Fatemeh breathed a sigh of relief. She didn't want to stop in Socorro if they didn't have to. If they waited until they reached Albuquerque, the telegrams might not reach the people she hoped to contact in time for them to help.

The three rode through the gate. The fort wasn't completely deserted. The general store was still open and there were still Indians out in front, displaying their wares. A few older soldiers milled about the grounds, attending to their duties.

Fatemeh hitched her horse at the rail in front of the general store. Stepping in, she approached the man at the counter. "I would like to send three telegrams. The first is to Mr. Luther Duncan in Mesilla. The second is to Mr. Onofre Cisneros in Ensenada, Mexico."

"An international telegram will cost extra, ma'am," said the man at the counter.

Fatemeh nodded. "I'm aware of that and I'm prepared to pay."

"Very good," said the man. "What about the third?"

Fatemeh took a deep breath, then let it out slowly. "To be honest, I'm not sure the best way to reach him. Perhaps you can advise me."

Ramon found the ride northward with Major Johnson's cavalry hot, dusty and slow. One hundred horses rode at a nice even pace behind the major. Ramon wondered if the major would still be in front once the fighting started, or if he was only there to avoid being choked by the dust.

As they rode, Ramon's new woolen, blue jacket and trousers began to itch. He longed for his comfortable gingham shirt and denim britches. He also longed for more water than he had in his canteen. He was relieved when they reached Fort Craig and he realized from the murmurings of the soldiers around him they were going to stop for the night.

Once they reached the fort, sergeants barked orders about where to set up tents and what to do for dinner. Ramon watched as the soldiers around him tended their horses and then began setting up campsites. Ramon looked around, confused, not really sure where he should be. A sergeant whose name he didn't know rode up. "Soldier, get with your squad and help them set up camp!"

"My squad?" Ramon looked hurriedly around. After a moment, he caught sight of Sergeant Forrest and Corporal Lorenzo. "I see them, now." He dismounted and led his horse over to the two familiar men.

Sergeant Forrest's eyebrows came together as Ramon approached. "I'd heard the major went out and rescued someone from a bounty hunter. Would that be you?"

Ramon felt his cheeks grow hot, but nodded. "That would. I seem to find myself without a...what's it called? Without a squad."

Corporal Lorenzo clapped Ramon on the shoulder. "We'd be happy to have you join us." The corporal showed Ramon where to take his horse and where to lay out his bed roll.

Ramon took care of the horse. When he returned, Sergeant Forrest was gone. "Where's the sergeant?" he asked.

Lorenzo nodded toward a nearby group of men. "He's checking on the other squad under his command. Two squads make a section and the sergeant is the section commander."

Ramon nodded, wondering if he would get the hang of all the military terminology. Once his bedroll was laid out, the corporal gathered the men together and they went inside the fort for food. After eating, Ramon returned to the campsite with his squad and fell into a deep sleep.

He woke early, roused by a bugle call. They ate a quick breakfast, accompanied by tepid coffee, then gathered their gear and resumed the journey northward. The men from Fort McRae were joined by two hundred more mounted soldiers under the command of a Lieutenant Colonel named Smith.

As they resumed the northward ride, Ramon occasionally caught sight of riders passing near the marching troops. He amused himself trying to decide where they were going or what they were doing. At one point on the third day out, Ramon saw three riders, maybe half a mile distant. He couldn't make out faces from that distance, but the group appeared to be two women and one man. One of the women seemed to be wearing a flat-topped hat like the one the bounty hunter Larissa Crimson wore. If it was her, he wondered where her hansom cab had gone and who the others were. Could she be on his trail again? Despite his concern, he never saw those particular riders after the one brief sighting and dismissed the notion it was Crimson or anyone else he knew.

Five days after leaving Palomas Hot Springs, Fatemeh, Eduardo and Larissa found themselves on the rail platform at Flagstaff. While Eduardo and Larissa went to retrieve the horses, Fatemeh stopped into the station's telegraph office.

An elderly gentleman with a wooden leg manned the counter. She introduced herself and asked if there were any telegrams for her.

"Fatemeh Karimi?" He squinted at her, as though trying to read her face through cloudy vision.

"Yes, I sent some telegrams from Fort McRae a few days ago and asked that the replies be sent here."

After a moment, the gentleman nodded. "Yes, I think I did get a couple of telegrams for you, Miss Karimi. Let me go check." He hobbled away with a step-clunk, the wooden leg resounding against the planks of the floor. Fatemeh wondered how he lost his leg. He seemed too old to be a Civil War veteran, but after a moment, Fatemeh realized he could have fought in the Mexican War a few years before that.

The man returned carrying two slips of paper and handed them to Fatemeh.

She read the first: WILL SET OUT FOR THE GRAND CANYON AT ONCE STOP ONOFRE CISNEROS.

The second was also concise and to the point: WILL DO WHAT I CAN STOP WILL CHECK TELEGRAPH DAILY STOP LUTHER DUNCAN.

"There were only two telegrams?" asked Fatemeh.

"Those are the only two I received," said the man. "I'd remember receiving more for a woman with a strange name like yours."

Fatemeh frowned, but put the two slips of paper in her satchel and left to meet with Eduardo and Larissa. When she arrived, they already had their horses saddled and were discussing the prospects of a meal before setting out for the canyon. Although it was early in the day and Fatemeh was anxious to be on her way to find Professor Maravilla, the rumbling of her stomach encouraged her to agree with her traveling companions.

She hoisted her saddle onto Husniyah's back and securely fastened the straps, then she put on the bridle. Giving the horse a pat on the neck, she climbed on and they sought out a place for breakfast.

Late that afternoon, Fatemeh, Larissa and Eduardo rode into view of the Grand Canyon. It was spring and the sun was still fairly high in the sky. Both Eduardo and Larissa were as captivated by the sight of the canyon as Ramon and Fatemeh had been. Fatemeh took her time and checked the landmarks against her memory. Finally, she pointed. "I think we'll find Professor Maravilla that way."

The three rode along the rim of the canyon for two more miles until Fatemeh recognized the place where the professor had set up his makeshift home and workshop. She climbed off the horse and found the trail that led down to the cave. The mechanical owl was gone, but Fatemeh was relieved to see the professor's books and supplies still there. It didn't appear he was gone for good.

Fatemeh left the professor's home and began her ascent to the rim. Near the top, she heard Larissa exclaim, "What in the world is that?"

Turning around, Fatemeh saw the professor bringing his owl in for a landing. He reached the canyon's rim about the same time she did. The owl extended its claws and slid to a stop near the travelers. The professor clambered out of the seat and lifted his goggles to the top of his head. He smiled broadly when he saw Fatemeh.

"How good to see you again," he said. Then he looked around at the others. "But where is Ramon?"

Fatemeh stepped up to the professor and took his hands. She introduced Eduardo and Larissa. "Have you heard about the airships from Russia?"

Professor Maravilla smiled. "I don't get much news way out here. Tell me more."

Fatemeh told him about the invasions of Sitka and Seattle and how the airships seemed to be traveling toward the southeast. She told him about the army's plan to find the airships and engage them in battle.

Professor Maravilla shook his head. "Ground troops would be virtually defenseless against airships such as you describe."

"That's why I would like you to build more of your owls to

help us fight these things," said Fatemeh.

Professor Maravilla sighed. "If I had supplies, help...then maybe..."

Fatemeh retrieved the two slips of paper from her pouch. "Luther Duncan is standing by in Mesilla. He can help us get supplies. We're here and ready to help you build the owls."

The professor nodded and pursed his lips. "We'd still need someone to fly the owls."

Fatemeh held up the other slip of paper. "That's where the pirates come in."

General Alexander Gorloff woke with a start as he dropped onto the wooden planking of his cabin's floor. He tried to get his bearings in the darkened room. After a moment, he found the wall and started to bring himself to his feet when the airship shuddered and his legs threatened to drop him to the floor again.

"What the devil is going on?" he asked aloud.

"*The* Czar Nicholas *is encountering turbulence,*" came Legion's familiar voice from the back of the general's mind.

"Say that in plain Russian!"

"*It is extremely windy outside,*" said Legion. "*The ship is being knocked about.*"

"How could that happen?" Instinctively, Gorloff fumbled around his nightstand for a striker before remembering that the ship used lights powered by electricity. They were based on a design pioneered by a German chemist named Herman Sprengel and adapted for the airships by Mendeleev with Legion's help. The general reached over and rotated the switch, turning on the lamp. "Can't you predict the weather? You seem to know about everything else."

"*Although the weather patterns of your world follow certain trends, even we cannot predict specific weather phenomena with complete accuracy.*"

Another shudder went through the ship and suddenly Gorloff's stomach fluttered. He felt as though he was falling. Casting about the room, he found his shoes and slipped them on. In his nightshirt, he ran out of the cabin and shot forward, almost tumbling downward toward the ladder that descended into the gondola. There he found Captain Makarov gesturing and shouting orders. The captain had thrown his jacket over his nightshirt, but otherwise looked as though he had been as rudely awakened as the general.

Looking out the window, the general could see the moonlit ground rising rapidly toward the airship. The captain opened the speaking tube and blew into it, sounding the whistle at the other end. "Stabilizer cables—heave on my mark." He waited a moment then called, "Heave!"

The ship shuddered and finally righted. The general looked out the window. They were no longer going nose-first into the ground, but they still descended rapidly.

The captain faced the general. "Our rudder is out. The stabilizer cables are also broken, but we have partial control. We can land safely, but we're going to need to make repairs."

"How long will that take?" asked the general.

"If we can get some men to a town for parts, I think we could be underway in two or three weeks," said the captain.

"Weeks?" roared Gorloff. "Can we afford such a delay?"

*"The delay is minimal. Any troops the United States will be sending will take much longer to reach Denver than we will need for repairs,"* said Legion. *"Perhaps they will send troops past Denver to our present location. That would only work in your favor."*

"What about cities?" asked Makarov, apparently hearing Legion's words as well. "Is there a city nearby?"

*"We are over Montana territory,"* said Legion. *"Based on our calculations, we should be approaching the town of Butte."*

"Very good," said Makarov. "Give me course and bearing and we'll get as close as we can."

Gorloff snorted, but realized there was nothing he could do about the situation. He nodded to the captain, then made his way back to his cabin so he could get dressed before they landed.

As the morning dawned, Fatemeh, Eduardo and Larissa held steaming mugs of coffee while Professor Maravilla listed out the materials he needed for the owls' construction including cloth for the wings and the tiny brass gears for the couplings. "The owl's framework is made of thin steel. It's pounded out to be as lightweight and strong as possible. I worked with a blacksmith in Flagstaff to get it just right."

"Do you think he could make more quickly?" asked Fatemeh.

"If he has the raw materials." Maravilla nodded.

Fatemeh took a sip of her coffee. "All right, then. We need to pool our money and see how much we have. Then I think we need to make a trip to Flagstaff and get in our orders for materials. I'll wire Luther Duncan in Mesilla and he can get us the things we can't find locally."

Larissa set down her coffee mug and leaned forward. "Pool our money? You didn't say anything about this being a common expense when we started out. I'm happy to help out where I can, but I need my money to live on."

"And if you don't help with expenses, there's a good chance you'll be spending that money in a new Russian America," said Eduardo. He took a sip of coffee, then set the cup aside. "Look, I was very young when this part of Mexico was invaded by the United States. My family adapted, but I don't want to see us invaded again. My uncle fought for the Union in the Civil War because he didn't want the Confederates taking over and allowing slavery here." He shook his head. "The Russians have an emperor. Do you think life will be better with them in charge?"

Larissa took a deep breath, then let it out slowly. "No, I don't want the Russians to take over, but I don't want to become penniless either. Why can't others share the expense?"

Fatemeh reached over and put her hand on Larissa's shoulder. "We'll find a way to pay you back. In the meantime, the money we have among us is all we've got. Since the blacksmith is local, maybe he can donate some time or supplies. Maybe it won't cost much, but we need to find out how much we have available."

Larissa swallowed hard, then nodded. "All right, I'm in. But I'll hold you to that part about finding a way to pay me back."

"God will light the way," said Fatemeh.

The Russians safely landed the *Czar Nicholas* and the *Czarina Marie* about two miles outside of Butte, Montana. The *Czarina Marie* also suffered damage from the windstorm, although not as severe as the *Czar Nicholas*. The Russian troops marched into Butte and once again the Russian flag was raised over an American town. They learned where they could obtain the materials they would need for repairs.

"*There are also many skilled workmen here in Butte,*" suggested Legion to General Gorloff. "*They could help you speed up the repairs and you could be on your way much faster.*"

Gorloff stood near a tree, away from the dirigibles, smoking a cigar. He shook his head. "No, I don't think so. Although I would like to get underway as soon as possible, there is a danger in sharing too many details about our craft with Americans. I would like that knowledge to stay in Russian hands."

"*We are distributed in the minds of many Americans as well as the Russians. To prevent the worldwide catastrophe you saw, you must also learn to work with the Americans, not merely dominate them.*"

"We *are* working with them," countered Gorloff. "Colonel Berestetski is an American, but I know we can trust him because you have assured me of that and I've seen examples of his goodwill toward us. I will need more time to trust the others."

"*We can assure you, all of the Americans whose minds we occupy are just as interested in averting world catastrophe as you are,*" said Legion. "*They are willing to go along with you because they believe you will work together. They are not interested in being dominated by you.*"

Gorloff lifted the cigar to his lips and took a long draw. He watched the smoke drift away. "Much as I enjoy these chats with you, there are times I would like my mind quiet. I wish you could leave for a time and allow me to be alone with my thoughts."

"*We can become quiescent at any point and leave you to your thoughts. All you need to do is ask.*"

"Would you come back when I needed you?"

*"We would."*

"Let me alone for ten minutes. I would like some time to myself." For the first time in several months, the general's mind was completely quiet. He smiled and smoked his cigar in peace.

By the end of the first week, supplies had started arriving at the Grand Canyon every other day. Larissa had purchased a wagon in Flagstaff. Every morning she was at the canyon, she would wake up at dawn, have breakfast, then go out and hitch two horses to the wagon. She drove the wagon into town and checked in with the blacksmith, Leroy Foster. He usually had a few more pieces of steel to load into the wagon. From there, she would drive the wagon over to the train station and see if there were any shipments. Often there was a bolt of cloth or a small box.

Once the rounds were complete, she secured the wagon as best she could, then found a hotel to spend the night. After breakfast the next morning, she retrieved the wagon, drove it back to the canyon, and unloaded the goods.

Professor Maravilla spent the balance of his evenings showing her how the clockwork owls worked. At first, she was dubious of the machines, but after watching the professor take several sunset flights around the canyon and learning more about how the machines worked, she began to long for the opportunity to fly an owl herself.

By the end of the second week, the professor had three complete owls and materials to build the remaining eight. On that day, the professor had Larissa sit in one of the owls. He had her show him everything she had learned in the evening sessions.

"I think you're ready for a test flight," he said.

"Really?" asked Larissa, wide-eyed. "Now?"

"You will need to practice with the owls if you want to fly them against these airships. There's no better time than the present."

"Okay," she said dubiously. She activated the striker on the steam engine's small oil burner. It only held enough fuel for an hour's flight—that would be their biggest challenge using the owls in combat. They had to get the owls to the battle and they could only fight for a short time.

Once the steam engine was running, she wound the owl's clockworks. She pulled goggles down over her eyes, then pushed the control rod in front of her forward and released a small lever near the base of her seat. The owl hopped on spring-loaded feet toward the canyon's edge. When Larissa had seen Professor Maravilla make flights, she found the action comical. Now she felt like her teeth were going to rattle out of her head. The mechanical owl made one more hop and suddenly, there was no ground under its feet and her hat was no longer on her head.

Larissa Crimson had trained herself to be a tough bounty hunter. She had faced down men with cold iron who intended to kill her rather than go to jail. She held her own in gunfights, pinned down and outnumbered. She always walked away to tell the tale. In those situations, she had learned to take her time, find her opponents' weaknesses and control them. Usually, the fact she was a woman was enough to slow her opponents and give her an advantage.

Larissa Crimson screamed like a little girl when she faced the bottom of the canyon and felt the wind whipping through her hair. The ground was coming up fast. There was no weakness she could exploit. The cold hard earth did not care she was a woman. Her mind flailed around looking for a way to control the situation.

After a moment, her mind focused on the levers in front of her. She did have control. She took a deep breath and pulled back on the control stick. The mechanical owl flapped its wings and straightened itself out. Then she saw the far edge of the canyon rapidly approaching. She gritted her teeth and moved the control rod to the right. The owl swooped over on its side and turned. She straightened out the control rod and looked around. She was flying over the Grand Canyon.

The bounty hunter laughed. She laughed at the ecstasy of flight and with relief she had not plummeted to her death. She looked around at the beauty that surrounded her on all sides and sighed. The reds, yellows, grays and greens of the canyon were all around her. Rocks jutted upward and outward in seemingly endless variety. The professor had said all this had been carved by a river at the bottom. How many years had that taken? Her mind reeled at the thought.

She pulled back on the control rod and lifted the owl slightly, then turned around and went back the direction she had come. Fatemeh and Eduardo had already made flights in Professor Maravilla's owls. Even so, she realized she saw the canyon from a perspective only three other people before her had seen. She noticed details of light and shadow she missed before. As she flew, she felt a few bumps of turbulent air. She remembered her lessons and glided smoothly through them. Not only was she in control of the owl, she was in control of the air and the very canyon itself—a canyon carved over centuries by a mighty river. She whooped aloud, realizing no dream would ever be out of her reach again.

Larissa had spent a lot of money helping to get materials for the owls and her backside was sore from hours in the wagon, going back and forth to Flagstaff, but suddenly all the effort was worth it. Even if this was the only time she ever got to fly, she was delighted she had taken Fatemeh Karimi up on this crazy scheme.

As Larissa considered that, an unfamiliar lump formed in the back of her throat. She realized she was sad these owls were being built for war. She pulled back the lever some more and the owl flapped its wings. More puffs of steam came from its tail. She was now high over the countryside. From this height, she could see no boundaries, just glorious forested land cut through by an even more splendid canyon. This was a sight that should be available to all. She vowed to finish the fight quickly. If Professor Maravilla was willing, she would stay with him and help him in his research. It suddenly seemed a much more noble pursuit than being a bounty hunter.

Checking her gauges, Larissa realized that she was running out of oil. She needed to land soon. She turned the owl back toward the rim of the canyon. Flying over the rim, she caught sight of the professor. She also saw seven men on horseback approaching. Larissa let the owl drift down near the ground, then pulled back on the control rod as the professor had shown her.

The owl bounced a couple of times when its feet hit the ground and finally skidded to a halt. Larissa unstrapped herself from the seat and sprang from the owl, drawing her six-gun as she did. The professor blinked at her in confusion, but a moment later, the seven men appeared through the trees.

The leader tipped his hat. "I am Onofre Cisneros, formerly captain of the good ship *Tiburón*. We were looking for Fatemeh Karimi."

"Oh," said Larissa. She holstered her gun. "We've been expecting you. Welcome."

"Yes, yes, we need as much help as we can get," echoed the professor. "Please join us." As the men climbed off their horses, the professor turned to Larissa. "How was your flight?"

"It was great." She remembered she was still wearing the goggles and pushed them up to the top of her head. Then she realized her hat was gone. "The only problem is that I lost my hat."

"Fortunately, it did not go far." The professor produced Larissa's hat from behind a nearby rock. He handed it to her with a flourish and a bow.

She dusted it off, placed the goggles back on the hat, and set it on her head.

The professor nodded, then led Onofre Cisneros and his men to a place where they could tend their horses.

"A detachment of American soldiers has been seen approaching from the northeast, sir." The airman who delivered the report snapped a smart salute.

"Thank you, Airman. Stand by." Captain Makarov looked toward the general.

General Gorloff shook his head. They had been grounded nearly two weeks and still had nearly one more week to go before repairs to the *Czar Nicholas* would be complete. However, the *Czarina Marie* was in full operating condition.

"How many men are there?"

"It appears to be a company of cavalry and a small artillery unit, sir," reported the airman.

Gorloff nodded. "Have the *Czarina Marie* wait until they've formed up ranks. Once they have, send her aloft, maneuver over their position and drop bombs until they're decimated or disperse."

*"General Gorloff, may we suggest that we be used to infiltrate the minds of some of the American military leaders. We could sway them to your way of thinking. It would waste less ammunition and cost fewer lives,"* said Legion.

Gorloff shook his head. *No, Legion, not this time. They would know what we are thinking. It would give their officers a great advantage.*

*"If we infiltrated their minds, we could keep them from reporting to their superiors,"* countered Legion.

"It's too much of a risk," said Gorloff, aloud. He looked from Makarov to the airman. "Carry out my orders."

The airman snapped another salute, turned, and left to deliver the orders to the captain of the *Czarina Marie*. Captain Makarov moved from one foot to the other as he nervously looked out the window.

"Legion, would you please allow Captain Makarov and I to have a private conversation—without listening to us?" asked the general.

*"Very well,"* said the entity from the back of the general's mind.

The general waited until he felt his mind go quiet and then stepped up next to the captain.

"We can dismiss Legion as easy as that?" said the captain.

"It would seem so." Gorloff nodded.

The captain reached up and rubbed his temples. "It is a relief to have some quiet after his continual chatter in my mind. When he first entered my mind, I thought I was going mad. Eventually I got used to it, but after months of chatter, the sense of encroaching madness has returned."

"I understand," said the general. "However, I think you are troubled by more than Legion's persistent chattering."

"On one hand, Legion aids us in our victories. On the

other hand, Legion seems content to treat our enemies as equals."

Gorloff pursed his lips and watched as the *Czarina Marie* dropped ballast and began lifting off from the ground. "Legion has articulated the differences between Russians and Americans better than any general or politician I have ever met. And yet..."

"And yet he seems to treat those differences as trivial, as though they are barely important." Captain Makarov finished the thought.

The *Czarina Marie* was now airborne and Gorloff could see the American forces. He retrieved a telescope from next to the airship's controls and studied the formation. Cannons were being wheeled around to face the grounded airship.

The captain continued. "Legion has shown us that if America becomes a real-world power, our countries will be at each other's throats. We likely would destroy the world. The only way to save the world is to keep America from becoming a world power. That much is clear."

"If America must be dominated, why does Legion treat them as equals?" Gorloff looked at the captain and shrugged. "I begin to wonder if Legion has a different objective than ours." He raised the telescope to his eye again.

A hatch opened on the bottom of the *Czarina Marie*. The first bomb was dropped just as the Americans were loading a cannon ball. An explosion rent the air. The shock wave sent ripples through the *Czar Nicholas*. Horses and men began to scatter. Another bomb fell from the *Czarina Maria* and soon another cannon was destroyed. Those men that were left began to retreat back toward the northeast.

The general passed the telescope to the captain, then put his hand on the captain's arm. "Whatever happens, we must be steadfast in our objective."

"Very good, General Gorloff." The captain raised the telescope to his eye and nodded appreciatively.

Fatemeh, Professor Maravilla, and Onofre Cisneros watched as six pirates in mechanical owls darted around each other over the Grand Canyon. They were getting the hang of operations and were practicing fast maneuvers so they could avoid bullets or anything else the airships might throw at them.

"Adapting the steam engines to use manganese peroxide, zinc and potassium chlorate rather than oil was a stroke of genius, Captain," said the professor with open admiration. "We have extended the range of the owls and the chemicals weigh far less than oil."

"Thank Monturiol i Estarriol in Spain. I just adapted his design for my submarine. I'm glad we were able to adapt it to the owls as well." Captain Cisneros turned toward Fatemeh. "We have owls, we have brave men and women to fly them. That leaves only one question. How do we use them to bring down the airships?"

"I've been thinking about that," interjected Maravilla. "Based on the newspaper reports from Montana, one ship dropped some kind of material as it lifted off. I'm guessing the material must have been ballast. If that's true, these airships must be balloons, but they're enormous. Hot air alone cannot make them stay aloft."

"You're thinking they must use hydrogen." Captain Cisneros nodded. "It would be easy to build some kind of bomb that could make the hydrogen in those ships explode."

"Precisely!" exclaimed the professor.

"Absolutely not." Fatemeh's hands were on her hips. "Our goal is not to destroy the airships. We merely want them to land. We want the Russians aboard those ships to surrender and leave."

Cisneros and Maravilla sighed together. To Fatemeh, they looked like two young boys who had been told they couldn't play a dangerous game. She had to fight not to laugh at their apparent disappointment.

After a moment Maravilla smiled and punched Cisneros in the arm. "If we don't destroy them, perhaps we can find out about them, learn what makes them work!"

"Then we can build our own airships," chimed in the former pirate captain.

Now Fatemeh did laugh. "That's the spirit! We have more

to gain if we don't destroy the ships than if we do."

"So, our objective is to get aboard and force them to land."
Cisneros nodded. "We'll have to scout them out, find their vulnerable points."

Maravilla rubbed his chin. "The reports from Montana said they had hatches on the bottom. Maybe we can exploit those."

Cisneros looked at his former crewmates flying around in the steam powered, clockwork owls. "It'll be like taking ships at sea."

"That's why I wanted you and your men," said Fatemeh. "You avoided taking lives when you captured ships. I believe you can do that with these airships as well."

"We should have the men practice with grappling hooks," said the captain. "In case they need to pull themselves up into an airship."

"We could also land on top," suggested Maravilla. "The owls' claws could grip onto the fabric at the top of the ship and allow someone to cut their way inside." The professor also looked at the pirates flying around. "That only leaves one last question. We have a dozen owls almost complete, but only eleven pilots. Should we finish all twelve, or should we use the final owl for spare parts?"

"Are those birds out there?"

All three whirled around at the voice of the stranger who had approached silently. He was a young man, not yet twenty years old. Fatemeh smiled broadly at the now-familiar face. "We'll need all twelve owls," she said. "Gentlemen, may I introduce our last rider, Billy McCarty."

Legion had traversed the galaxy. He had visited millions of inhabited worlds, but he had never interfered with the life he found there. He had observed and watched as some lifeforms lived in harmony with their worlds. He had watched sadly as others destroyed their own worlds, feeling helpless to prevent what he saw. On Earth, he thought he could prevent these creatures from destroying their own world, help them evolve into a peaceful society.

Legion had enjoyed interacting with Mendeleev. The scientist gave him some hope for humanity. However, Gorloff, Czar Alexander, and the others disturbed him. Even the American mayors tended to see life as a series of skirmishes and conquests. Many humans saw things in terms of one group dominating another. Gorloff was not content to come into America and bring stability. He had to vanquish the Americans. Legion performed calculations and looked toward the future again. This time, the world did not destroy itself quickly. Instead, it was ruled by a totalitarian Russian empire. Science and art were relegated to the realm of curiosities. The empire would become something akin to a castle and the other peoples of the world would become serfs, serving that castle.

However, the human spirit was strong. The oppression would not last. Eventually a people somewhere—perhaps the Chinese or the Africans would rise up against the empire and topple it. Perhaps the world would fall into chaos. Or, perhaps great weapons would destroy the world after all. Legion feared he had not saved the world. He had only delayed the inevitable. The answer did not lie with these military minds or the politicians. It lay with men like Mendeleev—men who could envision a better future.

Legion quietly listened to the private conversations of Gorloff and Makarov. They had grown fearful and distrustful. Such men could not save the world. Legion would start looking for the men who could help him fix the problems he had helped to create.

# CHAPTER FOURTEEN
## THE BATTLE OF DENVER

Colonel Peter Berestetski held onto a handrail in the staging area of the *Czar Nicholas's* underbelly. He looked out over the troops assembled there as the airship approached Denver. They looked fine in their sleek, navy blue jackets with brass buttons and gold piping. So far, they had not seen any action that marred their uniforms or matted the polish on their boots. The only ground troops they had encountered were the soldiers in Montana and they had been dispersed quickly from the air.

Berestetski wondered if he would actually have to fire a shot during the campaign. He would be thankful if he never had to raise his gun against another human being. He grew up as a farmer, not a soldier, and wasn't sure how he would do under the strain of actual combat.

As these thoughts played through his mind, the colonel realized Legion was being strangely quiet on the subject. *Legion?* he ventured silently—half-glad for the lack of voices in his mind and half-fearful the alien presence had left.

*"We're here,"* came the response, more distant than usual. If he didn't know better, Berestetski would have said Legion sounded tired.

*Is it likely we'll encounter any more resistance in Denver than we have in other cities?* asked the colonel.

*"Based on what happened in Montana, there is a high probability of encountering combat troops in Denver,"* said Legion. *"In our experience, soldiers have minds intent on killing. They cannot be swayed as easily as civilians who are seeking to understand a situation."*

Peter Berestetski swallowed and looked over at Major Kozmin, who stood nearby. The major was a hardened veteran of many battles. The colonel did his best to mimic the major's stern features that betrayed no outward sign of fear or doubt. He made a quick check of his sidearm and ammunition to make sure all was in order.

A short time later, an airman entered the bay and delivered a report to Major Kozmin. The major nodded to the colonel and then barked an order to the assembled men. They all stood, checked their weapons, then slung them behind their backs. The *Czar Nicholas* was nearly in position to deploy the troops. The airman, who acted as a runner, turned and left the bay.

General Gorloff knew the location of the Denver Mint from his time in Washington. It was located in the Clark, Gruber, and Company Bank Building at the intersection of two streets called 16th and Holladay. The airships would maneuver to a position near downtown where the troops would disembark. They would march to the bank, while the airships supported them from above.

A few minutes later, the airman returned and delivered another message to the major. The major pointed and soldiers released the latches that held the bay doors in place. Other soldiers dropped the rope ladders over the side and began their descent. Berestetski swallowed hard.

Once most of the soldiers had gone over the side, he watched the major take his place and begin the descent. The colonel then took his place at the top of the ladder.

There was a light wind that caused the rope ladder to sway as the colonel descended. Fortunately, Legion still helped him control his muscles and reflexes and he nimbly made his way down to the ground. As a farmer, he wasn't bad at climbing ropes into haylofts. However, he wasn't sure he could have made the full descent from the swaying airship to the street below without Legion's help.

Finally, the last few soldiers made their way down from the airship. The colonel watched for a moment as the two airships rose and airmen pulled the ladders back into the bellies of the craft.

The colonel and the major looked around and took stock of where they were. They had been dropped on an empty plot of land near the South Platte River. Briefly taking stock of the landscape, the colonel thought the South Platte hardly deserved to be called a river, it was so small. After a moment, the colonel saw railroad tracks. They would follow the tracks into the city until they reached 16th Street and then turn southeast toward the mint itself.

The colonel spoke to the major and they confirmed plans with each other. The major had his lieutenants muster the men and they began their march into the heart of Denver.

The march was fairly short, perhaps three-quarters of a mile. Colonel Berestetski shook his head when he saw the object of their quest. It was a squat, brick building—two stories tall with a small, castle-like tower on top. American troops surrounded the building. When they saw the Russians, they knelt on the ground, aimed, and then fired.

Legion reported that the Russians had lost six men. The narrow streets and surrounding buildings hindered the aim of the American soldiers. The Russian lieutenants had their men take position and return the American troops' fire. Legion estimated that perhaps one hundred American troops guarded the building.

Berestetski eyed the surrounding buildings. He ordered ten men to accompany him into the building across the street from the Denver mint. It was a general store. Inside, a stunned clerk held up his hands when he saw the smartly dressed soldiers enter the room.

"Is there anyone upstairs?" asked the colonel.

The clerk shook his head. "Nothing up there but storage." Berestetski wondered if the clerk was surprised he spoke English. Waving the thought aside, he sent five of the men upstairs to make sure everything was secure. He sent two more men out to retrieve the major, then turned to the clerk. "You should leave. This is a dangerous place."

The clerk nodded quickly and then darted out the door.

A few minutes later, Major Kozmin entered, accompanied by two dozen men. Some remained on the ground floor while others accompanied the colonel and the major upstairs to their command post for the battle.

*"From this vantage point, you should overtake the American forces within the hour,"* said Legion.

The colonel's eyebrows came together. He thought it was

strange Legion should refer to "you" rather than "we" after all the time they had spent together. He shook the thought aside and made his way upstairs to oversee the battle.

Ramon breathed a sigh of relief when he heard the order to stop riding. They'd been traveling north for so many days he'd lost track of how long it had been since they left Fort McRae. He climbed off his horse and led it to a place indicated by Sergeant Forrest. He gave the horse a pat and then formed up with the rest of his squad.

Forrest reviewed the men briefly, then dismissed them to set up camp. Ramon looked around. Wherever they were, it was beautiful. Pine trees surrounded them and scented the air. The ground was covered with lush grass. In the distance, to the west, were tall, snow-capped mountains. Ramon gathered they were in Colorado, but that was the extent of his knowledge.

There had been many rumors about where they'd find the airships. Originally, people thought the airships were making for Denver—perhaps to capture the mint just like the Texans had tried back in the Civil War. However, there was also a rumor that said the ships had been grounded in Montana and American troops had already engaged them. Another rumor suggested the airships might be bound for St. Louis, where they could virtually shut down all of the nation's interstate commerce. Still others speculated they were on the way to Washington, D.C. itself.

Ramon found himself dismissing those last two rumors. If there was any truth to them, why were they always marching north?

Soon after the campsite was situated, Forrest returned and addressed the men. "They've got a mess tent over yonder. Go grab yourself some food, then come back."

"Any idea where we are?" asked Corporal Lorenzo.

"We're just outside a small town called Littleton." The sergeant pointed north. "Denver's about ten miles yonder." Then, the sergeant motioned for the men to come closer. "Lieutenant

Stone says General Sheridan himself is camped here. He's summoned Colonel Smith and Major Johnson. I have a feeling we'll be seeing action soon."

Ramon was surprised to find his spirits lifted with the prospect of action. He really didn't want to go into combat. It was one thing to match wits with a lone gunman or stop a fight, but the prospect of facing a whole barrage of bullets and maybe artillery was downright terrifying. Even so, the ride north had been so mind-numbing, he found himself welcoming the change of pace.

He followed Lorenzo and the rest of the men to the mess tent where he retrieved a plate and utensils and went through a line. The cook served up a rather uninspiring and cold meal of jerky, beans, and partially fried potatoes. There was hot coffee, though, and Ramon gladly took a cup, then found a place to sit by himself so he could compose his thoughts. As he sipped the coffee, he made a face. It was weak compared to Fatemeh's brew.

Ramon found himself wondering where Fatemeh was and what she was doing. He couldn't imagine her sitting idly by during the invasion of the Russian airships. Still, he hoped she actually was somewhere safe and not trying anything crazy or foolish.

On the trip north to Denver, whenever the troops camped near a town, he noticed many of the men made their way into saloons and bought the services of the ladies there. Ramon sometimes joined them on their excursions to the saloons but was content to sip a beer and maybe smoke a proffered cigar. Even before he met Fatemeh, he'd never found the prospect of spending the night with one of the ladies in a saloon especially appealing.

As Ramon sipped his coffee, his stomach began to growl. Even though the food barely appealed to him, he dug in and cleaned his plate. Then he went back for one more cup of the thin coffee. Finally, he gathered up his plate and cup, delivered them to the man doing the dishes and rejoined his squad at the campsite.

Forrest ordered everyone into their bedrolls.

"Any word on what's happening?" asked Lorenzo.

The sergeant shook his head. "The general is still meeting with all the senior officers in the tent. Could go on all night for all I know."

The corporal pursed his lips and nodded, then turned around. "All right, men, you heard the sergeant. Let's get some shuteye."

Ramon sat down on the bedroll, pulled off his jacket and his boots, then climbed underneath the blankets. He looked up at the sky and watched as the stars came out. Even though he was exhausted, he had a hard time falling asleep. He found himself wondering if this would be the last night he would ever look at the stars. If a bullet caught him, would he go to heaven or would there just be no more Ramon Morales? He realized then he had never asked Fatemeh what she believed happened to a person after they died.

Eventually sleep claimed Ramon and his eyes drifted shut.

It felt like a mere moment passed when the shrill sound of a bugle startled Ramon awake. Stars still sparkled in the sky, but they had moved. By his best guess, it had been six hours since he fell asleep.

Ramon stumbled to his feet and began collecting his belongings so they could be packed on his horse. Forrest rode up and shouted orders that Ramon's half-awake brain really didn't register. He followed the rest of his squad to the mess tent, consumed a hasty breakfast of oatmeal and coffee, then followed them to the place where the horses had been corralled. He retrieved his horse and led her back to the campsite. There, he placed the saddle on her back and hefted the saddlebags into place. Once he confirmed everything was secure, he climbed on.

Within half an hour, the order was given to move out. Ramon snapped his reins and followed the other men. As they rode, the sky began to lighten somewhat and Ramon looked around. The force he was riding with had grown considerably.

As the sun cleared the horizon, he saw buildings clustered in the distance. Ramon realized he must be seeing Denver. Over the center of the city were two strange oval-shaped clouds. Once the troops were slightly closer, Ramon swallowed hard. He realized those things weren't clouds. They were the airships and they were the two biggest man-made things he had ever seen in his life.

Soon, a lieutenant rode up and assigned Corporal Lorenzo's squad to help a special unit that had accompanied General Sheridan's party from back East. The unit was already making its way toward Denver. Lorenzo's men hurried to catch up with them.

As they rode alongside the river, Ramon learned the unit was comprised of former members of the Army's Balloon Corps. The Balloon Corps had been disbanded during the Civil War, but some balloons still existed along with a few pilots who could fly them. General Sheridan had worked to get them to Denver as soon as possible.

In addition to the members of the Balloon Corps, there were several artillery units as well. Oxen trudged along, pulling howitzers and mortars behind them. They were the only kind of artillery Ramon knew about that could shoot far enough upward to have a chance of damaging the airships. However, he dreaded the thought of those shells coming back down and pummeling Denver.

Ramon's attention kept being drawn to the airships. They were long, grayish ovals with fins at the back. Hanging off the sides were boxes with something that looked like windmills pointing toward the rear. Underneath the large, ovoid portion of the airships was a box with sunlight glinting from the windows. Ramon figured they were too far away from the airships to see anyone inside anyway. What really caught Ramon's attention was the golden owl on each ship's keel at the bow. He smiled grimly, wondering what Fatemeh would make of these strange decorations.

Looking through the telescope, General Gorloff watched as the American troops advanced on Denver. "How many would you say there are?"

The general looked around when he didn't hear an immediate response from Legion. Captain Makarov's eyes shifted from side to side, as though he too was looking for someone to answer. Finally, he said, "Perhaps one thousand soldiers." His tone was apologetic.

"Legion, do you concur?" asked the general.

*"We're sorry, General, you had asked for privacy this morning. We were away."*

"There are American troops coming this way. I see cavalry, artillery and infantry units. Do you see them as well?"

*"We do,"* said Legion. *"Several of our components have left to scan them. We count 1,254 soldiers advancing on Denver. They out-number the Russian forces holding the mint and in the general store across the street, but, of course, you have the aerial advantage."*

"Is there a danger from any of the artillery they're bringing into range?" Gorloff's brow furrowed.

*"They are equipped with howitzers and mortars. The airships should gain altitude to be out of range, which will give you a clear advantage. It's unlikely they'll shell buildings in downtown Denver, except as a last resort."*

"Thank you, Legion." Gorloff turned to Captain Makarov. "You heard?"

Makarov nodded, then turned to his first officer. "Take us to an altitude of sixty-five hundred feet above sea level." He turned to the signal officer. "Request the *Czarina Marie* do like-wise."

Both officers saluted and carried out the orders.

Meanwhile Gorloff continued to observe the troops on the ground through the telescope. The infantry advanced first, moving toward the center of town, carefully making their way around buildings and searching for anything out of the ordinary. As the infantrymen entered buildings, they brought people outside and had them leave the area. The general nodded to himself, appreciating the prudence they demonstrated by getting civilians out of harm's way.

The artillery units advanced northward along the river. Gorloff guessed they were working their way to the field where the airships had deployed the troops. It made sense. That would give the artillery the best chance at either hitting an airship or sending shells into the area around the mint. Still, it would leave the cannons vulnerable to attack from above.

Gorloff turned his attention to the cavalry units. Some

followed the artillery along the river. Others worked their way through the streets of Denver behind the infantry.

Captain Makarov tapped Gorloff on the shoulder and pointed downward. The American infantry had apparently engaged the Russian troops stationed in the general store. It appeared some of the Americans had been killed and the rest were falling back and establishing a perimeter around the area.

The general found the motion of the American troops fascinating. There was an ebb and flow as men were placed into position and other men carried information to superiors. Gorloff had never quite pictured a battle in those terms before.

"I think the time has come to bring a little disorder to the American troops," mused the general. He pointed to two places where it seemed infantrymen were getting ready to fire on the mint.

Captain Makarov had the signal officer send a message to the *Czarina Marie*. Then he opened the speaking tube and ordered the ordnance men to prepare the bombs. The captain barked a series of orders to the helmsman and then watched the ground with his own telescope. When he was satisfied they were in the right position, he ordered the ordnance men to drop the first bomb.

There was a flash of light and a cloud of debris followed by a strangely muffled sound. As the smoke and debris cleared, Gorloff saw men lying on the ground, not moving. Infantry from the rear surged forward. Some cleared bodies and others formed into ranks, taking the place of their fallen comrades.

Captain Makarov had the helmsman move the ship slightly and ordered the release of two more bombs. The *Czarina Marie* was also dropping bombs on the soldiers below. The general noted the troops were beginning to fall back.

Turning his telescope around, the general saw the artillery units had reached the field. They were working to get cannons into position. However, he noticed there were more than cannons being set up. Something made of fabric and netting was laid out along the ground. It was attached to a basket and soldiers were unfurling hoses from machinery nearby toward the thing on the ground.

"Captain Makarov, are they preparing a balloon?" asked Gorloff.

The captain turned his telescope toward the artillery. "I believe so, sir."

"It looks as though the ground troops are falling back, perhaps we should turn our attention to the artillery," said the general.

The captain nodded and ordered the helmsman to turn the ship around.

"*There is a danger to the airships if the American troops manage to deploy the balloon,*" observed Legion.

"How much danger could such a balloon represent?" Gorloff shrugged. "I thought the Americans only used those balloons for observation."

"*If they have long-range rifles or a Gatling Gun and can ignite a spark within an airship, it would be destroyed.*"

Gorloff took in a deep breath and let it out slowly. He looked at Captain Makarov.

"I've got men on the swivel guns in the bow," said the captain.

"We might want some sharp shooters in position as well," said the general.

"Very good." The captain opened the speaking tube. "Lieutenants Chmil and Apraxin, arm yourselves with Berdan rifles and join the men at the swivel guns in the bow ports."

"Aye, aye, sir," came the reply.

As the *Czar Nicholas* drifted toward the artillery and balloon position, General Gorloff noted the balloon was nearly upright.

The Balloon Corps and the artillery units came to a wide, sandy floodplain near the river, unsuitable for construction but a good place to set up the guns and for the balloonists to launch their craft. Ramon helped the rest of Lorenzo's squad unfurl a great mass of fabric and ropes from one of the Balloon Corps' crates. Other men fired up some kind of machinery and began unfurling hoses. Overhearing various conversations, Ramon gathered the machines were hydrogen generators. The balloons would use the hydrogen to go aloft.

As they worked, Ramon saw the windmills hanging from the Russian airships spin up. The behemoths moved a short distance. Sometime later, doors opened on the bottom of the airships and something was dropped. When the things hit the ground, there was a flash of light and sound like thunder.

"They're bombing our troops," observed Lorenzo when he saw where Ramon was looking.

Ramon pursed his lips and nodded. He suddenly felt very exposed on the riverbank.

The men from the Balloon Corps had Ramon and Lorenzo help them attach a basket to the ropes on the flattened balloon they had pulled from the crates. The basket seemed large enough to hold two men and some supplies. The men at the hydrogen generators brought a big hose over and attached it to an opening on the balloon. Soon it filled and began to rise off the ground.

Ramon and Lorenzo grabbed ropes that dangled from the inflating gasbag. They staked the ropes to the ground as though they were setting up a tent. The balloon was soon full and the corpsmen closed a valve and disconnected the hose.

Ramon looked back toward the city and noticed one of the airship's propellers had started spinning again. The craft was turning toward them.

The sergeant saw what was happening as well. "We better get a move on."

A captain and lieutenant climbed into the balloon's basket while the sergeant lifted the cover from another wagon. Loaded there were a Gatling Gun, several rifles, and boxes of shells. Lorenzo had his squad line up as a fireman's brigade and they began passing rifles and ammunition to the men in the balloon. Finally, they passed along the Gatling Gun and its mount. Ramon found himself wondering how the balloon would lift off with all that weight.

Even as they were setting up the Gatling Gun, the captain in the balloon called out, "Cast off!"

The sergeant directed Lorenzo, Ramon and the other men of the squad to pull up the stakes. As they did, they watched the balloon ascend into the sky.

Ramon shielded his eyes from the sun. The balloon rose and the airship closed in. The two men in the balloon finally had the Gatling Gun set up and one of them turned the crank. Ramon could hear the pop-pop-pop of the gun firing shells at the mighty airship. He wondered how the gun could do any good against such a behemoth.

A hatchway opened in the bow of the airship and Ramon thought he could see a man leaning out, holding a rifle. He fired a couple of shots. They had no apparent effect.

One of the men in the balloon took up a rifle and fired toward the airship, while the other continued to operate the Gatling Gun. Ramon wasn't sure whether it was the prevailing wind, or the force of the bullets, but the balloon seemed to be moving backward, over the river. Even so, the airship was closing rapidly.

A moment later, one of the two men in the balloon scored a hit. The rifleman in the airship tumbled from the hatch and fell to the ground. Ramon turned away to avoid seeing the man impact the ground, even though he knew he was probably dead already.

Another hatchway opened on the airship and a small cannon jutted out. It fired and hit the balloon, which erupted in a ball of flame. Lorenzo ordered his men to take cover under the wagons to avoid being hit by fiery debris.

The artillery was finally set up and mortars began lobbing shells up toward the airship. However, as far as Ramon could tell, the ship was too high to be in range of the shells. From his vantage point underneath the wagon that had carried the balloon's armament, Ramon could see one of the hatchways opening on the bottom of the airship. He prodded Lorenzo. "We need to get out of here now!"

Lorenzo ordered his squad to move. Lorenzo and Ramon were climbing out from under the wagon to get to their horses when a bomb fell from the airship. The explosion sent Ramon flying through the air.

Major Kozmin summoned Colonel Berestetski to the window

of the general store. The *Czarina Marie* had maneuvered into a position where she was visible to them and had deployed signal flags. The colonel was ordered to investigate the place where he and his troops landed. According to Legion, that was also the place where American forces had set up artillery and had been shooting at the Russian airships.

"*It appears all the troops there are dead or in retreat,*" said Legion. "*General Gorloff would like you to spike the cannons to assure they are permanently out of action.*"

Peter Berestetski nodded and turned to a nearby sergeant. "Search the store, look for something to drive into the ends of the cannons and some large hammers. I'm guessing we must have something suitable at hand."

The sergeant nodded and recruited a couple of men to help him search the store.

The colonel looked out the window again. The ground forces around them were also retreating. He retrieved a rifle and went downstairs. There, he found the sergeant and the two privates ready with a pair of wheelbarrows loaded with hammers and large pieces of iron suitable for spiking any cannons that had survived the aerial assault.

Berestetski nodded his satisfaction. He ordered four armed men to accompany them, then motioned for the other men to follow behind him. Cautiously, he peeked out the door. Not seeing any living people on the street, he proceeded back toward the place where he and his troops had been deposited. The *Czar Nicholas* hovered over the river. The field was littered with bodies—many ripped apart and missing limbs. The colonel's stomach churned and he felt bile rise to the back of his throat. He gulped water from his canteen, then forced himself to evaluate the scene. "Legion," he said aloud. "Are any of these guns in usable condition?"

"*There are two at the north edge of the field that could be used again,*" said the alien presence.

Berestetski looked around and finally spotted the two howitzers Legion indicated. He pointed and the sergeant and his men drove their wheelbarrows in that direction, seemingly oblivious to the carnage around them.

The colonel wandered through the area in something of a

daze. He wondered if there was anyone who could be helped, but it appeared all the people on the field were dead. Many were badly burned—skin blackened and peeled from the bone. There was a decapitated corpse, but he saw no sign of the poor wretch's head. Staggering over to an empty wagon, he opened his canteen again and lifted it. Reaching the wagon, he saw two men who were not as bad off as the others he'd seen. The colonel was startled by Legion's voice.

*"Subject of interest: Ramon Morales."*

Berestetski knelt down by the man next to him and put his fingers alongside his neck. He felt a pulse. "He's alive," he said aloud. "What's that about subject of interest?"

*"We encountered this human twice before. It was soon after our arrival on your world,"* explained Legion. *"He has a companion named Fatemeh Karimi. She has demonstrated remarkable insight about us."*

The colonel looked around. "I don't see any sign of a woman here." He found himself glad of that. "Is this man a danger? It looks like he could use medical attention."

Legion was silent for a time. If he were dealing with a human, the colonel would have assumed he was taking time to choose his words carefully. *"This human could know about dangers to the operation. He should be treated and interrogated."*

"Very well. Alert the men on the *Czar Nicholas*. Have them lower a stretcher."

*"We have already done so."*

A moment later, a hatch opened on the bottom of the *Czar Nicholas* and a stretcher was lowered on two ropes. The sergeant and his men had finished spiking the two surviving howitzers and stepped up, leaving the heavy wheelbarrows behind. They hefted Ramon Morales onto the stretcher and watched as he was lifted up into the airship.

The colonel then looked around. He thought there had been two men on the ground. If there had been a second, he was now gone. Berestetski shook his head, and thought nausea and the strain of battle might be playing tricks on his mind.

A rope ladder was lowered from the airship. The colonel looked at the men. "Return to the general store. I will follow shortly."

The men saluted and left. The colonel ascended the rope ladder into the airship.

General Gorloff was waiting for him in the bay. The colonel saluted.

"Legion tells me he might have encountered the man you sent aboard," said the general.

The colonel placed his arms behind his back. "Legion mentioned something about a woman, but I saw no signs of her."

The general nodded. "This is no place for women. I can't imagine how she would be a danger to us."

Two medical officers lifted Ramon from the stretcher onto a rolling bed and carried him through a set of double doors at one end of the bay.

"It'll be interesting to see what this Ramon Morales knows about Legion," said Berestetski. He turned to the general. "How is the battle going?"

"The American forces are in retreat. However, I suspect they are merely regrouping and will attempt another assault. You should return to your post at the general store and stand by."

Colonel Berestetski saluted, then descended the ladder.

Corporal Jesús Lorenzo shook his head, but he could not clear the ringing from his ears. He looked around and saw soldiers in nearly black uniforms standing around a fallen comrade. He blinked a couple of times to clear his vision. After a moment, he realized the man was Ramon Morales. The soldiers lifted Ramon onto a stretcher attached by ropes to the great airship that hovered overhead.

Lorenzo willed himself to move. He darted to a position behind the hydrogen generators and watched the Russian soldiers. Ramon was lifted up into the airship. Lorenzo couldn't see that Ramon was alive, but doubted the Russians would bother taking him aboard the ship if he was dead. Once Ramon was out of sight, a group of men spoke to a Russian with epaulets. The men saluted the officer, then turned and left. A rope ladder descended from the airship and the officer climbed aboard.

Lorenzo took the opportunity to leave his hiding place. He made his way along the river toward General Sheridan's command post on the outskirts of town. As he walked, his vision and hearing began to clear. He looked down at himself and realized his uniform was a muddy mess and he'd lost his hat somewhere in the battle. Still, he crossed himself and thanked his namesake he was still alive.

After an hour of walking, the sun was low on the horizon and he saw the American camp. He turned and looked back at the two airships. They seemed like two unnatural gray clouds hovering over downtown Denver. As he turned back toward the camp, he caught a glimpse of something near the setting sun. Lorenzo raised his hand to shield his eyes. At first glance, it just looked like a flock of birds. However, there was something strange and jerky about their flight. They made their way to the ground west of the city.

Lorenzo estimated they were about two miles away. It was late in the season for birds to be flying north, but it was not impossible. Still, something about their flight seemed more mechanical than natural. He had seen enough strange things that day not to dismiss any possibility. Perhaps there was an airborne benefactor, or perhaps they were something worse than the airships. Or, it could just be birds.

Corporal Lorenzo weighed the prospect of a clean uniform and food against his curiosity. His curiosity won out. He turned and hiked due west to see what had landed.

Aboard the *Czar Nicholas*, General Gorloff climbed down into the gondola. He found Captain Makarov watching something through the window with great interest.

"Take a look toward the west. What do you see?" asked the captain.

The general shielded his eyes against the glare of the sun, then shrugged. "Birds. So what?"

"Use the telescope," urged the captain.

Reluctantly, the general raised the telescope to his eye and did his best not to look directly into the sun. He frowned when he realized that he was not seeing birds after all. They were some kind of machine built to look like giant owls. Their flight was jerky and little puffs of steam came from their tails. "What the devil are those things?"

"Could the Americans have developed some form of flying machine?" asked the captain.

"It seems unlikely the Americans could have developed something so sophisticated this soon," said Legion. "Some scientists and engineers have been working on flying machines and airships such as the one we're in. However, ornithopters are very sophisticated technology. We would be impressed if humans developed such things in this short amount of time with no prompting."

Gorloff wasn't sure what an "ornithopter" was, but he realized he didn't care. "Do they represent a threat?"

"They are likely more fragile than an airship or balloon, but they could be far more maneuverable," said Legion. "They will be difficult to shoot down. They are a serious threat and they are very interesting."

Gorloff frowned, unhappy Legion found these strange mechanical owls so engaging. He turned to the captain. "We need to keep watch on these things—whatever they are. Make sure men are posted round the clock."

The captain saluted. "Yes, sir."

# CHAPTER FIFTEEN
## DANCE OF THE OWLS

Fatemeh's owl skidded to a stop on top of a hill a short distance from Denver. She glanced at Onofre Cisneros, who had already landed and was unstrapping himself from his seat. He had spotted the hill they landed on. It would give them a good look at the airships and allow them to catch updrafts that would help them get airborne again in the morning.

The other ten owls drifted down and skidded to a stop around them. Cisneros' crew wasted no time and began unpacking their gear. Soon, they would have a campfire going and start cooking dinner. Fatemeh's stomach growled in anticipation. She unpacked her own bedroll from the storage compartment in the back of the owl and laid it out on the ground.

Larissa laid her bedroll out next to Fatemeh's. The bounty hunter looked at the airships hovering over downtown Denver. "They look mighty big."

Fatemeh stood with her hands on her hips and assessed the airships. "They are, but mostly they're just bags filled with gas. I'm guessing most of the soldiers are down on the ground."

Cisneros had retrieved a spyglass and studied the distant dirigibles. A moment later, Professor Maravilla joined him and looked at the sight with his own telescope. The professor began to laugh. He turned and summoned Fatemeh.

She walked over, followed by Larissa. Taking the telescope, Fatemeh looked at the dirigibles and then the buildings below. She swallowed hard as she saw the damage the aircraft had inflicted on the buildings of downtown Denver. Closer to the river, she saw ruined cannons and the bodies of men littering the ground. "I fail to see what you find so funny."

"Look at the bottom of the airships toward the bow," said the professor.

Fatemeh lifted the telescope to her eye again and even in the twilight gloom she could see the golden owls that adorned the airships.

Cisneros nodded appreciatively. "Tomorrow, the owls shall be dancing with one another."

Fatemeh handed the telescope to Larissa and continued to study the scene. "Do you see anything that affects our plans?"

The former pirate captain shook his head. "We attack in two teams of six. The professor and I will go first. We'll try to land on top, make our way inside and find a way to let the rest of you in. Then we'll see if we can force the ships to land."

Billy McCarty came over. "I still worry about the professor being the first one to go aboard one of those things. He may know our clockwork owls, but he ain't good with a gun like Larissa and me are."

The professor inclined his head. "We don't know exactly what we will find in there. Good with a gun won't help if you get lost on the way to the hatches."

Fatemeh held up her hands. "Billy has a point. Perhaps Larissa should go with Captain Cisneros and Billy should go with the professor. A second pair of eyes as you make your way through the ships won't hurt."

"I would welcome the help of Miss Crimson." The pirate captain cast a grin he meant to be charming toward the bounty hunter.

Larissa folded her arms and glared at Fatemeh, but remained silent.

The professor frowned but nodded. "Very well."

The smells of dinner cooking wafted toward those assembled by the ridge. Fatemeh's stomach growled louder. "Now that that's decided, I think we should go eat." She was grateful Cisneros had brought his cook from the *Tiburón* along and no one expected her to prepare food for the Owl Riders, as Billy had dubbed the group a few days before.

They gathered around the campfire and the cook, Juan de Largo, mounded a concoction of smoked fish, beans and chile atop tortillas and passed them around. Fatemeh bit into hers gratefully.

Larissa eyed hers skeptically then took a taste. Her eyes

went wide and sweat beaded on her forehead, but she nodded as she swallowed. "This isn't too bad. Wish it wasn't so hot."

Billy laughed. "Quit your gripin'. That there chile'll put hair on your chest."

Larissa narrowed her gaze at the gunfighter. A nearby shuffling sound kept her from firing back a retort.

Billy and the pirates stood, drawing their guns. A man in a blue American army uniform approached, holding his hands out where they could be seen. Several days' growth of beard peppered his chin and his uniform was covered with mud, but Fatemeh still recognized him. "Corporal Lorenzo!"

The soldier inclined his head. "Miss Karimi? What are you doing here?" He looked around at the others and his eyes fell on Billy. "What's this all about?"

"We're here to save you soldier boys," declared Billy.

Fatemeh finished her tortilla and fish in two hasty bites, then approached Corporal Lorenzo. She indicated the clockwork owls sitting nearby. "We think we have a way to fight the airships."

Lorenzo nodded slowly. "I hope so, 'cause we sure could use all the help we can get."

"Come," said Fatemeh. "Have something to eat. How is Ramon doing?"

The corporal licked his lips. "He was knocked unconscious by a bomb today. The Russians found him and took him aboard one of the airships."

Fatemeh felt like her knees were going to give way. She took her seat by the campfire again. "Tell us everything you can."

The next morning, General Gorloff arose before sunrise. He dressed, went to the ship's galley for a quick breakfast, then made his way to the gondola just as the sun was rising. Captain Makarov was already there, scanning the horizon near the place where they had seen the owls land the day before. A low mist covered the ground, obscuring the view.

The captain shook his head. "Perhaps they were just birds after all."

"There's movement to the south, sir," called the first lieutenant.

Makarov looked where the officer pointed, then handed his telescope to Gorloff. Sure enough, there was a roiling and swirling of the mist in the city streets and the general could just make out dark bodies moving within. The soldiers had regrouped for another assault on the ground.

"Signal the *Czarina Marie*," said the captain. "Get them into position."

"Something's approaching from the west, sir," called one of the officers.

Both Gorloff and Makarov whirled around. The general saw the strange mechanical flock bursting through the mist, toward the airships. Gorloff lifted the telescope to his eye. He clearly discerned owl-like forms, illuminated by the wan sunlight coming through the clouds. People sat within the owls, controlling them. He handed the telescope to the airship's captain.

"They mean to attack us." Makarov snapped the telescope shut and stepped over to the speaking tube. "I need men at the starboard gun ports right now—sharp shooters with rifles and cannoneers on the swivel guns."

Gorloff heard the muted acknowledgement and then moved closer to the window so he could get a better look at the approaching machines. He shook his head. "I wonder…is it even possible to fly those things and raise a gun against us?"

*"Do not underestimate the threat posed by the ornithopters,"* advised Legion. *"Those craft are capable of ramming the airships and they appear to have talons that could rip into the ships if they get close enough."*

There was a whistle from the speaking tube. The captain opened it. "Go ahead."

"Guns are ready. The mechanical birds are nearly in range."

"Fire when ready," ordered the captain.

The cannons on the starboard side erupted a moment later. Because of the ship's large size, the swivel guns were barely audible in the gondola. Despite the muted sound, they caused the airship to tip slightly on its side. When the ship righted itself, Gorloff shook his head in dismay. The mechanical owls had spread out and avoided the gunfire. "We missed them all."

"Fire again," ordered the captain.

Once more, there was a barely audible blast from the small swivel guns and the ship rolled. When the general could get a good view, he swore. "I count eleven still in the air. That's only one down. Legion, what do you advise?"

"*Ascend. The thinner the air, the harder it will be for the ornithopters to function.*"

The general gave a sharp nod to the captain, who pointed to the men at the controls. "Make it so."

The Owl Riders rose toward the airships. Hatches opened on the side of the closest ship. Fatemeh looked toward Cisneros, who was frantically signaling for the riders to spread out. She pulled back on the control rod just as little puffs of smoke appeared from the airship. Something whizzed by underneath her owl. Finally she understood the hatches were gun ports. She looked around and counted. All dozen owls were still airborne.

A moment later, there was more smoke from the gun ports. She pushed her control rod to the side, sending her owl into a wide arc. Looking down, she saw a cannonball smash into one of the owls. The fragile craft flew apart and she gasped, too stunned even to scream. Looking around, she saw all the other owls were still intact. She wasn't sure, but she thought it was Juan de Largo's owl that had been destroyed. A sob built in the back of her throat but she fought it down. She needed to concentrate on the task at hand and not give in to her emotions.

Fatemeh turned her owl back toward the airships and saw they were ascending. From experience over the Grand Canyon, she knew the owls could only go so high. She sought out Professor Maravilla and turned her owl toward his. When she was close enough he could see her, she waved. The professor waved back. She pointed sharply at the airships. He nodded, then looked at the owl flown by Captain Cisneros.

The professor reached behind him and moved a lever on the little steam engine. Fatemeh knew he was giving himself more power at the cost of time he could spend aloft. His owl began flapping mightily, shooting off toward the nearest airship. Captain Cisneros also put on a burst of speed and followed close behind. Two more owls—Billy and Larissa—soon followed.

As they continued to close the distance, Fatemeh heard popping noises. Sharp shooters in the gun ports were trying to pick off the closest riders. She signaled to the others. They also put on a burst of steam and moved in closer to the airships. They began flying in spirals and loops, hoping to distract the gunmen from their targets.

Billy followed close behind Professor Maravilla. He heard the zing of bullets over the roar of the wind. He took the controls with one hand and drew his revolver. Taking careful aim, he fired back at the men in the gun ports. He laughed when one of them ducked back inside.

Professor Maravilla and Billy flew up and over the airship. The professor lowered his owl's talons and descended. The metal claws ripped into the fabric that comprised the ship's hull. After a moment, he hit something solid, throwing him forward into the controls.

Billy guided his owl down toward the professor's. Leaning over, he studied the long gash left by Maravilla's craft. The metal talons of Billy's owl grabbed onto something solid and the owl lurched to a stop. As it did, it smashed into the professor's owl and it began to slide. Billy thrust out his arm to the professor. The professor shook his head and grabbed hold before his owl plummeted from the airship and fell to the ground below.

Maravilla and Billy looked down at the ship and saw steel girders they could hold onto. They descended through the gash in the hull.

Captain Cisneros and Larissa made a wide arc. Looking over at the captain, Larissa realized he was watching Maravilla. The sound of bullets whizzing through the air persuaded them to continue on. The captain took his owl up over the second airship's bow. He slowed, easing his craft downward. From her position, Larissa could tell he was coming in at a bad angle. One of the owl's talons caught, but the other missed. The owl swiveled and Cisneros jumped from his seat onto the top of the airship.

The captain's owl was now in Larissa's path. She banked suddenly and leapt toward the captain. He caught her by the collar as she nearly slid past, then hefted her toward his unstable purchase. Meanwhile, her owl continued out of control toward the airship's tail. The owl smashed into the tail and the airship lurched to the side.

Legion found himself fascinated by the prospect of humans developing ornithopters to attack the airships. He wanted to know more about this new group of humans and what motivated them. The Russians were angry someone had chosen to defy them. Legion expected defiance, so he wasn't angry. What he'd not expected was for the defiance to take such an inventive form.

The mechanical owls flitted about the airships. Although they were ascending, the airships had not risen high enough to be immune from the owls' attack. Two flew out of sight over the *Czar Nicholas*. A short time later, one of those owls plummeted to the ground even though it had been too near the ship to have been a victim of the swivel guns.

Soon after, a third owl landed on top of the *Czarina Marie* and a fourth plunged into her tail. The two riders sliced their way into the ship and disappeared. General Gorloff finally realized the *Czar Nicholas* might also have invaders aboard and he rushed up the gondola's ladder into the body of the airship.

The general peered around the giant gasbags, trying to see if there were any people in the ship's superstructure. Finally, the general spotted two people working their way down a ladder that ran alongside the gasbags. The general drew his sidearm and pointed it at the two invaders.

*"You cannot fire,"* said Legion. *"Remember what happened to the balloon the Americans were trying to raise."*

Gorloff swore to himself and vowed to wait until the invaders were closer. He fell into the shadows to wait.

As Gorloff waited, Legion allowed his attention to drift to the *Czarina Marie*. The *Marie's* captain had spotted two people in the superstructure above the gasbags. Fortunately, Captain Yudina had the wisdom not to fire his gun at the hydrogen bags. Instead, he went back into the gondola and ordered the gunners to leave their post and wait for the two stowaways.

Without entering their minds, Legion had no way of knowing the invaders' goals. However, if their only aim was to destroy the airships, he suspected they wouldn't have gone to such trouble to get inside. Legion wanted to see what the invaders would do. He allowed the gunners to answer the captain's order in the affirmative, then he sent commands through their neural pathways that prevented them from moving. If the invaders did prove violent and brutish, Legion could deal with them himself.

Legion then sent parts of himself to hover close to the people working their way down the ladders. The human who called himself Mauricio Maravilla spoke almost incessantly about what he saw. He was fascinated by the airship, and Legion could tell he admired the builder and honestly wanted to learn more.

The human called Onofre Cisneros was quieter and more cautious, but his eyes took in everything he saw. Legion sensed these humans possessed intelligence and imagination in great quantity. He needed time to see exactly what they would do.

Fatemeh looked around and tapped a glass gauge next to the steam engine that displayed the chemical supply. If the professor and Captain Cisneros didn't get the big doors open soon, she would have to land to avoid crashing. She pushed the joystick to the side and made a loop. As she did, she realized the gunners had stopped firing. She wondered if they had run out of ammunition or if something else had distracted them.

She reached back and tapped the gauge again. She had just enough fuel left to make a safe landing. As she began the turn that would take her back to the hill where they had camped the night before, movement from the airship caught her eye. The bay door fell open.

Fatemeh continued in a long arc, then flew toward the bay door. The owl's wings flapped furiously and she entered the darkened hold at the bottom of the airship. Carefully pulling the joystick back, she dropped the owl onto the floor. It skidded to a stop just before hitting the wall. Three more owls followed her in. The pirates unstrapped themselves and hopped out of their craft, drawing pistols. Billy and Maravilla grabbed hold of a set of ropes and pulled the bay door closed.

"I was worried you'd run into trouble," said Fatemeh.

"No trouble at all." Billy sported a cocky grin.

"In fact, the only thing we've encountered is something of a mystery." Professor Maravilla rubbed his goatee. "Here, let me show you." He led Fatemeh and the pirates into an adjoining corridor. A few steps took them to a steel support brace. Hiding in the shadows was a bearded man wearing a uniform with epaulets. He held an ornate pistol in his hand, but stood absolutely still.

Fatemeh peered closely at him. "Is he alive?"

Just then he blinked.

She jumped back, her eyes wide, but the man did not move. She took a tentative step forward and put her fingers against his jugular vein. There was a pulse, but he seemed completely paralyzed.

"What's going on?" Fatemeh narrowed her gaze, examining the man.

"Subject of interest: Fatemeh Karimi," said the man.

Fatemeh narrowed her gaze. "Luther Duncan spoke that way when I first met him."

"It was not Luther Duncan. It was us." The Russian was still paralyzed, all except his throat and mouth.

"Us?" Fatemeh looked the paralyzed Russian up and down. "There's more than one of you?"

"We are Legion."

"Madre de Dios!" A pirate named Ernesto made the sign of the cross. "He's possessed!"

"In a sense, your compatriot is correct, Miss Karimi," came the voice from the paralyzed man. "We reside within the humans on this ship. We are not General Gorloff. We are merely using him to communicate with you."

"What is your purpose?" asked Fatemeh.

Billy tugged on Fatemeh's shirt sleeve. "Miss Karimi, I don't think we have time for this ... weird conversation."

She shrugged him off. "On the contrary, I think we may have gotten to the root of the situation." She turned her attention back to the paralyzed man.

"We are travelers. Our purpose is to learn and explore," said the man.

"How do these airships help you achieve that purpose?" asked Fatemeh.

"An experiment. We sensed the Earth was on a path to destruction. Your species shows promise. We wanted to avert destruction if at all possible."

Professor Maravilla's eyes went wide. "You're from another world, aren't you? Mars, perhaps?"

"Much further than that," said the man.

Fatemeh nodded. She couldn't quite picture what the being that used General Gorloff looked like, but she realized it must be the same creature—or perhaps creatures—who had possessed Luther Duncan. Was it a spiritual essence or something more concrete? She yearned to know the answer, but sensed Billy was right and time was short. "The unity of the world is one of the tenets of my faith. I don't believe you can avert the world's destruction though war."

"We have come to realize it was a mistake to work through military minds. Perhaps we can revise our experiment before it's too late." The man's mouth went slack.

Maravilla tapped him, but got no response. He looked at Fatemeh and shrugged. "He doesn't seem to have any more to say."

"Then we better get to work." Fatemeh looked at the professor. "You should find a way to land the ship."

The professor nodded. "I suspect the controls are in the gondola." He turned and pointed toward a ladder that stuck up through the floor. "I'm guessing that's the way down."

Fatemeh looked toward the pirates who had accompanied her. "Go with the professor, in case there's trouble." They nodded and the four made their way to the ladder and down. Fatemeh turned to Billy. "Come with me. We need to find out if Ramon is aboard this ship."

Billy nodded. "I think there's crew quarters back that way." He pointed toward the bay where the owls had landed.

As they jogged down the walkway, she glanced up at the giant gasbags that filled most of the big chamber they were in, marveling at the ship's immensity even as she worried about Ramon.

Billy stepped past her, and drew his gun. "You better let me lead. Don't know what we'll find."

Fatemeh swallowed and nodded.

Billy led the way through the door and passed through the big bay. Fatemeh reasoned the space must be a staging area for troops and supplies. At the other end, Billy eased the door open. Beyond the bay was a corridor lined with doors. Billy went to the first door. It was labeled in Cyrillic script. His eyebrows creased as he tried to read what it said. Giving up, he pushed the door open. Inside were numerous gun racks and boxes of ammunition.

"This must be the armory," said Fatemeh.

Billy nodded and moved on to the next door. That one proved to be a nicely appointed stateroom. Fatemeh guessed it was probably the captain's cabin. They continued down the corridor checking each door. Most of the rooms were empty, but in two of them, they found men frozen in mid-motion, like the other fellow they had encountered on the walkway. However, none of them seemed inclined to speak.

As they reached the end of the corridor, Fatemeh felt a sinking sensation in her stomach. She realized Professor Maravilla must have reached the controls and figured out how to control the ship. They must be descending.

Finally, Billy and Fatemeh opened the last door at the end of the corridor. Inside, they found what appeared to be an infirmary with several beds. Cabinets containing first aid supplies stood against the walls. A man in a white jacket sat at a desk, frozen in place like the others; he held a pencil over a piece of paper.

A man in an American army uniform lay on one of the beds, his head turned away from the door. Fatemeh took a tentative step toward the figure on the bed.

He moaned, causing Fatemeh to stop in her tracks. She looked back at the doctor. He was still frozen. Her brows knitted, Fatemeh looked back toward the man.

The man in the uniform threw one leg over the edge of the bed and sat up, holding his head.

"Ramon!" called Fatemeh.

He looked up. "Corazón? Where are we?"

"We're aboard the Russian airship. I've come to rescue you."

Ramon's feet dropped to the floor and he tried to stand, but his legs gave way. He caught himself on the edge of the bed. Fatemeh and Billy sprang forward and stabilized him. Ramon looked over to the gunfighter. "Why is it that when I'm in trouble, the two of you are here together?"

"Got me," said Billy. "I've yet to get anything out of this deal."

Ramon looked over to the paralyzed doctor. "What's wrong with him?"

"I'm not sure," said Fatemeh. "As far as we can tell, everyone on this ship is under the control of some power, but I don't know how long that control will last."

Together, Billy and Fatemeh helped Ramon move forward. They left the infirmary and made their way along the corridor and toward the bay. As they moved, Ramon was able to take more of his own weight and finally could walk without assistance. When they reached the bay, they found Professor Maravilla and the pirates.

"We're over a bank—Clark, Gruber and Something. Looks like Captain Cisneros has gained control of the other ship. They're right behind us." The professor licked his lips, then inclined his head toward the stern. "I think we better get out of here. It looked like some artillery units are moving into position near the river."

"What!" Fatemeh put her hands on her hips. "Surely they don't mean to destroy the ship! Can't we get out of here?"

The professor took a deep breath, then let it out slowly. "I could probably manage to ascend, but I don't think we could get out of range in time. Our best chance is to get out of here and keep them from firing on us."

Fatemeh gritted her teeth, but nodded.

The professor tapped Billy on the shoulder and the two of them went to the ropes and opened the bay door. Wasting no time, the pirates dropped the rope ladder from the bay to the roof of the building below and began descending. Professor Maravilla and Billy followed them.

Fatemeh turned to Ramon. "Can you make it?"

He leaned over and kissed her briefly on the lips. "If you can, I can."

She took his hand and squeezed, then ushered him toward the ladder. Once he was a few feet down, she mounted the ladder and prayed the army wouldn't fire until they were clear of the ship.

General Alexander Gorloff was still trying to make sense of the strange conversation Legion had with the woman when four of the invaders ran past him and back into the bay. Several minutes went by, then just as suddenly as the paralysis had come upon him, he was released. He ran to the bay and peered down through the still-open door. Seven people stood on the roof of the Denver Mint. The general aimed his pistol and fired, scattering them. Several of the invaders drew revolvers and fired back. The general leapt away from the hatch and gritted his teeth.

Cautiously, he looked back through the open bay. The *Czar Nicholas* was rising. "Legion, what's happening?" called the general.

Silence was the only reply.

"Legion?" he ventured again.

Still, the alien presence refused to answer.

With a curse, the general holstered his sidearm and ran forward. "What's going on?" he called as he descended into the gondola.

Captain Makarov looked around with a sheepish expression on his face. "I'm not sure what happened. We were fighting off the mechanical owls and suddenly every muscle in my body froze up. We watched helplessly as men came in and took control of the ship. They flew it like experts."

The general's eyes moved from side to side as he thought. Silently he called for Legion again. As he did so, the truth dawned on him. "Legion has betrayed us." He ran to the window. "What's happening now?"

The captain pointed toward the ship's stern. "American artillery units are taking up positions along the river. We're attempting to ascend out of their range."

"Will we make it in time?" asked the general.

The captain shook his head. "I don't know."

Soon after the Owl Riders reached the tower-like roof of the mint, Billy saw the other airship lower its ladder to a nearby building. Larissa and the pirates began to descend. Billy looked back up toward the open hatch on the bottom of the airship they had just abandoned. The bearded man who had spoken to Fatemeh stuck his face over the edge. He recognized murderous fury intent on the man's features.

"Take cover!" shouted Billy.

The man in the airship began firing at them. Everyone scattered toward the walls and tried to make themselves into the smallest possible targets. Billy drew his six-gun and returned fire. He smiled as the four pirates did likewise and the man's face disappeared from view.

"That'll learn 'em."

A moment later, the airship began to rise. Professor Maravilla peered through the crenellations in the wall toward the river. "I think we better find a way inside the mint, and fast. It looks like they're loading those guns."

Billy found a trapdoor in the roof. A padlock held it closed.

He shot the lock, then kicked it aside. Throwing open the trap-door, he smiled at the sight of a ladder descending into the building. He looked toward Fatemeh. "Ladies first."

Fatemeh opened her mouth to say something, but a look from Ramon cut her off. She made for the ladder and he followed. The professor and the pirates were next. Finally, Billy mounted the ladder just as a series of thunder-like booms came from the river.

Billy was pulling the trapdoor closed when an explosion from above knocked him from his perch.

Fatemeh cried out as the explosion sounded from overhead and Billy fell from the ladder. He hit the floor with a thud that was barely audible after the blast. She rushed to his side and grimaced at the unnatural angle of his left arm. She reached up to check for a pulse when his eyes flew open and he sucked in a loud breath. "What the hell just happened?"

Professor Maravilla ran to a window. "There's debris raining down outside." He frowned and shook his head. "They must have ignited the airship's hydrogen with an artillery shell. The airship has been destroyed." He fell to the ground and put his face in his hands. "Such a waste."

"My arm!" cried Billy as though his brain had just registered the pain.

"It's popped out of its socket." Fatemeh looked at Ramon. "Hold him down." She moved to his side and grabbed his arm while Ramon got a firm grip on Billy's torso.

"What are you gonna do?" Billy's eyes were wide with panic.

Without answering, Fatemeh yanked and twisted Billy's arm. Billy screamed as his arm snapped back into its socket. A moment later, a sudden look of calm came over his features and he lost consciousness.

"What happened?" asked one of the pirates.

"He just passed out," said Fatemeh. "He'll be okay once he wakes up."

Just then, the door of the room they were in burst open.

Two soldiers aimed rifles.

"No one make any sudden moves."

The Owl Riders were taken to the Army encampment near Littleton. Fatemeh was relieved to see Cisneros, Larissa, and the pirates who had accompanied them. Apparently they had escaped their dirigible and took cover in a nearby feed store before the artillery began firing.

The Owl Riders were questioned by officers throughout the rest of the day. Finally, they were assigned tents near the edge of the camp. Larissa and Fatemeh were assigned to one tent while the men were split between two others. Russian soldiers sat outside a nearby tent.

"So, are we heroes or prisoners?" asked Larissa.

Fatemeh shook her head. "I have no idea." She ducked into the tent and lay down on one of the cots. She closed her eyes and began to recite a prayer she had memorized back in Persia, but never thought she would need in America. "Lauded be Thy name, O my God! Thou beholdest me in the clutches of my oppressors. Every time I turn to my right, I hear the voice of the lamentation of them that are dear to Thee, whom the infidels have made captives for having believed in Thee and in Thy signs, and for having set their faces towards the horizon of Thy grace and of Thy loving-kindness." She continued her prayer and when finished, she opened her eyes.

"Do you think it did any good?"

"You would be amazed at what prayer can accomplish." Fatemeh winked.

"I never really believed in prayer."

Fatemeh sat up. Reaching out, she took Larissa's hands. "You became a believer the minute you climbed in one of Professor Maravilla's owls and let it jump off the edge of the Grand Canyon."

Larissa inclined her head. "I'm not sure I know what you mean."

"I can think of nothing that took a bigger act of faith than that."

"I believed in the professor."

"And I believed God would guide the professor." With that, Fatemeh squeezed Larissa's hands and let go. "Now I pray God will guide the army toward wisdom and not rashness where we're concerned."

Larissa sighed. "Amen to that, sister."

The next day, Ramon awoke as a bugle sounded outside, rousing the soldiers. Used to sleeping on the ground, he rolled over and fell out of his cot. He rubbed his backside as he sat up.

Professor Maravilla threw his feet over the edge of the adjoining cot and rubbed the back of his head. "I had the strangest dream last night," he muttered. "I saw plans for the airship we'd captured. I saw how I could improve it. What's even stranger, I still remember it." He reached around for his bag, withdrew a sketchpad and began making notes.

A soldier stepped into the tent. "Private Ramon Morales?"

Ramon held up his hand. "That would be me."

"Get in your uniform and come along." The soldier stepped outside.

"Yes, sir." Ramon stood up. His uniform was folded on the ground near the cot. He quickly dressed and tried to brush off as much of the caked mud as he could, then stepped outside.

Ramon smiled when he saw Fatemeh outside her tent.

Maintaining his stoic expression, the soldier summoned Fatemeh and began walking toward the center of the encampment. Soldiers were climbing out of bedrolls and getting ready for the day. The smells of breakfast came from the mess tent and Ramon felt his stomach rumble. The soldier passed the mess tent and led them to a slightly smaller tent nearby. He lifted the flap and indicated they should enter.

Sitting behind a desk was a man familiar from many daguerreotype images. He had a mop of brown hair, turning silver at the edges. A long, angular mustache hung under an aquiline nose. A tuft of hair protruded from the man's lower lip. A round black hat sat on the table next to the man. Ramon snapped to attention and saluted General Philip Henry Sheridan.

"At ease, Private," said the general. "Please, be seated." He indicated two chairs in front of the table.

Ramon and Fatemeh sat down.

The general folded his hands and directed his attention to Fatemeh. "Miss Karimi, I am given to understand you led a force comprised mostly of Mexican nationals against the Russian airships that invaded the United States."

"Yes, sir." Fatemeh wrung her hands. "I'm a healer and I've come to believe that America is a good place to live. This invasion would hurt America like a disease hurts the body. I felt I had a cure."

"Hmph." The general folded his arms. "I would have preferred if you brought your plan to the army."

Fatemeh inclined her head. "Sir, I respectfully submit that if I brought it to the army, committees would still be discussing whether the owls could be built and Denver would be in the hands of the Russians by now. Most of your force would be dead."

The general barked out a laugh that startled Ramon. "Young lady, you may well be right. I honestly prefer the political tangle you've handed me to burying most of my men." He leaned forward. "However, the tangle is real. I'm afraid most of the men that helped you will have to be deported."

"Yes, sir." Fatemeh swallowed and nodded. "What about me, sir?"

The general sat back and folded his arms across his chest. "I suppose that depends. You're in the country legally. Have you considered becoming a citizen?"

"Very much so," said Fatemeh. "America isn't perfect, but I've found there's lots of good here. I'd like to stay."

The general smiled charmingly at Fatemeh. "We'd be glad to have you, young lady." Then his smile melted as he turned his attention to Ramon. "Private Morales, I understand you acted with extreme bravery on the battlefield. Your commander, Major Johnson, has recommended you for a commendation."

Ramon opened his mouth, but no words came out. He suddenly became more aware of his mud-stained uniform and made another effort at brushing it off. Giving it up as a lost cause, he adjusted his glasses and sat up a little straighter. "Thank you, sir," he finally said.

"Major Johnson has also informed me of the…circumstances under which you were drafted and your…relationship with Miss Karimi." He cleared his throat. "In light of your heroic service, I would be happy to arrange an honorable discharge for you." The general inclined his head. "However, we could sure use men like you in the army."

Ramon grinned briefly, then suppressed it. "Well, sir, I was grateful Major Johnson rescued me from a bounty hunter, but to be honest, I prefer civilian life to military."

The general nodded. "The major also told me about your situation with Randolph Dalton." General Sheridan's smile looked especially devilish framed as it was by the angular mustache. "If Mr. Dalton doesn't call off this ridiculous manhunt, several lucrative army contracts are going to disappear."

"Yes, sir," said Ramon. A moment later, the full weight of the general's words sunk in. "Thank you, sir!"

"Don't mention it." General Sheridan stood and saluted.

Ramon jumped to his feet and returned the salute.

"Now, get out of here," said the general. "You two have given me a *lot* of paperwork to do today."

# EPILOGUE
## ESTANCIA

A week of good-byes followed the destruction of the Russian airships over Denver.

Professor Maravilla continued to make sketches and write equations in his notebook. Ideas seemed to flow from him at a breakneck pace. Since he was in the country legally, he was allowed to go once he turned over his design for the clockwork owls. As a bonus, he was able to give the army detailed sketches of the Russian airships.

"They probably would have been satisfied with the plans for the airships," said Fatemeh. "I'm surprised you gave them the plans for the owls as well."

"I've seen numerous ways I can improve the design, my lovely lady." The professor straightened his red waistcoat and checked his pocket watch, as though he had an appointment. "I'm going to return to the Grand Canyon and build a new generation of flying machine. It'll be much easier now that I have help." He turned and smiled at Larissa, who stood beside him.

Larissa tipped her coachman's hat at Fatemeh. "Thank you. I used to think the only way I'd ever get the kind of respect and control I wanted was by being the best gunslinger around. You've shown me a new kind of world."

"Just remember, anything's possible." Fatemeh winked at Larissa. The two women embraced. Soon afterward, Maravilla and Larissa rode off toward Arizona.

Cisneros and his band of pirates were to be escorted to the Mexican border, but no charges would be brought against them. Like Maravilla, Cisneros found his mind flooded with new ideas. He gave the army the design for the chemical-reaction steam engine.

"I fear this has been an expensive journey for you and your men," said Fatemeh, "but I appreciate that you came when I called."

Cisneros took Fatemeh's hand and kissed it. "My lady, you kept me and my friends from being hanged as pirates. It was our pleasure to come to your aid." He began to turn away, but stopped. "Moreover this journey has proved very inspirational. I suspect I'll be a rich man again in a short time if half the ideas I've had pan out." He smiled and waved.

Fatemeh's brow creased as she wondered about both Maravilla and Cisneros. What was going through their heads? Were they inspired by the presence from another world that called itself Legion? If so, it was being quiet. She waved at Cisneros and wondered if she was waving at Legion as well.

The next day, Billy announced he was leaving. His left arm was in a sling and he complained the muscles ached, but was grateful Fatemeh had been able to set it back in its socket. One of the army doctors said he should have full use of his arm again within the month.

Because of his role in fighting the Russian airships, General Sheridan dropped all charges related to his activities at Fort Grant and rustling cattle bound for forts in New Mexico. "Being a law-abiding citizen might be better than stirring up trouble all the time," he said.

"So, where are you heading, Billy?" asked Ramon.

"I'm thinking about going down to Mesilla and looking up Luther Duncan. He seemed a decent sort. Maybe he can help me find an honest job."

"I hope so, Billy." Fatemeh smiled at him. "You're a brave and talented young man. You deserve better than the path you were on."

Billy frowned at those words. "You know, I think you're right. Is it just me, or does the world seem different somehow?"

"The world is always changing," said Fatmeh.

Ramon turned to Fatemeh as Billy stepped away. "Have you ever noticed that all of our best friends are outlaws and people with crazy dreams?"

Fatemeh smiled. "A lot of people think Bahá'u'lláh's dream of world peace and unity is a crazy dream. In Persia, I was an outlaw for following him. Good citizens maintain the status quo. It's the outlaws and the dreamers who change the world."

"So, what does that make us? Outlaws or crazy dreamers?"

"A little of both, I think."

Ramon took Fatemeh in his arms and kissed her.

The next day, Ramon, Fatemeh and Eduardo saddled up and began the ride south. Three weeks later, they reached Albuquerque. Once there, Ramon announced they would part ways.

"I look forward to getting back to the hot springs," said Ramon's cousin. "You should come with me and rest up a bit before moving on."

Ramon shook his head. "Now that the general has promised Randolph Dalton will be off my back, I have my own promise to fulfill."

Eduardo smiled and nodded. "Tell Aunt Sofia 'hi' for me," he said. "Make sure to send us an invitation to the wedding. I'm sure it's going to be a wild party."

"It will be, Cuz—if mom approves of Fatemeh."

"She will," said Eduardo. "They're birds of a feather, you know."

Ramon and Fatemeh waved as Eduardo rode off toward Palomas Hot Springs. Once he was out of sight, they turned to the southeast. As they rode, Ramon and Fatemeh spoke about where they might try to settle down. They discussed the possibilities of returning to Newhall in California, or going back to Las Cruces.

At the end of the day, the tiny village of Estancia came into view. The sun hovered just over the horizon as they reached the gate to the homestead Ramon's mom and dad had built. A burrowing owl stood on a nearby fence post. It did a little dance and chirped.

Fatemeh whistled in reply.

The owl bobbed up and down, then flew away.

"What about staying here?" asked Fatemeh. "I have a good feeling about this place."

Ramon shrugged. "I suppose Estancia's as good as anywhere else." Looking up, he saw his mom on the porch. Like Ramon, Sofia Morales was short and solidly built. She wore a simple blue gingham dress. Round spectacles were perched on the end of her nose. Her sleeves were pushed up past the elbows, as though she had been working on something when she saw Ramon riding up.

Ramon climbed off his horse. He wrapped the reins around the porch rail, then wrapped his mom in a big hug.

Fatemeh climbed off her horse, but hung back, holding her hands in front of her.

"Who is this?" asked Ramon's mom, looking around his shoulder.

Ramon smiled proudly. "This is Fatemeh, my fiancée."

"I hope she's a good Catholic girl," said Sofia Morales quietly to Ramon.

"Well…" said Ramon.

Sofia Morales stepped forward and took Fatemeh's hand.

"I'm pleased to meet you, Señora Morales," said Fatemeh.

Ramon's mom smiled and she looked back at her son. "She has better manners than you. I like her already." She turned back to Fatemeh. "Come inside and freshen up. Tell me how you met."

Ramon lingered on the porch as they stepped inside. He watched the sun sink slowly below the horizon. In a few hours, a new day would dawn. There was no stopping this journey into the future. He couldn't wait to find out what tomorrow would bring.

# ABOUT THE AUTHOR

David Lee Summers is an author, editor and astronomer living somewhere between the western and final frontiers. He edited *Tales of the Talisman* Magazine and three anthologies. *Owl Dance* is his seventh novel. His other novels include *The Solar Sea*, which was selected as a Flamingnet Young Adult Top Choice, and *Vampires of the Scarlet Order*, which tells the story of a group of vampire mercenaries who fight evil. His short fiction has appeared in such magazines and anthologies as *Realms of Fantasy, Cemetery Dance, Science Fiction Trails, Human Tales, 2020 Visions, Space Sirens,* and *Six-Guns Straight From Hell.* In addition to his work in the written word, David operates telescopes at Kitt Peak National Observatory. Learn more about David at **www.davidleesummers.com**

Made in the USA
Monee, IL
21 July 2023